HARD TIMES

Blayne Cooper

Spinsters Ink
2007

Spinsters Ink
P.O. Box 242
Midway, Florida 32343

Printed in the United States of America on acid-free paper
First Edition

Editor: Katherine V. Forrest
Cover designer: LA Callaghan

ISBN-10: 1-883523-90-7
ISBN-13: 978-1-883523-90-9

Dedication

I always have to give a shout-out to Bob. His patience, love and partnership are a big part of what make my life worth living. I love you more every day.

But this book is dedicated to my sister Mandy. It's a great feeling knowing that as I march through life someone has my back. Even if that someone might give me a hard pinch when I'm not looking. Don't get too comfortable. My revenge will happen when you least expect it and be twice as bad. Someday we'll be black-and-blue old ladies together. Isn't sisterhood wonderful? I love you.

Acknowledgments

This story is a little grittier than my usual tale. But despite my best efforts to indulgently wallow in drama, I continue to discover that I'm not a very dark person at all. So when I felt lost among my own words, I turned to my friends for encouragement and advice. They never let me down. Susan and Steph, your support helped make this book happen. As always, thank you.

My editor, Katherine Forrest, worked hard to make this a better story. Her efforts show in the final product. On a personal note, and as one who has been much edited, I can happily say that her laid-back style was a breath of fresh air. Thanks a bunch.

About the Author

Blayne Cooper is the author or co-author of a variety of fiction ranging from mystery/romance to outrageous parody. While she enjoys the challenge of working in multiple genres, it's writing about the humor found in everyday life that gives her the most pleasure. The University of Oklahoma College of Law grad loves travel, reading and spending long, sleepless nights crouched over her computer in search of the perfect words that will make people laugh or weep uncontrollably. She's still looking, but having a great time on the journey.

Lorna
1986

"C'mon, baby, just a little more, please?" He inched his hands just a bit further under her blouse.

It was cold outside on the porch and his fingers felt warm and comforting against the smooth skin of her belly. It had been a dreary, overcast winter's day and at nearly seven o'clock it was well past dark. Lorna Malachi chuckled and placed her hand over Nathan's, torn between encouraging him and pushing him away.

"Ah, c'mon, please?" he begged in a hushed tone, his face close to hers.

The words tickled her eardrums and Lorna felt herself lean into his touch, her body's natural response blocking everything else out. "Nathan," she groaned softly, nuzzling his neck. She sighed when his fingers sank deeply into her thick auburn hair and tilted her head way back so his lips could find hers. "Mmm . . ." She pulled away just slightly. "Nath, I—"

The porch lights flicked on. "Lorna, is that you?"

At the sound of her little sister's voice, Lorna jerked away from her boyfriend.

"Daddy says it's time to come inside and eat." The girl's voice held a note of pleading that Lorna understood all too well.

"Coming, Meg," she answered on an uneven breath. She glanced at the shivering ten-year-old girl whose hands were stuffed into the pockets of a raggedy pair of jeans. Maybe she could fit in enough hours of overtime to buy her another pair next week. "Go back inside, honey, it's cold."

With a mind of her own, Meg ventured a little farther out onto the porch and shyly gazed up at Nathan. Nathan was the cutest boy at the Burger Palace, where he and Lorna worked after school.

He blew out a frustrated breath, a stream of fog exiting his nostrils and swirling around his head as he gave Meg a tiny, good-natured wave. "Hey, kiddo."

Meg turned big blue eyes, a Malachi family trait, on her sister. "Sorry," she mouthed.

"Is Dad mad?" Lorna stepped forward and ran her fingers through her sister's dark curly hair, frowning at its disorder. Had her mother even combed it today?

Meg nodded and her eyes locked with Lorna's. She quietly replied, "Isn't he always?" as she glanced back inside the house. "Hurry."

"Everything'll be okay." Lorna gave Meg a playful pinch, hoping to see her smile. It didn't work. She spoke without turning away from her sister. "I gotta go, Nathan. I—"

"I know." Nathan rolled his eyes and hopped off the porch, his sneakers crunching on ice-crusted snow. "I know."

"I'm sorry." Lorna shooed Meg back inside, but she hesitated at the door, her fingers tightly wrapped around the frigid doorknob.

Nathan cocked his head as he tugged his car keys from his jacket pocket. "Hey, is everything okay?"

No. "Sure." She took a deep breath and steadied her trembling hand. "I'll see you after homeroom tomorrow?"

"You bet," he said brightly, already over his earlier frustration. "And Lorna?"

"Hmm?" She finally looked over her shoulder and raised her eyebrows in question.

"Only a few more months till we graduate. Then we can get in my car and just keep driving." He kicked at a snowdrift, sending a spray of powder onto the porch. "We'll never see snow again."

She smiled, wishing things were truly that simple. "See you tomorrow."

"Later." Nathan took off jogging toward his car.

So far dinner had been tense and quiet. The sight of her mother sporting a fresh black eye and her father a split lip hadn't helped the mood.

Lorna restlessly picked at her dinner, wishing she were anyplace but home. The dining room was so hot it was stifling, and even though she'd changed into a pair of lightweight shorts and T-shirt, a thin sheen of sweat covered her body.

"So." Her father set down his coffee cup, and looked directly at Lorna, who fought hard not to shrink under his penetrating gaze. "How was your exciting shift at the Burger Palace?"

Oh, God, here we go. Her stomach twisted but she didn't look away. "Fine."

George slammed down his cup sending coffee splashing over the sides. "You're not knocked up, are you?"

Lorna closed her eyes to keep from rolling them. "Not this again."

Her father snorted. "You can't tell me you and that faggot Lindstrom boy don't get it on in the freezer or storeroom or somewhere." He stuck his finger in Lorna's face. "Don't think I'm taking in any little bastards because you can't keep from spreading your legs."

At the end of the table Meg began to sniffle.

Lorna's face turned to stone. "I'm not preg—"

Her father waved a dismissive hand at her. "Shut up. I don't expect little sluts like you to tell me the truth anyway. Naomi, where's my fuckin' coffee?"

With jerky motions, Naomi Malachi began refilling her husband's cup, her mouth drawn in a thin line. "If Nathan Lindstrom is a faggot then how would Lorna get pregnant? Immaculate conception? Besides, if she was knocked up, she'd never tell you anyway. I know I wouldn't," she added under her breath.

George's eyes narrowed and his ruddy face darkened a shade, making his fair eyebrows stand out vividly. "When I want your damn opinion, I'll beat it out of you, bitch."

In an explosion of motion, he backhanded his coffee cup across the dining room table. Coffee flew everywhere and the cheap cup shattered against Meg's plate, sending a spray of ceramic chips and burning liquid onto her face and T-shirt.

Her heart pounding, Lorna shot to her feet and scrambled around the table. "Meg!"

"Goddammit, George!" Mrs. Malachi shoved her husband hard and he responded with a vicious slap that sent her reeling into her chair.

"Lorna?" Meg whimpered, holding her shirt out from her body with her fingertips. Coffee dripped from her chin.

"Shh . . . Ignore them." She began tenderly wiping Meg's face with a napkin. "Maybe they'll do us a favor and kill each other."

"I heard that, little slut," George roared, fending off another of his wife's blows as she reached across the table for him.

"Don't move, Meg." Lorna carefully picked a shard of glass out of her sister's arm, leaving a tiny spot of blood in her wake. She tried to block out the sounds of her parents hitting each other and yelling obscenities. "You didn't get burned, didja?"

Meg glanced down at a pink spot on her arm and rubbed it, wincing. "I—I don't think so."

Lorna's brows drew together as she gently grasped Meg's chin and turned her head to the side. What she saw caused her heart to clench so hard she felt faint.

A fresh bruise.

Suddenly she felt like she couldn't breathe. *How could I have missed that?* "Where'd you get this?" Her voice was unusually harsh and she instantly saw fear reflected back to her in her sister's eyes.

"I—I—I—" Meg didn't seem to know what to say. Her parents had suddenly stopped screaming and fighting and were looking right at her, their gazes burning a hole through her. "I fell," she said listlessly, then her face crumpled and she began to cry again.

Dazed, Lorna just stood there. She'd heard her mother use that same excuse a hundred times. To neighbors. To family. To the police. She remembered with sickening clarity the first time she'd said the very same thing and the shame that had accompanied it. But hearing the words fall from her ten-year-old sister's lips made her blood run cold like nothing ever had.

"Shut the fuck up, little girl." George's handsome face twisted into something grotesque that was all sharp angles and shadows. "Anything you got, you had coming to you." He pointed at her. "Just remember that."

Lorna whirled around, eyes blazing. "Which one of you did this?"

Her mother guiltily looked away, but her father met her gaze squarely, defiantly.

A surge of crystalline hatred engulfed Lorna. "You hit her?"

Mrs. Malachi had always taken the brunt of her husband's abuse, though the scar bisecting Lorna's right eyebrow testified to the fact that she hadn't escaped her childhood completely unscathed. But George had never, *ever* touched Meg.

The hair on the back of Lorna's neck stiffened and a pulsing anger sang through her blood, making her limbs tingle in anticipation. "Well?" she demanded, still glaring at her father.

"Lorna, don't!" Meg was sobbing so hard it was difficult to understand her. She grabbed her sister's hand and held on for dear life. "I spilled the milk. It was m-my fault. It was me!"

Lorna pried her hand from Meg's and stepped back around the small table until she was standing toe-to-toe with her father. He wasn't much taller than she was, but danger emanated from his pores.

Her voice dropped to its lowest register and Lorna spoke slowly to make herself painfully clear. "If you ever touch her again I'll call the police and have you tossed back in jail."

For a second his face remained motionless, then, to everyone's surprise, he burst into laughter.

Lorna's eyes narrowed.

George leaned closer to his eldest daughter. "You think they can stop me from doing what I want in my own house? Pah!" He made a face as though he smelled something rancid. "You're as stupid as your mother."

Lorna swallowed, then nodded once. Her voice was so calm it sounded foreign to her own ears. "I guess you're right." And he was. "The police won't do anything." A short lifetime of experience had already taught her that.

A smug smile planted itself firmly on her father's face. "Looks like you finally understand things."

"I'll tell you what I understand. I understand that if this happens again, I'll stop you myself." Lorna's stormy blue eyes glinted with unspent rage. "I'll *kill* you."

Mrs. Malachi began choking on her coffee.

George crossed his arms in front of his chest and raised one eyebrow. "Suddenly so brave and—" His eyebrow went even higher, "—cocky, girl? I didn't know you had it in you." He smirked at his wife. "Maybe she is mine after all."

Lorna's rage finally spilled over. "Not Meg!" She banged her fist on the table, sending a full ashtray clattering onto the floor. "She's just a girl and she's never done anything to you. Don't—You—Touch her!"

The wiry man's amusement quickly melted into anger. "You don't have the guts to kill anyone. You—Are—Nothing," he mocked. His face was so close to Lorna's that she could taste strong Irish coffee and stale BelAir cigarettes. "You think just because you're bringing home a few dollars from the Burger Palace you can tell me what to do? Me?" he roared, spittle flying from his lips, his voice so loud that Lorna's ears rang.

"Lorna, please, let's just go to my room, okay?" Meg's face, except for a lurid red streak across her right cheekbone, was as white as snow. "Let's just go."

Emboldened by anger and fear, Lorna swallowed hard. "You don't have to be afraid anymore, Meggy. Daddy's not going to do it again, right?" She pinned him with her stare, willing him to, for once in his life, act like Nathan's, or anybody else's, father.

George spread his hands wide and mildly said, "Of course I won't."

Stunned, Lorna let out a loud puff of air. She blinked a few times. "You won't hit her?" she clarified cautiously.

"Let me see your face, Meggy." George walked around Lorna and grasped Meg's face with a tender hand. After giving the bruise a careful inspection, he glanced back at Lorna, leaving his hand in place and stroking the soft skin with his thumb. "It looks fine to me."

Lorna shook her head. "It's not fine. She doesn't deserve to be hit for accidents!"

"I'm okay. It doesn't hurt much," Meg swore, shooting a nervous glance at her sister. "Thanks, Daddy." Hesitantly, she leaned into his touch, closing her eyes in delight as he stroked her cheek.

"It doesn't hurt?" George smiled sweetly at Lorna, then whipped his hand across Meg's cheek with a blow so stunning it sent her sprawling across the kitchen floor like a rag doll. "Then I guess I didn't hit you hard enough the first time." He snorted. "That'll teach me."

For a long second everyone froze in horror.

George began to laugh, his voice shredding the silence. "Aren't you going to kill me, Lorna?" He pointed at himself with taunting fingers. "Here I am. Here I am! Here I am!"

A blood-red veil draped over Lorna's vision. Meg's reborn cries sounded far away and barely registered over the rushing in her ears. "Bastard," she hissed as she grabbed a steak knife from the table, and, with a lightning-fast swing, buried it to the hilt in her father's stubbly neck.

The look of surprise on George's face as blood spurted from his throat in a steady, hot crimson shower was almost comical. With a surreal sense of disconnectedness, Lorna watched him helplessly grab at the knife, and then tip over like a wobbling bowling pin.

Did I do that?

Mrs. Malachi began screaming George's name over and over and

Meg looked at her sister with panicky, wide eyes. "L-L-Lorna?" she screeched wildly, too petrified to move a muscle.

George was making gurgling sounds and thrashing around on the linoleum like a beached fish, but Lorna ignored him completely and stepped over his writhing body to make her way to her sister.

Meg pushed to her feet and, heedless of the red speckles that covered the older girl's shirt, flew into Lorna's arms, squeezing her with all her might. She tucked her head under Lorna's chin and held on for dear life.

Lorna closed her eyes and pressed her lips to Meg's head. "He won't hurt you or anybody else again," she said quietly. She wondered for brief moment if she should feel sad or, at least, the tiniest bit of regret. But she didn't, her mind only recognizing a relief so profound that her body began to shake.

It was finally over.

Meg blinked slowly, her eyes transfixed on her father. "Did you k-kill him? Is he really dead?"

George was still now, lying in a thick pool of dark blood, his eyes fixed and open, staring dully at the stained ceiling.

Lorna licked dry lips, the scene before her horrific in its beauty and finality. Her eyes filled with tears, but they weren't for George Malachi. "Yes."

Meg squeezed her tighter and whispered, "Good."

Kellie

Fourteen years later . . .

It was nearly midnight and tiny points of light dotted the lake just outside the floor-to-ceiling windows. In her hollow, five-bedroom house, Kellie Holloway sat alone in the middle of the living room floor, a pristine, endless sea of shadow-draped white surrounding her. White carpet. White curtains. White walls. Miles of sterile nothingness.

Kellie's features had been described as classic: a strong but feminine jawline, a straight thin nose, high cheekbones. But today, unlike most days, she didn't look her best. Her clothes were askew and feet more used to high heels than sneakers were bare.

She hiccupped and swallowed against the burn of stomach acid and whiskey. Her hiccup echoed in the room that was utterly empty, save for an empty booze bottle to her right, and a full bottle of pills to her left.

Her life was finished. Done. It had taken only six months for it to evaporate before her eyes, and every second of it had been unadulterated hell. Sure, she'd spent the last month in the bottom of a bottle, trying to forget about how everything good in her life had trickled through her fingers like grains of sand. But that hadn't kept this day from arriving. She could stall many things, but ultimately, she couldn't stop time. It had just kept ticking away, maddeningly. Relentless.

Every stock. Every bond. Every penny. Everything she'd worked so hard for and loved, hell, even the things she'd hated, were all gone. The business that she'd built from the ground up, the very essence of what she was, no longer existed. It was as though the first thirty-seven years of her life had been a total waste, her very identity obliterated.

Her business partner and on-again, off-again girlfriend had even stolen her clothes when she'd left her two days ago. "Bitch," Kellie seethed brokenly, looking at her hand and seeing double. Puzzled, she wiggled her fingers. "I hope the next woman you screw gives you the c-c—," she hiccupped, "the clap."

They were *definitely* off-again, for good.

"Well you didn't remember these, didja, Ms. I-can't-be-with-you-when-you're-like-this." Kellie triumphantly held up a bottle of her ex-lover's prescription painkillers and shook them wildly. In addition to her former girlfriend's stunningly complete job of divesting Kellie of her possessions, a repossession crew had removed every stitch of furniture from her house. But somehow they'd left the contents of her medicine cabinet untouched.

She had jack shit but she'd be damned if her teeth weren't pearly white!

She fell back on the soft carpet and stared at the blurry ceiling. The room was dark save for a soft golden glow that came from the harbor lights peering in through her massive windows. "I wanna die." The thought startled her and she said it again, not quite believing that she actually meant the words. "Whoa, I do." Her voice dropped to a raw whisper. "I really just want this all to be . . . be over. I'm so tired . . . of everything."

She let the pill bottle tumble from loose fingers and she started to cry again as she pressed the palms of her hands against puffy eyes. "I don't want to be here." She gestured aimlessly at the grand, but barren room. She hugged her whiskey bottle to her chest. "I just want to go to sleep and never wake up."

Well, then. It was decided. How amazingly simple. She doubted her parents had given that much thought toward her conception. Why shouldn't she treat her death as cavalierly as they'd treated the creation of her life?

When she'd pulled the pills out of the medicine cabinet earlier that evening, she'd only meant to keep them as a defiant gesture because she had nothing else. But now, now, they could be put to good use. They were painkillers, after all.

And she was nothing if not in pain.

She sat up and blinked slowly as she glanced around the foreign-looking room. "This is the end of my wonderful, miserable life." She wondered briefly why there was no soundtrack. At the close of every tragedy there was a fantastic, dramatic soundtrack that swept the audience away, horns wailing, violins weeping.

Real life was so disappointing.

With a resigned sigh she stuffed her mouth full of pills, closed her eyes, and put the whiskey bottle to her lips. She thought that her heart should be pounding. But the beat was slow and steady. Resigned. *Three*, she counted down, *two, one* . . . a deep breath, *die*. She tipped the bottle back and a single drop of whiskey drizzled into her mouth, dissolving a lone, disgusting-tasting pill.

"Ugh." She gagged. Then her stomach heaved and the pills shot from her mouth as she threw up all over her shirt and the carpet.

"Oh, crap. Crap!" She curled up on her side and coughed a few times, her head spinning. "I can't even kill myself right!" she howled. Drool connected a long strand of obsidian-colored hair to her cheek. Out of the corner of her eyes she could see the hair and the sight made her laugh, an insane cackle that was as much tears as anything else.

She hadn't cried as her world had come crashing down around her. She'd been brave or drunk and so she'd been able to hold every ounce of pain she felt inside. But now that she'd begun to sob, Kellie found she couldn't stop.

A loud rap on her front door finally caught her attention.

"Ms. Holloway, this is the police. Open the door, ma'am."

Kellie stood on long, wobbly legs and began to stagger to the door. "Ya, right! Sure it's the police," she yelled in a hoarse, sarcastic voice. "I know it's you, you repo jerks! Well, there's nothing left for you to take. Check your stupid clipboards. You already hauled away my entire life."

Halfway to the door, Kellie tripped over her own feet, and skidded face first across a large expanse of carpet, smearing puke down her body and along the flooring. Her vomit-soaked shirt felt hot against her skin and she whimpered as she tried to peel carpet fibers from her tongue.

"Ms. Holloway, we're coming in." The firm voice floated over her.

"Oh, come in then for chrissakes," she moaned bleakly, rolling over and throwing her arm over her eyes. "See for yourselves, then leave me alone."

At the edge of her senses she heard the front door open. "See? There's nothing left for you to take." *Nothing.* "Now get out."

"I'm afraid we can't do that, Ms. Holloway." This time the voice was closer.

She opened one slate gray, very bloodshot eye . . . and looked up at a stout policeman. Next to him was another impatient looking uniformed officer. She blinked with exaggerated slowness. "Who the hell are you?"

The nearest officer reached down, grabbed Kellie by the wrist and hauled her to feet. The second officer recoiled at the stench of whiskey and barf. "Kellie Holloway," he announced, holding his nose with one hand and waving his other in front of his face, "you're under arrest for Fraud and Larceny in the Third Degree."

"What are you talking about?" Kellie jerked upright, ignoring the stabbing pain the motion caused her head. "I lost my business, I didn't commit any crimes."

"You have the right to remain silent—"

Wild eyes flicked from one impassionate face to the other and she began twisting from the man's iron grasp. "I'm not a criminal!"

The second officer glanced at his watch and rolled his eyes and continued, "Anything you say can and will be used against you—"

Kellie's face contorted and she bared her teeth. "I don't want to be silent! And I sure don't want another scum-sucking lawyer in my life!" She caught sight of the nearest officer's gun and saw her way out. She lunged for it with her free hand and managed to unsnap the safety strap and wrench the gun from its holster.

Two sets of eyes widened. "Jesus!" Both officers grabbed for the gun at the same time Kellie began to twist away.

"Uff!" A hard elbow to the gut knocked the wind out of her and she fell forward into one of the officers, struggling frantically. In less than two seconds, all three people were on the floor, a mass of flailing, striking limbs and wild yells.

"Let it go!"

"You let it go!"

"No! You—"

BANG!

Chapter 1
Two years later . . .

"Built in 1972, Blue Ridge Women's Correctional Facility is located twenty miles from the nearest town and nestled safely in the mountains."

Kellie wished the guard with the big Fu Manchu mustache would stop his impromptu travelogue from hell. She rattled off her social security number to a large, dark-skinned woman behind a Plexiglas window.

"Waist and length?" the woman asked.

Kellie just looked at her. "Huh?"

"What's your pant size, honey? I don't have all day."

"I-um. A 10. Or maybe an 8 depending on the cut and where the waist sits."

The woman rolled dark eyes. "Waist and length measurements only. Does this look like Bloomingdale's to you?"

"It does to me," shouted a woman from the back of the room.

"Shut the fuck up," the guard barked, tossing an aggravated glance in the direction of the outburst.

Kellie's eyes widened as fear coursed through her. "How about thirty-one waist, and, uh . . . maybe thirty-two length, I guess."

The dark-skinned woman pursed her lips then handed her a pair that read 30x34. A few minutes more and she'd filled a cotton laundry bag with other clothes and handed it to Kellie through a large hole in the glass. Inside the bag was also a small bundle of papers with the words Blue Ridge Inmate Rules emblazoned in bold letters on the top of the first page of the packet. Kelli frowned. She never had been very good with rules.

"Change clothes when you get to your cell and put your jumpsuit in the laundry bag." Bored, the woman looked behind Kellie at the next newbie prisoner and hollered, "Next!"

Kellie took the hint and stepped forward, clutching her stack of clothes, the dust from the bag making her sneeze several times in quick succession. She stood as far away from the other new prisoners in the reception area as possible. At least her parents, mortally shamed by her arrest and subsequent trial, had ponied up bail money, allowing her to spend blessedly little time behind bars. Until now.

There had been a few chatty types on the bus over from County jail, but she wasn't one of them. Why waste time talking to criminals? She'd remained quiet, absorbed by the ugly scenery and small snowflakes as they stuck to the window and melted.

The guard waiting for the prisoners continued with his monologue. His voice was a dull monotone and he knew every word by heart. "Blue Ridge has two housing wings. Maximum security holds eighty women. Pray you never see the inside of that building. Medium security, the paradise where you've been assigned, holds one hundred and sixty women.

"Infractions of prison rules will cause one of four things to happen: One, loss of privileges. Privileges include being allowed to work, take classes, participate in visiting day and having more than one hour per day outside your cell. The second consequence for violating prison rules is time in solitary confinement."

The black prisoner behind the Plexiglas chuckled. "That'd be the hole, ducklings. You don't wanna end up there."

The guard smacked the Plexiglas with his baton, but didn't seem particularly angry over the interruption. "Three, transfer to the maximum security wing."

Kellie felt numb as the words rolled over her. She couldn't believe she was here, couldn't believe the jury had found her guilty, couldn't believe that somehow *this* had become her life. God, she would still kill for a scotch and soda and a quick, painless way to make all of this go away.

"In addition to the two housing buildings," the guard droned on, "there's a cafeteria, a work center, a garden, a gymnasium, and, of course, the exercise yard. Rules for each building and area are posted on the bulletin boards and on the paperwork in your bags." He turned to face the waiting women. "Learn them." He lightly smacked his baton against his palm. "Live by them." *Smack.* This time a little harder. "And we'll all get along just fine." *Smack!* He cocked his head. "Or not."

The guard's grim face, and his shiny baton with its well-worn handle, left Kellie no doubt what the fourth, unspoken, consequence of breaking the rules would be.

"Holloway, you're in cell . . ." The guard gave a cursory glance at the paper in his hand and shook his head. "Fourteen-hundred-B with Mally." He snorted. "Lucky you."

They paused at the cell door and when Kellie didn't move, he gave her a shove. "Welcome to the first day of the rest of your wretched life."

Kellie bit back a curse as she bounced off the wall.

The guard laughed and kept walking as he escorted another new prisoner to the end of the cellblock.

The door was made of a sheet of metal, not bars, and it was thick. She entered the cell with her heart in her throat. Her palms were sweating and she was a little dizzy at the prospect of what she would find inside.

Kellie left the door open as she entered. She had been told it would close and lock behind her. Stupid, she knew, but she couldn't help herself, the fear that she'd been holding in since the jury foreman had said those hateful words, rose to the surface with alarming speed. She sniffed hard, willing the tears not to come. *Years. God, oh, God. I could be here for years. What has Cindy done to me?*

Stunned, she took in her surroundings. County jail had been a filthy cesspool of humanity, but she'd always consoled herself by the fact that her stay there would only be for a short time. But this . . . this was her new home.

The eight-by-eleven-foot cell was painted a pale blue and held a set of bunk beds with white sheets and cream-colored blankets. There was a metal desk with an attached metal bench, and a six-drawer dresser at the end of the room. High above the dresser was a small barred window that allowed some natural light into the cell. Oddly, the room smelled faintly of wood chips, though all the furniture appeared to be metal or hard plastic.

A plastic-framed picture of a dark-haired little girl, a few tattered paperback novels, and the fact that the bottom bunk had bedding on it, were the only evidence that someone lived in the room.

"I can just imagine my gorilla woman roomie now," she muttered.

Kellie began to dig into her bag and pulled out a T-shirt and pair of jeans. She perched on the lower bunk and exhaled wearily, covering her face with her hands.

"The bottom bunk is mine and I shaved my legs yesterday so I won't be a gorilla again until the end of the week."

Kellie's head jerked sideways to find a figure in the doorway. A woman who looked to be in her early thirties with wet, reddish-brown hair and a ruddy complexion was standing there, looking very irritated. She had a bath towel draped over well-toned shoulders and a lean, strong-looking build accentuated by a slim waist and shapely thighs that strained at the confines of her blue jeans. *A cyclist's physique.* Kellie's eyes were drawn to the edges of a lurid, green tattoo peeking out from the sleeve of her blindingly white T-shirt.

The stranger was a good three inches shorter than Kellie's five feet eight, but somehow she managed to be utterly imposing, filling the entire cell with her presence from the doorway. Kellie instantly decided that although her expression was just a little too hard and guarded for anyone to call her pretty, there was something undeniably interesting about her face.

"Earth to newbie." The woman waved. "Are you still in there?"

"I'm-I'm sorry," Kellie murmured worriedly, snapping out of her appraisal. "You probably heard that ill-advised gorilla comment . . . I didn't . . . I mean." She audibly gulped, fear coursing through her. "Just sorry. My name is Kellie Holloway."

"Lorna." Lorna cocked her head, damp hair curling at the nape of her neck. She sized Kellie up, and sighed, apparently determining that she wasn't a physical threat.

Experience, Kellie instantly deduced, had been this woman's wicked teacher.

"If you're sorry, then why are you still sitting on my bed?"

Kellie sprang to her feet and scrambled to the back of the cell, clutching her bag of clothes to herself.

Lorna quietly padded inside.

Kellie closed her eyes against a sudden wave of claustrophobia. Or maybe it was the fact that she'd been more than two days without a drink. Despite her former girlfriend's accusations, she hadn't considered herself an alcoholic, just an active, social drinker. But now she wasn't so sure. Adding even one more person to the small space made her ill.

"Uh oh. You don't look so hot," Lorna observed mildly.

Kellie swallowed hard, her gaze desperately flickering around the room. Even convicts needed a sink and toilet, didn't they?

Lorna scrubbed her head with her towel. "You can stop looking, a toilet isn't going to pop out from underneath the bunk beds. During orientation didn't they tell these were dry cells?"

Kellie drew in a couple of deep breaths to settle her nerves. The woman's voice was a little deeper than she'd expected based on her size, but not unpleasant. "Umm . . . the guard blabbering on and on—was that considered my orientation?" She forced a chuckle and tried not to feel the trickle of cold sweat that snaked its way down her back. "And what's a dry cell? One where they don't serve alcohol with the room service?"

Lorna stuck her head outside the cell. "Hey, Roscoe, you fat fuck," she yelled. "Nice job orienting the newbies!"

She turned back to Kellie and draped her towel over the bed frame to dry. "Princess, you can get anything from alcohol to Oxy and back to Hershey's chocolate again with enough money. But dry cells mean we have shared showers and toilets."

Kellie took a tentative step forward, and did her best not to look terrified. She scowled at being called a princess but wasn't about to correct the woman before her. Was her new roommate a serial killer? Or maybe an arsonist or child molester? A chill chased its way down her spine. The possibilities were endless and all bad.

"You don't have to be afraid of me," Lorna told her simply. "Unless you piss me off, that is." Then she caught the unconscious widening of Kellie's eyes . . . and flinched. "You might as was well get comfortable instead of huddling in the corner." Lorna gestured with her chin. "You can use the bench to take a load off."

Kellie drew in a deep breath and did her best to hold the smaller woman's gaze, which was intense and concerned at the same time. "I won't be here long enough to care. My lawyer says he'll appeal and—"

Lorna rolled her eyes. "Very funny. You—" She stopped when the offended look on Kellie's face evidently told her she wasn't joking about her appeal. "Uh . . . Never mind."

"What were you going to say?"

"Nothing."

"Yes, you were." Kellie's ire began to rise. For months the police and even her own lawyer had treated her as though information was on a need-to-know basis only. And *she* didn't need to know. She couldn't stand it for another second. "Dammit! What was it?"

Lorna shrugged one shoulder. "Your lawyer told you not to get too used to being here, right?"

"Yeah." Kellie lifted her chin. "He was right, I don't belong here. So?"

"And the reason you shouldn't get too comfortable is because he was doing up the paperwork for your appeal at this very moment, right? And he said for you not to worry because your appeal was rock solid."

Anxiety began to swirl in Kellie's belly. "He *should* have a good basis for the appeal. I *don't* belong here," she insisted defiantly, even as her confidence began to flag.

"Then you'll be one of the very few."

Lorna looked as though she was guilty of the crime that had landed her here and had never bothered making any bones about it.

Kellie really didn't want to hear the rest of what this woman had to say. It was already hitting way too close to home. Could they have had the same lawyer? She didn't want to believe she could have been so easily had. But somehow she couldn't stop herself from saying, "Go on . . . you were telling me about the lawyer thing."

"You're sure?"

"More than sure."

"I'll bet that your lawyer also said that you shouldn't expect to hear from him for a while because he'll be soooo busy working on your appeal that he'll be hard to reach."

Kellie's mouth dropped open. That's exactly what the man had told her as she was shuffled out of the courtroom, the word guilty still ringing in her ears.

Lorna gave her a sympathetic look. "Same story, different day. We've all been there and we're all still here." She sat down on her bed and stretched her legs out with a groan. "So you might as well have a seat."

It took Kellie a few minutes, but she finally got the nerve up to make her way back to the metal desk where she set down her bag and began rooting through it with short, irritated movements. "Surely they gave me some humongous white tube socks to go with my tacky blue jeans and white T-shirt."

Lorna snorted softly.

"I'm going to look like a reject from The Outsiders," she mumbled.

Lorna made a face as Kellie passed by. "Showers and bathrooms are out the door and to the right at the end of the block." She wrinkled her nose. "Showers are only open twice a day for thirty minutes. You've got twenty minutes left today and then you'll have to wait until tomorrow."

Kellie discreetly sniffed herself and heard a faint, "Go to hell, Mally," drift back into the cell as a guard she presumed to be Roscoe walked by. "Ugh." She had been in a nervous sweat all day, the bus to the prison had smelled like a combination of body odor and rotten eggs, and this was her second day in her Day-Glo orange jumpsuit. "Umm . . . So I can go shower right now?"

Lorna settled back on her bunk with her hands behind her head. She allowed her eyes to drift closed and a soft sigh to escape her lips. "Feel free. Please."

"Mally?" *Isn't that what the guard had called her?*

One of Lorna's eyes popped open and Kellie was taken aback by the raw anger she saw there. "I didn't say you could call me that. And you now have eighteen minutes to get clean."

Reeling from Lorna's sudden change in demeanor, Kellie didn't say another word. Hugging her entire bag to herself, she marched out of the cell and into the unknown.

Lorna Malachi had just begun to doze when there was a loud rapping on her cell wall.

"Where's the newbie?"

Lorna sighed and opened her eyes to find Roscoe and Chul, a small Asian guard who was generally pleasant when he wasn't with Roscoe, standing in her doorway. "What?" she answered groggily. "Oh, c'mon! You rolled my goddamn cell just last week!"

"Nobody is searching your cell, Mally. Unless you have something to hide, that is." He glanced around, clearly hoping to see something out of place. "Some contraband here maybe?" He yanked out her desk drawer and turned it upside down, spilling its contents onto the concrete floor.

"Not only are you a bastard, but you can kiss my Irish ass."

"Where's Holloway?" Chul asked as he leaned against the cell wall, ignoring the other guard and the pencil that came to rest at the toe of his boot.

"She's in the shower, removing the stink from one of your buses." Lorna directed a cool gaze at Roscoe. "That's still allowed, right? I mean, if we didn't shower—" She wrinkled her nose, "—we'd smell like you."

Chul snickered.

Heat invaded Roscoe's cheeks. "You always gotta be a smartass, doncha?" He took an angry step forward and reached for his baton. "I—"

"You know showers are allowed," Chul said, interrupting Roscoe and sighing as he stepped between him and Lorna. "Don't you two start with your bullshit. I'm almost off shift and I'm too tired to deal with it."

What served as Roscoe and Lorna's relationship went back to Lorna's days in the maximum-security wing. It had taken both of them years to make the move to medium security. The difference was, Lorna had easily adapted to the more relaxed setting, but after nearly six years, Roscoe still had an impossibly long way to go.

Chul gave Lorna a warning look and she replied with a contrite look of her own.

"C'mon, Roscoe." Chul pushed off the wall with a groan, then dusted his hands off on his pants. "Let's go get Holloway."

Lorna sat up and scrubbed her face. "Whaddya need her for? She can't be in trouble already, can she?" But even as she said the words she knew they weren't true. Trouble followed some people like their own shadow. And after only one brief meeting, she suspected that Kellie was one of those unlucky souls.

"She belongs next door with Murano." Chul chuckled, happily taking the opportunity to needle the older man. "Seems Roscoe here forgot his glasses today and assigned all three of our newest residents to the wrong cells."

"Don't worry, I'll go get her," Roscoe said, his sudden smile bordering on a leer.

"I'll go." Lorna stood, visions of the last time she saw Roscoe in the shower room. The repulsive memory invaded her mind and made her feel like puking. She easily recalled Roscoe's gray uniform trousers around his ankles, his large belly flapping with every grunting thrust as he pumped in and out of a hapless inmate, who made a show of pretending she was enjoying what was happening. "I was gonna head down to the showers anyway."

Roscoe drew in a breath to protest, but Chul grabbed him by the wrist and began to tug him from the cell. "Thanks, Lorna." He lightly backhanded Roscoe's chest. "C'mon, let the next shift deal with Holloway. She can bunk in this cell tonight and we'll check her in next door in the morning. So long as she's accounted for, we're covered."

Roscoe slowed to a stop, clearly not wanting to go anywhere but the shower room.

"Besides," Chul persisted, "Joo-Eun sent me with brownies today and I haven't had a chance to eat them."

Roscoe grumbled a string of profanities but allowed himself to be distracted in favor of Joo-Eun's best dessert.

The hallway was empty and Lorna approached the shower room with a growing sense of dread. It should have been crowded right before closing. Instead, it was as still and quiet as a grave and soon she realized why. There was a lone woman standing outside the cell nearest to the showers. She was keeping watch.

"Shit." Lorna picked up the pace, and flew past the heavyset woman who was supposed to be guarding the door. She burst into the cell and came to a skidding halt at the scene before her.

Two women surrounded Kellie, who was half-naked and bent over the desk. A firm grip in Kellie's hair held her head down hard against the metal.

Gagged and fighting wildly, Kellie cried and let out muted screams as the hand of the tallest woman disappeared between her legs.

Oh, Christ. Lorna wanted to turn around and mind her own business. She really did. But, she realized wearily, there would be no one else to help the new woman. No one would bother. It was her or nothing.

Lorna kicked at the set of bunk beds, making them clank hard against the concrete walls. "What the fuck is going on?"

Caught by surprise, both women stepped a pace away from Kellie, as far as they had room to go.

Kellie flew upright, and instead of bolting, as Lorna expected, she lit into the woman closest to her, catching her in the shoulder with a wild haymaker.

The woman stumbled backward, her hands flying to where she'd been struck. "Hey!" Regaining her balance, she rushed forward only to be stopped in her tracks by a withering glare from Lorna.

"Don't do it, Laverne," Lorna warned, adrenaline surging through her and very nearly making her twitch. "Get out of here while you still can and take that useless bitch still standing outside the doorway with you." But she knew she wouldn't be rid of Katrina Nowak, the head bitch, so easily.

When Laverne hesitated, Lorna grabbed Kellie by the shoulders and pulled her close. "Are you all right?" When Kellie didn't answer she gave her a firm shake, scattering blood droplets everywhere. "I said, are you all right?" Her voice and firm demeanor forced Kellie's wild gray eyes to focus on her.

Kellie's nose was bleeding and misshapen and she was shaking like a leaf. "I ju-just wanted a shower." Her eyes filled with tears. "I'm no-no-not okay."

"Long time no see, Mally. What the fuck do you think you're doing in my cell?"

The thick, sickeningly familiar southern accent scraped across Lorna's nerves, reminding her of darker times when she heard it on a daily basis. The hair on the back of her neck stood on end and a bolt of white-hot hatred, unpolluted by pity or compassion, tore through her. She struggled to keep her composure.

"Get dressed," Lorna ordered Kellie softly, guilt swirling in the pit of her stomach. *My fault. Christ, having her come here alone her first day was stupid. I know better.* "And go back to my cell."

"I think I need a doctor," Kellie said in a nasal voice, one hand on the bridge of her nose. Petrified gray eyes darted to the other women, who were now prowling around them like leopards moving in for a kill. "I—"

Lorna merely shook her head, her eyes never leaving Kellie's. She cupped Kellie's cheek, feeling warms tears run over her hand. "Go now."

Katrina let out a frustrated breath, her voice a dangerous rumble. "This is none of your concern, Mally."

Furious, Lorna wheeled on Katrina, a tall, gangly prisoner with icy Nordic features and a cruel smile. "I'm making it my business, bitch. I heard you were coming over from maximum security, but I couldn't believe the administration was that dumb. If you're here, who's running hell?" From the corner of her eye, she saw Kellie scramble toward the bench where she'd left her bag and yank out a T-shirt. *Hurry.*

Katrina's expression was dead. "Such a funny girl."

Lorna merely crossed her arms over her chest and waited.

"It looks like you're wrong about the administration," Katrina began. "You never were a very good judge of people. They constantly disappoint you, don't they?"

It was a split-second decision. "Do you know who that woman is?" Lorna demanded, pointing at Kellie and moving directly in front of Katrina to draw her eyes off the panicking brunette. She widened her stance and centered her body over her feet, making a note to go for the nose first.

Katrina looked confused. "She's new. And—"

Eyes blazing, Lorna made herself as clear as she knew how. "I've already claimed her. She's my cellmate and she's my family now."

Kellie's mouth dropped open and her busy hands froze. "What are you talking about?" she screeched, too confused and terrified to keep quiet. Her gaze flicked to the door. "Guards!" she hollered desperately. "Help!"

The woman next to Laverne paled and glanced nervously around the cell. "Fuck. I'm outta here."

"Shut up!" Both Katrina and Lorna yelled at Kellie in unison.

Katrina took a step forward and Lorna stopped her with a firm hand. "Don't touch her," she said in a low voice that came directly from her gut.

Katrina's jaw tightened and her hands shaped into fists. "You're lying, Mally. Seems my new friend doesn't even agree that she's one of yours. You must not be very persuasive." Katrina wrenched her arm from Lorna's hand.

Lorna merely raised a single eyebrow and waited.

"Don't tell me you suddenly started craving pussy! You couldn't have changed your mind that much since we were cellmates."

Lorna shoved her face farther into Katrina's personal space. "You are one sick bitch," she whispered disgustedly. "You always were."

"I learned from the best." Katrina clucked softly. "Don't you remember? We cut our baby teeth on tasty inmates like this one."

Lorna's stomach lurched at the bitter truth of that statement. Her heart was pumping double-time and she kept Laverne in her peripheral vision. One kick to the gut or crotch and she wouldn't be a problem. "You don't seem to be understanding me, dumbass. The newbie doesn't have to approve of or even be told about what I decide. Who gives a damn what she says? She's my family now. Under my protection. Hands *off!*"

Katrina's eyes turned to slits. "There's a difference between her being your family and you just not wanting me to have her, Mally. That's not playing fair."

Lorna's head snapped sideways. "DO AS I SAID and get the fuck back to my cell!" Tiny droplets of spittle flew from her mouth as she roared, her eyes flashing dangerously.

Kellie bolted from the cell in nothing but her bloodstained T-shirt and underwear. She slipped on the damp floors on the way out, banging her hip against the tile. She let out a muted cry, but didn't stop as she crawled the rest of the way to the door and fumbled for the handle.

She heard more yelling and then a fight erupt behind her, but she didn't care. She ran as fast as she could, catcalls following her as she made her way back to Lorna's cell. *Aren't there any guards in this place?*

She slammed the door shut behind her and ran a trembling hand through her hair. "Oh, God. Oh, God." Her nose was still sluggishly bleeding and her skin crawled in remembrance of Katrina's touch. She sat down on the bottom bunk, and used the hem of her T-shirt to stem the flow of blood.

Before she had a chance to do anything else, Roscoe strode into the cell.

"The cell block is buzzing," he drawled slowly, taking in Kellie's bloodied nose and tear-streaked face. He didn't look surprised, but he didn't look happy either. The guard sighed. "Mally do that?"

Kellie looked away and shook her head, the motion causing her nose to throb even more.

Impatience and a shocking level of anger invaded his voice. "Protecting her won't do anything for you."

"I'm not protecting her." Kellie's temper flared. Where was he when she needed him? "It wasn't her. It was—"

"Save your breath!" he snapped. Roscoe struggled to gentle his voice and clumsily moved closer to give Kellie's arm a sympathetic pat. "I know you're new. So let me lay things out for you. Mally is a bad egg. But all you have to do make sure that she's punished for hurting you is to tell me what happened." Confidence filled his smile. "And I'll make sure she gets exactly what she deserves."

Was he deaf? "But she didn't touch me."

His nostrils flared. "Of course she did. She left her cell to find you, didn't she?"

"Maybe," she began hesitantly, feeling confused. "I don't know." For a brief second she considered telling him that it had been Lorna who had assaulted her. Surely that would mean the guard would separate them for good. She didn't want to be part of some bizarre Jerry Springer convict family. But something about Roscoe's eager expression worried her.

"Well?" He tapped a foot that looked too small to go with the rest of his enormous body. "I ain't got all day. Lights out is coming soon."

"Umm . . . She didn't touch me," Kellie finally repeated.

"Okay," he said, clearly irritated and not doing a very good job of hiding it. He began milling around the desk. "If she didn't do it, who did? Such a shame a pretty face like yours is already damaged goods." His gaze traveled down her body and settled between her legs for several long seconds before finally sliding away. "What else was . . . damaged?"

Suddenly, Lorna appeared in the doorway cast in light and shadows. Her mouth was bleeding lethargically and a lurid scratch ran from eye to chin and divided her cheek.

The women's eyes locked and Lorna slowly shook her head no, silently mouthing, "Don't do it."

Torn, Kellie bit her lip.

"Holloway?" Roscoe repeated, drawing out her name as he moved around the room.

For a long second Kellie sat on the razor's edge. Lorna's expression didn't change, but her eyes screamed a warning that Kellie found herself unable to ignore. "I—I um. I just tripped, is all." *Right. Even this schmuck won't believe that.*

Roscoe slapped the metal desk with an open hand, his head snapping sideways. "Bullshit!"

Lorna's eyes briefly closed as if relief, then she strolled all the way inside, keeping her back to the guard as she breezed past him. "Here to put Holloway in her new cell? What took you so long?"

Roscoe's glare burned a hole in Lorna's back as he moved to her laundry bag and peered inside. His mouth moved but no sound came out for a few seconds. Then he waved a dismissive hand. "She'll be moved when I'm good and goddamned ready." Frustration leaked into his voice. "Maybe tomorrow, maybe never. I know how much you enjoy having roommates."

Kellie had no idea what was going on, but despite Lorna's earlier statement, which seemed to indicate she'd taken some sort of bizarre proprietary interest in her, going anyplace with Roscoe was rapidly becoming an equally unsettling option. Best to stay put.

"Fine, Holloway," Roscoe began derisively, "if you want to be Mally's dog—"

Lorna's back straightened.

"—Be my guest. Just don't come crying to me when she does worse than a bloody nose."

He stormed out.

Lorna leaned over the desk, bracing her hands on the cool metal as her head sagged. Kellie was as angry as she was frightened. "Why didn't you want me to tell the guard what happened? You saw what she did to me!"

With visible effort, Lorna pushed away from the desk. "This is truly your first time, isn't it?" she tiredly asked.

"I'm a little too long in the tooth to be a virgin, don't you think?" Kellie said in a clipped voice. "Besides, that Katrina woman didn't get quite that far. Though it wasn't for her lack of trying. If you hadn't kicked that bunk and . . . well . . ." She let the sentence trail off, her throat constricting around the words.

"I meant your first time in prison," Lorna clarified gently. Her hand went to her lip. "Goddammit." She let out a hiss. "That hurts." She plopped on the bed next to Kellie, who scooted as far away from her as she could.

Lorna looked stung by the action.

Kellie sniffed a few times, glad her throbbing nose had finally stopped bleeding. Though she was pretty sure it was broken. "Yes," she finally uttered. "I'm a prison virgin." She knew her voice was rough with anger. Anger at the wrong person. But she couldn't help herself. "As if you couldn't tell."

Lorna's brows contracted. "Didn't you ever see any prison movies?"

"No."

"Never talked to a relative who'd recently come out of the joint? Uncles? Cousins? Your dad?"

Kellie blinked. Lorna had asked her question as though she couldn't believe the answer could be no. Rather than offend this volatile woman again, she settled on mumbling, "I'm not close to my family."

Lorna looked at Kellie like she was an alien. "Not even a boy-friend who—"

Kellie glared at her with bloodshot eyes. "I *said*, I've never known any convicts and I don't know what to do, okay? Up until a few months ago my life was not a bad Loretta Lynn song! Besides, after ten minutes I was already in trouble. That should tell you something."

Kellie gestured widely. "None of this is my fault." She blinked a few times, reality crashing down on her and a hint of desperation invading her voice. "I—I don't know how I'm going to do this."

"You'll find a way," Lorna corrected mildly, scooting back farther on the bunk and leaning against the cool wall. "But there are some things you'll need to learn."

"But how do I learn them without getting killed in the process?"

"You just do. It's not easy . . . I know." Lorna looked like she wanted to say more, but couldn't. "Look, the most important thing to know is that you never, ever, rat out an inmate to a guard. Never."

"Even for trying to rape me?" Kellie asked bluntly.

"Even for trying to kill you."

Kellie's hands balled into frustrated fists. "But shouldn't the murderers be in maximum security!"

Lorna smiled grimly. "Maybe. But it costs three times as much to house a con in maximum as it does medium security. The state's only got so much money. So even the worst of the worst can find their way here over time. And you had the very bad luck to meet one of the worst today."

Kellie eyes flickered over Lorna. She felt an unwelcome tingle of attraction for her rescuer. "Only one?"

Lorna bristled. "Fuck you, Holloway. I'm happy to let you figure things out for yourself." She crossed her arms over her chest and looked away, eyes on fire. "Having any roommate is a pain in the ass . . . But one who is a bitch to boot isn't something I'm going to put up with."

Kellie flinched at the harsh words. "I . . ." She swallowed. "I'm sorry. I didn't mean it that way. I don't know what I'm saying. I'm . . . Just go on. Please." *I need all the help I can get.*

But Lorna waited until Kellie was literally squirming. "The guards are always hanging around here, but as you found out today, they aren't everywhere. You have to live with the other women, not so much the guards. The inmates exterminate rats, even ones who are just scared or who are just telling the truth. Period."

Kellie gaped. "They would kill me?"

Lorna shrugged a well-toned shoulder. "They would try."

Kellie closed her eyes, feeling more tired and dirty than she had before. And that was saying something. A drink would go a long way toward dulling this nightmare. "Jesus."

Lorna hadn't spoken to anyone for this long in years and, though it was foreign, it wasn't unpleasant.

Kellie wrapped her arms around herself and began to sway.

Lorna frowned and studied the woman next to her. "Drug stupid, huh?"

"What?"

"What are you coming off of?"

Kellie sniffed and glanced away. "I don't know what you mean."

Lorna inclined her head. "Oh, yes you do. You're detoxing. So which is it? Drugs or booze?"

"I am certainly not detoxing! Do I seem like some crackhead druggie or smelly wino to you? I'm not detoxing."

Lorna gave her a pointed look. "You're not, huh?" She grabbed Kellie's hand, which was shaking like a leaf, and held it up for inspection. "You coulda fooled me."

Kellie yanked it back.

Another shrug. "Fine. So you're not drying out. I guess you just look *exactly* like someone who is." Lorna glanced at Kellie with a knowing eye. Unexpectedly, her hand shot out and she grabbed Kellie's chin so she could move her face from side to side as she examined her. "Booze, I think."

"Maybe I just look like someone who was wrongly convicted, whose face was pounded in, and who was nearly raped!" Kellie said from between clenched teeth. But what she really wanted to do was scream at the top of her lungs. She wanted to hit this woman. Or maybe shake her within an inch of her life. But when she looked down at her own hands they were trembling so badly she couldn't have done it if she tried. She tucked them under her armpits and whispered, "Christ."

"How long?" Lorna asked in a voice so matter of fact that Kellie forgot to lie.

"A little more than two days."

Lorna let out a long breath, hoping that Kellie wouldn't get the DTs. Dealing with someone who felt like shit on toast was one thing, hallucinations, however, freaked the hell out of her. She wrestled with herself for a moment before saying, "There are medicines in the infirmary that will—"

"So," Kellie interrupted in a nasal voice, changing the subject to something equally depressing. "Am I your dog like that guard said?"

Lorna winced and allowed herself to be distracted. "I don't want or need a dog."

Kellie just kept right on going as though Lorna hadn't spoken at all. "God, how can I be someone's prison bitch on my very first day!" she wailed miserably. "My life is a bad cliché. If only my man had run off too I'd be a Lifetime movie of the week." Briskly, she rubbed her arms. "I'd try to escape if I had a place to go."

"The things I get into," Lorna murmured under her breath. "Look, you're clearly a bitch." She gave Kellie a direct look. "But you're not my bitch. And more importantly, you're not Katrina's."

When Lorna said Katrina's name her voice dripped with so much hatred that Kellie gulped. She eyed the other woman warily. "But you said—"

"I know what I said." Lorna turned to face her. "Don't you get it?" She shook her head a little, trying to remember what the real world was like. It had been so long. "You were just about to become Katrina's property unless you could fend her off." She scratched her chin. "And, no offense, but it didn't look like you were fending her off."

Kellie glanced down at herself. Her shirt was covered in blood, her hair looked like she'd been in a wind tunnel, she stank, and she was still in her panties. "No kidding. I'm not really much of a fighter." The skin beneath her eyes was already starting to turn purple and her vision was a bit blurry. And her nose hurt.

Lorna idly examined bruised and torn skin on her own knuckles. "Look, I felt bad for sending you to the showers alone on your first day and I didn't want Katrina to have the satisfaction of claiming you." She shook her head a little, obviously as surprised by what she'd done as Kellie. "So I claimed you for myself as part of what's mine."

"You said I wasn't your bitch!" Kellie said desperately. Clearly she couldn't trust this crazy, violent woman.

"Shut up."

"But—"

"Jesus Christ, just shut up and listen!"

Reluctantly, Kellie bit her tongue and sat on her hands. She had to bounce up and down a little to keep herself from talking.

Lorna rolled her eyes at Kellie's resentful expression. "I wasn't kidding when I said I hoped Roscoe was coming to move you to another cell. God! You have a listening problem and it's already pissing me off."

"I guess I'll never be voted 'Most Popular Convict,'" Kellie said flatly. "I'm crushed."

Lorna looked as though half of her wanted to strangle Kellie while the other half wanted to laugh.

Kellie held her breath.

Finally, a reluctant grin twitched at the corner of Lorna's mouth.

"You were saying?" Kellie said with exaggerated politeness, knowing she'd already pushed her luck beyond what was wise with this volatile woman.

"If you're part of someone's clan here it means something. It means protection and belonging and most women respect that because that's all we have. We make our own families. It's not a sexual thing," Lorna assured her hastily. Then she winced. "Well, at least it's not with me. There are all sorts of relationships that we create that have special meaning here. Sisters, cousins, spouses, even grandmothers."

Kellie scrubbed her forehead roughly. "You declared ownership over me like a piece of property," she said hotly, unable to stop herself. "I'm not some hunk of meat."

Lorna snickered. "Of course you are. We all are. What's important is that you have the power to hold on to what's yours."

Her eyebrows jumped. "And you have the power?"

Lorna stretched out her legs and yawned. "You're here, aren't you?"

Kellie wiped her eyes, not believing how much had changed in her life in the last hour. But at least Lorna didn't seem hell-bent on rape. "So, who else is in this clan of ours?"

Lorna gave her a tired, wan smile. "So far it's just us. Now go make me some coffee and gravy, bitch. And get off my bed." She was clearly joking and mimicking someone else's voice.

Valiantly, if half-heartedly, Kellie played along. "Screw off, deadbeat. I'll sit down and bleed anywhere I like." She carefully felt her nose with trembling fingers, crossing her eyes as she tried to assess the damage.

"Ah." Lorna grinned. "We're just like real family already." But her smiled faded before she'd even finished saying the words. She licked her lips, grimacing at the metallic tang of blood. "Who needs the outside world, huh?"

Kellie's lower lip trembled and she whispered, "I do."

The bleak vulnerability of the response tugged at Lorna's heartstrings. Something that hadn't happened in a very long time. She laid a cautious hand on Kellie's arm, and Kellie's breathing stopped. Their eyes met and held for the second time that evening. Kellie was suddenly aware of the warmth of Lorna's palm. Just that much unexpected human kindness felt so good it brought tears to her eyes for the umpteenth time that day. She doubted she would have been as gracious had their positions been reversed. For the first time in years, she felt ashamed of her own selfish, and very unalterable, nature.

"I won't hurt you." Lorna looked down at her hand as though it weren't her own, and with brows drawn, she self-consciously removed it. "Katrina will hurt you if she gets the chance. But I won't." Her voice broke and she turned away, embarrassed. "I'm not like *him*," she uttered in a barely audible voice.

Despite Lorna's fervent statement, the tension between them eased and settled into something tolerable. Kellie didn't think Lorna knew she'd said that last bit out loud. And who 'he' was, Kellie decided, didn't really matter. "I believe you," she heard herself whisper in return. She had no idea why those words were so important to Lorna, but it was clear that they were.

"Okay." Lorna nodded once, quickly regaining her composure after a few hard swallows. "So long as we've got that settled."

With more tenderness than Kellie expected, Lorna examined her face. "Your nose is busted for sure," she murmured, lifting Kellie's chin higher as she continued her once-over. "You could go to the infirmary, but because nobody knows you, I'm afraid it would start rumors that you're squealing about who hit you."

"Oh," Kellie said glumly. "I hadn't thought of that. So I'm stuck with the face of a hockey player now?" Her teeth began to chatter as her body's craving for something to drink intensified and the shock of what she'd just been through settled in.

"Do you want me to try and fix it?" Lorna asked, letting her hand drop to her side. "Your nose, I mean. I'm good at that." Unexpectedly, she smiled, and Kellie nearly gasped as she saw years peel themselves from Lorna's already youthful face. "Then we can go back to the bathroom and wash up a little in the sink."

"The bathroom?" Kellie's voice was filled with dread. They would have to walk past Katrina's cell to get to there. Then again, holding it for years didn't seem like much of an option.

Lorna's face hardened again. "The showers are locked and Katrina won't be using those bathrooms. From now on, she's using the ones on the far side of the cell block."

"How do you know?"

Lorna nearly growled. "Trust me, I know."

Do I have a choice? "Can you make my nose straight again?" Kellie gingerly touched the swollen skin, feeling the misshapen cartilage.

Lorna eyed her speculatively. "I can try. I fixed my own a few years ago." She squared her shoulders and lifted her chin a little, unconsciously responding to Kellie's appraisal as the brunette gave her the once over.

She had a cute, slightly upturned nose that Kellie considered quite attractive. "Are you a doctor?"

"Absolutely," Lorna said seriously. "And an astronaut, scientist and Indian chief in my spare time."

Kellie's lips curled into a faux smile. "I knew you were a doctor because of your wonderful bedside manner."

"At these rates, what do you expect? But if you want someone else, I can refer you to the nurse in cell fourteen-oh-four-A. Unfortunately, she prescribed rat poison to her last patient."

Laugh or you'll never stop screaming. "Uhh . . . Not surprisingly, I'll pass on her. If you fix it, will it be painful?"

"Terribly, Princess."

Kellie positioned herself on the bed so that Lorna had easy access. She chuckled uneasily, praying this wasn't as stupid as she feared it would be. "Have I mentioned that I'm vain?"

"Have I mentioned this was really gonna hurt?" Lorna carefully laid her fingers on either side of Kellie's nose. They were blessedly cool against her heated skin.

Kellie blanched, her courage rapidly failing. "Maybe you shouldn't actually—"

To the sound of Kellie's shriek, Lorna quickly snapped the bent nose back into place. "Too late."

"Argh!" Blood again began streaming from Kellie's nose as she screamed.

Then the lights flickered.

"Uh oh."

Kellie froze, her hands covering her nose and mouth. "Uh d'oh, whad?" Nervously, she glanced around. *What more can happen!*

"That means bathrooms have already closed and lights out is in three minutes."

"But—" Kellie gestured angrily at her face and hopelessly stained shirt. "I thought we were going to wash up."

"So did I." Lorna began digging through one of her dresser drawers. Over her shoulder she tossed a plastic box, forcing Kellie to awkwardly snatch it out of mid-air or be hit in the head with it.

Kellie stared at the box of Wet-wipes as Lorna began to peel off her T-shirt. Her eyes were irresistibly drawn to Lorna's lean back and the intricate tattoo on her bicep.

"Better hurry," Lorna told her, grabbing a fresh shirt from a different drawer and quickly tugging it over her head. Her hair was just a little curly now that it was nearly dry.

Kellie began wiping her face hastily, doing her best not to cry. Her nose felt straighter but it was completely numb and she was pretty sure that wasn't supposed to have happened.

There was a loud clicking sound from the door as the lock that had been holding the door open released.

A few seconds more and Chul swept by the room, his boots clicking against the floor with every rapid step. Glancing inside he saw two bodies and closed the door so quickly that Kellie barely saw him. She grabbed another wipe and hurriedly cleaned her sticky chin, glad she couldn't smell the blood.

Then the room went black.

Kellie sucked in a nervous breath. Out of the blue, a warm hand came to rest on her shoulder and she nearly jumped out of her skin. The hand gave her a gentle squeeze.

"It's all right," Lorna promised quietly. "It's not as dark as you think. Your eyes will adjust."

The cell door clicked again and then a heavy deadbolt slid into place. Kellie jerked at the sound. "Is it—?"

"Locked until morning," Lorna confirmed quietly, "yeah."

Kellie released a shaky exhale. Her insides were quivering and she felt even sicker than she had a few minutes ago. The room was dark, and cramped and, suddenly, it was unbearably hot. *I can't breathe.* "I guess . . . I mean, I suppose you get used to the sound of the lock every night, huh?" The words sounded thin even to her own ears.

Lorna glanced at the back of the cell and upward toward the small window that allowed slivers of moonlight to sneak into the room. She took a step forward, placing herself in the silvery light, and letting it drape itself over her face. Then she turned, sighed, and shared the unvarnished truth. "No."

Chapter 2
The next night . . .

A low moan woke Lorna from a dead sleep. She blinked in the darkness, painfully reminded of her battered lip when she licked it unthinkingly. "Ouch."

Another moan.

There was a moment of confusion as Lorna sat up. "Meg? I'm comin'. Don't be afraid."

"Huh?"

Not Meg. Someone else. Ugh, I hate that dream. Lorna's mind whispered, *What's that new woman's name again? Ah, yes.* "You okay up there, Princess?" she muttered wearily, throwing her arm over her face.

The beds shook a little as Kellie whimpered out a faint, "No."

Lorna let out a long sigh and rolled over to toss her legs over the side of her bed. As she stood, she listened to the rain patter against the thick glass of the tiny window. The occasional flash of lightning lit the cell. "What's wrong? Your nose hurting? I have some aspirin in my toiletry bag."

Kellie was huddled up into a miserable, shivering ball.

Lorna laid a hand on her shoulder and her palm was instantly soaked with a cold sweat. *Shit.* "Holloway?"

No response.

"Kellie?" This time louder. Lorna gave her a hesitant shake and Kellie rolled over onto her back, her body twitching every so often. Even in the weak light Lorna could see that she was pale and that her nose was terribly swollen. Her slitted eyes were colorless.

Kellie's face contorted in pain. "My st-stomach hurts."

Lorna sighed and rested her forehead against Kellie's mattress. Her voice was quiet in deference to the thin walls and sleeping women in the cells all around her. "I know. You need to go to the infirmary." She glanced over her shoulder. The clock said one o'clock.

"I can't believe that my bitch ex was right." Kellie's voice shook. "I *really* need a drink." She squeezed her eyes shut. "If I just could have one. Just one and I'd be fine."

Lorna filed away the surprising information about Kellie's ex being female and simply nodded. "Hang on. I've got something to drink."

Kellie shot up, blinking dazedly as her head spun. "You do?" she asked eagerly. "Thank Christ! I'll pay you back somehow. I swear I will."

Lorna rifled through the bottom drawer of her dresser. After a few seconds, she tugged out two tall plastic bottles from among a pile of T-shirts.

Kellie's quivering hand shot out and grabbed the bottle, instantly she began working the lid. A second more and the bottle was at her lips. "Fuck!" She choked a little and wiped her wet chin with the back of her hand. "You tricked me! This is water!"

Lorna twisted off her bottle cap and took a long sip. "I never said it was alcohol. I don't drink that poison," she said after she drank a few gulps.

Then she went back to her dresser only to return with two small white tablets in her hand. Lorna handed them to Kellie and made a shooing motion. "Go on, take a few more sips and then I'll call the guards and we'll get you to the infirmary for some real drugs. If I scream long enough, they'll eventually wander down." She sighed and added in a murmur, "I hope."

"And the entire cellblock will hear?"

"Yeah, I guess."

Kellie took another sip of water, scrunching up her face as though she were drinking gasoline. "If you scream for the guards and they take me to the doctor, what will keep people from thinking you're the rat? Ohh . . ." She lurched forward, her arms drawing inward to her belly.

Lorna grimaced. "Cramps, huh? And your head is throbbing too?"

Kellie swallowed and closed her eyes. "How did you know?"

Lorna almost decided not to answer, but somehow the darkness lent a note of intimacy to the conversation, and she found herself willing to share just a tiny bit of history with this stranger. "When I was a kid my mom used to quit drinking every couple of years or so. It never stuck for more than a few weeks." She paused and shrugged. "I knew the signs."

Lorna offered Kellie her hand, but she didn't move. "I'll help you walk," she clarified a bit impatiently. "The guards sure as hell won't."

"W-what about what the other inmates will think of you?"

Irritated, Lorna shook her head. "I don't give a shit what anyone thinks about me. They all know me, and besides, I can take care of myself if you haven't noticed."

But Kellie's will was resolute. "But s-still, it could be dangerous for both of us, right?" She looked right at Lorna.

"I . . . I don't know." Lorna would have said 'no' only yesterday, but with Katrina in the cellblock things had just gotten a whole lot more complicated. Lorna threw her hands up. "Maybe," she admitted reluctantly, her teeth grinding together.

Kellie handed back her bottle of water and cradled her head in her hands. "Then I'm st-staying right here. Right here." She continued to rock back and forth. "Besides," she let out a painful chuckle, "if you're in danger how can you protect me?"

Lorna put a hand on her hip. "What makes you think I'll continue to protect you?"

Kellie stopped speaking for a few seconds and clenched her teeth to keep from crying out in pain. "How would it look if one of 'yours' was hurt after you made such a big deal of claiming me? I'm sure everyone knows about it by now. No, you need to keep an eye on me. At least for a little while."

Kellie moaned again, her stomach lurching violently. "Maybe I will go the infirmary. If someone kills me while I'm there th-then I won't feel like this anymore." Sweat beaded on her forehead.

Lorna set the bottles on the desk. "You're not going to die."

Kellie's smile was icy cold. "Don't be too sure. Th-There's more than one way to skin a cat."

There wasn't even a hint of teasing in Kellie's voice and a wave of uneasiness swept over Lorna. "What does that mean?"

"Nothing."

"What does that mean?" Lorna asked harshly. "Another way to skin a cat?"

Kellie glanced up, looking a little befuddled. "What? It's just a saying."

Lorna positioned herself right in front of Kellie. "Don't even *think* about offing yourself in here," she said in typical blunt fashion. "Don't even think about it."

Kellie squeezed the sides of her head. "I was just joking," she protested ineffectually. "Jeeze."

Lorna's face was deadly serious. "It didn't sound like that to me."

There was a long silence filled only with the sounds of far off thunder and two women breathing. Seconds ticked away until Kellie said, "Well, I w-was joking." This time she could meet Lorna's gaze.

Lorna released a shaky breath. "You shouldn't joke about things like that."

"Now is not a good time for a lecture." Kellie bared her teeth like a rabid dog. "I don't need another mother."

"And I don't need to come back to my cell to find a stinking corpse hanging from the bed frame!" Lorna shot back. "Don't you dare do it, Holloway!" She clenched her hands into fists. "Don't you fucking dare or I'll . . . I'll . . ." Her eyes flitted back and forth as she thought of a suitable threat.

"Kill me?" Dramatically, Kellie bit her knuckle and let her eyes go wide as saucers. "Oh, no. Not that."

"Very funny."

"And I don't stink."

"Then what smells like an animal carcass?"

With every fiber of her being Kellie wanted to deny it, but even through her damaged nose she could tell that Lorna was right. "Tomorrow. I'll get cleaned up tomorrow. Honest."

"We've had inmates who wouldn't wash before. If the guards don't hose 'em down, the other inmates will. And it won't be pretty."

"I just didn't feel like it today, okay?" She rubbed her temples then her hands shot to her stomach. "Lorna?"

Lorna briefly considered climbing back into bed and pulling the covers over her head. "Do you ever shut up? I'm really starting to regret the fact you know my name."

"Was feeling like puking one of those symptoms you know so much about?"

Lorna's eyes widened. "Shit!" She leapt for the plastic waste paper basket under her desk, thrusting it under Kellie's chin.

Kellie began heaving her guts out.

Lorna shifted from one foot to the other, not knowing quite what to do. Whenever her mother hit this stage, she would smash dishes against the wall to make herself feel better. Then she would go to bed and expect Meg and Lorna to pick up the broken glass and clean up the vomit. By the next day she'd start drinking again.

Awkwardly, Kellie tried to push the hair out of her face, but stray strands kept escaping.

The motion snapped Lorna out of the past and, unable to watch her struggle, she moved Kellie's hands away and replaced them with her own, lifting the hair out of the way. *Soft and thick, just like it looks.*

She tried to block out what she was seeing, hearing and smelling, but it was no use, her own stomach roiled. Blood wasn't a problem.

Broken bones, prison tattoos, and shockingly violent altercations that would send most women running for the hills or an asylum, she could handle them all. But a little barf, and her stomach began to whirl and churn like a cork in the sea.

It took forever, but finally Kellie was left with only the occasional dry heave. And finally she was finished with even that and set the waste paper basket to rest on her outstretched legs. She tilted her head back, eyes closed in abject misery. "Jesus."

Lorna gently released Kellie's hair and let her hand come to rest on Kellie's forehead. The skin was slick and clammy. She used the hem of her T-shirt to tenderly wipe it off.

Kellie opened her eyes, but didn't move to stop the compassionate attention.

Lorna headed toward the desk with a relieved sigh. She began stripping out of her T-shirt again.

"You must be a good mother," Kellie said hoarsely, wishing she could see Lorna's face to gauge her reaction.

Lorna snorted. "Why would you say something that crazy?"

Kellie wondered if she was serious. Lorna had given her more care in the last hour than anyone had in her entire life. She waited, but quickly realized that Lorna's question was genuine. Kellie limply gestured toward the desk where she'd seen a photo of a little girl. "Your daughter has your eyes."

"Here." Lorna handed her back the water bottle and sat down in front of her, her back against the opposite wall. "Feel free to keep it," she joked weakly. "And that's not my daughter, it's my sister."

"Mmm . . ." Kellie put the bottle against her cheek. "Big age gap."

"Not as big as you think." A bitter sigh trickled out. "The photo is . . ." *All I have left.* "It's old."

Kellie waited to hear more, but she was only mildly curious and when Lorna stopped talking, she didn't press the issue. She drank greedily, then moved the cool bottle to her forehead. "I'm sorry. I know it's late. You must be tired."

"I'll be okay."

"I'll do my best to be quiet so you can get some rest," Kellie promised, barely able to speak over the pounding in her head. She tried to stand but Lorna leaned over and held her down with one hand.

"I'll take the top bunk tonight." Lorna's voiced brooked no disagreement. "If you stay on the concrete you'll catch your death, so you can use my bunk, if you want."

"Thank God," Kellie said. "I don't think I could made it back up the ladder."

Lorna's forehead creased. "Then why did you offer?"

"Vomit rules of etiquette?"

"Miss Manners would pee her pants with pride." Lorna yanked off Kellie's damp sheets, then deftly climbed the ladder at the head of the bed, making sure to lie on the blanket rather than directly on the tattered mattress.

Kellie leaned back against the bed frame, the cool floor having chilled her legs to the bone, but she didn't care. "I'm not usually this much trouble."

Lorna shucked Kellie's pillowcase then pulled the pillow over her head and held it there. "Promise, Princess?" she muttered into the mattress.

Kellie wrapped her arms around herself and stifled a moan as her cramps returned with a vengeance. She didn't comment on what appeared to be her new nickname. She'd been called far worse by people who knew her far better. "Not really. No."

Lorna chuckled quietly, a gesture that was equal parts amusement and worry. "Somehow I knew that."

Chapter 3
A few days later . . .

It was seven fifteen in the morning and the sleepy, grumbling inmates were lined up outside their cells with Chul and a female guard that Kellie hadn't seen before taking head count. Once everyone was accounted for, it was time for announcements.

"As you know," Chul began in a bored voice, "today is phone call day with visiting hours right after."

There were a few muted cheers and to Kellie's surprise, a few groans too. *I guess not everyone likes keeping up with things back home.* Chul and the female guard, whose hair was styled in a wild array of thick braids that reminded Kellie of Whoopi Goldberg, carried a small canvas moneybag. The guards started at the other end of the block and began talking to each inmate.

Lorna leaned over slightly and whispered, "Can you call collect?"

Kellie chewed her lip. She didn't think her lawyer's secretary would accept a collect call. "No."

"Okay, then you prepay for long distance calls. They come in thirty-minute increments."

Kellie nodded. That should be enough time to see how her appeal was going.

"If you're going to make calls or have a visitor you get to eat first and then you'll be escorted to the reception area."

"The place where I got my lovely prison clothes?"

Lorna quirked a grin. "Exactly. And since it's Chul and Elaine who will be taking you today, you'll get to pay the real phone rate."

A heavy feeling settled in Kellie's chest. "How much is long distance? That was always included in my cell phone plan. I don't have any idea how much the per minute charges are, but I have eight dollars."

"A half hour costs thirty dollars."

"What the hell!" Kellie screeched in disbelief. She felt as though she'd been punched in the gut. "I can't afford that!" *My how the mighty have fallen. I used to pay more than that for my wine with dinner.*

The inmates around them began to laugh and were only quieted by a stern look from the female guard. Nobody wanted to lose her privileges today.

Chul made his way to Lorna and they exchanged friendly bobs of the head.

"Hi, Elaine," Lorna said to the large female guard whose chest was bursting from beneath her tight gray uniform. Her boobs were nearly the size of Roscoe's. "Long time no see."

Elaine Johnson smiled brightly, her large white teeth flashing impressively. "Hey, Lorna. There was an unexpected opening so I was working the minimum side of the fence for the last few months." She buffed her fingernails against her uniform.

"Ooo, lucky you. Is it the paradise that it's rumored to be?"

Elaine glanced around at the dreary concrete walls. "Compared to here?" Her ample body shook as she chuckled. "Oh, yeah. They've got cable TV in all the cells, and all new gym equipment last year. And get this—" She nudged Lorna conspiratorially. "Three women from some hair salon in Barston come in once a month to cut hair.

They even sell those fancy shampoos and soap when they come. The women eat it up."

Lorna let out a low whistle. "That beats the beauty school drop-outs we get. And nice shampoo, huh?"

"Absofuckinlutely. That stuff might sell well here."

The women exchanged knowing looks. "It just might."

Kellie vowed to ask Lorna what those looks meant later.

Chul moved in front of Kellie and opened his mouth to speak.

"Wait," Lorna said.

Chul's gaze slid sideways. "Yeah?"

"I umm . . . I need a phone card today."

"Lorna Malachi wants a card?" His voice cracked at the end like he was a surprised teenager.

Elaine stared at her, unmoving.

Lorna dug two twenty-dollar bills from the front pocket of her blue jeans. The maximum amount of cash an inmate was allowed to keep in her cell or on her person was ten dollars, but cost of phone calls alone rendered that rule impossible to enforce. "Just 'cause I've never made a call before, doesn't mean I can't," she said, irritated by their shocked faces. "A woman can change her mind."

Kellie turned to her cellmate and stared along with the guards. *Never made a call? Ever?*

Lorna rolled her eyes at them all and stuck out her hand. "Just give me the damn card, will ya?"

Elaine was the first to regain her senses. She stuck her hand in the moneybag, but hesitated. "I thought you were saving for when you finally get sprung."

Lorna crossed her arms over her chest, not saying another word.

"Jeesh. Don't get all huffy. Here's your change." Elaine pulled out two fives and handed them to Lorna.

"Hey, Elaine, I don't believe what Lorna is telling me." Chul pointed to his nearly non-existent buttocks. "Quick, check out my ass."

Without thinking, Elaine looked at his butt. Which, of course, looked the same as always. When Chul began to laugh, she realized she'd been caught in one of his favorite jokes . . . again. She scrunched her face and groaned. "No winged monkeys." She shook her head. "Quit trying to be funny and give the woman her card." Then she smacked his slender forearm. "You know I hate looking at your scrawny ass!"

Elaine turned to Lorna and waggled her eyebrows. "Good for you, girl." She lowered her voice. "Make whoever you're calling talk dirty to you. At least it will help you get your money's worth."

Lorna's scowl faded and her eyes took on a slight twinkle. "Thanks for the advice."

"Instructions and expiration date are on the back on the card," Elaine said.

Laughing, Chul moved on to Kellie. "A card for you too, newbie? There must be someone you're itching to tell how horrible this place is. You sure look the part of the much-abused felon." He gestured toward her bruised, sallow face. Between detox and her run-in with Katrina, Kellie knew she didn't quite look as good as death warmed over.

Kellie sighed. According to the information in her prison packet a new worker could earn five dollars and ninety cents a month. Or if she passed some ridiculous tests that she actually had to pay to take, she could tutor other inmates in basic education subjects or job skills and earn from twelve to forty cents an hour. No wonder the black market thrived inside Blue Ridge. "No card till summer, I'm afraid," she said glumly.

Chul shrugged. "Suit yourself."

When the guards were finished collecting money, Elaine leaned against the wall and repeated the words she said every week. "People with visitors step forward." About a third of the women formed their line, then filed in behind Chul, who led them to the cafeteria.

Elaine yawned, showing off a few gold molars. "Those using the phone, step forward." That left only a half dozen women in the rear. At the end of the block, Kellie spotted Katrina. When it came to her, however, she wasn't surprised she had no one to visit or call. But why was Lorna still standing next to her?

Lorna gave Kellie a gentle shove and pressed the phone card into her hand. "Go make your call. You won't be able to rest until you talk to your lawyer and know what's going on."

"But what about you?" Kellie's eyebrows drew together. "Why would you do this?"

Lorna's eyebrow twitched. "This is for me. I'm tired of hearing you complain that you haven't heard from your attorney yet."

Kellie wasn't buying that. "Lorna—"

Lorna glanced down and swallowed a couple of times. "Look, I've got no one to call. You might as well take it."

With Elaine in the lead, the second line of women began to move.

Kellie wanted to ask Lorna about her family, the girl in the photo, or maybe some friends she had on the outside. There had to be someone, didn't there? But there wasn't time. Instead, she accepted the unexpected gift with as much grace as she could muster.

A few seconds ago Kellie had felt like the dark cloud that had held her in its grip for so long was raining on her again. But now . . . "Thank you," she said sincerely, pulling Lorna into a quick hug and giving her back a slightly awkward pat, very aware that Lorna's body had stiffened with the contact.

Lorna stepped back and motioned her forward. "G'wan. And, Princess?"

Kellie jogged to catch up to the back of the line. "Yeah?" she called out.

"If you get your lawyer to talk dirty to you, keep it to yourself, okay?"

Kellie smirked. Her lawyer was seventy-five years old, bald as a cue ball, and she was pretty sure he had a penis, something that disqualified him from all things romantic or sexual in Kellie's book. "No way," she answered as she walked backward. "I'm going to share every lurid detail so you get your money's worth."

From opposite ends of the hall, their eyes met and both women's faces relaxed into smiles.

Kellie's heart fluttered. Something was happening.

Chapter 4
One month later . . .

"Why is everyone in such a hurry?" Kellie's gaze flitted around the cafeteria. "Are they all on their way to throw up?" She stepped aside as two women ran past her out the cafeteria doors. Doing her best not to retch, she pushed her plate away.

The dimly-lit room was painted drab pink, and nearly as depressing as the meals that were served there. They only had fifteen minutes to eat and if the guards heard them utter a single sentence, they would be ordered out of the room. If they were talking that meant they were finished eating.

Lorna's eyes twinkled. "You didn't like the chipped meat on toast?" She stood and picked up her tray. She'd long ago given up on enjoying the taste of food and now ate every bite purely out of habit. Even her lima beans and strawberry Jell-O were long gone.

Kellie shivered and dropped her fork into the enormous pool of brownish-gray gravy that covered a pile of something else that was brownish. "I couldn't help but notice it's not called chipped *beef* on toast, which would be disgusting in its own right."

Lorna gave Kellie a sideways glance as they filed into the back of a line to place their trays on a conveyor belt. "You need to eat." A step forward. "You're getting too skinny."

Kellie gave her jeans a quick tug up. They were seriously drooping. "Food and I aren't on speaking terms yet." Then she noticed Lorna's brow furrow and quickly added, "But I'm feeling a little better." And she was. Her skin was still unusually pale, and she was having trouble sleeping through the night, but after nearly a month in this place her stomach cramps were finally gone. Unfortunately, they'd been replaced by a persistent craving that was nearly more than she could stand.

She'd barely put her tray down when Lorna yanked on her arm. "Hurry up!"

"Why are we hurr—Hey!" She stumbled a step as Lorna tugged a little harder.

"We get to go outside today." They skirted around two older women who gave Lorna a respectful nod as she passed. "First time since before Thanksgiving!" she said, her voice full of youthful excitement.

"We can't go outside. We'll freeze. There's still snow on the ground!" Kellie laid a hand on Lorna's thin, navy blue sweatshirt identical to the one she was wearing.

"Doesn't matter." They took their place at the end of a line that snaked around a blind corner. "The calendar and the warden tell us when we get to go outside. Not mother nature." She bounced up and down a little and peered over the shoulder of the woman in front of her.

Kellie smirked. "You're really excited, aren't you?"

"How can you tell?" Lorna deadpanned.

Kellie shuffled forward several paces, her grin stretching muscles that felt sorely out of use. "I can't imagine."

Lorna grinned and wiggled her eyebrows and Kellie was struck by how appealing she was. Neither bitchy, nor deceitful, nor pretty in a centerfold sort of way, she wasn't the type of woman Kellie was usually attracted to at all. A study in contradictions, there was something oddly compelling about Lorna that was both edgy and safe at the same time. And then there was her smile . . . It could, alternately, make Kellie's knees go weak with its splendor and her heart ache with its sadness.

Kellie laughed warmly at Lorna's rampant enthusiasm. "You're hot," she murmured, a note of surprise and appreciation peeking through. Then color suddenly drained from Kellie's face so rapidly she felt a little dizzy. *Jesus Christ, did I say that out loud?*

Lorna groaned. "Duh."

"Duh?" Kellie repeated, stunned. They moved forward another step. "So you agree?"

Lorna gave her a funny look. "Why wouldn't I? It's true."

"Well . . ." Kellie frowned. "It is. But—" *How vain is she?*

"Just not in bed."

Kellie's feet froze and her mouth dropped open. "What?" she said a little louder than she'd meant to.

"I said, I'm not hot in bed," Lorna repeated slowly, as though Kellie were a dull child.

"No?" Kellie said weakly, disgusted at herself for being vaguely disappointed. "That's really more than I wanted to know."

"Hey, what's wrong with you?" Lorna gave her a poke in the belly. "Did that chipped meat melt your brain or something?"

Kellie shook her head a little. "I'm surprised to hear you agree is all." She let out a slightly huffy breath. "Most people aren't that frank." *Or arrogant!*

"Well, most people don't sleep in a concrete cell with the temperature turned down to next to nothing. If they did, they'd wear socks to bed too!" Lorna defended hotly.

Kellie just looked at her.

Lorna's brow creased. "You're really weird sometimes, you know that?"

Ramona, the woman from the cell next door, who was standing directly behind the pair, began to snicker, causing Kellie to turn and sneer in her general direction.

"Hey, Ramona." Lorna lifted her chin at Ramona and gave her

a puzzled but friendly wave. "Since you're suddenly obsessed with the temperature, Kellie, I thought you might like to know that you won't freeze." Then she pointed toward the front of the line that was moving way too slowly for her tastes. "Hurry it up, ya heifers! You all wear size double XL!"

A chorus of laughter mixed with a few muffled curses rang out in the hallway. But the line did begin to move a little more quickly.

They turned a corner and Kellie was standing in front of a table manned by Chul and Roscoe. Bored, Roscoe tossed her a lightweight poly-filled coat. It was puffy and had a few stains and crudely sewn tears, but it smelled like lavender laundry soap. "Next," Roscoe called out gruffly, looking right over Lorna's head.

Lorna let out a sigh of relief. "Let's go," she urged Kellie. "Now."

"She needs a coat too," Kellie said, unable to keep the irritation from her voice. She was beginning to hate that man.

Roscoe smiled, showing off tobacco stained teeth. "She does, huh?"

"Yes."

"No, I don't," Lorna quickly inserted, tugging on Kellie's sleeve. "Let's go."

"No, Mally, she's right." Roscoe stood and his big belly pushed the pile of coats forward several inches. "You might sue if you catch a chill. I wouldn't want you to get sick." His voice dripped with sarcasm.

"Oh, man." Chul rubbed his temples and looked like he wanted to slug Roscoe. "Not again! Here—" He reached for a jacket to give to Lorna.

"No," Roscoe growled, causing Chul's hand to still.

Lorna did her best to keep her emotions in check. She was losing precious time outside. "Large."

Roscoe handed Ramona a jacket as though Lorna wasn't even there. "Next."

"I said, large," Lorna ground out, adding a reluctant, "Please," at the end.

In an explosion of violent motion, Roscoe shoved a jacket into her hands and pushed her forward with all his might. "I said *next,*

Mally! Get yer ass outside!"

Lorna surged forward, arms flailing, nearly falling flat on her face before Kellie caught her. She whirled around to face Roscoe, her chest rising and falling rapidly.

Chul's eyes grew and he mouthed, "Oh, shit."

"Don't," Kellie said quickly, grabbing hold of Lorna's sweatshirt and doing her best to pull her toward the door. She could feel the waves of anger pouring off her like water cascading down a waterfall. "I want to go outside." *And this is spinning out of control.*

Her pulse began to hammer as every last inmate held her breath to see what would happen next. "Please, Lorna." Kellie wondered if here, in front of so many others, Lorna would be willing, or even able, to give in and let her have her way.

Lorna's and Roscoe's gazes locked, steely and cold. But after several charged seconds, Lorna allowed Kellie to lead her away. "Asshole," she muttered darkly, looking over her shoulder one last time as Roscoe began to laugh. "Ungh!"

"Don't let him get to you," Kellie said in what she hoped was a more soothing than terrified voice. "You got a coat, didn't you? C'mon." She picked up the pace, putting as much distance between Lorna and Roscoe as quickly as she could. "I think it's even sunny outside." And for the first time, Kellie pushed open the large metal doors that led to the prison yard.

A blast of cool, fresh air tinted with the scent of pine and water greeted them. One side of the yard faced the maximum-security wing, a fence at least fifteen feet high and coiled with ring after ring of razor sharp barbed wire separated the two worlds. The remaining sides of the yard looked out to evergreen-filled fields with the first hints of spring grass beginning to peek through the small patches of blindingly white snow. And beyond it all, piercing a cobalt-blue sky, were the mountains.

Kellie had learned that the yard was one of the most dangerous places in the prison. Groups of women, most divided by color or race, were clustered around various tables or pieces of recreational equipment.

Kellie drew in a deep breath and moaned in unexpected pleasure, the explosion of light and riot of color making her squint and smile. "God, I didn't remember it being this good outside!"

"I know," Lorna agreed softly.

And she did, in a way few people could, Kellie realized.

Their sneakers crunched on the gravel as they stepped farther away from the building and Kellie slid into her coat, grateful for the meager protection against the cool, stiff breeze. She tilted her head toward the sun, and allowed its rays to soak into her face. "Lorna, this is so—" When she looked over at the other woman, she had to clamp her hand over her mouth to keep from laughing out loud.

A good six inches of Lorna's arms were hanging out of a jacket at least two sizes too small. So small, in fact, that it wouldn't zip closed. "That dickhead Roscoe gives me a size extra small every year!" she whined, giving Kellie a pathetic look.

Kellie kept her hand planted firmly in place and told herself that the way Lorna looked wasn't funny.

"But if I wear more clothes than this," Lorna tugged at her sweat-shirt that was layered over a white T-shirt, "I bake all morning."

"What's with you and Roscoe?" Kellie's nose was already beginning to leak from the cool air and she sniffed a few times. "He doesn't seem to love anything more than messing with you."

Lorna's gaze dropped to her sneakers. "Roscoe and I go way back."

Kellie's curiosity was piqued and she wiggled a little in anticipation of learning something new. "Way back where?"

Lorna gestured to the maximum-security yard. "Everyone has stuff in their past they don't want to talk about." She glanced back up at Kellie. "Don't you?"

The intensity in Lorna's eyes left Kellie feeling a little off balance. "I—I . . . Of course."

Lorna relaxed a little. "I wasn't going to hit Roscoe or anything. Despite what you might think, I'm not crazy."

Kellie gave her a wary look and gracefully allowed Lorna to change the subject. For now. "I know I don't know you very well, but it looked to me as though you were about to explode like a nuclear warhead."

Lorna cracked a tiny smile. "While that's always a possibility, it's more likely I would have yelled at him and ended up in the hole for a couple of days."

"Days?" Kellie knew the guards had to keep order, but days of solitary confinement just for yelling seemed a little excessive.

Lorna nodded slowly and wrapped her arms around herself and tucked her hands under her armpits. Unconsciously, she moved a little closer to Kellie.

"You're shaking!" Kellie wanted to enfold this woman in her coat and snuggle closer to her. A warm feeling pulsed through her at the mere idea. Whoa. "Can't you just go back inside and get a jacket that fits? Roscoe has had his joke." Then the last group of inmates, followed by Chul and Roscoe, exited the building. Chul locked the door behind him. "Never mind," she said dejectedly.

Lorna sucked in a big lungful of air and grinned despite the fact that she looked ridiculous and was already miserably cold. "It's okay." Her voice was resolute. "I'll just do what I do every year."

"What's that?"

"Wish that a bolt of lightning would hit that bastard Roscoe directly between the eyes."

"Not that I don't think that's a valid wish, but . . ." Kellie tilted her head back and surveyed the clear blue sky. "It's not likely to come true."

"Then I'll have to settle for playing ball." Lorna motioned toward a basketball court with ten women anxiously clustered around a woman pumping air into a basketball. The other inmates had already fanned out to different parts of the yard that held a scattering of wooden picnic tables, a small dirt track, a few pull-up bars, and a surprisingly well-maintained volleyball court that was filling up fast. "Do you play? Some exercise would probably do you good."

Kellie's eye caught the mountains in the distance. She'd never been an outdoor person, never been camping and rarely did as much as visit the city park. But suddenly the barbed fence between her and the trees made her want to burst out in tears. She wanted to be there. She wanted to be anywhere but here. Kellie bent at the waist feeling as though someone had punched her in the gut.

Lorna gently touched her arm. "Kellie?"

With effort, Kellie pushed aside the ache in her chest and straightened. "Sorry. I suck at all things sporty." The nape hairs on her neck suddenly lifted and her gaze traveled around the yard. The other inmates and even the guards were watching. "What are they doing?" she said under her breath, feeling like a beetle under a microscope.

Lorna hopped up and down a few times to send some warm blood pumping through her legs. "I think they're watching us to see if I'm going do something about the way you dragged me away from Roscoe and to see if I'll take your jacket." She glowered. "The jerks."

Kellie blinked a few times. "They're waiting for what?" Had Lorna actually done that to someone else? "Why would you—?"

"This isn't all that hard to figure out, Kellie," Lorna said patiently as she stuffed her hands into her jeans pockets. "Pretend we're dogs. I'm alpha. That means I get the biggest hunk of meat. And you, as not alpha, get the scraps." She opened her arms wide and indicated her child-sized coat. "And this is a scrap."

Part of Kellie wanted to laugh in Lorna's face. She didn't take anyone's scraps! And yet, a bigger part of her realized that Lorna was deadly serious and that the roles they were playing here, whether they aligned with how they felt inside her or not, weren't a game. "I shouldn't have tried to pull you away from Roscoe," she said quietly.

"Please don't be sorry." Lorna lips tensed. "I'm glad you didn't want to see me do something stupid. It's . . ." She paused, struggling for the exact right words. "Well, it's been a long time since anyone cared what happened to me."

"Lorna, I do care." And it was the truth. Though she'd had precious little experience with friends, Lorna seemed like she would be a good one, and the unexpected consequence was that it made her want to be a good one in return.

"Listen," Kellie started tentatively, hoping that she hadn't misread her cellmate completely. But it was hard not to feel connected to a person who'd held your hair out of the way while you puked your guts out and didn't turn away from you when you felt your worst. God, she wished Lorna was gay. "I know I need more help than you do, but that doesn't mean we can't help each other. I think in this place it's good for someone to have your back, right?"

Lorna's smile stretched her face and crinkled the skin around blue eyes the color of the ocean at dusk. "Absolutely."

For a second Kellie was dumbstruck, not so much by what Lorna had said, but by her heart's soaring reaction to making this woman happy, if only for a second. This was something new and she wasn't sure whether it was more disconcerting or wonderful.

Shaking it off, she squared her shoulders and took the next step, which meant swallowing her pride. It took more than one swallow, but she finally put her hands on her own jacket zipper. "You can take the coat."

"No." Lorna's hand shot out to stop her. "Just because the others think I would or should do that, you don't have to." She squeezed Kellie's hand gently and looked up at her from beneath thick lashes, uncertainty written all over her face. "Okay?"

A gust of wind blew a strand of Kellie's hair into her face and suddenly, Lorna reached out with her other hand and gently tucked it behind Kellie's ear. Warm fingertips grazed her chilled ear and Kellie gasped a little at the unexpectedly intimate gesture.

Lorna slowly let her hand fall.

Kellie studied her face, but Lorna's face was closed. She was still an enigma.

Lorna stuffed her hands back into her pocket and gave a little shrug. "I guess I'm gonna play b-ball. We've only got forty-five more minutes." But she didn't move.

Kellie really didn't want to be alone, but she couldn't even dribble a basketball and Lorna was obviously longing to go. *This is your life now. You can't stick to her like glue every second or she'll go crazy and ditch you. Then where will you be?* "Have fun." She did her best to smile reassuringly. "I'm gonna go walk on the track and stretch my legs."

Lorna exhaled, visibly relieved. "Great," she said, still a little awkward. "I know this is going to sound racist, but stay away from the black women."

Kellie's hackles rose. "But—"

Lorna held up a hand. "They don't know you. And that means they don't trust you. That could change with time, but for now, give them respect and stay away from them."

Kellie's eyebrows lifted briefly. "It's respectful to ignore them completely?"

Looking both amused and worried, Lorna said, "You really are green as a little sapling, aren't you? Let me give you the Fisher-Price rules of prison yard relations."

Kellie rolled her eyes, but listened.

"Don't stare at them. Don't sit on those benches." She gestured. "Don't even walk near them. Those are theirs. Don't start a conversation with Janelle. She's the skinny one with the short Afro and a tattoo on her neck. She's their leader."

Kellie scrunched up her face. "The one with the spider web tattoo? Gross. I remember her from the cafeteria."

Lorna nodded her approval. "Good. You're paying attention. Janelle's actually pretty cool, but don't talk to her unless she talks to you first." The corner of her mouth quirked. "Bad manners would reflect poorly on me and then I would be forced to discipline you to save face."

Kellie's eyes narrowed, but Lorna just glared right back.

"Don't think I wouldn't, Princess."

Kellie threw her hands in the air. "Fine."

"The black inmates aren't standing together by coincidence, you know. There's strength in numbers."

"Are they a gang?" Kellie's wary gaze slid sideways. She'd never seen all the women of Blue Ridge's medium security wing at once. Even in the cafeteria they ate in shifts, based on their cell and work assignments. But now that she had seen them as one big group, she shivered a little, wishing she hadn't.

"Them? Nah. They just stick together. Black gangs are more common at the men's facility upstate. Same with the Mexicans. No, it's the women by the weight benches who are pissant wannabe gang members." Lorna's lips thinned. "They're bitches who never stop looking for trouble. They control most of the illegal trade that goes on here and in maximum security." Her voice dropped an octave. "Stay away from them too, Kellie. I mean it."

Kellie turned to see a cluster of white women who were huddled together. A chill ran down her back and settled cold and hard in the pit of her stomach. Katrina was among them.

But even as Lorna was telling her to stay away from Katrina she could see there was some sort of connection between her cellmate and the blonde woman. The vibe they gave off was something close to a dysfunctional family. Lorna and Katrina clearly despised each other. But that didn't change the fact that a slender, but very real thread, seemed to tie them together.

Creepy.

"You don't have to tell me twice. They won't even know I'm here. Can I at least walk the track?"

"If you see any women who've paired off, are walking along the perimeter while keeping an eye on the guards, be careful. That's a sign they're going to make trouble for someone by giving her soft candy."

Kellie gave her a blank look.

"That's prison slang for anything from a punch or two to a thorough beating," Lorna explained.

"Hey." Kellie covertly gestured toward a woman who was standing as close as any prisoner dared to the fence that separated maximum and minimum security. "What's she doing?"

"Signing."

Kellie frowned. She had a cousin who was deaf and had seen him talk with his hands when they were children, but these awkward, exaggerated motions didn't look familiar at all. "That's not sign language."

"Sure it is. It's just not any language you'll see in the outside world. See?" Lorna tilted her chin in the direction of the maximum-security exercise yard. "It's how she talks to the small chick on the bench there."

Kellie followed Lorna's gaze to a slight dishwater blonde who looked as though the wind might blow her away. She watched the pair gesture excitedly until a guard hurried over to the woman in the opposite yard and hauled her inside the prison by the scruff of her neck. "What were they saying?" she wondered out loud.

There was a long pause.

Kellie turned. "Lorna?"

Lorna glanced away from the dejected woman who was jogging away from the fence as if, for some reason, she didn't want to tell Kellie. It seemed . . . private somehow, even though she and every other prisoner who wasn't wet behind the ears knew what was going on.

"Were they making a drug deal or something?" They had clearly violated some rule by talking to each other.

Lorna sighed. "I love you." Her gaze shifted to Kellie. "That's what they were saying to each other."

Inexplicably, Kellie felt a lump rise in her throat. "Oh."

Lorna trotted off to the court, high-fiving a few of the women as she stepped into the paint. A tall woman who was dribbling the ball came toward Lorna.

"Could that slut stand any closer?" Kellie mumbled, suddenly grumpy.

The inmates split up into teams without saying a word and Kellie decided they must have played together many, many times.

"Okay, to the track." She began to walk away, doing her best to hold her head up high and not look away from the other inmates she passed. *Don't show that you're afraid,* Lorna had told her on only her second day at Blue Ridge. *Even when you're falling apart on the inside, be strong on the outside.*

The track was a little bumpy, but she had been right, stretching her legs did feel good. She was halfway around her second lap when she heard her name being called.

"Hey, chica . . . Kellie, hold up." Ramona trotted up beside her.

Ramona was small, maybe five feet two inches and one hundred pounds sopping wet. But she was a little like Lorna in that she had a presence that belied her size. Her curly hair was styled into a mullet that Kellie deemed nothing short of a tragedy; but her round face was open and friendly and her full lips were almost always curved into a smile. "It's a beautiful but cold day to be outside, yes?" Her Mexican accent was as thick and spicy as salsa, but after years of hiring laborers from south of the border, Kellie wasn't too bad at deciphering the Spanglish that was so common in Blue Ridge.

Kellie tilted her head back, feeling the sun on her face again. *Be nice,* she warned herself. *So what if you won't have anything in common? At least someone is talking to you who doesn't look like she wants to hurt you.* "It's great."

Ramona seemed to relax a little. "How's it going?"

"Okay," Kellie allowed, sneaking a quick peek across the yard and to the basketball court just in time to see Lorna miss a shot from the free throw line.

Ramona pulled up the collar on her jacket. "Even though you're right next door, I don't see you too much. You've been here what, a few weeks now?"

Kellie knew exactly how many days, how many hours—she checked her watch—and how many minutes she'd been in this place. But she doubted that Ramona wanted that much detail. "That's about right."

Ramona looked at the dark circles under Kellie's eyes with friendly concern. "I don't hear you throwing up at night anymore. You must be doing a little better, sí?"

Embarrassed, Kellie's stomach clenched. "You heard that?"

Ramona made a soft clucking sound. "You aren't the first woman to detox here, chica. Don't look like you want to crawl under a rock. You should have seen me my first time here."

She'd been coached not to pry, but she wasn't the one who brought it up. So . . . "You've been here more than once?"

"Sí. This is my second time. I'm a year into a nickel." She gave Kellie a rueful look. "My parole didn't take so good, you know?"

Kellie didn't know, but she nodded politely anyway.

"So how it is *really* going?"

Unable to contain herself, Kellie threw her hands in the air. "How the hell do you think it's going? This is prison . . . *prih-sun* . . . it's going terrible! It sucks!"

Ramona let loose with a big belly laugh that was all out of proportion with her diminutive size.

And after a grouchy huff or two, Kellie joined in.

"Of course it sucks," Ramona said. "What did you think it would be like? This isn't a . . . umm . . . how do you say? Country Club prison?"

Kellie began her third lap and her eyes were drawn to row after row of wicked-looking barbed wire. "No. It's not."

"But it could be worse," Ramona reminded her as she jogged alongside. "You could be all alone and not a part of Lorna's *familia*." She chewed her lower lip thoughtfully for a few seconds before adding, "She's been alone too long. At least I get letters and visits from my Eduardo and my sons. She has no one. But now you both have someone too. *Usted es ambas mujeres afortunadas.*"

Apparently Kellie's Spanish wasn't as good as she thought it was. But she managed to pick out a few words. "We're lucky?"

Ramona slapped her on the back as they passed a couple of very slow walking, older women. "Yes! It's good that you share Lorna's bed. She gets much respect."

"We're not . . ." Kellie stopped herself, deciding to let the others think what they would. The closer they believed she was to Lorna, the better. "You're right. It would be a lot worse to be all alone."

Pleased, Ramona nodded. "I've known Lorna since she came over from maximum. Even back then she was good to me. Today I saw how you tried to protect her from that *cabrón* Roscoe. You did right. It's nice to see her happy."

"You think Lorna's happy?" Kellie asked, knowing she sounded surprised. *Who could really be happy here?*

"Of course! This is the second big difference in her life here."

Kellie slowed down so that her longer stride matched Ramona's. "What do you mean? And what was the first?"

"Nuh uh." Ramona waggled her finger. "The first is her story to tell. But you are the second. I see her talking to you." She shrugged. "Me and Lorna, we say hello, sometimes we end up on the same bathroom cleaning shift, and sometimes she asks me about my sons and husband. But I've never ever seen her talk to anyone for more than a minute or two. She is polite but . . ." She made a motion at her lips as though she was locking them and tossing away the key.

"Mmm. Maybe she just didn't have much to say?"

"Maybe," Ramona allowed doubtfully. "Or maybe she had not found the right person to talk to." Then her large, dark eyes began to grow with alarm. *"Mierda!"*

Kellie's heart began to pound. "What?"

"Hello." The icy voice came from behind Kellie and sent a chill down her spine. "What are you doing so far away from your protector?" Katrina, who was wearing a soft leather coat and a scarf, circled around the women, her posse of friends flanking her. She smiled at Kellie.

"You'd better get out of here," Ramona inserted bravely, her gaze flicking toward the basketball court on the opposite end of the yard. "Lorna won't like you messing with her woman."

"I don't give a shit what Mally likes or doesn't like!" Katrina hissed, her face twisting with sudden fury. "And she's not her woman." She gave Kellie a condescending look. "Mally doesn't like you that way, does she?"

Kellie wanted to tear her eyes out.

"Shoo," Katrina made a flicking motion at Ramona who turned worried eyes on Kellie for a split second before turning and bolting like a bullet out of the barrel. "You guys too," she instructed her posse, who grumbled about walking halfway around the track for nothing, but obeyed nearly as quickly as Ramona. "Kellie and I have private business to attend to." She reached out and ran her fingers down the soft skin on Kellie's cheek. "Don't we?"

Kellie swatted the strong hand away. *Oh, God. Where is Lorna? Or the guards?* "Get your filthy hands off me!"

"Tsk. I'm not going to hurt you." Katrina's voice was smooth as silk. "We just got off on the wrong foot before. Things can be different now. You should know, Holloway, that I'm more than just the average prisoner."

"You are?"

"Absolutely! I can tell you're a go-getter who will do whatever it takes to win." She jerked a thumb at her own chest. "That's what it takes to succeed here. I'm like that too. Hustle's the name of the

game. Nice guys get shoved out of the way." Her face was dead serious. "In fact, I dream of the things I can do here, especially with you
by my side."

Kellie looked at her like she was insane. "Am I supposed to
believe that bullshit?"

Katrina smiled guiltily like a small child who was trying to get
out of trouble by being cute. "It would make things a lot easier on
you if you did."

Kellie's stomach roiled at the thought of spending one more
minute in this vile woman's presence. "Get away from me before I
call over the guards."

Katrina laughed. "My good buddy Roscoe?" She took a step
closer to Kellie. "He likes to watch, you know. Here you're either
fucking the guards or another inmate. And I haven't seen you with
any guards . . . I'm sure he wouldn't mind if I called him back to my
cell one night while you were visiting me."

Kellie turned up her nose. "I'd rather die."

Katrina pursed her lips. "Nothing so dramatic as all that is required.
But," she shrugged lightly, "no matter. You'll come around eventually."
She studied Kellie's face for a few seconds. "And just to show you
there's no hard feelings between us, I have a gift I'd like to give you."

"You already tried to give me your *gift,* remember?" Every word
was painted with pure revulsion. "I didn't want it then either." She
tried to move forward but Katrina blocked her path once again,
clearly delighting in Kellie's growing distress.

Katrina waggled her index finger at Kellie. "This is a different
gift. And you haven't heard what it is yet."

Despite her fear, Kellie got right up in the taller woman's face. "I
don't want anything from you. How much clearer do I have to make
that?"

"Not even a drink?" Katrina tempted sweetly. "Free of charge for
you." She winked. "For old times' sake."

Kellie paled.

"I figure you for a Scotch lady. Was I right?" Her voice made it
clear that she was confident that she was. "I've got some in my cell.
And not the cheap stuff either. This is single malt."

Katrina's tongue snaked out and she slowly licked her lips as though she'd just taken a long satisfying drink.

Kellie's knees felt weak.

"It's so rich and smooth. Remember the warm feeling of it in your mouth and the pure pleasure when it slides down into your throat, pools in your belly and then seeps into your blood?"

Every cell in her Kellie's body screamed, Yes! Without her permission, her mouth began to water. "I—I—" She closed her eyes and turned away. *Jesus. It would be worth it. How much could one drink hurt? I won't lose control again.* "I don't . . . I don't want it." But she didn't even sound convincing to her own ears.

Katrina looked at her with a knowing expression and with a tender hand, she lifted Kellie's trembling chin. "Yes, you do," she said gently. "I understand what you need. I can see it in your eyes and I can give it to you."

Kellie swallowed hard. "You—you can?"

"That's what I'm good at," Katrina said, reassuring and calm. "Giving people what they need. Easing their suffering."

Kellie jerked her chin away, doing her best not to blurt out that she'd go down on Katrina here and now for that bottle. "Okay," she admitted shakily, "I *do* want it." Blazing eyes fastened on Katrina's. "I want it so badly that I'm willing to do almost anything to get it."

Katrina smiled like a Cheshire cat, her pale hair fluttering in the breeze around her head. "Then—"

"Almost."

The smile began to falter.

"And spending even five seconds with filthy trash like you doesn't come close to qualifying." She smiled at the stunned look on Katrina's face. *Didn't expect that, didja, bitch?*

Katrina's hands shot out and she grabbed Kellie's biceps, strong fingers digging in as she roughly yanked her close.

Kellie let out a muted scream, but quickly quieted as Katrina's grip tightened and became painful. Her tiptoes were barely touching the ground and their bodies were touching all along their lengths. She could smell chipped meat on Katrina's breath and her stomach lurched.

"You think you have it better with Mally?" Katrina spat, her eyes flashing wildly.

Kellie didn't even dare breathe and hot tears welled up before she could stop them.

"Do you?" Katrina gave her violent shake.

"Yes!" Kellie cried raggedly.

"Think again." Katrina's mouth was so close to Kellie's that their lips were almost touching. "She's *twice* as bad as I'll ever be. You're sleeping in the snake's lair, inches from her fangs, and you think you're safe? What you are is a goddamn fool! You don't know who you've gotten involved with, newbie."

Kellie lifted her chin defiantly. "Yes, I do."

"Really?" Katrina lowered her voice to a wicked purr. "Did she tell you that she's a cold blooded murderer?"

Kellie's eyes widened.

Katrina tightened her grip even more and Kellie bit her lip, not wanting to give Katrina the satisfaction of seeing her cry. Her hands felt like they were being pricked by millions of tiny needles as they began to go numb.

"Did Mally tell you that she liked killing? How the hot blood tasted?"

"You're lying!"

"How the blood felt slipping between her fingers?" Another vicious shake. "Hmm?"

"No!" Kellie squeezed her eyes closed and tilted her head back, then she slammed it forward, bringing it down hard against Katrina's forehead and nose.

The bigger woman dropped her like a sack of potatoes and they both fell to the ground, dazed.

Kellie hissed in pain. "Christ!" The ground was cold against her bottom and for a few seconds the world spun. With effort, she tried to roll up on her knees, but she gave up quickly and settled for a cold seat back on her butt. Her head throbbed in time with her heart and she blinked a few times, trying to bring the two bodies that were rapidly approaching into focus.

Katrina was first to her feet. She looked down at Kellie with deadly intent, a thin line of blood leaking from her forehead and nose, which was now bent at a funny angle. Her mouth twisted with rage. "Bitch! I'm gonna kill you!"

"Katrina?" The voice came from behind her and just as Katrina turned around, she was struck on the side of the head with a basketball traveling at a stunning speed. The force of the blow knocked her right off her feet and she landed flat on her back with a loud "uff!" as the air exploded from her lungs.

Then warm hands cupped Kellie's cheeks and began to stroke them. "Are you okay?"

Kellie closed and opened her eyes a few times, hearing the shrill sound of police whistles in the background. She rubbed her eyes with the backs of her hands that were still tingling. Sunlight lit Lorna's hair, bringing out fiery auburn highlights. The corners of her mouth curled upward. *Oh, how pretty.* "Lorna?"

Lorna dropped to her knees directly in front of Kellie. "Yeah, it's me." Visibly upset, she lightly ran her hands down Kellie's arms, then legs, to see if she was injured. "I'm sorry." She shook her head angrily. "That bitch didn't have a shiv or anything, did she?" She pushed up Kellie's jacket. "No. No, blood," she babbled, tugging down the jacket. Then she lifted her eyes and saw the goose egg forming on Kellie's forehead. "Shit."

Kellie's shoulders sagged with relief, "Boy, am I glad to see you."

"You shouldn't be." Lorna was fuming. "I got to playing and lost track of everything else. I'm so sorry."

"S'okay. Didja win?"

"What? I don't know!" She carefully lifted Kellie's head. She gently grazed her fingers over a large knot that was already purpling and winced in sympathy.

A high pitching keening sound caused both women to look sideways at Katrina who was curled in a ball on the ground, bloodied hands pressed to forehead and nose. Had she been making that sound since she hit the ground?

"You head butted her and broke her nose?" Lorna asked, eyes wide, amazed. "Holy shit!"

Kellie nodded slowly and winced at the throbbing sensation that made her feel as though her head might explode. But this time, when she tried to focus, she could clearly see her cellmate and a nervous Ramona standing directly behind her, shifting from one foot to the other. "Katrina deserved it."

Lorna's eyes narrowed dangerously. If looks could kill, Katrina would be picking out her pitchfork, and sharpening her cloven hooves and horns. "Hell, yes, she deserved it. And more."

Katrina was finally able to stand on wobbly legs just as her friends showed up along with Chul and a huffing Roscoe, who looked as though he were about to have a stroke after jogging across the yard.

Relieved that the guards were paying attention to Katrina for the moment, Kellie asked, "So how deep is the shit I'm in?"

The question sounded remarkably childlike and Lorna bit back an indulgent smile. "Semi-deep. What happened today will spread like wildfire and every prisoner will know by tonight." She took Kellie's hands, frowning at their coolness, as she inspected them for injury. "How does it feel to be a tough chick?"

"I'm mostly afraid, Lorna," Kellie said unevenly. "I don't feel so tough."

"I know exactly what you mean," Lorna murmured, doing her best to produce an encouraging smile. "But that'll be our little secret. Most of the others will think twice before messing with you now, Princess." There was an unmistakable glint of pride in her voice. "You did good."

"Thank God for small favors." Kellie's mood brightened a bit.

"Then there's Katrina." Lorna winced. "She's going to want to murder you just to save face. Now she hates us both and she's a dangerous enemy, Kellie."

Kellie's smile evaporated.

A string of barked profanities made both women jump. "And Roscoe's pissed," they said in unison.

Kellie felt a painful twinge in her forehead. "Does this look as bad as it hurts?"

"Lemme see." Lorna checked the bruise and then Kellie's pupils to see if they were the same size. Reassured, she pulled Kellie's head to her chest in a surprise hug. Then she raised her eyes and surveyed the yard, making sure that every woman interested could see exactly what she was doing. "You've got a good bump. But you're still the prettiest woman in the yard."

Kellie's ears perked at the quietly spoken words, but Lorna didn't seem to be aware she'd said them out loud.

Lorna tucked Kellie's head under her chin and gently stroked her hair with shaking hands. She placed her lips near Kellie's ear. "Do you feel like you're going to barf or are you dizzy?"

Kellie took stock of herself, and decided that even though she was in pain, she'd been in a helluva lot less comfortable positions. "No."

Lorna exhaled loudly. "Then you probably just got your bell rung. It sucks, but you should be okay."

"What's going to happen to you?" Kellie asked, not moving an inch away from Lorna, whose name was currently being featured in Roscoe's ranting profanities.

"Nothing that wasn't worth it ten times over." The warm tone of Lorna's voice told Kellie she was forgiven for getting into trouble. But her heart sank as she realized that this time her cellmate was going to end up paying right along with her.

Lorna seemed as content as Kellie to stay right where she was, so neither woman made an effort to move. The guards would be dragging them inside soon enough. "Trust me." She smiled rakishly. "I haven't had that much fun with a basketball in years."

Both women snorted softly, each enjoying the closeness, though neither was ready to talk about it just yet.

Kellie let the warmth of Lorna's body chase the cold away. "We're in trouble, huh?"

"Oh, yeah, Princess," Lorna whispered right into Kellie's ear. "Big trouble. If you don't see me for a few days, stick with Ramona, okay?"

But right that second, wrapped tightly in her friend's protective embrace, Kellie didn't want to ruin the warm glow that seemed to bubble up from her belly by thinking of the future. For once, the present was more than enough.

Chapter 5
One month later . . .

"What did we do to deserve this again?" Kellie dunked her mop into a bucket of murky water. She leaned her forehead against the handle, her muscles protesting this unfamiliar labor. She and Lorna were in the shower room, and despite the much darker circumstances the room irresistibly reminded her of her high school days and school facilities.

It was nearly lights out and they were still working hard. Chul sat just outside the door to the showers, reading a magazine as he patiently waited for the women to finish their chore.

"This isn't punishment."

Kellie hummed her agreement. She'd gotten her first taste of punishment after her altercation with Katrina, lost her yard privileges for two weeks, and spent the time cleaning the cafeteria's grease trap and the urinal in the guard's break room, among other choice duties.

Katrina, on the other hand, had received no punishment whatsoever. After a private conversation with Roscoe that left him smiling for two days, she'd managed to convince him that she'd suffered enough already. After all, she'd needed four stitches. Then there was poor Lorna, who had somehow been pegged as the instigator of it all. She'd spent an entire week in the hole.

Kellie had been fuming at the injustice of it all. But Lorna, who'd emerged from solitary confinement unusually quiet and a little more introspective, had taken it in relative stride, assuring Kellie that when she had come to her aid she knew exactly what she was doing. Katrina's disrespect for her family couldn't go unaddressed, she'd explained seriously, or else every Jane and Juanita would think they were ripe for the picking. Whatever that meant.

"This is cleaning and it was our turn," Lorna continued. "We should have Ramona and Dusty helping us, but they're sick." She scrubbed the bathroom drain with a worn scouring pad. "Damn flu is sweeping the block."

Kellie regarded the long set of rubber gloves that covered her hands. "Please, God, let us avoid it. If I never throw up again, it'll be too soon."

Lorna gave her a sympathetic glance. "You're feeling a little better now though. I can tell." The color had returned to Kellie's face and the dark circles under her eyes weren't nearly so pronounced. Even the knot on her forehead, which had made her look like a mutant unicorn for a few days, was gone.

Kellie did her best to smile. "I guess I'm not going to die after all." Though she didn't sound a hundred percent certain of that fact. What Katrina had offered still haunted her. "I still feel . . . not right, I guess. But, believe it or not, it's easier to deal with how I feel without having to deal with the highs and lows that come with drinking too."

"Really?"

"Hell no! Drinking made it all better! It rocked!"

Lorna burst out laughing and Kellie felt the air leave her chest at the sight. When Lorna smiled a natural smile, not the snarky or reluctant one that she displayed most often, she was truly beautiful.

An undeniable truth settled in Kellie's gut.

I want to kiss her. What is wrong with me? Katrina made it perfectly clear that Lorna's straight. She would never want me in a romantic way. Kellie distracted herself by pulling the mop from the bucket of water and moving to the corner of the showers. There was a brownish stain that was slowly coming up and it was easier not to think about whatever vile thing it was when she could consider Lorna's appealing laughter instead.

"I suppose you had a maid do this for you back home," Lorna said absently, her head bent as she went about her task.

Kellie frowned. "I had someone come in twice a week to clean. But I seriously doubt she was down on her hands and knees like you are."

Lorna lifted a challenging eyebrow. "Don't you think there are any working-class people who put in an honest day's work?"

"Nobody I know puts in an honest day. They might work hard for what they want, but inferring honesty from their actions would be a bit of a stretch."

Lorna made a noncommittal grunt. Her hair was damp at the temples and a line of sweat dripped from her chin. "Whatever."

A flash of irritation took hold of Kellie. "I wasn't a millionaire or anything. I was just comfortable." She peeled off her sweaty gloves with a loud snapping sound. "The reason I know my housekeeper didn't work this hard is not because I think all laborers are lazy, but because nothing in my entire house was as clean as the drain you just finished scouring."

Lorna pushed to her feet and unscrewed the cap on an enormous bottle of bleach. She began to sprinkle the liquid across the floor. "Having a maid sounds pretty rich to me. Must take a lot of money to be able to pay someone to do the little things that most folks just do for themselves."

Kellie's chest clenched at the way Lorna saw her. She was far from a spoiled diva. "When you put it that way it makes me sound like I was a rich sloth. My money was tied up in my business and I worked at least fourteen hours a day, six or seven days a week." Indignant, she added, "I hardly sat around eating bonbons!"

Lorna shrugged. She'd wasn't even sure what a bonbon was. "If you say so."

Kellie sniffed. "I do."

Lorna clucked softly and shook her head. "Sounds like someone likes to get in the la-ast word," she said in a sing-song voice.

"Do not!"

"Do too!" they blurted in unison.

Two sets of twinkling eyes met and they both began to laugh. When they were finished laughing they were still looking at each other. Lorna felt the heat rising in her cheeks and, unsettled, glanced away for a few seconds to gather herself. An unfamiliar sensation of attraction danced through her bloodstream. When she looked back, Kellie was working again and whistling quietly.

The women continued to clean in relative silence for a few minutes until Kellie screwed up her courage and said, "Hey."

Lorna's head lifted in question and she pushed a lock of thick hair from her face with her forearm.

"Thanks."

Lorna's eyes widened a trifle. "For what?"

"Just . . . for everything so far." Kellie wanted to do more to express her gratitude, but she didn't know where to start. *Keep it simple and to the point.* "I don't know what I would have done if you hadn't stopped Katrina. I—"

Lorna waved her off and focused on her scrubbing. "Don't worry about it."

"I'm not worried," Kellie insisted. "I'm just trying to be nice."

"Why?"

Kellie began counting to ten under her breath. She only made it to three. "This is the sort of conversation that makes my blood pressure go up. I'm being nice because I'm grateful!"

Lorna glanced up to see if Kellie was teasing. But, to her pleasure and surprise, there wasn't a trace of smugness in Kellie's expression, only a little exasperation "You'd have learned things without me. You'd have learned the hard way, but you'd still have learned." She went back to work.

Kellie smiled wryly. "The hard way hurts. In case you haven't noticed, I'm into maximum pain avoidance."

Lorna blew a damp strand of hair from her cheek with a sharp puff of air. "No kidding. Don't go thinking you know everything already just yet though," she warned in a semi-serious tone.

"I won't." Kellie crossed her heart. "This is nice. Just talking I mean."

Lorna answered without thought. "What's really nice is being alone together."

Kellie's eyes widened a bit.

The reaction wasn't lost on Lorna. "They seem more interested in my . . . in our business than their own. I like not having the urge to box their ears for listening in, is all." She shrugged one shoulder, looking as though she wanted to crawl into a hole somewhere and die. "That's what I meant about being alone with you."

"Oh." Kellie released a plastic smile. She fought not to box Lorna's ears. It was one thing not to be interested in her. It wasn't like that hadn't happened before, especially with unavailable straight women, the kind you knew you shouldn't be interested in, but who somehow managed to break your heart anyway. But it was another thing altogether to look like you'd rather munch on rat poison than consider the idea that there could be benefits to being alone together.

"My first impression of you was wrong," Lorna said suddenly. "You can be a good listener when you want to."

Her face was so apologetic that Kellie couldn't help but forgive her on the spot. *Ugh. I'm making myself wanna barf.* "I'm working on that," she said a little sheepishly. "But . . . umm . . . Do you ever notice that we mostly talk about what's happening in the world?"

Once they'd grown comfortable together, Lorna had peppered Kellie with questions from everything from whatever happened to Prince and the Revolution to what it was like to use a cell phone. Apparently, occasional but restricted Internet access and television, which Lorna rarely bothered to watch anyway, weren't quite enough to keep her up with the times. "Or we talk about things that will help me figure out how to be a better convict."

Lorna smiled. She liked talking about those things. It made her feel connected to both Kellie and the populations outside Blue Ridge's walls.

"But we never ever talk about you."

Lorna's smile fell away. "So?"

Kellie awkwardly wrung her mop dry and dumped the contents of her bucket down the drain in the middle of the room. "God, this is sickening!"

Lorna gathered up all the cleaning supplies except for a single mop and jug of bleach and carried them to a small closet located in the changing room next to the showers. She opened the door with a key she'd been wearing on a black shoelace around her wrist and began to put items away in specially labeled spots that made sure everything was accounted for.

"So . . ." Kellie continued, gripping her mop a little tighter. "I want to know about you too."

A six-foot high concrete privacy wall separated the two rooms and the women, though they could easily hear each other when they spoke.

"We don't talk all that much about your life on the outside either, Kellie."

"That's only because you don't ask more. I love to talk about me. It's been my favorite subject for most of my life. Ask anyone."

Lorna could hear the flopping sound of Kellie's shower shoes as she moved around the room. "I respect your privacy."

Respect. Who knew the word was so heavily used in prison? "It's not disrespectful to want to know about the person you're living with."

Lorna hung a dishrag on a plastic hook on the inside of the closet door. "Don't forget that we aren't living together by choice, Kellie."

Stung, Kellie suddenly felt like a fool. She clamped her jaw shut and turned away. She wasn't going to let Lorna hurt her feelings a third time.

Flustered, Lorna closed her eyes. The sudden silence in the room was deafening and she felt the weight of her error. She was glad for the tiny privacy the wall gave her. "F-fuck," she spluttered, feeling as though she'd been there so long she didn't have any manners left at all. "I didn't mean that the way it sounded. I don't know what's wrong with me today." She smacked herself in the forehead. "It's like all of a sudden I'm tongue-tied and can't say what I really mean."

"Whatever," Kellie grumbled between clenched teeth.

"Not whatever. I'm sorry." Lorna leaned against the wall and shook her head. "In a way, you *are* my cellmate by choice. If I kicked up a fuss to the right people, they'd realize you should be next door and probably have Roscoe or another guard get off his dead ass and move you. I haven't done that because—"

"Because you don't want to deal with Roscoe?" Kellie ventured in a jaded tone, mopping the corners of the room.

"No," Lorna corrected firmly. "Because I like rooming with you. You're smart and different from most of the women in here. I'm not worried you're going to steal my underwear."

Kellie's face scrunched up. "Someone's actually done that?"

"Oh yeah, and that's not the worst I've had stolen. Did you know that tampons can have a higher black market value than cigarettes under the right circumstances?"

For a moment, Kellie forgot to clean. "This place is barbaric!"

"No shit, Sherlock. You're just now coming to that conclusion?"

She crossed her arms over her chest. "If you're so happy rooming with me and talking to me, why do you wish we weren't having this conversation?"

Lorna groaned. "Jesus, are you always this difficult?"

"Yes."

"Ask a stupid question," she muttered, rolling her eyes at herself. Then, in a louder voice, she called over the wall, "What's there to say about me?" Another trickle of sweat, this time borne of nerves and not work, trailed down her cheek. She was about to wipe it away when she caught sight of the soiled gloves she was wearing and stopped herself. She removed the gloves and tossed them in an empty bucket. "Trust me, I'm beyond boring."

Kellie coughed at the burning sensation caused by the scent of rising bleach. "We gotta hurry and finish up here, Lorna. Or we're going to end up with brain damage. And I'll bet you're not boring."

Lorna snorted quietly. "That's a bet you'd lose."

"Uh huh," Kellie said tauntingly. "Never mind." She leaned on her mop for a moment. "It's clearly *me* who's afraid of discussing personal things."

Lorna lifted an eyebrow at the patronizing tone. "Okay, what do you want to know?"

"No, no. Never mind. If you don't trust me enough to tell me, I understand." Now Kellie felt a little guilty. She knew Lorna would be stewing over what she'd just said and she suspected it was just the path to get her the information she wanted. *Is a little harmless manipulation between friends really so wrong?*

"If you're ashamed of something about yourself," Kellie continued, "and you don't want to tell me, I'd understand that too." A sliver of guilt, an emotion so foreign it felt mysterious, assailed her. "I really would." Then she realized she was starting to believe her own bullshit. *Great. So much for manipulation.* "Don't tell me anything, okay?" she said with as much sincerity as someone who was about to get her way could muster. "We barely know each other and I—"

"Jesus Christ, Kellie. Just ask already." She was finished in the closet and she fiddled impatiently with the rusty lock. Chul would take the key from her on their way out.

"I wanna know what you're in for."

Lorna jerked at Kellie's words. She hadn't been expecting that.

Kellie poked her head back into the changing room, her long hair shifting over her shoulder as she eyed Lorna warily.

"Okay, you asked for it." Lorna drew in a bracing breath. "You know those tags on mattresses? The ones that say, "'Do Not Remove Under Penalty of Law'? Well, being the rebel that I am, I—"

"Lorna," Kellie rolled her eyes, "I'm serious!"

Lorna took the mop from Kellie's hands, soaked it with bleach, then gave the room one last quick wipe down, turning all the showers on, one by one, to wash away the last of the bleach. She said with a deep sigh, "Not here, okay? Can we talk back in our cell?"

Kellie nodded. "Okay. Does that mean we're ready to go?"

"Yeah. The rinse is the last step." After taking Kellie's gloves, Lorna quickly stashed the mop with the other cleaning supplies and walked back into the showers. She tugged her T-shirt and bra off in one swift motion, exposing her naked torso to the warm, damp air. As Lorna dropped the garments on the damp floor, she caught Kellie staring at her, lips parted, gaze fixed. "What are you waiting for?"

Kellie licked her lips, feeling light-headed from the flow of blood that had taken a sudden turn southward. Lorna usually dressed and undressed in the privacy of darkness and somehow they were never in the shower room at the exact same time. This was a rare treat.

"Never mind." Kellie sighed and stripped out of her clothes in record time. She began to rinse off, flinching a little as the hot water hit her skin. Water cascaded down her head and after a few seconds her body adjusted to the heat and she sighed in pleasure as it beat against the small of her sore back.

Kellie indulged herself in a good long lascivious look at Lorna that made her toes curl. She could never act on her lust, but there was no harm in looking. In fact, she wouldn't be the only one. She'd noticed that Lorna seemed to have caught more than one woman's eye.

A large white dollop of suds snaked down Lorna's slender neck, firm breasts and muscular stomach only to disappear between her legs and she casually swiped it away.

Kellie had to bite her bottom lip to keep from whimpering. No human had ever wanted to be a glob of bubbles more than she did at that very moment.

Lorna was nearly finished rinsing her hair when her gaze tracked Kellie's. "Do I have something on me?" She glanced down at herself through a cloud of steam, trailing a hand up her stomach and over her breast to brush aside the suds to see whatever it was that Kellie found so fascinating.

Kellie nearly passed out at the sight. But somehow she managed to get things together enough to plant a neutral, almost innocent expression on her face. "It's your tattoo . . . it's sort of hard not to notice."

Lorna shifted slightly as she looked down at her arm in disgust. "I hate the damn thing and wish I could cut it off."

Kellie stared at her with wide eyes. "That's a little extreme, isn't it?"

"Let's go, ladies!" Chul hollered, rapping on the door. "Lights out in ten."

"C'mon." Lorna hastily shut off her water, her wet fingers slipping on the knob, and dashed for the changing room. "If we're not in our rooms by lights out there'll be hell to pay."

"So why are you here at Blue Ridge?" Kellie cocked her head to the side. "What crime did you commit that's kept you here for so many years?"

Lorna's jaw worked, but she kept her mouth tightly clamped shut.

"Are you embarrassed by whatever it is you did?" Kellie ventured, not paying any attention to the guard who swept by their cell, barely breaking his stride as he peered inside and quickly moved on.

"No."

"Would you do it again?"

Lorna felt as though the wind had been knocked out of her. "You don't ask easy questions, do you?" She chuckled a little nervously.

"Well?"

"I wouldn't want to ruin my life again. But under the same circumstances . . . I don't know what I'd do."

"Katrina said . . ." Kellie swallowed. "She told me some things about you."

Lorna straightened.

"Some things that scared me," Kellie continued honestly. "A lot."

"What?" Lorna demanded, anger draping over her face and filling in every tiny line like a stone mask. "What exactly did that troublemaking bitch say?"

Kellie gulped audibly but kept her voice steady. "That you're a murderer. And that I wasn't safe anywhere near you."

Lorna froze again, a mixture of fury and dread coursing through her.

"But I didn't believe her," Kellie added quickly, unable to push away the tiny shard of doubt that had lodged itself in her mind. "At least I tried not to."

The air went out of Lorna's lungs. *Oh, Kellie, sometimes the truth is the worst of all.* "I just . . ." She lifted a hand and let it fall. "I'm not a crazed, violent person. I don't want to hurt you or anybody else."

The lights went out and the door closed and locked itself. Grateful for the momentary distraction Lorna said, "That really freaks you out, doesn't it?"

"It *is* freaky." Kellie rubbed the goosebumps that had arisen on her bare arms. "Doesn't it bother you?"

Lorna nodded seriously. "Bother? Yes. Frighten? Not for a lot of years. Wanna know something my very first cellmate told me that made me feel better?"

Intently, Kellie leaned forward. "Please."

"When that door locks at night, don't think of it as locking us in."

Kellie blinked. "No?"

"No," Lorna agreed conspiratorially. She gestured toward the hall. "Think of it as locking the rest of the criminals out."

"Huh." Kellie scratched her chin. "I . . . I guess it does do that."

Lorna was a little proud of herself. It wasn't easy to comfort someone when there was almost nothing comfortable about her situation. "Well—"

"That just begs the question, 'Who am I locked in here with?' I feel like Katrina knows something important." Kellie searched Lorna's face in the darkness, unsure she'd recognize the truth from a lie. "I feel like you're hiding something from me."

Lorna's nostrils flared. "I don't owe you any explanations, Kellie. My past is private."

"I don't want your damn biography! I just want a little reassurance. You're not an ax murderer or something, right?"

Lorna didn't even breathe.

"Right?" Kellie asked again with growing alarm.

A sigh broke free and Lorna ran a shaking hand through her hair. "Of course I'm not an ax murderer." *An ax and a big steak knife are two totally different things, right?* "Katrina just has a huge mouth and is trying to frighten you into her bed. Forget about her."

Kellie cocked her head to the side, her eyes narrowing. "Why?"

"Why? What?"

"Why does she care if I'm in her bed?"

Lorna gave Kellie a look like she was crazy. "Have you looked in the mirror lately, Princess?"

A smile flashed on and off Kellie's face. "I appreciate the compliment, but Katrina's no slouch. My guess is that she could have her pick of most of the women here even without bullying them into it. She doesn't need me. And after what happened on my first night here, she can't think I'd ever come to her willingly."

"Okay," Lorna allowed. "If she can hurt me by screwing you or screwing *with* you, all the better. She just enjoys fucking with people. Me in particular."

"I can't put what Katrina said out of my mind!" Kellie stared bleakly at the far wall. "It wasn't just what she said, but the way she said it." She shivered at the memory. *"Murderer."* She swallowed a couple of times and jacked up her courage. "I have nightmares that you kill me in my sleep."

A hollow ache split Lorna's chest and she turned onto her side to face the cold concrete wall as she covered her ears with both hands.

Lorna lay silently on her narrow bunk, tears pooling behind her. "You first."

"I'll tell you why I'm here, but I thought . . . well, why don't you go first, okay?" Lorna's voice was uncharacteristically hesitant.

"Umm . . ." Kellie pushed herself into an upright position. "Okay." She could hear Lorna move closer to the edge of the bunk above her. "Do you want the whole story or just the conviction list?"

Lorna's eyes widened a bit. "There's a list?"

"A short one, yes," Kellie admitted, laughing a little at the surprise in Lorna's voice. Then she paused before saying, "You know, I never thought this would be my life."

Lorna let loose a soft, but jaded chuckle. "I don't think any of us dreamed of going to prison when we were girls, Kellie. I don't remember playing 'convict' Barbie."

Keep things as light as you can. It's clear she's freaked out about something. "Even Barbie wouldn't look good in black horizontal stripes.

And these dreadful sneakers. An outrage!"

"Agreed. Although the cute but sniveling Ken would make a perfect prison bitch."

Lorna appeared so delighted by that prospect that Kellie softly laughed. "If you say so. When I said I didn't think this would be my life, I meant that back home I had a plan. A real plan." She smiled a little as she remembered. "It was on paper and everything. Had a big house and a blood red, vintage Jaguar convertible that was sweet enough to make grown men weep with envy, and hot blondes melt like butter."

"Crying men, sexy blondes dripping everywhere," Lorna said thoughtfully, a lopsided grin curling her lips before slowly fading away. "Were you happy?"

"I had everything I'd ever wanted! You'd have to be in a coma not to be happy in my situation!"

"Is that a yes?"

Flustered, Kellie blurted out the only thing she could think to say. "I—I was on plan!"

"O-kay," Lorna said hesitantly. "I guess that means yes."

Kellie gritted her teeth, but her frustration disappeared as the silence between them lengthened. "I'm not sure," she said finally. "I thought I was. I—I tried to be. But looking back, my girlfriend only wanted a free pass on the gravy train and I was so stressed-out all the time that I started drinking to relax. One drink after work became two. Then two turned into three." She made a face. "I stopped counting after I started thinking in terms of how full or empty the bottle was."

"That's probably a bad sign," Lorna deadpanned.

"Ya think?" Kellie huffed. "I was working day and night. I needed . . . something." She frowned as she considered her life from the inside out, and not the other way around, for the very first time. It wasn't as pretty as she thought it would be.

"I didn't have time for friends and I blew my family off for so many years that almost none of them will have anything to do with me now. I was so busy working toward getting where I wanted to go that the journey sucked."

"Family and friends weren't in the 'plan'?"

Kellie closed her eyes, a bleak feeling sweeping over her. "Not really, no. Once upon a time, a million years ago, I thought about settling down. Maybe even adopting a baby or something. But then I realized how much of my resources a family would take, so that got scratched off my list in favor of a swimming pool and more networking."

"Kel, your plan sucked shit."

Kellie exploded with a surprise burst of laughter. Charmed by a frankness she'd encountered a precious few times in her life, she smiled at the use of the diminutive form of her name. No one had called her Kel since she was in grammar school. "I guess it did. I thought I knew where I was going." Her gaze flitted around the dark room. "And look where I ended up."

"Mmm . . . Your life took a detour," Lorna said thoughtfully, and for a moment Kellie wondered whether she was talking about her or herself.

"A thirty-month detour."

Lorna's eyebrows jumped. "A two-and-a-half-year sentence?"

"Eligible for parole in eighteen months with time served and good behavior, but I digress. Okay, back to my *E! True Hollywood Story*."

"Huh?"

"Never mind. Things were going along swimmingly at home when money started disappearing from the books." They'd never talked like this and it felt better than Kellie would have ever believed. Even though she detested the subject matter, opening up to someone made her feel a tiny bit lighter. "I was the majority owner of a business that bought private and commercial property and got it ready for new development."

"What does that mean?"

Kellie thought about putting the spin on her job; she never did like the way the absolute truth sounded. But, she was forced to admit, if ever there was a night for the absolute truth, or as close as she could muster, this was it.

"It means," Kellie said, "that I hired wrecking crews to annihilate anything in between me and a flat, dead piece of dirt. I'm probably responsible for half the ugly strip malls filled with dollar stores and cheap nail salons in the state. But, every once in a while I'd buy a piece of crap property, usually something that was the subject of a recent foreclosure, and put some spit and polish on it, then resell it for an obscene short-term profit."

"That's called flipping, right?" Lorna was suddenly excited. "I've watched some television programs on that. Read a book on it too!"

"Really?" Kellie blinked a few times in the darkness. "Why?"

"Because of my job here, of course, and, well . . ." Lorna paused. "We'll talk about that later. Keep going."

"Okay, so if it was worth it, I'd flip it. But that's the exception to the rule and not really my main business. Like I said, I generally buy the places from a bank or desperate seller, level them, clean up the lot, and then sell the more palatable piece of land to developers."

"But sometimes you fix up buildings or houses, right? So are you a carpenter or do you hire folks to do that? That's so cool! There are a lot of old places that just need a little TLC to bring them back to their former glory. Once, in the TV lounge, I saw a show about a Victorian home that—"

"Whoa." She hated to burst her friend's bubble. "I've never lifted a hammer in my life and tender loving care was not even remotely part of my business plan," Kellie corrected with an internal wince. "Those things take time and patience. I didn't have those things when it came to making money. It takes thirty to forty-five days to flip a dump, but I can flatten a structure and haul the mess away in more like seven to ten days. Even if I could make more money by flipping, the added profit rarely made up for the added time and labor. Total destruction is the way to go."

Lorna made a sour face but kept her voice neutral. "Oh."

"Did you think I did something more glamorous?" A defensive edge tinged her words. "The work might not be using my education in the job, but there was good money in it."

"Take it easy. I didn't know what to think," Lorna answered honestly.

Kellie exhaled unhappily. "Anyway, at first I thought the missing money was just a mistake. I asked Cindy—my business partner, whore, shyster, ex-girlfriend—to look into it, and she told me every-thing was fine. I had a few other partners who were silent investors. But Cindy was the only one I really worked with on a regular basis. So I trusted her and I continued to spend money and buy and sell property as usual. One month last year I had eleven properties all being worked on at same time. I had more illegal immigrants on the payroll than Wal-Mart!"

Lorna had no idea what she was talking about. "Umm."

"That was a joke."

"Oh."

"Anyway, I was framed."

Lorna rested her chin on her arm and gave the bunk below hers a doubtful look. "Were you really? Because I have to tell you, this place is *full* of innocent people."

"Don't confuse my being framed with being innocent. Even I'm not that delusional. Some of my investments didn't pan out while more money began to disappear. And it took more and more cash to cover them, more money that I *thought* I had, but really didn't." Kellie swallowed hard as she recalled the feeling of helplessness that had settled in her chest and simply stayed. "Everything seemed to unravel after that. No matter how hard I worked, no matter how many deals I put together, I couldn't catch up."

"That sucks."

"Sucks?" Kellie laughed humorlessly. "What took fifteen years to build, my whole adult life since college, was sitting in ruin inside a year! Bill collectors called day and night. Repo men hauled away my stuff. We weren't all that close to begin with, but my parents, who are big shots in the local real estate market, were so mortified by what was happening that they were too ashamed to even talk to me.

"And then there was Cindy." Kellie's voice dropped to a gravelly growl. "She blamed me for everything and starting bringing up conversations and events that never even happened. I thought I was losing my mind! The few lousy friends and business associates I thought I could trust never even returned my calls." Her voice broke. "I was dead, only my body didn't know it."

Lorna climbed down off her bunk and Kellie sat up, making room for the other woman on the mattress. "Was it really that bad?" She settled in next to Kellie. "To feel like you were dead just over your job?" Even in the worst of times she had clung to whatever it was she had left in this life, which was never much.

"It wasn't just a job. It was my whole life. So, yes, I felt like I was dead," Kellie said with absolute conviction.

"So how did you handle it?"

"You know the answer to that," Kellie said, pantomiming taking a drink.

Lorna nodded. "Let me guess . . . martinis?" She wasn't even sure what those were. But they sounded like something fancy business people would drink.

"Mmm . . . Good choice. I adored those and Cosmopolitans. Scotch and soda and I were torrid lovers for quite some time. And let's not forget the occasional drink right out of the bottle."

"Yuck."

"Yuck," she agreed softly. "I dug myself in deeper and deeper until I didn't know which end was up and I didn't care." Kellie found herself not wanting to share this last part, but now that she'd started, she couldn't just stop. "I couldn't stand to look at myself in the mirror anymore. I was everything I hated. A failure. A loser!"

She wrapped her arms around herself as she thought back to that night. "The police came to my door with a warrant for my arrest. Cindy had gone to the DA and had somehow gotten him to believe that I'd stolen from the company. I think she slept with the bastard."

Lorna turned and gazed at her. Much to her dismay, she couldn't see her eyes. "Did you steal?"

"No!" Kellie glared at her. "It was Cindy! She'd been ripping me off forever." She smiled a cruel smile. "Too bad for that traitor whore that my Jag was paid for so I had something to sell. That let me hire a mouthpiece, who then hired a forensic accountant and a private detective. Together they found enough evidence against Cindy to get me acquitted at least on that charge." Kellie's face lit up with all the anticipation and delight of a child on Christmas morning. "Ha! The bitch will go to trial this year. I can't wait to testify against her!"

"But if you were acquitted—?"

Kellie sighed. "There's more. I didn't want the police to take me into custody. I didn't want to be alive at all. I'd drunk enough whiskey so that I was nearly numb and . . . then taken some pills." Her throat constricted a little as she spoke. "And somehow there was a gun and . . . it wasn't my fault. I swear!" She let the words drift off, feeling a weight on her spirit that wanted to crush her into dust.

Lorna took her hand and Kellie gave it a squeeze. It was strong and smooth with just a few calluses on the palm. A nice hand, Kellie decided.

"You did something really stupid, didn't you?"

Kellie let go, and then shrugged. "What did I have to live for?" She turned her head and looked at Lorna questioningly.

Lorna shivered at the bleakness rolling off Kellie. "There are always things to live for!"

"Never mind," she said dully. What had made her think that Lorna would understand? Nobody understood. "It doesn't matter now anyway."

"It does matter, Kellie. It—"

"I went for the policeman's gun."

"Uh oh."

"We wrestled for it and it just went off. I don't even remember pulling the trigger." After it had happened, Kellie hadn't felt guilty. She hadn't felt anything at all. It was just a terrible mistake. And she'd been so drunk she couldn't think straight.

Even now bits and pieces of the evening were a messy haze. But it was getting harder and harder to deny the ache in her gut that she felt every time she thought of that young police officer she'd shot. He'd barely looked old enough to drive, much less be a cop. "The bullet hit his femoral artery and the doctors couldn't save his leg. Thank God he lived."

Stunned, Lorna blew out a long breath. "Damn."

"It was touch and go for a long while. He'd lost so much blood. It was everywhere." The memory of it made her queasy. Sticky and hot, it had literally covered her and the two officers, making them all resemble extras from a slasher film. "He lost his leg, but he lived."

"Holy *shit*," Lorna hissed softly. "You maimed a cop?"

Kellie flinched at the words. "If he'd just left me alone none of this would have happened! I just wanted to die. I didn't want to hurt anyone. They shouldn't even have been in my house!"

"I'm not a big fan of the cops. But it sounds like the guy was just doing his job. And it sounds like him comin' to your house that night saved your life." Lorna frowned. "Why are you making excuses for what happened?"

"But you—"

"Nuh uh," Lorna intoned firmly. "I might not want to talk about my past. But that doesn't mean I deny the truth about it."

Stung, Kellie scooted away. "I didn't want my life saved. And I told you the shooting was an accident. I'd been drinking!"

Lorna's jaw clenched. She wanted to be sympathetic, she really did, but Kellie was going too far. "Don't excuse your actions with the booze. Not with me," she said harshly. "Nobody poured that whiskey down your throat."

Why can't I make you understand? "It was Cindy's doing! The cops shouldn't have been there in the first place. It wasn't my fault someone got hurt. None of it was my fault! So what do I have to feel bad about?" But even as she said the words, she felt a far away echo of their emptiness.

"Jesus Christ. The guy's career is toast, not to mention the fact that his new mandatory nickname is Peg Leg Pete, and you sound like a teenager making excuses for missing curfew?"

"Who are you to judge me?" Kellie shot back defensively her eyes burning. "Who in the hell do you think you are, Lorna Malachi?"

Lorna's body stiffened at the stinging anger directed her way. "I know exactly who I am. Exactly."

"And that's a murderer. Something I'm not!"

Lorna's mouth snapped shut at the undeniably true words. They glared at each other for a few seconds before Kellie looked away. Quietly, but quickly, she moved off Kellie's bunk and climbed the ladder to her own.

Kellie fell sideways and punched her pillow, but it did nothing to quell the fury surging through her. Anger at herself for what she'd just said and anger at how she'd let her life get to this point. She knew that she'd just jeopardized weeks of hard-earned friendship with a few heated words. "Lorna—"

"I'm nobody to judge you, Kellie." Lorna's voice was distant, but firm. It held none of the honest openness only moments before. "Nobody at all." She crossed her arms over her chest and sourly regarded the ceiling. "Go to sleep."

Kellie closed her eyes. *Crap.* "You chickenshit! I bared my soul to you and told you everything that happened. And now you're going to be a big baby and pout and not reciprocate?"

"I'm not pouting." Lorna leaned off the side of her bed. For a second it looked as though she was going to strangle Kellie, but instead, she whipped her pillow at Kellie's face. "So there!"

"Uff." Kellie peeled it from her head and was surprised to see Lorna's head upside down in front of her, her hair hanging down in soft waves, a tentative, conciliatory smile playing at her lips.

Reluctantly, Lorna admitted, "Okay, I was pouting a little. And you were right, I guess I was judging you a little."

A sigh. "And I hurt your feelings."

Lorna nearly denied it, but held her tongue. It was true.

"I'm sorry," they both said in unison. And in that moment, both women knew they'd leaped an invisible hurdle.

"I'm not climbing down again," Lorna said bluntly, though the words didn't carry any heat. "My feet are cold."

"You can't hang upside down like that for much longer. Even in the dark I can see that your face is turning red." Kellie reached out and boldly stroked Lorna's cheek with gentle fingertips. "Yup," she heard the slight tremor in her voice and swallowed hastily. "It's warm." Then she felt the soft skin beneath her fingers grow from warm to hot and she smiled inwardly.

Lorna disappeared, but Kellie decided not to allow the retreat. Before Lorna could voice a complaint, Kellie climbed the ladder to the upper bunk. She stared down at her new friend. "Sit up."

Lorna shook her head firmly. "Nuh uh. I'm finished talking for the night. It's late."

"No way. You said you'd tell me." Then Kellie's forehead creased as she got a good look at Lorna's face. Was that fear she saw glittering in those pretty blue eyes? "What's wrong?" she asked gently.

Lorna's eyes widened slightly, but she couldn't seem to make her mouth work.

Kellie tried another tack. "Did you ever have a sleepover when you were a girl?"

Puzzled by the question, Lorna muttered, "Once or twice. Until my dad starting hitting on my friends, that is."

Kellie went a little slack-jawed. "Umm . . . okay, pretend this is one of those times, minus the part with your dad." Kellie gave her a gentle nudge. "Scoot."

Lorna pulled the blanket up to her chin, her gaze darting around the room. "That—that's not allowed!"

Kellie rolled her eyes. "You've got to be kidding! Most of this place, including the guards, think we're lovers. Sometimes T-bone and Deshawna go at it so loud across the hall that they wake me up! Nobody will care."

"But I would never do that to you," Lorna whispered seriously. "I just wouldn't."

"Do what to me?" Kellie's eyebrows drew together. "What are you talking about?"

Lorna jerked upright. "Nothing. Here." She moved over so quickly that Kellie's head threatened to spin. Lorna sat up and allowed Kellie to move alongside her and the bunk creaked under their joint weight.

Kellie softened her voice and her gaze. "Time to spill your guts, tough girl."

Stunned by the almost magnetic pull coming from Kellie, Lorna began to speak, clearly just wanting this all to be over. "Okay, here's my story."

Kellie braced herself.

"I stabbed my father in the throat and killed him. The end."

"What?"

"I think you heard me the first time," Lorna told her softly, her fingers wound tightly in her blanket.

"I guess I did." Kellie waited for more information, but Lorna seemed content to allow her some time to process what she'd already said. *Stabbed? Sweet Jesus.*

After a few minutes of charged silence, Kellie said, "That's it? No more killings?" She gave her a skeptical look that dared her to lie. "Just the one?"

Lorna's eyes widened. "Isn't that enough?"

Kellie was lightheaded with relief. "Of course it is. And it's horrible and scary."

Lorna lifted her chin a little. "That's what I figured."

"But I was still imaging way worse." A rueful laugh bubbled up. "And let me tell you, I have a *vivid* imagination."

Lorna made a face. "No wonder you have so many nightmares."

But Kellie wouldn't be distracted. For once, this wasn't about her. "I know there's more to the story than you killed him. The end."

Lorna blinked a few times. "You mean you want to hear more?"

"Of course, Lorna. You've been at Blue Ridge forever. I didn't think you were here because of parking tickets."

Lorna shifted uncomfortably.

"It was self-defense, right?"

Lorna slowly shook her head and now it was Kellie's turn to feel uncomfortable. "Premeditated?" She winced at how high her voice suddenly sounded.

"Depends on if you believe the district attorney who prosecuted me."

"I want your side of the story. Tell me."

Lorna focused on the wall as she spoke. "My dad was a bastard."

"He used to hurt you." It wasn't a question. Going on instinct, Kellie reached up and with a tender touch, traced the slender scar that bisected Lorna's eyebrow, and continued to trace it. Lorna nodded, doing her best not to lean into the touch. "He used to hurt everyone," she corrected. "He was a mean, no good drunkard. I was seven and I stepped on the remote control for the television set and broke it." She shook her head a little. "He was so mad." Lorna's voice sounded smaller than usual. "He picked up the phone and threw it at my head. I needed fourteen stitches."

Angrily, Kellie bit back a curse. "What about your mother?"

Lorna shrugged. "She was just like him. Drunk a lot. Gone a lot. She rarely hit me, but she and my dad would beat on each other constantly." Her nose was starting to leak and she sniffed a few times. "One night I found out he was beating up on my little sister, Meg."

Kellie's gaze darkened. "The cute little girl in the photo?"

A small smile appeared. "Yeah." The lump in Lorna's throat made it hard to speak. Kellie removed her hand and it was all that Lorna could do not to grab it and place it back against her face. "And I knew that once he started hitting her, he'd never ever stop." Lorna turned her gaze to Kellie. "I don't know how I knew it then, but I did, deep down inside. Mama wasn't going to stop him. Meg couldn't stop him. The police didn't care and were never going to save us. *I* had to be the one."

"How old were you?"

A pause. "Seventeen. But I was tried as an adult."

Kellie closed her eyes. "Oh, Lorna," she whispered, dismayed. "I knew you'd been here a long time, but your entire adult life? Jesus."

"He practically dared me to do it." The timbre of her words changed and her voice took on a faraway quality as she relived the terrible moment. "And when he hit Meg right in front of me . . ."

"You stopped him for good," Kellie finished gently, sighing along with her friend. She pulled the blanket tighter around her legs to fight the chill that was coming from within. "That doesn't make you a murderer."

Lorna was deadly serious. "Yes, it does, Kellie. Just because we're friends . . ." She paused. "We are, right?"

Kellie nodded and indicated their close proximity. "I haven't had many, but I'm pretty sure we qualify."

Lorna let out a shaky breath that was all relief. Once, years ago, when she thought she'd made a real friend, she'd made the mistake of telling Katrina what she'd done. She'd even boasted about it, hoping to enhance her reputation as someone not to be reckoned with. Lorna had cried about that, but not until years later. "Okay, well, us being friends can't change what happened."

"Well, it does to me," Kellie said decisively, eyes blazing with conviction. "There were extenuating circumstances. You were abused." She gestured wildly. "Shit, you must have had the worst lawyer on the planet!"

"It doesn't help when your own mother testifies against you at trial."

The air wheezed out of Kellie's lungs. And she thought her own mother was bad! "But what happened wasn't your fault. You were protecting a child! Lorna, you *were* a child!"

"I had a choice," Lorna corrected in a no nonsense way. She began counting options off on her fingers and it was painfully clear this was something she'd memorized long ago. "I—I could have walked away from him. I could have backed down. I could have run away with Meggy. I could have called social services. I could have done anything but what I did. I could blame everyone else for what happened, but that would just be lying to myself. I take responsibility for what I did. And for everything that happened after."

Kellie did her best to give her a reassuring smile. Her head was still spinning and her stomach wasn't very far behind. "Okay," she said quietly.

Lorna smiled back, tears still glittering in the wan light. "You're safe in here. No more bad dreams."

Kellie shook her head vehemently and whispered, "No." Then her smile faltered. "At least not about you."

Chapter 6
One month later . . .

Lorna set down her sandpaper and gave the dresser an approving look. The piece of furniture was solid oak with a deep black finish that glistened in the harsh neon lights of Blue Ridge's workshop. Nearly as tall as Lorna, it was a custom order that had taken more than a month of hard work and would sell for just over three thousand dollars.

She pulled open one of the drawers, grunting softly in approval when it slid silkily on its runners.

"Wow."

Lorna glanced over her shoulder and smiled. "Hey." She hadn't spoken to Kellie in hours. The noise from the saws and sanders had drowned out everything but Lorna's thoughts. And though she'd forgotten Kellie was behind her, the other woman had never strayed far from Lorna's thoughts.

Kellie let out a low whistle. "It's gorgeous."

Lorna's ego purred contentedly. "You think?" She wasn't one to fish for compliments. But she was good at precious few things in life, and this was one of them. It was a fine piece of furniture and she couldn't help but want to bask in Kellie's admiration, even if just for a few moments.

"Are you kidding?" Kellie gave her a playful swat on the back, tossing down the rag she was using to stain a table.

Lorna thrilled at the friendly contact.

A few low whistles sounded from the back of the room. Lorna wasn't sure whether they were directed at the dresser or her cell-mate.

Kellie looked worlds better than she had only the month before. With the addition of a few pounds, her features had softened and a few days of being outside in the yard in the spring sun had given her skin a healthy glow. Her bruises, at least the ones on the outside, had faded and she had more spring in her step.

Still, Lorna knew, she wasn't sleeping through the night.

Without thinking, Lorna reached up to rub the smudge of wood stain from Kellie's face. Her hand was halfway there before she realized what she was about to do. Confused and embarrassed, she glanced away and shoved her hand in her blue jean pocket. Rocking back on her heels she said, "Thanks."

Kellie's eyebrows drew together over Lorna's strange behavior. "The dresser is gorgeous, Lorna. Really. I know at least a dozen people who would die to have something so beautiful in their homes." Appreciative eyes lifted from the dresser . "You have real talent."

Several women working nearby chimed in with their agreement.

Lorna inclined her head as she examined her work critically. It had taken a lot of years of practice and training, but she was finally at a place where she knew she could be justifiably proud of her workmanship. "S'okay," she agreed with a poorly hidden grin. Then she picked up a dust rag and began to wipe down the wood. "How's your end table going?" It was a simple stain job but Kellie had been at it for hours.

"How does it look like it's going?"

Terrible. "It looks much better than the one you did last week," she offered encouragingly. "And that one was your best job yet."

"That one had to be sanded down and stained all over again."

Oops. "And this looks nothing like that." Lorna refused to let her eyes linger over a large drip that was currently running down the table leg. "Great job!"

"Whatever you say," Kellie said halfheartedly. She put the lid back on her can of stain and then gathered up her rags for the laundry bin.

Ramona, who was busy admiring the tall dresser, snickered at Lorna's attempt not to hurt Kellie's feelings. "Nice try, chica."

Machines all around the room shut off as the women began cleaning up the workshop. A line formed where the inmates would painstakingly check in every single tool or other piece of equipment they had taken out.

"Mind your own business," Lorna said from the corner of her mouth, her eyes on Kellie as she crossed the room.

"Tsk," Ramona chided. She slid off her safety goggles and did her best to rub out the indentation the strap had made in her thick curls. "Love makes everyone a liar. When I ask my husband how I look in my party dress, do you think he tells me the truth?"

Lorna's head snapped sideways. "I'm just being nice," she protested. "Love has nothing to do with it."

Ramona laughed. "You aren't that nice!" She batted her eyes innocently. "And you don't think she's pretty?"

A little exasperated Lorna whispered, "Of course, I think she's pretty!"

Ramona smiled.

But Lorna waved off the smug look. "That means nothing. Everyone with eyes thinks that. It's not even a matter of opinion. Look at her! It's a fact."

"How about sexy?" Ramona firmly believed she knew the answer to the question. But she wasn't above trying to make Lorna say it. "Do you find her sexy?"

Lorna instantly blushed to the roots of her hair, a sight that Ramona had never come close to seeing. Ramona bit back a laugh. Lorna had it bad. "I guess I know the answer to that."

"Everyone thinks that too," Lorna insisted again, but deep down she knew she wasn't on sure ground.

Ramona gave her a skeptical look. "If you say so."

Lorna's stomach dropped. "Don't they?" But she could see that Ramona was going to beg off before she had even started to speak. "Scratch that. Do *you* think she's sexy?" Ramona, who was utterly straight, was also as hot-blooded as women came. Lorna doubted her husband would be able to stand for a week after she was released from prison. Surely, she would admit the obvious.

Piercing blue eyes bore into Ramona's and she began to sweat. She licked her thick lips twice. It was obvious by the look of rapt attention on Lorna's face that her answer was very important. Luckily, she could be honest. "I can see that she is attractive, yes. And I can see that others might find her sexy, but she is my friend," Ramona said, choosing her words very carefully. After all, this was Lorna's woman she was discussing. "Antonio Banderas is sexy. My Eduardo is sexy. My *friends* are not sexy."

"Oh," was all Lorna could think to say, feeling even farther adrift. *Couldn't you find someone sexy and have her be your friend too?*

Confusion swirled around Ramona's head like a swarm of bees. Lorna clearly acted as though Kellie was her woman in every way possible. They fought like a couple. They shared the intimate looks that lovers do. They spoke to each other, standing close together, in the low tones that lovers use. And when someone looked at Kellie too long, she could practically hear Lorna grinding her teeth. So why then did Lorna seem so puzzled?

Suddenly, Ramona snapped her fingers. "You don't think she loves you yet? But you share lust, yes?" The slight woman made a sexy purring sound. "*Que bueno.* Lust is good too! Love can come with time. I don't think you should worry. I can see how much she cares for you."

Lorna's eyes narrowed.

"Aye! Never mind." Ramona studiously attended to her wiping. "Mind my own business," she murmured. "I know. I know."

Lorna bent and filled her dustpan with a fragrant pile of sawdust and woodchips. "Right." She set the dustpan on a wooden bench and leaned forward to sweep underneath it. *Her needing my help or even us being friends is not the same as loving me. And even if she could love someone like me, I could never—*

"Let's go, ladies!" brayed a guard who was sitting on a stool in the corner. He checked the clock on the wall that was covered by a black metal cage and then his wristwatch. "Five more minutes!"

Another guard who was manning the metal detector at the front of room yelled, "You gotta hot date tonight with another ugly fat chick?"

"No," the guard on the stool replied calmly. "I stopped screwin' your wife a couple of years after you got married."

The inmates began to laugh as the guards shot each other the bird.

Ramona decided a quick change of subject with Lorna would be best for her continued well-being. "I saw you talking to Jennings. I don't think she's ever going to change her mind."

Patrice Jennings, with her perfectly trimmed salt-and-pepper hair, was Blue Ridge's woodshop business administrator. Her office faced the back of the shop, and allowed Patrice to look out onto the shop from behind a large, thick glass window. The office was filled to the brim with stacks of papers, cardboard boxes and files. What time Patrice didn't spend in front of her computer, cursing, she spent at her calculator cursing. The inmates considered her their own more attractive version of Ebenezer Scrooge.

"I know it's her shop. I know." Lorna gestured. "I know! But I've got the money for materials, and to grease her palms, and I'll work over my lunch or during rec time. She never leaves that damned office anyway and she can see what I'm doing the entire time. If I start now and make parole on time, she won't have to store what I make."

Ramona lifted her eyebrows in question.

"If I don't make parole I'm going to kill everyone in here, so she can keep the damn thing!"

Ramona paled a little. She was never sure when Lorna was teasing and when she was stone-cold serious.

"Jennings has let other cons do it before and you know it. Sweet

Cheeks built her own coffin, and Jennings used it as a file cabinet until Sweet Cheeks took it with her when she left, remember?"

"Mmm . . . I prayed for that Sweet Cheeks woman." Ramona shook her head. "A coffin painted hot pink is not a normal thing to do." She pushed her lips together as she thought. "I wonder how she got that thing on the bus to town?"

"Beats the hell out of me."

Kellie joined them and held the dustpan while Lorna filled it again. "What's up?"

Lorna didn't say a word so Ramona filled the silence. "For years Lorna's been asking Jennings to let her build something for herself for when she gets out of this place. Lorna always asks—"

"And she always says 'No,'" Lorna supplied sourly. "But it doesn't hurt to try. What else do I have but time?"

Kellie's gaze strayed to the office and a rail-thin black woman who was polishing her glasses. "Why does she say no?"

"Who the fuck knows? My money should be as good as the next con's." Lorna glanced at the clock, then hurried out of her apron. She balled it in her hands. "You'll get this stuff?" She gestured toward Kellie and the broom and dustpan.

Kellie nodded. "Sure."

Ramona smiled sweetly as she stuffed her goggles into her pocket. The women had to buy their own. "Take mine too, please?" Ramona tossed Lorna her apron.

Lorna snatched it out of midair and jogged back to the laundry bin. The room had to be spick-and-span before they were allowed to line up at the metal detector and leave for dinner and a few women were already waiting impatiently at their workstations.

Kellie hung the broom back in its slot, a speculative look on her face.

"What are you thinking?" Ramona asked curiously, having to reach on to her tiptoes to put the hand broom away.

Kellie plucked the hand broom from Ramona and fitted it into its place, deep in thought. She didn't have enough money to bribe the administrator, and she'd been branded a troublemaker after her incident with Katrina. Neither the guards nor administrators were eager to do her any favors. Still, she wasn't without things to offer. "I don't honestly know."

"Oh, no." Ramona warbled, her mullet bouncing with the shaking of her head. "That sounds dangerous. I don't like the look on your face, chica." She leaned against a table. "And neither will Lorna."

"She's not my keeper, Ramona." Kellie said absently as she took her place back at her workstation.

"Does she know that?"

Kellie gave her a half smile. "Probably not."

Chapter 7
July 2002

Kellie was still struck by the silence that came with nighttime. Prison was such a noisy place; full of bells, the hum of machines, raised voices, and the general chatter of too many bodies crammed into too small a space. Except for the occasional sexual escapade from their very active neighbors across the hall or the soft click of the guard's boots, it was as quiet as a grave. Restlessly, but mindful of the woman sleeping in the bunk above her, she fluffed her pillow, trying to get comfortable.

Lorna's slightly husky voice broke the silence. "It's after midnight, you should be asleep."

Kellie opened her eyes and looked at the bunk above her. "How'd you know I was awake?"

"You're not snoring."

Kellie blinked a few times, her vision slowly adjusting to the dim light. "I snore?"

"Yes."

Kellie wiggled deeper into her pillow. "Well, next time ignore my question like usual. I didn't need to know that. It's bad enough my nose isn't straight anymore. I look like a slow and inept boxer."

"It's barely noticeable. And what little bit is noticeable is actually better."

"Liar!"

"Believe what you want, but it was too perfect before. Now it has more character. And I don't ignore your questions and you know it." Lorna rolled over and propped her head up on her hand. "Why are you so cranky?"

Kellie sighed. "It's like my mind is racing or something. I feel like one of those pathetic polar bears in the zoo that does nothing but pace back and forth in her cage. Isn't that enough to make anyone cranky?"

"Animals *sleep* in their cages." Lorna stretched her arms out in front of her, reaching for the ceiling that too was far away to touch. "Everyone knows that. Forget polar bears. Didn't you ever have a dog?"

"Nah. I begged for one for the first ten years of my life, but eventually I gave up. My mom said they were dirty and left too many hairs on the furniture. How about you?"

Lorna nodded. "Once. A black lab puppy named Kirby. My mom accidentally backed up over him on our driveway when I was ten. She didn't tell me she'd done it. That night we had a nasty ice storm. The next morning on my way to school I found him frozen solid . . . squashed. That afternoon I had to chip all the bits of him off the driveway with a snow shovel. I never wanted a pet again after that."

"I can't imagine why." Kellie grimaced. "Ugh! Are *all* your childhood stories disgusting and traumatizing?"

Lorna snorted softly. "Not really. Even my family managed a few good times now and then. It's the bad memories that stick though, you know? One sound or smell and they come rushing back whether you want them to or not. It's like they're seared into my brain."

"Don't you think they can get better over time?"

Lorna thought about that for a moment. She knew something about hauntings of the past. "I think . . . not always. Not the ones that burn way down in the pit of your stomach. Those are there for good. You just have to hope you're lucky and do your best not to dredge them up very often."

Pensively, Lorna glanced up at the small window that allowed moonlight to penetrate the room. "Someday I'll be some pathetic old lady with Alzheimer's and I won't remember what year it is or even my own name. But I'll still see Kirby splattered on the concrete every time I see an Alpo commercial."

The thought of Lorna being all alone made Kellie's heart hurt. "Maybe when you're an old lady someone will be there to remind you who you are," she said softly.

Lorna sighed. "Maybe." But it was clear she was doubtful. "So why aren't you really sleeping? More bad dreams?" She'd heard Kellie whimpering about the shooting. The dreams seemed to be getting worse and worse, interrupting her cellmate's sleep almost every night.

"I don't know." Kellie scrubbed her face with the back of her hands. "I can't remember what I was dreaming about." Even after lying awake for what seemed like half the night, a vague sense of unease still clung to her like a foul perfume. She plucked at her T-shirt, which was damp with sweat.

"Lorna?"

"Yeah?"

"Don't you miss being touched?" Kellie slid her hand under the soft cotton of her T-shirt and skimmed the smooth skin covering her belly, the light touch raising goosebumps and causing a brief shiver. "At first I missed the sex more," she confessed. "Not that I don't still miss it like crazy," she admitted freely. "But now there are times when it's a toss-up between that and the feeling of someone's body pressed tight against mine, feeling her heartbeat, just being close, even if it doesn't last."

A sudden, wistful craving for human contact made Lorna want to burst into tears. But as she always did, she ruthlessly tamped it down until it was dust. "I miss a lot of things. But what good would it do to think about what I can't have? It won't change anything."

Kellie wasn't sure what exactly Lorna was saying. Surely she realized she could have a girlfriend if that's what she wanted. But maybe she was so straight that the thought of touching another woman wasn't within her realm of possibilities. Then again, she'd learned that it wasn't uncommon for straight women to make the best of their situation at Blue Ridge and pair off with another woman. Those with husbands and families on the outside often had lovers on the inside. It gave them a sense of normalcy, sexual companionship and sometimes, under the most difficult of conditions, love.

"Does it have to change anything?" Kellie asked. "Can't what we're doing just be talking and wishing?"

"No." Flat. Inflexible.

"Ugh! Maybe you've been in for so long that you don't feel anything at all anymore?" Kellie snapped, her hands balled into fists. She slapped them down angrily. "This place is perfect for someone like you!"

The long silence that greeted Kellie's words gave her more than enough time to wish she could suck back her words. "Oh, damn. Lorna—"

Scalded, Lorna struggled to breathe. "Just because I don't go on and on about it until other people want to wring my neck doesn't mean I don't hurt for all the things I miss every single day! Sex is only one of those things." Her eyes dulled. "You—you think I'm a robot or something?"

Lorna sounded as hurt as Kellie had ever heard her, and a sliver of danger, one she doubted even Lorna herself was aware of, threaded her voice. Like an injured animal, the way Lorna protected herself was to lash out. Even though Kellie was well past being physically afraid of her cellmate, Lorna's upset or anger always caused anxiety to rip through her like a frigid wind. Somewhere along the way Lorna's friendship had become the bedrock beneath her feet, sturdy and vital to her balance. The thought of that shifting terrified her.

"Of course you're not a robot," Kellie answered quickly, her heart pounding. "I wasn't thinking when I said you didn't feel things. That was stupid."

"Just because we're not the same doesn't make you better than me. I feel every bit as much as you do."

Kellie's hopes at being forgiven quickly sank like a stone. When Lorna was truly upset, she was beyond listening. "I know you do. I'm sorry."

"Then what was that goddamn comment about this place being perfect for someone like me?" Lorna moved close to the edge of the bed and wrapped her hands around the metal frame, squeezing hard enough for her fingers to ache. "White trash, you mean? Or maybe violent?"

The startling vulnerability in Lorna's voice caused Kellie to sit straight up in bed. She ran trembling hands through her disordered hair, a heavy sensation filling her chest. "Believe it or not, I meant practical. You're one of those plucky people!"

"*Plucky?*"

Kellie's eyes widened. She'd never heard that word said as though it were a curse. "You're a survivor. No matter what. You seem to see everything so clearly and reasonably when all I want to do is scream at the top of my lungs and chew through the fence to get to the outside world. I was frustrated that you deal with things so well and . . . and I just don't!" Dismayed, she swore, "That's all! I didn't mean it the way it sounded."

"You know what I *feel* the most?"

Kellie cringed. "Pissed off at my big mouth and me being an asshole?"

"You deserve for me to say yes. But, the answer is no." Lorna sank into the thin mattress and closed her eyes. "Fear. That's what I really feel. Mind-numbing, soul-aching fear."

It was the last thing Kellie expected to hear from the most confident person she'd ever met. She cocked her head and listened hard. *Oh, no. No. Please don't let her be crying!*

"Kellie, do you know the most likely thing to happen to me once I leave this place?"

"No, not really."

"It's for me to do something mental and end up right back here."

It was a startling admission. Kellie pushed aside her bed sheet and swung her feet onto the cool floor. "You're wrong. That's not what's going to happen." Her stomach twisted. She'd never considered for even a split second that she could somehow end up back in prison after leaving this hellhole far behind her. But this was the only adult life Lorna knew. "You're too smart to let that happen."

Lorna's voice was a bare whisper. "Even if you're right, and I don't end up back here, I don't know how to . . . be with anybody. What if I'm free but I end up all alone anyway?"

Kellie closed her eyes against the raw pain she could hear coming from her friend. "You won't."

"I—"

"For once just don't argue with me, okay?" She couldn't stand the thought of someone as caring as Lorna ending up all alone. She willed herself not to cry. They both couldn't fall apart at the same time. "Please?"

Lorna impatiently wiped at her eyes. "Okay, okay."

Kellie started to relax. "Umm . . . When you say you don't know how to 'be' with somebody are we talking love or sex or—"

Restlessly, Lorna picked at a snag in one of her sheets. "I mean I don't know how to have a real relationship. The only one I've ever had was just kid stuff."

Though Kellie'd had a couple that had lasted several years, in the end, they were abject failures. But there were things that she believed to be absolute truths. "You are a good person. You're kind and smart. Anyone would be damned lucky to have you. Well, you won't be alone for long."

Lorna's eyes filled again. "I had this teacher in the fourth grade, she was nice to me even though I missed a lot of class to stay home when Meg was sick or my folks were too hungover to fend for themselves. Everyone liked her, the kids, the other teachers. Her friends came to class once and brought flowers on her birthday. She always had clean clothes and a job. I want to be like her, not like my parents. Not . . . Ugh! I don't know what I'm saying," she said harshly. "I know I sound stupid, like I'm begging to be reassured or something. I'm not usually like this."

"Everyone has self-doubts."

"I hate that."

"I know. But I know this too. Loyal people, the kind you can trust with your secrets, who would be there for you no matter what, the kind who hold you when you're sick and whose smile makes your knees melt, they're impossibly rare. When some lucky man gets a shot at you, Lorna, he's going to grab hold and hang on for dear life. And if he doesn't, well, then he's a damn fool. The only way you're going to end up alone is if you want to be."

Lorna swallowed a few times before she could speak around the lump in her throat. "Thank you for saying that."

"You can tell me when things are bothering you. Who else do you have to spill your guts to?"

"No one."

"My point. Talking won't change things but it might make them seem more manageable. I can be a good friend to you, Lorna, but I can be an even better one if you let me inside just a little."

"I—" Lorna swallowed thickly. "I'd like that, but it's . . . hard."

It was a sentiment Kellie knew all too well. "I'm coming up." This time it wasn't a question. She climbed into the top bunk and slid under the covers next to Lorna. There wasn't an inch of space between them and she pulled Lorna to her, and for once, she didn't feel a scintilla of resistance to her touch.

The warm sensation of Kellie's skin was such a simple comfort that Lorna lay there, stunned for a few seconds, her arms wound tightly around her friend, her head resting just below Kellie's chin. Overwhelmed, she sank into her, allowing herself to revel in the contact she'd been craving for months. Holding in the tears became an impossible task, and once she let go of one, there was no stopping them.

Kellie held her tenderly until she was all cried out, or at least until the worst of the storm had passed.

"I don't know why I did that." Her voice was raspy and tired.

"It doesn't matter why, Lorna. No matter what it is, you're still entitled."

Lorna's heart constricted when Kellie shifted slightly and pushed her hair off her forehead, dropping a feather soft kiss there. A tremulous smile flickered off and on her face. "I was supposed to make you feel better so you could go to sleep."

Kellie murmured into cleaning-smelling hair. "Stay where you are. It's my turn to take care of you."

Lorna's body went rigid and the tips of her ears burned at her neediness. "I don't know how to act when you do."

Kellie swallowed hard. "We'll manage, Lorna. You'll see."

They shared a moment or two of silence, but it was comfortable, and something familiar between them.

Kellie waited, doing her best to be patient as Lorna's breath warmed her chest. Though she wanted to drag Lorna across the divide, kicking and screaming if need be, this was a chasm of trust that Lorna had to cross on her own.

Finally, Lorna's body relaxed again.

Relief coursed through Kellie, but she felt some anxiousness as well. She wasn't exactly an expert at this friendship thing. And Lorna needed a very good friend at this moment.

Lorna cleared her throat, then whispered. "I miss my sister. I think about her a lot and wonder what happened to her after I . . . I don't feel sad when I think about her, but when I think of how much of her life I've missed . . . sometimes it's hard to breathe."

Kellie held Lorna a little closer. "Tell me about her."

"Okay." Lorna's chin quivered for a second, but then she let out a slow breath and seemed to grab hold of herself. "Meggy was a really quiet kid. She followed me around everywhere." An old memory suddenly came into focus, one that made her smile sadly. "She had a crush on my boyfriend and used to sneak peeks at us through the window when he was dropping me off from a date. Then when I finally came inside the house she'd creep into my bed and make me tell her all the things I did on my date."

Kellie let go of a melancholy grin. "*All* the things you did?"

"I left some things out."

A fiery tendril of jealousy wormed its way through Kellie's guts. "So what was he like?" *Masochist!*

Surreptitiously, Lorna inched her icy feet closer and closer to

Kellie's warm legs. She wasn't going to make contact. She just wanted them close enough to share some of the heat. Only another inch or two and . . .

"Christ!" Kellie levitated a couple of inches off the bed, taking Lorna with her. "What the hell is that?"

"Oh, shit! Sorry."

"It's okay. You don't have to move. God knows those things need some warmth."

"But—"

"Stay put," Kellie growled playfully. "I'm fine. I just wasn't expecting that."

"You asked about Nathan. He was okay. Sweet. Nice. A cute guy who tried to make me forget about what was happening at home while I was with him."

Kellie fought the urge to ask just how cute.

"He was a high school hockey player who dreamed of a scholarship but wasn't quite good enough to get one. I couldn't make bail, of course, and he came to see me in county jail before my trial. I don't think his parents were too thrilled about it though. He kept looking over his shoulder as if his dad was going to show up and kick his ass. Even in my neighborhood murderous girlfriends were looked down upon." She snorted a little. "Snobs."

Kellie let out a weak laugh and Lorna joined in.

"Well, it was just that one visit. He said he'd look after Meggy, but," Lorna sighed, "there wasn't really anything he could do. He hung around for a few months after I was arrested, but time marches on and, eventually, so did he. He said in a postcard that he was sorry about everything that had happened. I believed him."

Asshole. I would have at least waited . . . well, at least until the trial was over! There wasn't the slightest bit of longing in Lorna's voice when she said his name and Kellie was ashamed that she was glad. "It sounds like he was thoughtful when it came to Meg. No wonder you and your sister liked him."

"Meggy was crazy for him though she denied it when I teased her about it. She was sweet and goofy and funny."

Kellie felt Lorna smile.

"School was hard for her, but she wasn't dumb or anything," she was quick to point out.

"I would never think that."

"By the end of her kindergarten I was working with her every night. That seemed to help and she started doing a lot better."

"Where was your mother during all this?" Drunk, Kellie suspected, resentful that a teenage girl was left to do a parent's job.

Lorna thought for a second. "You know, I have no idea."

"She didn't cook?"

"Nah. Meggy and I did the cooking. Or I would bring home burgers from the place I worked."

"Grr . . ."

"It wasn't a big deal, Princess." Lorna patted Kellie's belly, then, unexpectedly, she laid her hand there and began a slow rub as though she were petting a well-loved puppy.

The touch made Kellie's skin tingle and she bit back a groan of pure pleasure.

"Mom was a rotten cook," Lorna continued, wholly unaware that her innocent touches were coming perilously close to undoing Kellie. "It was safer to make things for ourselves. Besides, I liked to cook."

"Were—" the word came out all smoky and warm and Kellie paused and tried again. "Were you a good student?"

Lorna shrugged and admitted that she did okay. She hadn't been all that interested in school though she liked reading and was reasonably good at math.

"Meg was pretty," Lorna said suddenly. "If she's still alive, I'll bet she has a handsome boyfriend or husband. I might even be an aunt by now."

"Jesus, Lorna, you don't even know if she's alive?"

A pained expression flashed across Lorna's face. "I hope she is . . . but God only knows who my mom hooked up with once my dad was gone. She wasn't the sort of woman who could get by on her own. She brought a date to my trial."

"Incredible!"

Very aware of how damp Kellie's T-shirt was from her tears, Lorna sniffed a few times and moved her head. "I'm sorry." Awkwardly, she sat up a little and tried to wipe off the cloth. "I should—"

"Shh. I don't mind your ice block feet and I certainly don't care about my damned T-shirt. Lie back down and tell me why you lost track of someone who was obviously so important to you."

Lorna didn't move.

"Lorna, us being this close . . . physically, I mean, does it bother you?" Kellie knew how she felt about it, but she certainly wasn't going to force this level of intimacy on anyone.

Slowly, Lorna shook her head, her eyes still glistening in the gray light.

Kellie just opened her arms and, wordlessly, Lorna snuggled back against Kellie, her head on the pillow so they faced each other as they spoke.

"I saw my sister once at my trial. It was the first time I'd ever seen her in a dress." Lorna's voice was a mixture of fondness and sadness. "Mom brought her and then let me know that she didn't want my bad influence in Meg's life anymore and that they weren't coming ever again."

Kellie's eyes glinted with sudden rage.

Lorna saw it instantly and reached out and gently squeezed and released Kellie's hand. "I didn't expect her to come and visit me. Prison is no place for a kid."

Oh, Lorna, it's no place for you either.

"I guess I didn't understand what she really meant at the time. She said they weren't coming to visit, not that Meg would disappear from my life forever. I wrote and wrote, but never got a single letter in reply. Finally, I got one of my letters back stamped 'addressee unknown.' So I stopped sending them."

"But not writing them?" Very occasionally, Kellie would catch Lorna writing at the desk. Lorna never said what she was doing and always tucked the neatly folded pieces of paper into the bottom drawer of the desk when she was finished. And although Kellie burned with curiosity over what the carefully penned notes said, she'd never had the heart to sneak a peek.

"It's silly I guess, but when I write them I feel like I'm talking to her. I've never been able to bring myself to pitch 'em."

"Lorna, it's not silly at all."

A few more hot tears spilled down Lorna's cheeks and splashed onto their shared pillow. "Years ago I paid a guard to run some Internet searches on Meg's name. She printed out the results and brought them to me. There was nothing except for a few newspaper articles where she was mentioned as my sister after my arrest."

Sometimes, Kellie mused, *life's so unfair that it literally knocks you to your knees.* She reached out and wiped Lorna's cheeks with the back of her knuckles. The skin was soft and damp and she longed to kiss it. "I would have given anything for a sister that spent time with me and cared how I did in school. You were a good sister and I'm glad Meg had you."

Lorna beamed one of those smiles, albeit a little watery, that turned Kellie's insides into jelly. "Thanks."

"You know, it's like you said, talking doesn't change things, but it can make them feel more manageable." Blue eyes shone with gratitude and something more. "It's mainly nice not to feel like I'm alone."

"You're not," Kellie said simply. "So you wanna know what I miss?"

"Besides the sex and sleep?"

"Promise you won't laugh?"

"Duh." Lorna gave her a little poke. "If it's funny I'll totally laugh."

Kellie decided she couldn't find fault in that. Lorna laughing, no matter the cause, was a good thing. "I miss the rain."

Lorna blinked, her gaze drawn upward to the window. "What's there to miss? Last week it rained every day. We didn't get to go outside even once."

"Late at night when I'd finally stop working, I used to open my patio doors and sit in a soft recliner and listen to stormy nights. I loved the burnt-sulfur smell of lightning and the earthy, fresh scent of rain. I have ever since I was a kid when I used to put on my swimsuit and play in the backyard."

"I didn't think you liked being outside much."

"I usually don't. I'm not into hiking or canoeing or whatever it is people do in those remote places like Minnesota or Wyoming. But now that I can't go out whenever I want . . ."

Lorna hummed in understanding. "Not being able to have something makes you want it twice as bad."

Kellie smirked. Her cellmate already knew her too well. "Maybe more."

Lorna's face took on a far-off expression and a smile played at her lips. "Worms."

"Huh?"

"Rain and wet soil smells like worms to me. When I was a kid we used to catch big fat ones after a big rain and then use them to fish off the bridge in town. I like the smell of rain too. It's the outside." Wistfully, she added, "It's being free."

It was a strange feeling to be understood so completely. Kellie's spirit soared.

Their eyes met and Kellie's heart clenched. "Forgive me? Please?"

Lorna look confused. "For what?"

"Because I hurt your feelings earlier with what I said."

"Kellie?"

"Hmm?"

Lorna glanced down and lifted her hand to ever so gently trace Kellie's very kissable lower lip with the tip of her index finger.

Kellie's heart began to thunder.

Lorna's eyes lifted from Kellie's mouth and in a breathy voice she said, "Do you really think my smile could melt someone's knees?" She searched Kellie's face intently.

Yes! "I—" Kellie's tongue felt clumsy and thick as her mind raced. Was Lorna actually flirting with her? "I—"

Expectantly, Lorna's eyebrows edged upward. "Yes?"

"I—" Like a deer in headlights, Kellie was frozen in Lorna's gaze.

Kellie bit her lower lip. Lorna was rapidly becoming temptation personified. If she didn't get a grip on this, the next year and a half was going to be hell. "When you meet the right, umm, guy. His knees will be melting all over the place. I'm sure of it."

Lorna released the breath she was holding and offered up a tepid smile. "Thanks."

Kellie wanted to die. The perfect moment had strolled up to her, slapped her in the face, and then left her sucking its wake as it exited their cell.

"Maybe you should go back to your bunk," Lorna said awkwardly. "It's crazy late and I feel like I've run a marathon."

Kellie let loose a string of internal profanities. "Okay." Kicking herself, she flipped off the sheet and thin blanket and began to climb down.

Lorna stopped her halfway down with a hand on the side of her head.

Kellie glanced up, intentionally not looking into Lorna's eyes. It would be too easy to drown there. "Yeah?"

Impulsively, Lorna leaned forward. She meant for the kiss to land on Kellie's cheek, but at the last second her friend moved and the kiss ended up half on, half off Kellie's soft mouth.

Both women let out soft gasps of surprise.

Lorna let her lips linger. "Good night," she whispered finally, still so close their mouths were touching. When she pulled away, she looked as shocked by what had just happened as Kellie.

Stunned by the loving gesture, Kellie stilled. Then she slowly lifted her hand to touch her own cheek where Lorna's kiss still burned. "You kissed me?"

Terrified and disturbingly aroused, Lorna wanted to escape. *Shit! She's not even safe around me.* "I—I—I won't do anything else. I swear!"

Kellie's forehead crinkled. "What are you talking about? You kissed me, you didn't kick me in the teeth." She offered up a cautious, but warm smile. "It was a nice kiss, too. One of the sweetest I've ever had."

"You'd better get in your own bed, Kellie," Lorna said seriously as she sat on her hands.

Kellie didn't move.

Lorna's face turned beet red. "I mean it!"

"What is going on?" Kellie demanded, ignoring Lorna's words and climbing back into the warm nest on the top bunk. "You're shaking."

Lorna scooted away from Kellie was though Kellie were on fire. "I said go!"

"Shh . . ." Kellie glanced at the cell door. "Do you want the guards coming in here?" She laid her hand on Lorna's leg, only to have Lorna jerk it away.

Kellie's eyes flashed. "What the hell is going on with you? And don't say it's nothing! It's not nothing!"

Lorna wrapped her arms around her own stomach and bent slightly at the waist. "I'm sorry. I didn't mean to do that." She began rocking back and forth. "You were just so close. And you're so pretty. And . . . and . . . I just couldn't help myself!" Pleading eyes lifted from the bedcovers and pinned Kellie. "I'm sorry. I would never hurt you."

"You *didn't* hurt me," Kellie clarified, struggling to gentle her voice.

"You don't understand." Heartsick, Lorna whispered, "I wanted to."

Kellie's jaw sagged. "After everything we've b-been through, I find that hard to believe."

"Believe it!" Lorna's words spilled out in a rush. "I'll talk to Chul. Or maybe Elaine. Yeah, Elaine. I think she's got early shift tomorrow. If I throw some money their way I can get one of us transferred into a new cell. It might take a few days but—"

Kellie held one hand up. "Stop! I don't want to transfer cells and I certainly don't want a new cellmate."

Lorna's stomach twisted. "You need one, Kellie. It's getting harder and harder for me."

Kellie grabbed her own head as though she wanted to tear her hair out. "*What* is getting harder and harder?"

"It's getting harder and harder for me not to touch you!"

Kellie searched Lorna's face for any clue as to what was going on in her friend's head. "And you think touching me is bad?"

Lorna nodded slowly, then closed her eyes. "Yes," she hissed.

Kellie sighed and leaned back against the wall. There were so many things that needed discussing she hardly knew where to begin. "You know that I'm a lesbian, right?"

Lorna nodded again. "When you said Cindy was your girlfriend I didn't think you meant just friends."

Kellie tried not to sound as hurt as she felt. "So you think it's bad to be a lesbian?"

Lorna frowned. "Of course not."

Kellie's mouth worked but no sound came out.

"Besides, just because you're gay doesn't mean I can do anything I want to you."

"No kidding," Kellie deadpanned. "But I still have no idea what you're talking about!"

Lorna threw her hands in the air. "Haven't you seen it? Haven't you heard it? What do you think Katrina was trying to do to you your very first day here?"

Kellie's expression cooled. "Katrina was trying to rape me, not kiss me."

"She was trying to control you! Haven't you ever seen a big male dog grab a smaller one and start humping it? That's what being physical means here. It's not like the regular world where you meet someone and go on a date or something. At best it's using someone as some pathetic replacement for real-life companionship. At worst it's raw power, domination and violence."

Kellie's gaze softened. "It doesn't have to be like that."

"But-but that's how it is!" Every word felt like a struggle. Why couldn't she make Kellie understand what was so clear? "I want to control you even though I know it's wrong. I feel like I'm the one losing control!"

"Is that what you meant when you said you wanted to hurt me? You want to touch me?"

Lorna's mouth went bone dry and her cheeks flushed bright red. "Yes. I—I—"

"You can tell me," Kellie prodded tenderly. "We're best friends, right?"

"I think so, but—"

"Lorna!"

Resigned, Lorna shook her head. Patience was not among Kellie's virtues. "Yes, we are."

"So that probably means you can tell me anything." Kellie tapped the bed with a rapid, almost frantic motion. "Now would be a good time."

Eyes slightly hooded, Lorna drew in a deep breath and looked up at Kellie from behind thick auburn lashes. "I want to kiss you."

Kellie's eyes sparkled and she let out a breath that was all relief. "Thank God."

A tiny, confused smile cracked through Lorna's distress. "That doesn't bother you?"

Kellie beamed. "Do I look upset?" She wriggled on the bed like a happy puppy. "I'm thrilled and flattered."

An enormous weight tumbled off Lorna's shoulders, making it a little easier to breathe. At least Kellie wasn't repulsed by the idea of her interest. Then she winced inwardly. *At least not yet.*

Kellie couldn't hide her surprise. She was about to mention that Lorna had never talked about women in a sexual way, but then again, except for a brief mention of her high school beau that she'd had to drag out of her, Lorna hadn't talked about anyone that way. Lorna was too passionate to be asexual, Kellie decided, so she just assumed she was straight . . . and very private. But now . . . "Have you been with other women here?"

Lorna pulled her knees to her chest and rested her forearms on them. This whole conversation made her want to crawl out of her skin. But she'd started down this path with that pathetic attempt at a kiss and now there was no turning back. "No."

"What about men?" They weren't all as revolting as Roscoe. One or two of the guards, in fact, had the freshly scrubbed look of someone just out of the military and were undeniably good looking.

Lorna shook her head. "Male or female, anyone who was ever interested in me here . . . they always wanted to push me where I didn't want to go. I've never wanted anyone."

Kellie's face fell.

"Until now," Lorna added quickly, not wanting there to be any confusion on that point. "I just don't know what to do."

Kellie let out a slightly frazzled chuckle. "If that's all that's bothering you, we can work with that, Lorna. Nobody knows what to do at first. Luckily, practice, which I love by the way, cures all things."

"But there's more." Lorna screwed up her courage. Perspiration began to bead on her forehead and she wiped at it nervously. "And this is the bad part."

Kellie saw the raw fear in Lorna's eyes. She longed to reassure her, but she couldn't do that until she truly understood what was going on.

"I don't *just* want to kiss you. Sometimes, I want to hold you down and kiss you. I want to *make* you want me to kiss you. I want to be the one calling the shots. I want you to want to touch me. I want to control you." Lorna's face twisted in revulsion. "Just like Katrina."

"Lorna." Kellie laid her hand on Lorna's arm, visibly relieved when she didn't jump at her touch. "You're nothing like her."

Lorna's gaze darkened with shame. "You wouldn't say that if you knew more about me. I'm more like her than you know."

Kellie filed that conversation away for the future. "Look," she said with complete frankness, "I don't know everything about you. But I know a lot. You're not a passive person normally. I'm not surprised that you'd want to be dominant in bed, too. That's not a bad thing. In fact," she smiled reassuringly, "it can be a very good thing."

"Dominant in bed?" Lorna croaked, a bit of the blood draining from her face. "I was just talking about kissing!"

Kellie's eyebrows disappeared into soft dark bangs. "You've never even thought about things going further than that? Maybe in a dream or just a harmless fantasy?"

The color returned to Lorna's cheeks with such astonishing speed that she felt a little dizzy. "Maybe . . . I mean, yes."

"Because you're attracted to me?"

"You knew that." It wasn't a question.

Kellie shook her head. "I *hoped* that." Carefully, she moved a little closer to Lorna while still allowing her some space. "When you thought of us together . . . were you violent toward me?"

Lorna rested her head against her upraised knees and drew in a shaky breath. "Sort of."

There was a pause before Kellie said, "Tell me what happened."

Close to tears, Lorna turned to her cellmate. "I don't think of this all the time or anything. But sometimes I imagine what it would be like to hold you down and I make you say things to me and . . . um . . . do things to me."

"Things?" Kellie cleared her throat to remove the huskiness she could hear there. "Things," she repeated, proud that the word sounded completely normal.

"Touch me . . . Kiss me. Jesus, Kellie!" she blurted. "You get the idea!"

Kellie would have found herself incredibly turned on were it not for Lorna's horrified expression. "Fantasy and reality aren't the same thing. Just thinking about something or being curious about it doesn't make your actions real."

Lorna swallowed. "But what if some of these fantasies are things you'd like to do in real life? Even if you think they're wrong?"

"In your fantasies how did I react when you—" Kellie gestured vaguely "—did whatever it is that you did?"

Lorna cringed as she waited for Kellie's inevitable anger. "You liked it."

But Kellie merely nodded, then took Lorna's hand in her own and threaded their fingers together. "Did you hurt me physically?" She brought Lorna's hand to her lips and softly kissed it.

Why isn't she mad? Slightly mesmerized by the effect of Kellie's loving touch, Lorna stared at their joined hands before trying to pull away. But Kellie had anticipated the move and held on with gentle, but firm pressure. "I—I . . . No." Confusion colored Lorna's husky voice. "I was in charge and I put your hands and mouth wherever I wanted them."

Desire flooded Kellie and she stifled the low groan that threatened to escape.

"But I didn't physically hurt you."

"Mentally then?"

"I bossed you around! I *commanded* you. That's not how things are supposed to be when you care about someone." Lorna slapped her hand down on the mattress. "You are the most contrary person I've ever met. You hate people telling you what to do!"

"Normally that's true, Lorna. But the rules in bed are a little different. I'm not at all averse to someone else being in charge. I don't think I'd want that exclusively," she admitted after giving the matter brief but serious consideration. "But often? Or even most of the time and with the right person? Absolutely."

"But why do I even want that? What's wrong with me?" Lorna covered her eyes with one hand. "Just thinking about it makes me feel like shit!"

Kellie's voice was low and held more than a hint of anger as she said, "Nothing is wrong with you. And maybe you feel the way you do because you've been in this dysfunctional pit your entire adult life! Sex does not equal manipulation, Lorna. What you're talking about is something that happens every day in normal relationships with happy people."

Lorna couldn't help but say, "That can't be true."

"Jesus, you're not fantasizing about us being dressed head-to-toe in latex and you branding me with hot irons until I scream for mercy, are you?" Kellie snapped.

Lorna's eyes widened. "Do people actually do that?"

"Uh huh."

"Well . . . Not me!"

Kellie gave her a direct look. "Then let me give you a little perspective from someone who hasn't lived your chaste life. What you're fantasying about is *not* abnormal. It doesn't even qualify as kinky! It's just you expressing a normal part of your personality."

Lorna still looked doubtful.

Kellie's hands twitched with the need to shake Lorna until she got what she was saying. "Do you think I'm a reasonable person?"

Lorna blinked at the non sequitur. "Hardly."

Kellie rolled her eyes. "*Most* of the time do you think I'm a reasonable person?"

Lorna shrugged one shoulder and did her best to be diplomatic. "I guess."

"Then you need to trust me on this. I wouldn't let someone do something to me that I didn't want. I was fighting Katrina tooth and nail, wasn't I?"

A little of the tension in Lorna's gut uncoiled. "I remember."

Kellie rubbed the back of Lorna's hand with her thumb and mentally gave a little cheer. "In your fantasy, did I say no to any of your advances?"

Lorna shook her head. "You didn't want me to stop what I was doing."

Kellie smiled affectionately. "I don't blame me."

Lorna tried not to smile herself, but it was getting harder and harder. "I'm being serious."

"I know you are." Kellie lifted Lorna's chin. "But you need to know that you can trust me to take care of myself where you're concerned. Look at me."

Lorna's darting eyes instantly locked with Kellie's and both women melted a little under the other's heated gaze.

"Trust me," Kellie said, on the verge of begging, or crying, or screaming. She couldn't be sure which.

"I do trust you, Kel," Lorna whispered back. "More than you know."

Mollified for the moment, Kellie let a little more of her heart show in her eyes. "I think I have a crush on you," she said softly.

Lorna let out an unexpected giggle, shaving off some of the hard, world-weary years of confinement from her face. "I think the feeling is mutual." She leaned forward and tenderly brushed her lips against Kellie's, trying to put everything she felt for this woman into a single kiss.

For a second, Kellie was too stunned to return the kiss. But when she sensed Lorna grow hesitant as though she might pull away, she murmured, "No," and pressed their mouths tightly together in a staggering display of passion.

The bed creaked loudly and the heat between them ratcheted up several degrees as their bodies came together. *Jesus*, Lorna's mind sighed. Kellie's lips were as soft and delicious as they looked and she instantly ached for more. Her heart hammered in her chest and slick moisture gathered between her legs.

Kellie moaned out loud when Lorna's tongue demanded entrance into her mouth for a bold taste. The kiss was sweet and hot and not the least bit tentative as tongues swirled together and fought for dominance.

"Easy," Lorna whispered, even as she feasted on Kellie's mouth again and again. Stopping was the last thing on earth she wanted to do, but her hands were itching to get Kellie out of her T-shirt and panties so she could lose herself in the warm, musky skin that lay beneath. And that was something she wasn't ready for. At least not yet. "Easy, Princess." She eased back a few inches to study Kellie's face but didn't loosen her grip on the other woman.

"You want me to stop?" Kellie drew her tongue the length of Lorna's lower lip and Lorna felt it all the way to the tips of her toes. " 'Cause I don't want to, but I will."

Lorna's eyes slammed shut. "No. I mean, y-yes," she stammered. "I mean . . . argh!"

Kellie drew away. There would be more nights for kissing and getting to know the firm body so close to hers.

When they finally separated, faces hot and flushed, they were panting softly. Stunningly aroused, Lorna had no idea what to say.

Kellie rested her forehead against Lorna's and gave her an affectionate smile that somehow managed not to be too lustful. She had been kissed more times than she could count and yet this admitted novice had reduced her to a quivering mass of goop in a matter of minutes. *Amazing.* "That was . . . It was . . ."

"Hot." Lorna pushed a damp strand of unruly hair from Kellie's forehead. An uncertain look swept across her face. "Right?"

"Smokin' hot," Kellie agreed readily. "Hot and amazing."

Lorna grinned, relieved. "I—" She turned her head as she heard footsteps start and stop just down the hall. "Shit," she whispered harshly. "Roscoe's checking inside the cells."

Most of the guards didn't bother shining a light into the cells after bed check, unless they were conducting a surprise raid. But Roscoe was notorious for being bored while working the nightshift as well as being an asshole. It was a dangerous combination. "Better go. If he catches you up here he'll get a clue that I actually like you and you'll have a new cellmate by morning."

Kellie nodded but couldn't resist giving Lorna one last sound kiss before she scampered off the bunk. She had just pulled up her sheet when the strong beam of a police issue flashlight landed on her head. She squinted against the bright light, only seeing a large shadow through the glass window in the door. The light lingered long enough for her to give him the finger. Then it traveled up to Lorna and the light disappeared as he moved down the hall.

"Lorna?"

"Yeah?"

Kellie turned onto her side and rested her head on her arm. "Thanks for trusting me."

Lorna could hear the smile in Kellie's voice and it made her own mouth curl in return. "Have sweet dreams tonight, Kellie."

"Yeah." Kellie sighed wistfully, her voice floating up to the top bunk. "I just might."

Chapter 8
One month later . . .

A large loading truck weighted down with fragrant planks of cedar, pine, maple and sheets of particleboard sat parked in the loading bay of Blue Ridge Women's Correctional Facility. The summer sun beat down on the inmates as the hot wind ruffled their white T-shirts.

Elaine pulled off her hat, wiped her damp forehead with the back of her hand and leaned against the prison wall. She crossed her arms over her ample chest and watched Roscoe and Patrice Jennings. She spent as much time watching them as the inmates.

After looking around to see if anyone was paying attention, Lorna casually strolled past Elaine, pausing only for a few seconds to say something and press what looked like an envelope into her hand.

Kellie squinted against the dust swirling around the loading bay as she watched the exchange from behind a tall stack of boxes. "Don't do something stupid, Lorna," she said to herself. "Please."

Lorna trotted back over to her cellmate and bumped shoulders with her. Unusually cheerful she asked, "Why the long face?"

Kellie was about to answer when Roscoe pointed and ordered in a loud voice, "Holloway and Katrina, take the maple then the cedar." The truck had nearly been unloaded, but they were behind schedule and the big man was noticeably on edge.

Kellie and Lorna exchanged worried glances.

Lorna's belly tightened, and her heart began to thud fast in her chest, her body's instinctive reaction to potential danger. Word was out that Katrina had been poking around in their business. And Lorna had no doubt that she would love to get a few minutes alone with Kellie. Her cellmate had told her how Katrina had offered her alcohol and one glance at Kellie's pained face told her how close she'd come to accepting the offer.

Roscoe examined the plastic clipboard in his hands and drew a meaty finger down the inventory list. "Mally and T-bone, you get the pine then the particleboard. Let's go! The rest of you back inside with Officer Johnson and Ms. Jennings."

The woodshop administrator, dressed in a white cotton blouse and a sharply pressed fitted skirt that sat a couple of inches above her knees, frowned, then strode over to Roscoe, her heels clicking on the concrete. Patrice Jennings leaned close to him and spoke quietly.

Roscoe's scowl deepened, but he nodded his agreement. "Murano, take Holloway's place. Ms. Jennings wants a word with her."

Laverne made a lewd gesture as she shouldered by Kellie. "Teacher's pet."

But Kellie merely rolled her eyes. She took a step forward to follow the group of women who were moving off the loading dock, but was pulled up short by a strong hand and fingers that wound around her wrist.

"What's going on?" Lorna whispered uneasily. "You and Jennings are awfully chummy lately."

"Don't worry about it." Kellie recognized tension around Lorna's eyes, but chose to ignore it for the time being. It wasn't as though Lorna told her everything that she did, right? "Everything's fine. Be careful with Katrina, okay? Don't let her drop a board on your head or something."

Lorna's jaw muscles bunched and released. "You didn't answer my question."

Surprised by Lorna's tone, Kellie's eyebrows jumped.

Roscoe tossed his clipboard onto a box of sandpaper and tugged up his sagging belt with one hand. "Let's go, Mally and Holloway."

Frowning a little, Kellie gently disengaged her arm from Lorna's grasp. "You worry too much. Go unload your wood before you get in trouble."

Lorna's gaze softened. "Kel—"

The other inmates had already disappeared into the building with Elaine. Ms. Jennings was impatiently tapping her foot as she waited to escort Kellie back to the woodshop office.

"Trouble in paradise, Mally?"

Lorna spun around and flexed her hands, trying not to think about how good it would feel to wipe that smug look off Katrina's face. Then she caught sight of the fence and what lay so tantalizingly just beyond her reach. It was enough to make her chest ache. *Nobody is worth ruining my chances at parole. Nobody.*

She'd thought more about her freedom in the past few months than she had in all her years at Blue Ridge. Getting to know Kellie had given her a glimpse of something simple and profound that she never thought she'd experience. Happiness.

"Hey, Roscoe, you don't mind if I work with my old pal Mally, do you?" Katrina asked in a syrupy voice. "We've practically been neighbors for months and months but we haven't had any time at all together."

Roscoe appeared as though he would refuse the request. He'd taken to referring to Katrina as 'that Polack dyke' the last few weeks, which meant that either Katrina had cut back on his kickbacks or, based on his especially wrinkled uniform, his wife had left him again and he was more pissed off at the world than usual. But after a few seconds of consideration, Roscoe merely shrugged. "Whatever. Just get to work or you'll both get written up."

Ramona Murano quietly paired up with T-bone, a scrawny dark-skinned woman with a permanent scowl and beady yellow-green eyes that reminded Lorna of a malnourished kitten. They headed for the truck before a fight could break out. Lorna usually did a good job of avoiding Katrina. Having them forcibly paired together would likely end up with someone bloodied or tossed into the hole. Or both.

"Better get those gloves on." Katrina winked at Lorna. "I wouldn't want you to get a splinter."

Unsettled, Lorna jerked her leather work gloves from her back pocket and tugged them on with short, angry movements. Her shoes sounded loud on the truck floor as she trudged to the very back, her mind shifting to Kellie's weird behavior. She didn't trust Ms. Jennings and there was no reason that she could think of that Kellie would need to speak with her alone.

The women each loaded several long planks of wood into a pile. "So," Katrina began, "what's it like to be Kellie's bitch?"

Lorna bit her tongue, refusing to be baited as she bent over to add a knotty piece of pine to the stack. Its pungent scent wafted upward and completely overtook the odor of the cedar that was stacked nearby. One of the boards was so green that it was still a little sticky. "Half the stuff they give us is crap," Lorna grumbled, making a mental note to lay claim to the pieces of wood as soon as she could.

Katrina added a few more planks to the mix.

"Whoa! Hang on."

Katrina's grin was challenging. "Too much for you to carry?"

Lorna examined the pile. "Probably."

Katrina clucked a few times and lifted her end of the pile, intentionally not stepping aside for Ramona and T-bone. The two smaller women had to shimmy between Katrina and the wall of the truck to get by with their load. "Mally." Katrina gritted her teeth and adjusted her grip. "You're nothing but a shadow of your former self."

Bored with the conversation already, Lorna used her powerful thighs to bend and lift her end of the load. "Good."

Katrina began to walk backward, her arms straining under the weight of wood. "What the hell happened to you? People used to fall all over themselves to get five minutes of your time or to get the hell out of your way. Now all you do is make fuck-me eyes at your cellmate."

"You know what happened." Lorna's arm muscles stood out in vivid relief against her ruddy skin. "Do not slow down, Katrina!"

"I don't know anything," Katrina snapped, "other than the fact that you turned chicken and betrayed your friends."

A wave of anger swept over Lorna. "You were never my friend! I grew up, and got smarter, and got the hell away from you. Get over it and leave me and mine alone."

Though her face was red from exertion, Katrina stopped at the bottom of the ramp from the truck to the cement slab in front of the bay. She managed a glare. "I don't want to get over it. I want you back in the fold where you belong. Helping me. Working with me."

"You're insane."

"That's never been proven."

Lorna snorted. "You want to be a team?"

"Yes."

Lorna saw a flicker of sincerity behind Katrina's frosty exterior. But as quickly as it came, it vanished. "Bullshit. You want to use me or kill me, whichever will give you more pleasure at that moment."

Anticipation filled Katrina's voice and she licked her lips excitedly. "Killing is so permanent, but using each other would be . . . normal. And last longer. We can have fun again, Lorna. Just like before . . . only better. Being bad isn't nearly as fun alone."

"You really are crazy if you think I'd ever go back to that life. Back to being like you . . ." Lorna let every bit of revulsion she felt for Katrina show on her face. "Whatever it is your twisted mind has convinced itself that we had together is nothing but a figment of your imagination." Her voice shifted into a growl. "Even if I could forget what a disgusting excuse for a human being you are, I'd never forgive what you tried to do to Kellie."

"Nothing happened, you know that."

"That wasn't from your lack of trying. Rape is low even for you. You're lucky you didn't succeed."

"If I had, you really couldn't have stopped yourself from hurting me, could you?" Katrina looked oddly pleased by the prospect.

"No," Lorna admitted, suddenly upset that it was clear Katrina still knew her so well. "Nothing would have stopped me. Now, move it!"

Lorna pushed forward, but stubbornly, Katrina held her ground, her sneakers squeaking a little as she was pushed back only a few inches.

A trickle of sweat snaked down Lorna's cheek. It itched and she couldn't scratch it. She had better things to be doing than sparring with this idiot. Her eyes smoldered and her voice dropped to its lowest register. "Last chance, Katrina, move or be moved the hard way."

Katrina chuckled. "Why, Mally," she said, in a voice far more placid than her expression. "If looks could kill I'd be dead right now. If I can't convince you of how good things can be with me, maybe I can convince your whore instead? I've got a lot to offer her, you know." She waited until comprehension dawned on Lorna's face. "That's right, a few sips of what's in my cell and I'll bet she'd come crawling to me for more. You always did have impulse control issues, didn't you?"

Katrina grinned from ear to ear. Every ounce of fury that rose in Lorna's eyes brought her that much closer to the woman she once knew. "Think about where my hands were on Kellie." She hummed a little in pleasure just remembering. "Her skin was so sweet." She waggled her eyebrows. "And especially damp where I was touching."

"Shut up."

"No, thank you."

Lorna's chest was rising and falling fast, hate swelling within her like a hurricane roaring up the coast. "You're wrong, Katrina. I don't want to kill you."

Katrina couldn't hide her surprise. "No?"

Lorna's body shook as she spoke, all designs of self-control swept away with the wind. "I want to hurt you and *then* kill you. I'd be doing the world a favor." She drew in a breath and prepared herself to knock away the boards before Katrina could use one as a weapon.

Katrina let out a hoot. "Yes! Now *that's* the old Mally I've been missing! The rage feels good, doesn't it? Comfortable. Like an old friend."

Roscoe stalked down the ramp and stopped behind Katrina. Incredulous, he looked at Lorna as he spoke. "This isn't your first load, is it?"

"It wouldn't be if you hadn't paired me with Cruella here," Lorna told him, exhaling shakily, another bead of perspiration dripping from her forehead. *Get me away from her, Roscoe, before it's too late!*

"Cruella?" Katrina affected a wide-eyed innocent look. "Now that hurt my feelings."

Roscoe's eyes narrowed and in a flurry of motion he gave the back of Katrina's knee a sharp rap with his baton. "That's not all that's gonna get hurt if you don't move it!"

Like a box of rocks, Katrina collapsed onto the hot pavement, her limbs akimbo. The planks she was carrying crashed on top of her, then thudded against the ground as she lurched sideways and let out a piercing shriek.

Roscoe stared down at her and shook his head in faux regret. "Ooh. That's gonna bruise."

Lorna couldn't help it, the tension in her began to plummet and she laughed. It was nice to see Roscoe's anger directed at someone who really deserved it for a change.

Roscoe's beady eyes found Lorna. "When are you two slags gonna kill each other already and give my acid reflux a break?"

Lorna scrubbed her face with one hand, and then stretched out her tired arms. There was no good response to that question, so she didn't answer at all. As much as she told herself not to let Katrina get to her, all it took was thinking of her and Kellie in the same room for her blood to alternately boil or run as cold as ice.

Since she and Kellie had kissed she'd become unbearably over-protective. She knew that. Kellie had, she was forced to admit, been more patient than she deserved, reassuring Lorna in hushed tones that they could take things slowly. Offering her simple touches and looks, all filled with sweet affection. If only Lorna hadn't done and seen so much during her time in Blue Ridge that made it almost impossible for her to relax and enjoy Kellie's friendship and more. She knew with shocking certainty that the monsters that lurked in the shadows here, waiting to crush you, were very real.

She'd been one of them.

And now she had to apologize to Kellie for how she'd behaved this afternoon. If she weren't careful, she'd ruin a good thing before it had a chance to blossom. *What a mess.*

Ramona and T-bone were back and ready for another load. "Umm . . ." Ramona looked at the scene before her. "You need some help with this mess, chica?"

Lorna shook her head.

"Nobody needs any goddamn help," Roscoe said impatiently. "Get your asses inside and get your next load! I'm missing my Sunday afternoon poker babysitting you bitches. This truck should have been unloaded an hour ago!"

T-bone moved so quickly she nearly tripped over her own feet with Ramona lingering only another indecisive second.

Silently, Katrina rose to her feet, dusted herself off, and began gathering the scattered boards. When the last board had joined the pile, she glanced up and shot Roscoe a look so filled with hate that, to Lorna's surprise, he unconsciously backed up a step.

Then Katrina turned her gaze on Lorna. *Jesus. She's dead inside.* Lorna tried not to feel the shiver that chased its way down her spine. Wasn't the saying that some dogs were all bark and no bite? She had to admit that wasn't the case with Katrina. She bit hard and often. And had rabies to boot.

"Big mistake, Mally," Katrina said grimly as she dusted herself off. She stretched out her back, a streak of pain flying across her otherwise impassive face. "When your world turns to shit, remember that it was your own doing."

Lorna let loose with a cold smile of her own. "Don't worry, Katrina, been there, done that."

"Hurry it up," Roscoe muttered as he rapped his baton against his open hand. Then he quickly padded across the loading bay and began hassling Ramona and T-bone's progress.

This time Katrina and Lorna went about their tasks without a word, each swimming through her own sea of dark thoughts.

• • •

Lorna sank down onto the bottom bunk and stared at the far wall, too tired to dig out her towel and toiletries kit just yet. Her gas tank, both physically and emotionally, was teetering on empty. She needed to apologize for her behavior earlier today, but her confrontation with Katrina still had her spoiling for a fight. She wanted to kiss Kellie and kill her at the same time. Now wasn't the time for a deep talk.

Kellie could tell by Lorna's unsettled demeanor that something had happened. She waited, but her cellmate said nothing. "So," she prompted, "nothing happened with Katrina?"

Lorna gestured toward the table. "Whatcha writin'?"

She held up the blank piece of paper and gave it a little wave, trying not to focus on the fact that Lorna had completely blown off her question. "Nothing."

Lorna hitched up an eyebrow. "Fine. Don't tell me."

Kellie's eyes narrowed and a resentment she didn't know she was harboring flared to life. "It's not like you tell me everything," she pointed out tartly.

Lorna laid back, crossed her arms behind her head and closed her eyes. "I don't have any idea what you're talking about."

"I saw you give an envelope to Elaine today. And this isn't the first time. I know you're not writing to anyone on the outside. And I find it hard to believe that you and Elaine are exchanging love letters."

Lorna cursed softly. She felt like a fool for thinking she'd been so careful. "It's . . . It's not." She lifted a hand, and then let it fall to the bed.

"Legal?"

Lorna's stomach dropped. "No, it's not legal. But it's not that bad, Kellie."

Kellie was about to explode. "*What* is not that bad?"

Dismayed, Lorna shook her head. "I don't want to involve you."

Kellie looked away, her shoulders sagging just a bit. "If that's the way you want things. Fine."

"What does that mean?"

"It means exactly what I said." Kellie turned back around to face Lorna. "Aren't you at least going to ask me how things went with

Jennings?"

Lorna gave her a wary look, surprised at being let off the hook so easily. Once Kellie grabbed hold of something, she was like a dog with a bone. "Okay," she said cautiously, "how'd it go with Jennings?"

Kellie couldn't help herself. She crossed her arms over her chest. "Fine."

Lorna waited for her, but when it was clear that Kellie wasn't going to say anything, she spat, "Goddamn you, Kellie!"

"It sucks to be kept in the dark like a dim-witted child, doesn't it?" Kellie shot back. "I don't need a convict thinking for me, or deciding what I should and shouldn't know."

Lorna flew off the bed. "You think this convict can't guess what you're sitting there doing?"

Kellie gave her a blank look at the non sequitur. "Huh?"

"You've had that blank paper in front of you for days with that far-off expression on your face."

Kellie sneered. "You don't know anything!"

Suddenly, it was too much for Lorna: not knowing how to act or be in love, unresolved sexual tension, the uncertainty of this new friendship and unending anxiety over an old enemy, even Kellie herself.

Fuming, Lorna said, "Let's see." She put a finger to her temple and tapped a few times as though she was puzzling something out. "You don't sleep well because you have nightmares. Speaking from experience, I'd say that something is eating you up inside. Hmm . . . I wonder what that could be?" In a far-off way she knew she should stop what she was doing, but the urge to push Kellie away won out. "It must be really bad," she added sarcastically. "What have you ever done that's bad? Absolutely nothing, right?"

Kellie wrapped her arms around herself and squeezed her eyes shut. "Stop it, Lorna."

"C'mon, Princess, you know what it is." Lorna cocked her head and waited. "I'll give you a hint. It's some basic emotion that separates us from the apes. One that you avoid like the plague. Guilt."

Kellie's eyes flew open, then narrowed. "I mean it. Shut up. You don't know what you're talking about."

"Don't I? Soooo . . . what does guilt have to do with that useless, blank piece of paper you've been staring at for days—could it be an apology letter to the man your selfishness and stupidity turned into a cripple? A letter that you're clearly too stubborn and self-absorbed to write?"

That was a direct hit in the heart and Kellie looked down at herself as if to verify that she wasn't actually bleeding. Was she really so easy to read? "Bitch!"

"Kel . . ." Lorna let out a ragged breath and gentled her voice. "I've never seen anyone eating themselves up from the inside out the way you're doing. You need to come to terms with what you've done so you can move forward."

"What makes you an expert on what I need?" Kellie balled up the paper and threw it with the force of a missile right at Lorna's head. "How do you know what I'm writing? Have you been spying on me?"

The ball struck Lorna between the eyes, bouncing off her before she could swat it away. "I don't need to spy!" she snapped viciously. "That trashcan is mine too."

Kellie's mouth dropped open. "You *read* one of the letters I'd started? It's not bad enough that the guards invade what tiny bit of privacy I have left. You're going through my mail too?"

As angry as Lorna was, she had to look away. "I just saw the name at the top. Nothing else."

Kellie didn't bother to conceal her hurt. "I would have expected something slimy like that from Katrina. Not you."

Lorna reacted as though she'd been slapped and a large part of the steam that fueled her anger evaporated on the spot. Betrayal was scrawled all over Kellie's face and it caused her own stomach to ball into a solid knot. "I—I have to go."

"Don't you dare run out of here!" A little shaky at the knees, Kellie sprang to her feet. They'd argued plenty of times, had even hurt each other's feelings, but this was the first time the knives had come out.

Lorna yanked open her dresser drawer and pulled out her toiletries kit and a wad of clothes, disappearing out the cell door before she could do any more damage to their already tattered friendship.

Steamy water rolled down Lorna's face as she roughly scrubbed her hair. Most of the other cellmates were parked in front of the television in the lounge, enjoying their favorite Sunday evening programming. So she allowed herself to do something she almost never did: feel sorry for herself and lick her wounds.

She thought of her early years at Blue Ridge, the ones filled with violence and resentment. She'd taken her life sentence very literally, and it left precious little room for hope. Twenty years was more than an eternity and more than a terrified teenager could contemplate. There had been no reason to act like a human being or care about anyone. Kindness and compassion? Those were only valued in the outside world. Here they were weaknesses waiting to be exploited.

Maybe she hadn't started off as a bad person, just confused and searching to belong to something . . . anything. But one lost and lonely day at a time, that's exactly what she'd become. Even more than the rage that Katrina had all too easily evoked in her, the feeling of lashing out at Kellie, of hurting her and taking even momentary pleasure in it, unerringly reminded her of that pathetic young woman she'd worked so hard to outgrow. "One step forward and two steps back," she murmured.

She closed her eyes and scoured her face, her eyes stinging from the combination of soap and sweat. Her skin flushed and tingling, she let the spray beat against her tired shoulders and contemplated whether she'd permanently messed things up with Kellie.

"Shit," she whispered harshly, refusing to let the tears come. She heard the splat of sneakers crossing the wet shower room floor.

Kellie stood before her, waves of anger pouring off her and crashing all around them.

Their eyes locked.

Kellie looked as though she wanted to hit her, and Lorna lifted her chin, then forced her arms to fall loosely at her sides. Her eyes dared Kellie to step forward, her body was coiled with tension. If

Kellie tried to hit her, she would defend herself because that was the way she was hardwired and her spirit demanded nothing less. But she'd never raise a hand in retaliation. Not to her.

Kellie gasped a little at Lorna's pose. Was she actually expecting physical violence? *Of course she is. The people who were supposed to love her unconditionally beat her and each other. It's what she knows best.* Consciously, and very visibly, Kellie unclenched her fists, relieved when she saw Lorna finally suck in a breath.

She'd stalked into the showers intent on giving her cellmate a blistering ass-chewing. And then they were going to kiss and make up, whether Lorna liked it or not.

Adrenaline still coursing through her, Kellie took in the entire scene before her. Lorna was shrouded in a misty cloud of steam, her skin flushed and pink. Her hair was slicked back from her face and water cascaded down her firm body, rivulets disappearing into a thatch of fiery-colored hair between her legs.

Kellie stormed forward through the strong spray of the shower and into Lorna. Hot water soaked through her T-shirt and jeans as she backed Lorna up against the gray wall.

Lorna gasped as the cool concrete came into contact with her overheated skin. She fought to stay calm as Kellie pinned her tight. Chests heaving, their bodies were molded together as they both waited to see what would happen next.

"I want to control you!" Wasn't that what Lorna had said? Kellie could see the other woman fighting with herself. Fight or flee. Seize or be seized.

Lorna's heart thundered and her agitation smoothly morphed into deep arousal. Her gaze dropped to Kellie's soft lips and she began to pant. She voiced her need in a succinct, heart-wrenching way that Kellie could have never expected. "I'm starving."

Kellie looked into the heavy-lidded eyes so close to hers and understood completely. "I know." *Seize!* Unable to wait another second, she claimed Lorna's mouth in a scorching kiss that soon became more vital than oxygen.

Slippery tongues fiercely dueled, as they tasted each other with unabashed ferocity. Then in an explosion of motion, their hands were everywhere, raking over heated skin and leaving trails of electricity in their wake, roughly pushing aside clothing as guttural moans of pleasure echoed off the shower room walls.

Kellie tore her mouth from Lorna's and attacked her succulent neck. Kissing. Sucking. *Biting.* As though she would never get enough.

Lorna's eyes slammed shut, a deep moan rent from her throat. She threw her head back as far as the wall would allow. "Oh, God." She was on fire. Everywhere. Kellie's wet jeans created a delicious friction against her hypersensitive skin and mindlessly, she thrust her hips forward.

Something inside her was screaming to take control, but the hands possessing her so completely were making rational thought impossible. It was all she could do to hang on as her body was played like an instrument in the knowing hands of a relentless master. When Kellie reached up and roughly squeezed her breast, her center began throb.

Lorna threaded her fingers in Kellie's silky hair and pushed her head down, guiding that devouring mouth to her aching nipple. "Yessss!" she breathed hotly, sensation singing through her and making her eyes roll back.

Kellie worshipped Lorna's breasts with single-minded devotion. She cupped Lorna's sex with her palm, her own knees shaking when Lorna brazenly pushed forward to meet her touch, burying her fingers in silky heat.

Kellie kissed her way up Lorna's body, but left her hand exactly where it was. She could feel Lorna's heart pounding against her chest. She stopped when they were face to face, mesmerized by Lorna's glistening lips, which she tasted once again. Pulling away just a fraction, so close they were still breathing each other's air, she lifted her eyebrows in question. "Inside?" She wiggled the fingers between Lorna's legs for emphasis, the motion making her partner's entire body convulse.

A bolt of heat shot through Lorna and she nodded frantically. She couldn't be more ready. "Yes! *Please*, Kel." She reinforced her words by covering Kellie's hand with her own, pulling inward.

Kellie's heart soared and she leaned forward even harder and pushed upward, forcing Lorna onto her tiptoes. Lorna took Kellie's lower lip between her teeth and gave a sharp tug urging Kellie forward.

Willing her hand not to shake, Kellie pushed a finger inside Lorna. *So tight and hot.*

Mouth parted, Lorna released Kellie's lips and looked deeply into her eyes, sharing every exquisite sensation. She groaned softly. Kellie was enthralled. Sweet, *Jesus, I'm going to come just watching her!* She gently stroked Lorna's clit with her thumb, thrilling at the stream of whimpers that poured from Lorna. The other woman looked as though she wanted to do something . . . to take control of the situation. But she wasn't sure how.

"Lorna, do you want—?"

"Just don't stop." A dark blush began working its way up from the top of Lorna's breasts to her cheeks.

"Never," Kellie vowed. She added a second finger to the first and she thrust upward stopping instantly when Lorna gasped in . . . pain? She froze, her eyes round with sudden concern. "Lorna?"

"Shh." Lorna kissed the corner of her mouth, speaking in husky tones. "It's okay." Her gaze dropped and she shook her head a little, scattering droplets of water and sweat from her forehead. "I've just never—"

Kellie's eyes widened even further. *She's never? And I just . . .* "Oh, God. I—I—I didn't know. You said you had a boyfriend and-and I wouldn't have . . . not here." Desperately, she glanced around. *Her first time shouldn't be in the showers.* "Not like this. I—"

Lorna wound her arms around Kellie in case she got any bright ideas about going anywhere. "Never is a lot shorter than it used to be, doncha think?" she teased gently, placing several steamy kisses on Kellie's face. Then she slid her hand under Kellie's T-shirt and bra, not stopping until she cupped a soft breast. She squeezed, and at the same time, thrust down on Kellie's hand.

This time Lorna's moan was languid and borne of pure pleasure.

She swallowed hard, excitement thrumming through her; her normally deep voice an octave below normal. "Don't stop touching me."

Kellie shuddered as Lorna pinched and rolled her nipple in a way that drove her wild. She nodded frantically, eager to please this woman. "If you're sure . . ."

Lips moved to her ear, tickling the sensitive skin there as they softly breathed, "I *need* to come. *Now.*" She ran her hands up Kellie's sides until her fingers found taut nipples. She squeezed.

And that was all it took for Kellie, who orgasmed under the onslaught of Lorna's persistent lips, hands and sexy-as-hell words. She clutched at Lorna, who held her securely as her body swam with more pleasure than she thought possible. She actually felt a little lightheaded.

Lorna rained kisses down on her, as she caught her breath. The kisses reignited the fire in Kellie's belly. Determined to give Lorna her own release, Kellie thrust forward again and again, using her thumb to trace the spot she knew gave the most pleasure at the end of every delicious stroke. This was easily the most erotic thing she'd ever experienced. She'd craved it for so long she could scarcely believe it was happening at all. "You are so hot I can hardly stand it."

Lorna's breathing increased and her legs shook. Kellie felt the flesh around her fingers begin to clamp down as Lorna rode her hand.

"That's it, baby," she whispered against salty skin, drawing her tongue along the length of Lorna's jugular. *Sooo close, but having trouble letting go.* She moved up to nibble swollen lips. She stopped her thrusting, quelling Lorna's mewling protests with another kiss. "Relax."

"I—I can't," she wailed between pants.

"Sure you can." Kellie eased back just a fraction to make sure that Lorna's footing was sure. "Relax. Feel this." She drew soft, slow circles around Lorna's clit.

Lorna squeezed her eyes tightly shut, the blush on her chest darkening several shades as she leaned into the touch.

"Tell me what you need me to do," Kellie cooed, grasping Lorna's bottom with her free hand and massaging it. "Tell me."

"I don't—" Lorna shook her head in frustration, sending out a spray of sweat and water everywhere. She widened her stance, her eyes rolling back in her head. "Faster!"

Kellie obeyed instantly and Lorna surged forward and held Kellie in a grip so powerful it hurt, biting her lip as she silently responded to Kellie's touch, quaking with the force of her explosion.

Lorna released a ragged breath, a million emotions racing across her face as Kellie tenderly placed a single kiss on her chin, then her cheeks, her forehead, and finally her trembling lips. When the soulful kiss ended she rested her arms on Kellie's shoulders, still a little dazed. "I—I don't know what to say." She smiled tentatively. "How do people normally react when someone rocks their world? Wow."

"You knew exactly what to say." Kellie beamed. "Very wow." She leaned forward for another kiss.

Then the shower room door opened.

Kellie instantly wedged herself between Lorna and the door. Then she stood there, dazed after the passion they'd just shared, but still cognizant enough to feel foolish. Her protect Lorna? Ridiculous.

She half expected Lorna to laugh. But instead, a warm, wet hand clasped her shoulder and gave it a gentle squeeze as they stepped out of the spray of the shower together.

In strolled two women, towels draped over their shoulders, small toiletry kits in hand. Their gazes instantly found the room's other occupants.

"Told ya," T-bone muttered out the corner of her mouth to the woman standing next to her.

"T-bone," Kellie greeted in a casual tone, before her lips tightened. "You should consider keeping better company." Memories of Laverne standing by and doing nothing while Katrina assaulted her rose up and left a bitter taste in her mouth.

"Hello, asshole," Lorna greeted Laverne from over Kellie's shoulder. "T-bone, leave."

T-bone just looked at her, blinking.

"Do I really have to add 'now'?" Lorna asked calmly.

The thin woman instantly bolted from the shower, her flip-flops echoing loudly on the gray concrete floor as she left a light spray of water in her wake.

Kellie's eyes widened and she spun around. "What are you doing?"

Lorna ignored Kellie, placating her with a gentle pat on the hip. Her gaze bore into Laverne's. "I want you to tell your good buddy Katrina just what you saw here tonight." She wound a possessive arm around Kellie and surprised her by placing a light, but astonishingly sensual kiss on her lips.

Lorna's kiss was so provocative that Kellie nearly forgot they had an audience and was mortified when the languid moan that filled the shower room turned out to be her own. Wasn't she supposed to be the more experienced of the two?

Lorna's actions reinforced the claim she'd already staked, making the sexual element, which had been assumed but not witnessed, absolutely clear. Kellie was hers in every sense of the word and woe to the person stupid enough to forget it.

Smirking a little at the shocked look on Kellie's face, Lorna cocked her head and glared at Laverne. "What are you waiting for?"

Laverne nearly tripped over her own feet as she bolted from the room.

"What was that?" Kellie asked again, as soon as they were alone.

"A little reminder to Katrina." Lorna rubbed Kellie's back. "She pushed my buttons today and I'm pushing back. She can't stand the fact that I've never responded to any of her disgusting advances."

Kellie's stomach tightened. "Disgusting?"

Lorna smiled reassuringly. "Only because they were coming from her."

Their eyes met and they smiled a little shyly, even after what they'd so recently shared.

Things suddenly seemed strange between them. Different. Kellie felt closer to Lorna than she ever had, but at the same time there was a palpable tension between them. Sex hadn't erased the hurt and anger she still felt over their last argument. Nothing but talk-ing—something that Kellie had until now avoided with her other lovers—would do that.

"Lorna." "Kellie," they began at the same time.

A tinge of pink rose up in Lorna's cheeks.

All Kellie could think about was kissing Lorna again. "Ask me again why I've been spending time with Jennings."

Lorna didn't hide her surprise or relief at the question. "Why have you?" She grimaced, bracing herself against the answer. "Is it because she's pretty?"

Kellie was floored. "I—what are you talking about?"

Lorna's shoulders sagged and she trained her gaze on her feet, wiggling her toes nervously. "You know what I mean. She wears nice dresses and suits. She's pretty and . . ."

Kellie looked at Lorna as though she were insane. "I don't care what she looks like!"

Lorna glanced back up. "You don't?"

Kellie sighed. "Christ, Lorna, do you think I would have . . ." She gestured aimlessly. "Do you think we would have done what we've just done if I was interested in Jennings?"

Lorna didn't bother to lie. "I don't know how things are supposed to be between us. Especially now."

And with that, Kellie realized that Lorna was just as bad at relationships as she was. It was a surprisingly liberating feeling. "I'm interested in you, Lorna, and no one else."

A tentative smile appeared. "Yeah?"

"Yeah," Kellie confirmed softly. "You said you don't know how things should be between us. They can be any way we decide. What is it that you want?" There was no doubt about what she felt. If they were on the outside, Kellie would be on Lorna like white on rice. But being together in prison wasn't exactly voluntary.

A beaming smile threatened to break free. "I want you to be . . . more than friends."

"I'm sorry, I'm too busy," Kellie said wryly.

Lorna wrapped her in a bone-crushing hug. "You're the luckiest woman in the joint!"

Kellie's entire body shook as she laughed, her sopping wet jeans clinging to her. "No, you are!"

"I know," Lorna said seriously, her heart showing in her voice. "So you and Jennings?"

"I've been spending extra time with her because I'm teaching her how to put her spreadsheets in Excel."

"That's a computer thingie, right?"

Kellie nodded.

"Jenning's paying you to teach her?"

"Sort of. In exchange for her letting you work on your own piece of furniture." Kellie grinned, more than a little proud of herself. "You can start next week."

Lorna's voice held a note of wonder. "She's really going to let me build something?"

"She really is."

Lorna blinked a few times, every feature colored with disbelief. "And *keep* it?"

"And keep it," Kellie confirmed softly, her heart aching over the simple things her friend had been denied for so long.

Lorna fought back tears. "Thank you."

Kellie sucked in a satisfied breath. Hours of tutoring one of the most annoying bitches she'd ever had the displeasure of meeting just became worth it.

"I'm such an asshole sometimes!" Lorna exploded as she began stalking around the room and gesturing wildly. "You do something nice for me and I picked a fight with you about it." Her eyes begged for absolution and she reached out to cup the other woman's cheek. "Forgive me?"

Lorna's words had seared a hole in her gut.

Slowly, and knowing full well that what she was about to say was more than a little callous, Kellie marshaled her strength. "No."

Lorna's jaw sagged.

Kellie's eyes narrowed. "You can't be an asshole and then just say you're sorry and expect me to make nice. Either you trust me, or you don't. And if you don't," a lump rose so fast in Kellie's throat that she had to swallow a few times before she could speak without her voice breaking, "then this ends now." *Before you take my heart so completely that there's little chance of me getting it back.*

Lorna could only stare. "After . . . everything . . . You'd really do that?"

Kellie felt about two inches tall. But she was resolute. "I wouldn't want to, but I wouldn't have a choice."

Eyes ablaze, Lorna rasped, "We always have choices, Kellie. Haven't you learned that by now?"

Jaw clenched, Lorna shut off the nearby shower. "C'mon." She took Kellie's other hand in hers and began leading her to the door. "I need to show you something."

Chapter 9
A few minutes later . . .

Lorna led Kellie down a seldom-used hallway that ended with a series of storage rooms that were generally off-limits to inmates unless they were on work assignments. Hair still damp and loosely braided, each woman was comfortable in her standard-issue gray gym shorts, well-worn sneakers and ever-present white T-shirts.

"Where are we going?" Kellie whispered, constantly looking over her shoulder to see if a guard or stoolie inmate had spotted them. The mere fact that they'd been alone for more than one minute meant they were somewhere they shouldn't be.

"We're going to one of the rooms where the kitchen keeps a stash of supplies. You wanted to know about Elaine, so I'm showing you. Now, shh . . . no more talking, okay?"

The hallway was mostly dark, except for the residual light that streamed in from another hallway that led to the cafeteria and was about twenty yards away.

Lorna carefully ran her hands around the doorframe.

Kellie watched in awe when she pulled out a small chunk of frame that had appeared seamless from the front. A second more, and she removed a hidden key from the notch and began working the lock.

Kellie shifted uneasily from one foot to the other. "What is—?"

Lorna pressed two fingers against Kellie's lips and raised an eyebrow in warning.

The key slid in silently and Lorna opened the door that led into a pitch-black room. She pushed Kellie forward, then, with a final quick glance down the hall, stepped in right behind her. She closed the door slowly so as not to make a sound.

They were in a storage room filled with cardboard boxes full of cereal and napkins and the like. The heat was stifling and the lone light from the tiny flashlight cast everything, including Lorna, in deep, sinister shadows.

Tall wire shelves sagged under the weight of dozens of enormous cans of generic ketchup, pickle relish, corn and other foodstuffs. Kellie examined an industrial-sized can of horseradish and her face twisted in disgust. So *that* was the hideous taste in the meatloaf.

But try as she might, she couldn't find anything out of the ordinary. In fact, early in her stay at Blue Ridge, Kellie and several other inmates, along with Chul, had helped bring noodles and cooking oil from another room that looked exactly like this one. "Okay, I give up." Kellie moved aside an enormous pack of paper napkins. "I don't get any of this."

"You will. I—" Lorna's head snapped toward the door and she clamped her hand over Kellie's mouth. "Shh." She warned her to stay quiet with a worried look a split second before she clicked off the tiny flashlight, plunging them into darkness. "Footsteps," she breathed in a voice so low that Kellie barely heard it.

The clomping sound of footsteps, growing louder and louder with every thump of her heart. *Shit. Shit. Shit!* She froze when a shadow appeared beneath the bottom of the door and stayed. She didn't dare breathe.

The shadow shifted, and then disappeared altogether and the dull thudding of shoes filtered into the storeroom.

Lorna let her hand drop from Kellie's mouth.

"Jesus," Kellie muttered under her breath, her chest aching from the strain of her furiously hammering heart.

The footsteps and then the shadow returned. The door handle began to rattle as the lock was tested.

Kellie gulped, hoping the sound wasn't as loud as she feared. *I'm going to pass out. I know it!*

Finding the door locked, whoever was on the other side apparently lost interest and moved on.

"If we get caught you're going to get in trouble right along with me. And you don't want that, right?" Lorna said.

"I—"

"Just let me show you what I came here to show you and then we'll go." She grabbed a large cardboard box from the second shelf and set it on the floor. Lorna used her thumbnail to pierce the tape that held the lid closed, blinking a little perspiration out of her eyes, she put the flashlight in her mouth so she could hold the lid open and still shine the light inside. "Go ahead," she urged. "It won't bite."

Kellie reached in and lifted out a bottle of expensive shampoo, glowering a little when she realized what was in her hand. The box was full of them, bottles of all shapes and sizes, many with brand names that were only sold in high-end salons.

"I like the stuff in that skinny bottle myself."

Kellie squinted at the bottle. "That's the same kind you gave me." She'd never heard of the brand, but it smelled divine and she loved the unexpected gift Lorna had given her after she'd completed her first solo project in woodshop.

"So?"

"You said you bought the shampoo from the cave!" Blue Ridge's tiny store, where prisoners could purchase up to ten dollars worth of personal items per week, was located in the basement near the loading bay. The eight-by-ten-foot room was understocked, overpriced, perpetually damp and unreasonably dark. But in a surprisingly cheerful move, prisoners referred to it as the "cave" and not the "crypt," a term Kellie thoroughly believed was more apt.

"I got it right from Elaine . . . wholesale. You *assumed* I meant from the cave."

The absurdity of it all nearly made Kellie laugh out loud. Half these women were so scary-looking that if she'd met them on the sidewalk before she'd arrived at Blue Ridge, she'd have crossed to the other side of the street rather than pass them by. And now these same inmates were primping for each other? She scratched her temple. "Let me get this straight. You're running a black market girly shampoo business with items that I could barely afford on the outside?"

Lorna scowled. "Is that so hard to believe? Jesus, you really can be a snob sometimes. Women are women no matter where they are. And at least some of them will always want to feel pretty. Even here." And she had the cash to prove it.

Kellie couldn't have disagreed more. "What are you talking about? We wear dumpy clothes. Ugly shoes. We do manual labor that ruins our nails, leaves blisters and calluses on our hands, and half the time, by the end of the day, we end up smelling like members of a chain gang. The food is loaded with salt, fat and chemicals. You look beautiful. The rest of us look like heaping piles of dung!"

Lorna trained the light on Kellie's face and smirked. "You're PMSing, aren't you?"

Kellie refused to dignify that question with an answer and set the bottle back inside the box and selected another. She gave it a little shake. "So this is all you're selling?"

Lorna's back stiffened and snatched the bottle out of Kellie's hand. "You were expecting kiddy porn?" She stuffed it back into the box and did her best to smooth back the tape so that if anyone cared to look, it would appear to be unopened.

Kellie flinched at the poorly veiled hurt in Lorna's voice. "I didn't mean for it to come out that way. Is this really worth risking your chances at parole? And how is Elaine involved?"

Lorna's entire demeanor shifted into something harder and far more edgy. "*Nothing* is worth losing my parole."

Kellie's words came out more angry than frustrated. "Then why are you doing this?"

Lorna looked surprised by question. "A tiny bit of black market activity, especially with harmless stuff like this won't make a difference one way or the other. Unless the warden herself catches me, the most that would happen is I'd lose privileges and get all my inventory swiped." Her T-shirt was starting to stick to her sweat-slicked belly and she plucked at the damp cotton. "Even Roscoe would let himself be bought off over something little like this."

Kellie blew her bangs out of her face and wrinkled her nose. The dust in the room made her nose itch and she was on the verge of sneezing. "Can you afford to buy your way out of trouble?"

"Money's okay." Lorna hummed a little as she thought. "Not as good as peddling ass, dope or extortion, mind you. But it's still pretty good."

Kellie felt a little ill. "Oh."

"Elaine takes a hefty slice. The biggest slice, really. But she brings in the goods, so she's taking a big chance when it comes to her career. I do the rest, and then I give her most of the money. She deposits my cut in an outside account."

"How do you know she's not ripping you off?" A surge of anger welled in Kellie. Business was business no matter where it was conducted or who was conducting it. Everyone had an angle. She'd learned that the hard way.

Lorna hiked one shoulder. "I don't know that she won't eventually screw me. How do you know that Jennings isn't lying to you? How do you know that she'll really let me work on my own piece of furniture?"

Kellie winced. Lorna had a point. You had to trust someone.

"Neither of us can be sure about what we're doing. Nobody can. But Elaine shows me the bank statements every month and we've got it set up so she can put money in, and I'm pretty sure she can't take any out. It's not foolproof, but I trust her enough to take the risk." Lorna's eyes narrowed. "If she screws me over I could rat her out too, and she knows it." She relaxed a little. "Now when I get out I'll have a little nest egg that will get me started."

Kellie nibbled on her lower lip. "I see." She stepped aside so that Lorna could put the box of shampoo back on the shelf.

Lorna's face fell. "You're disappointed in me, right? I'm breaking the law."

Kellie shook her head. While she didn't condone criminal activity, this wasn't like life on the outside. A lot of things that were a given in the real world simply didn't apply here. More to the point, she was no saint in any world and didn't expect that of anyone else. "I'm worried for you," she corrected gently. "You take too many risks."

"Then take another and be my girlfriend."

"I—I wasn't expecting that," Lorna said, a little stunned.

"I know you said you wanted to be more than friends. But I want to be sure what you mean. I'm just so crazy about you! Please, at least think about it. It's not like you said before." She recalled a heartfelt conversation they'd had weeks ago. "We're not just using each other. We're good for each other. You're the most important person in my life."

Kellie was well aware that a dingy closet was about as romantic as . . . well . . . a dingy closet. And when Lorna didn't answer for a few seconds she began to fidget. Maybe she'd assumed too much too soon?

"I'd like that very much," Lorna said as Kellie's panicky voice snapped her out of her surprised stupor. "You're the most important person in my life too, Kellie." There was a long pause. "It's . . . Have you ever felt so ashamed of something you've done that you couldn't even talk about it?"

Suddenly dismayed, Kellie swallowed hard. Her first reaction was to say no, but the sinking feeling in the pit of her stomach was nudging her toward the opposite answer. It was getting harder and harder to push this subject out of her mind. But that never stopped Kellie from trying. "Is that how you feel?"

"Yes."

"If I don't tell you the whole story, someone else will. In fact, I can't believe that hasn't happened already. I've been living on borrowed time." She ran her fingertips down Kellie's arm, raising the fine hairs there with the gentle motion. "I'm sure you've already heard nasty bits and pieces."

Kellie's mouth began to water at the tantalizing touch and she found it hard to focus on what she was saying. "I—I've heard things that don't sound like you."

"Ahh . . ." Feigning calm, Lorna said, "those would be the bits and pieces."

"In that case, I might get freaked out," Kellie admitted. "But we'll get through it, Lorna."

Defiant, Lorna shook her head. "You can't know that."

"Shut up." Kellie buried her face in Lorna's soft, fresh-smelling hair. "I do know that."

In the dark closet, they stood there together, holding each other, until they both started to believe. "Promise, Kel?" Lorna whispered hoarsely.

She sounded like a scared little girl who still dared to hope and Kellie felt tears pool in her eyes. Somewhere along the way she'd begun to feel her friend's pain like her own. How in the world had that happened? It was wonderful and scary as hell all at the same time. "Yeah. I promise."

Chapter 10
That same night . . .

It was nearly lights out when the women made their way back to the cellblock. A cluster of people stood outside the cell waiting for them.

Katrina separated herself from the group and let loose with a wicked smile before walking backward down the opposite end of the hall, her eyes and that sickly grin riveted on Lorna the entire way. Then she stopped and waited.

Lorna's feet froze and her stomach dropped. "Oh, shit." She'd seen that look before and in an instant she realized she'd made a grave error in pushing Katrina as far as she had today.

Kellie's head snapped sideways and her eyes widened a little at the fearful tone of her friend's voice. "What?"

Lorna clinched her teeth together, dread swirling in her belly. "I don't know."

A cluster of guards was waiting outside their cell and the women moved forward slowly, their anxiety building with every grudging step.

"There you are," Roscoe said. He rapped his clipboard with thick knuckles. "I thought I was going to get to sic the dogs on you, Mally."

He sounded so disappointed that he'd missed that opportunity that the tiny hairs on the back of Kellie's neck lifted in outrage.

Roscoe tugged up his sagging pants with one hand. "You both just made it before lights out."

Lorna smiled politely at the guard. "I thought you were off shift, fat ass. But I'm flattered that you came back to see me."

Kellie rolled her eyes. Not again.

Roscoe surged forward, pushing his face no more than an inch in front of Lorna, who didn't even flinch. "I don't think you'll be flattered long."

Foul air tickled her mouth and cheeks and Lorna coughed at the nasty smell of his breath.

With a look of supreme satisfaction on his face, Roscoe backed up a step. But his smile faltered when Lorna dismissed him with a look of utter disgust.

Lorna had the sudden urge to take Kellie's hand, but didn't dare. Still, she couldn't help but move a little closer to her, so close that their shoulders were touching.

Lorna struggled to stay calm. Unlike the maximum security wing, where guards never worked alone, in the medium security wing that was the norm. Two guards together weren't unusual, if the task called for it, but three guards together outside a prisoner's cell meant trouble. And then there was Katrina and her posse, who were still brazenly watching them from the end of the hall.

Kellie let out a deep sigh of relief that Lorna and Roscoe had apparently retreated into neutral corners. At least for now. Unable to keep the worry from her voice, she gazed questioningly at Chul and Elaine. "What's up, guys?"

Chul nudged Roscoe who handed over his clipboard. Frowning, the Asian man ran his finger down a list of cells and names. "I know it's late, but we're reassigning you tonight." He passed the board back to Roscoe.

Lorna felt as though she'd been socked in the chest as the air in her lungs burst out in a rush.

Clearly uncomfortable, Elaine managed a sympathetic look. "You wanna help Holloway get her things together?"

Roscoe opened his mouth to interject but Elaine fended him off with a stern shake of her head. "They don't need us digging through their things. This isn't a search," she reminded him.

Kellie said, "What do you mean reassign? I'm leaving Blue Ridge?"

Roscoe guffawed. "Did you think you were magically going home? You're just getting a new cell, bitch."

A growl erupted from Lorna's chest and she pinned Roscoe with a lethal glare. "How much is she paying you?"

Roscoe's eyes narrowed. "What the hell are you talking about?"

Lorna's hands shaped fists. "You crooked piece of shit!"

"You're calling *me* crooked?" Roscoe took a menacing step forward.

"Hey," Elaine soothed, inserting herself between Lorna and Roscoe. "This isn't such a big deal. It's only one cell down. And—"

Lorna continued to glare at Roscoe over Elaine's halo of black braids. "You son-of-a-bitch."

Chul yawned. "Go inside and get your stuff, Holloway. Don't make this worse. This isn't the Holiday Inn and you don't get to pick your room."

Kellie looked terrified, her voice rising with her panic. "I don't want to go anywhere!"

"You're not," Lorna ground out. She tore her eyes off Roscoe and trained them on Katrina, who was still watching them intently from down the hall, her long body leaning against the wall, an inscrutable smile still plastered on her face.

"Oh, yes she is," Roscoe corrected sourly. His hand came to rest on his baton. He'd used it once already today for a good purpose, and he looked all too happy to do it again. "Or would you like to continue to cause trouble, Mally?"

Like children gathered around a playground fight, half the cell block was now out of their cells, standing in the hall in their pajamas or gym shorts, watching the scene before them unfold with morbid fascination.

"Back inside!" Chul barked. "Anyone who misses lights out gets a visit to the hole!"

A chorus of grumbles rose up but quickly quieted as most of the prisoners disappeared back inside their cells.

Not Katrina. She pushed off the wall with one hand and gave Lorna a cheeky wave. Then she winked. Leaving no doubt in anyone's mind that she was the one responsible for Kellie's sudden relocation.

Lorna's entire body tensed and her nostrils flared. "Bitch," she seethed under her breath. "You couldn't just leave us alone, could you?"

Ramona, who had been watching silently up to this point, padded up behind Lorna and awkwardly patted her shoulder. "Don't do it, chica," she whispered.

Lorna whirled around and slapped Ramona's hand away, her own fists flying up in a protective gesture that still managed to appear aggressive.

Ramona swallowed hastily, her eyes popping wide open with fear as she raised her hands in surrender. "It's just me."

Lorna sighed and let her hands fall to her sides. "Sorry," she murmured. She wanted to scream or cry or fight. *Anything* to make this all go away.

Ramona said, "I'll take care of Kellie while we're rooming together. And you'll do the same for my cellmate, Dusty, yes?" Ramona and her cellmate had roomed together for years and both were teary-eyed over the unexpected reassignment.

The harsh fluorescent lights blinked and, instinctively, they all looked up. Three minutes until lights out.

"Dammit," Roscoe mumbled, shaking his head. "Chul, go flip the manual override for Mally's and Ramona's cells." He gestured between the large black woman and Kellie. "Elaine, you deal with Holloway. I'd rather deal with a loser like Mally than someone who thinks she should be treated like she's visiting a spa."

Lorna was beside herself.

From the corner of her eye, Kellie caught sight of the look on Lorna's face. She followed her gaze to Katrina, and then looked back to Lorna. Before her next heartbeat she knew exactly what was going to happen.

The blood fled from her face. "Lorna, please don't . . ." Desperate to stop the inevitable, she reached out to stop her.

But it was too late.

Violently, Lorna shoved her way past Roscoe and began striding down the hall, anger shimmering off her body. As she burned a path forward, the few women who dared missing lockdown to see the show scrambled out of her way the way a herd of gazelle bolts when a lioness enters its midst.

Lorna moved in and out of the shadows as she marched toward Katrina, reminding everyone that her fearsome reputation had been earned with blood, sweat and tears. But mostly blood.

Roscoe grunted in satisfaction and nodded a little. "Now I don't mind that I had to stay late." He scraped his fingers through his heavy five o'clock shadow as he scratched his chin. " 'Bout time those bitches finally killed each other."

Kellie's eyes bulged. "Jesus! Shit!" She tried to scoot between Elaine and Roscoe, but their bulky bodies slowed her progress. "Stop her!" she cried as she surged forward and popped out from between them like a cork shooting from a champagne bottle.

Elaine parroted Kellie's curse. She lunged for Kellie's wrist and somehow managed to grab hold of it and clamp down with surprisingly strong fingers. "Stay put, Holloway. That ain't your fight."

Frantic, Kellie cried, "Then *you* do something!"

Katrina didn't retreat when she saw Lorna coming. Instead, she sucked in a deep breath through her nose and stared deeply into her opponent's eyes. Then, both women released smiles that bordered on sensual. If they couldn't be allies then enemies was the only other option. No one had the luxury of being neutral in Blue Ridge.

Even through her cloud of fury, Lorna had the presence of mind to be very aware that this wasn't like the night she'd killed her father. Not at all. Though she utterly believed he'd gotten exactly what he deserved, she hadn't been thinking when she stabbed him. She'd just reacted. It had been like breathing. Instinct. Survival.

Tonight she was aware of everything. Every move she was making. Every breath. Every heartbeat. The soft sound of her shoes on the floor. The smell of the bleach used to clean the floors every Sunday mixed with the scent of sweat. Kellie's panicked voice seared into her brain. Her skin tingling with fear and anticipation.

Even the thought of violence sometimes made her sick. And yet she accepted that it was just another part of life. The respite from that had been a balm to her soul, but had been too good to last. This confrontation had been years in coming.

A mask dropped down over Katrina's face and her color rose as she began slowly moving toward Lorna, limping slightly from Roscoe's earlier strike with his baton, teeth bared like a rabid dog.

Cheers and hoots rang as inmates stood barely inside their cells, their necks craning as they strained to see what was happening. An eerie chant sounded. *"Fight. Fight. Fight."*

Using every ounce of her strength, Kellie broke free from Elaine and sprinted after Lorna, long dark hair flying out behind her as she exploded down the hall. It took several strides before she could hear Elaine and Roscoe, finally prodded into action, behind her, their heavy steps quickly growing distant.

The cells went dark all at once, but emergency lights in the ceiling left a small amount of light in the hallway and cast everyone in a weird red glow. Doors began to automatically close, muffling the disappointed voices of those locked inside.

Then Kellie was on Lorna's heels, reaching out. "Stop!" She dove forward and managed to make just enough contact to send them both crashing to the ground. "Stop it!" Kellie yelled, throwing herself on Lorna's back.

"Get . . ." Lorna struggled wildly. "Get off me!"

By sheer luck, Kellie dodged a flying elbow. "No!" The two women tussled a few seconds, rolling twice until they were face-to-face with Kellie sprawled on top of Lorna.

Then their eyes met and they both stilled. "Katrina's not worth it, Lorna. She's not."

Tears wanted to come, but Lorna pushed them back, her eyes blazing instead. She couldn't, however, stop the slight quivering of her lower lip. "She did this. She's controlling us!"

"I know," Kellie said seriously, her breathing still fast. "But she's not worth your freedom and that's what she wants. A new charge this close to your parole hearing will finish you."

Lorna's eyes brimmed with tears despite her resolve otherwise. *I can't lose you now that I've finally found you! Everything will be different now.* "She's ruined everything," she whispered.

Kellie's gaze softened and for the first time in forever, she let everything she was feeling for a woman show on her face. "You're not losing me."

And then Katrina was upon them. "Couldn't wait till you were back in your cell to be mounted, Mally?" Her voice rose to a screech that the entire cellblock could hear. "Oh, I forgot, you don't *share* a cell anymore."

With no chance at deflecting the kick that Katrina was drawing back for, Lorna pulled Kellie to her chest and used all her might to twist them both over so that her back would take the brunt of the blow. She closed her eyes and sucked in a breath as she readied herself for the explosion of pain . . .

That never came.

Elaine shoved Katrina against the wall with her forearms and pushed the tip of her baton in the small of her back. The guard looked as though she were about to have a heart attack from running down the hall. Perspiration flowed freely from her temples and her upper lip was soaked. "Attempted battery." She paused to take a much needed breath, "—and missing lights out?" Elaine made a soft clucking sound. "Not good. Not good at all."

Katrina grunted as her face was pushed against the concrete wall, her teeth scraping against chipped paint.

Roscoe yanked Kellie and Lorna up by the necks of their T-shirts. His chest was heaving from his short run. "Looks like Holloway is going to get her first taste of our private accommodations."

"The hole?" Lorna sputtered as she found her feet and smoothed down her bunched shirt.

Roscoe smirked, "Now, Mally, you know that we prefer to call it protective custody." Chul began walking toward him from the opposite end of the hall, but the big man waved him off. "Too late now anyway, ya chickenshit gook," Roscoe grumbled.

Lorna forced herself not to freak out. She hadn't told Kellie much about protective custody, mainly because she knew that just the concept scared the crap out of her cellmate. "What for? She didn't do anything!"

"The dyke missed lights out. That's mandatory time in solitary according to the warden and she'll probably get the box or the loaf," Katrina supplied helpfully as Elaine slapped handcuffs on her wrists, pinching the thin skin. "Ouch!"

"What's the box?"

Katrina grinned slyly. "Think of it as a steam room at the gym, bitch."

Elaine sighed. "It's not a steam room. It's a behavior management tool."

Kellie's eyebrows rose. "What does that mean?"

Elaine looked at her shoes. "The Box" was a technique so harsh that even a fair share of guards were uncomfortable with its use. "It's a warm room where prisoners go to . . . well . . ."

"To bake," Katrina interrupted. "And sweat like a pig in heat. And squirm. And be in hell. It's fucking torture!"

Lorna really couldn't disagree, so she bit her tongue and prayed for the night to be over. Solitary, or anyplace else that Katrina wasn't, was starting to sound good.

Kellie appeared faint. "Thanks for that *gruesome* description."

Katrina smiled sweetly. "I live to serve."

"I'm almost afraid to ask." Kellie shot Lorna an apprehensive look. "But what's The Loaf?"

Katrina laughed gleefully. "She hasn't told you? Why do you think she's so hollow-eyed when she comes back from the hole? Hard-ass went on a hunger strike for the last month of a six-month stint back in ninety-one." Even though Katrina's anger at Lorna was clear, her eyes were alight with excitement and her voice held a note of admiration that bordered on some sort of twisted form of awe and affection. "The warden had to order her to be fed through a tube! It was fuckin' great!"

"Lorna?" Kellie prompted, searching Lorna's face.

Lorna tried stalling. Sometimes, as part of the rehabilitation effort while in the hole, prisoners were fed only one thing: The Loaf. How could she accurately describe the disgusting, heavy bread-like substance that was made from flour, water, eggs, shredded carrots, and boiled potatoes all mashed into a dense log and served twice a day in one-pound slabs in a way that wouldn't give Kellie a heart attack?

"Well," Lorna began carefully, "it's just food. But you should eat it no matter how it tastes because that's all you'll get. Just eat it, okay?"

Katrina started laughing all over again. "Do as your *master* says not as she did, right, Holloway?"

"Hush." Elaine gave the tall blonde a small shove forward as they started down the hall. "One of these days nobody is going to care enough to stop Lorna . . ."

Roscoe gave Lorna and Kellie a push in the same direction. In a sing-song voice he added, "And somebody's gonna end up dead. Just do me a favor and don't make me wait too long, ladies."

"I know which *somebody* that's going to be," Katrina snarled, throwing both Lorna and Kellie a look.

Lorna thought she caught a split second of humanity behind the glare. But in the blink of an eye it vanished, making her wonder if it had ever been there at all.

She regarded the woman who had dared to call herself her friend very seriously. "So do I."

Kellie, Katrina and Lorna sat on long steel benches in a holding cell as they waited to be led to protective custody. They'd been sitting there for hours, staring at each other in stony silence.

"I'm afraid," Kellie whispered, her gaze straying to the bench on the opposite side of the room and Katrina, who had her eyes closed and her head resting against the cell wall. "I don't know what to do."

Lorna said firmly, "You do what the guards tell you and don't make trouble. The hole is shared by maximum and minimum security. It's all the same there and you're treated like the worst of the worst. The guards there are different. If you give them shit they won't just knock you around, Kellie. Be careful."

Gun-metal gray eyes widened.

Lorna smiled kindly. "Don't worry too much. Your mouth is the only thing that ever gets you into trouble and you're not allowed to talk to the guards anyway."

Kellie rolled her eyes. "What else?"

Lorna shrugged. "There's not much else to it. Do as you're told. You may or may not be allowed to order a book from the library. Be obedient and your chances will go up considerably."

Kellie wasn't much of a reader, but the chance at having any means to relieve her boredom was one she embraced with relish. "I can fake obedience."

"Good girl."

"How much of the day do I spend in my cell?"

Lorna let out a deep breath. "Twenty-two and a half hours a day."

Kellie blinked stupidly. "Wh-what?" she screeched. Only Lorna's, sudden, but firm grip on her arm stopped her from levitating off the bench. "What about going to eat, shower, exercise?"

Katrina snickered. "Don't worry, your meals are delivered just like room service."

"*You,* shut the fuck up," Lorna snarled. "You're why we're here in the first place!"

Katrina affected an innocent look. "And here I thought murder was why you were here, Mally."

Kellie wound her fingers in Lorna's T-shirt and pulled her back onto the bench. "Fighting's only gonna make this worse."

"Pussy-whipped." Katrina laughed softly and closed her eyes.

"Lorna?" Kellie gently laid her palm on Lorna's face and directed her friend's attention squarely on her. "Forget about her."

"Bu—"

"Just let it die."

They stared at each other.

"How can you look at her that way?" Katrina suddenly asked Kellie. "Like she's *so* special."

"She is special. And you're a pig."

Katrina laughed lightly. "Anything I am, she is too."

"Hardly."

"She *still* hasn't told you, has she?"

A low growl erupted from Lorna's chest.

Delighted, Katrina clapped her hands together like an excited little girl. "Go on, Mally. Tell your dog."

"Shut the fuck up." Lorna's voice was so low and deadly that Kellie's heart began to pound.

"Oh, you want *me*—" Katrina jerked her thumb toward her own chest, "—to tell her? Why didn't you just say so? Once upon a time, there was a snot-nosed teenager. And—"

Lorna leaned forward and put her elbows on her knees. "I don't want you to continue breathing."

"Too bad," Katrina sniped. "This isn't like the cellblock. You know the drill, one scream and the guards come running. Lay a single finger on me and you'll just spend twice as long in the hole."

Lorna sat back, and let out a calming breath, seeming to relax a little. "You're just jealous that someone cares whether I live or die and nobody is ever going to give two shits about your miserable existence."

Katrina blanched, but quickly regained her bravado. She put a hand to the side of her mouth as though blocking her words from Lorna and speaking only to Kellie. "Don't you love how she's all sweet and docile until she gets around me? We bring out the best in each other. She fights it, of course. But she always was stubborn. In fact," Katrina scratched her chin thoughtfully, "we might even be soulmates."

Kellie blinked. Katrina, the delusional bitch, wasn't joking.

Lorna's expression grew grave, maybe even a little sad. "If I could take back what happened to you, Kat, I would. Even now."

Katrina's face flushed beet-red so fast that Kellie wondered if her head might explode. It wasn't an unpleasant thought.

"Don't even go there. Don't you . . . Don't you do it!" Katrina spluttered.

"But it's past time that I did," Lorna said gravely.

Katrina ground her teeth together so loudly that Kellie's own mouth ached.

Katrina punched the wall, leaving a lurid bloodstain on the cement. "Shit!"

Kellie's eyes widened. She could only guess what was coming from Lorna and suddenly, now that the moment was finally here, she decided that she didn't want any part of it. Lorna was all she could depend on. "Stop, Lorna." She shook her head wildly, scattering her dark hair over her shoulders. "This is none of my business."

"I'm tired of this hanging over my head. If I don't tell you now, Katrina will only tell the parts she wants you to hear. Or it'll just be someone else."

The room was heavy with foreboding. Even the stagnant air felt thick and the hum of the lights seemed unnaturally loud. Kellie wiped moist palms on her legs. Then Lorna began speaking with such a quiet intensity that it captured Kellie completely and Katrina faded from the scene.

"When I first came to Blue Ridge I was a little like you were. Afraid of my own shadow, and totally off balance. Everything that was happening seemed like it was happening to someone else, like it was someone else's pathetic life. And when it finally hit home that the someone was actually me, it felt like the world was ending."

Kellie nodded mutely, a little shook-up that Lorna's feeling had so closely mirrored her own.

"But most of all I was angry. Angry for everything I lost. I wasn't really a resentful person before, you know? I know that sounds weird, after going through what I did as a kid. But up until the day I killed my dad, I was able to cling to the good times and forget the bad ones as fast as I could. But that night . . . in our kitchen . . . I turned everything upside down. Once I crossed that line and let myself *feel* everything there was no going back. It was like what was left of my innocence bled out onto the floor right along with that hateful bastard."

"You saved your sister," she reminded Lorna quietly.

"That's what I thought I was doing, but I was a fool. I traded one problem for another and left my sister alone with a woman who spent our rent money on lottery tickets, liquor and smokes. And while she didn't seem to get her kicks off hurting people like my dad did, it wasn't as though she was above violence herself."

"You had a bad childhood. Who didn't? Boo-fucking-hoo," Katrina mocked. "Anyone want to hear my sad story?"

"No," Kellie and Lorna said in unison.

Already on the verge of being upset, Kellie let her heart do the talking. "Lorna, you weren't a fool and you weren't selfish. You were just a scared, cornered kid who fought back."

Lorna patted her friend's leg. "It's okay, Kel." Lorna's eyes were soft with unconcealed affection and a hint of fear. She cleared the hoarseness from her throat. "Anyway, by the end of my first month at Blue Ridge I was a mess. I had the shit kicked out of me on a regular basis and I was stabbed in the hand after I sat down at the wrong table in the cafeteria."

Kellie closed her eyes in empathy, easily visualizing the small white scars on Lorna's right hand.

"A week later, two inmates cracked my ribs when I struck up a conversation with the wrong woman in the yard."

"How . . ." Kellie paused to try to flush her mind clean of thoughts of someone attacking Lorna. The fact that she'd been so young and vulnerable made it all the more heart-wrenching. "How do you know when someone is the wrong woman?"

"You don't always know who is safe to talk to and who isn't. That's why you watch and learn first, and act last."

"She's just like Yoda with the advice, isn't she?" Katrina drawled.

Lorna had to count to ten under her breath. "The wrong woman in this case was a newbie like me who had already been claimed by a hardcore con. We met on the bus to Blue Ridge. She looked so lonely walking around the track that I ventured over and said hello. Big mistake." Lorna sighed loudly. "Big. And someone explained to me, just like I explained to you on your first day, that the guards weren't the solution to my problems."

"Was it Katrina?"

"Ramona," Lorna replied, "was in her early thirties back then and even more of a pistol than she is now. It was about that time that I was approached by the hardcore con. She headed up the meanest, most violent gang in maximum and conducted her drug business from the inside as though she was living in some fancy condo and not behind bars. She put the 'B' in bitch and was nothing short of brutal. And she ruled with an iron hand, took what she wanted, whenever she wanted. She wouldn't have asked God for permission if it meant going straight to hell."

Kellie's accusing gaze shifted to the sullen blonde. This description was starting to sound familiar.

Lorna shook her head as she caught Kellie's train of thought. "Nuh uh. Katrina wasn't the big cheese. That was Lucille. And she was badder than Katrina on her worst day."

Lorna scrunched up her face. "For some reason Lucille took a liking to me and after a few months of my stumbling from one bad situation to something worse, she offered me a job doing anything and everything."

"And you took the job." Kellie doubted that refusing someone as powerful as Lucille was described was even an option.

"Oh, yeah." Lorna chewed her lip, looking very much like a woman on her march to the gallows. "I took it all right. At first, I told myself it was just to survive. That I was tired of getting the crap beat out of me. But . . ." Her eyes narrowed. "When I joined up with Lucille and her pack, things got so much easier. They promised me I would never be alone again and they were right."

"They were?" Kellie asked, surprised.

"Picture it as the evil sorority, rich girl," Katrina chimed in. "There was sisterhood to spare."

"All I had to do," Lorna continued, "was shut down any part of me that had an ounce of feeling and decency so what was going on around me couldn't touch me." A bitter laugh burst from her chest. "Little did they know I'd been doing that my entire life. I was a natural!" She snapped her fingers, giving her younger self no quarter. "No problem."

The rawness of Lorna's voice scraped across Kellie's nerves, making her soul cry out. "Lorna—"

"And then, before I knew it, the bad wasn't just around me. I was part of it, rolling around in it like a pig in the mud. Thick as thieves . . . literally."

Kellie avidly watched her cellmate's face and found nothing but self-loathing and regret there. *Oh, Lorna.* "I doubt you had a choice. It sounds like you were made the sort of offer that would have been dangerous to refuse."

"Don't make excuses for me. Lucille would have made it hard, but she wouldn't have killed me for saying no. At least I don't think so. She wanted the women around her to be nearly as hungry as she was. And to be honest, by the time Lucille asked me, I didn't want to say no."

Kellie squared her shoulders. "That's your measure of whether you had free will in a situation? That so long as you might not be murdered, you were really free to choose whatever option suited you? That's a little harsh, even for you."

Lorna groaned. "I did *everything* that came with being connected to Lucille, including marking myself as one of her gang." She gestured toward the tattoo that covered her shoulder and upper arm, her face twisting in revulsion.

Kellie reached out and touched it, suddenly understanding on another level what Lorna had just said. "They're actually on you. That's why you'll never be alone?" Tenderly, she grazed the symbols marking Lorna's lightly freckled skin and she glanced up.

Lorna nodded in bleak confirmation.

Katrina lifted her arm and tugged up her T-shirt, showing off a nearly identical pattern that was etched into her in dark green ink. "I like mine."

Lorna jerked her own shirt back into place. "You would."

Unfazed, Katrina said, "It ties us together forever, Mally. Two of a kind."

Kellie's stomach began to churn and a sickening whisper in Katrina's mocking voice rang out in her head. *Soulmates.* "Lorna, you aren't like Katrina!" she blurted. "I don't care what errands you ran for some Queen of Maximum Security. Yeah, yeah. You were bad. But I know you. You're gentle. And not just with me. I've seen you help other women."

Lorna said to Kellie, "I need you to understand that I didn't just do what I had to do to get by. I got rich-stinking-rich in the black market. And I'm not talking about selling shampoo. I mean the bad stuff, Kel."

Kellie froze for a second. "How bad?"

"Bad."

"Don't you think that's why they call it the *black*, and not sunshine-yellow market?" Katrina suddenly speculated.

Kellie didn't even turn her head to acknowledge the words. Once they were all released from the hole, she was going to find a way beat the crap out of Katrina if it was the last thing she did. "Likes knives or something? Real weapons?"

Lorna's back straightened and she mechanically answered, "Yes. More than one woman was sliced open with something I'd sold."

"Drugs?" she asked with as much confidence as she could muster, knowing how they repulsed Lorna.

Lorna didn't even hesitate. It was important that Kellie understood it all. "Anything I could get my hands on. Smack. Crack. Pot. Pills. And I sold them to women every bit as desperate as you were for a drink when you first arrived at Blue Ridge. If I had gotten hold of you back then, you'd be my puppet on a string right now. Offering me money, favors, your body, anything for a fix. Which I wouldn't have thought twice about denying you until it suited my purposes."

Kellie paled and swallowed a few times. It wouldn't have taken much to plunge her into hell those first few weeks. And Lorna had gladly done that to someone else? God.

Katrina sucked on one of her torn knuckles. "Instead of you being on top, you're her puppet, Mally," she said in a matter-of-fact voice. "Lucille is rolling over in her grave and laughing her skinny ass off. She always said you were weak."

With effort, Kellie looked into glistening blue eyes that were foreign and familiar at the same time. "Did you . . . hurt people? Physically, I mean."

Lorna's face burned but she pushed aside the almost overwhelming urge to look away. "Yes."

Silence.

Kellie had to know if it was the worst thing possible. "Murder?"

Lorna's eyes widened and instantly found Kellie's. "No! Rough stuff, sure, but nothing like that."

"Don't you remember?" Katrina supplied helpfully. "She scratched murder off her list of accomplishments *before* prison."

Lorna shot her a lethal glare.

Kellie's mouth was as dry as dust when she said, "Rape?"

There was a long pause, before Lorna began to stutter, "I—I—I—"

Kellie's stomach dropped through the floor. "Holy shit! Who *are* you?"

"I never did that," Lorna said quickly, looking as guilty as sin despite her words. "But I . . . I saw it happen." She licked her lips worriedly. "Lucille was disciplining her newbie girlfriend." She looked away as the words trailed off.

"Don't stop now!" Katrina sneered. "You're just getting to the good part! This is where you try to explain how someone as *good* and *kind* and *special* as you just stood there and watched while Lucille took your friend from the bus with a police baton."

Lorna covered her face with her hands. "We weren't friends!"

"And that made it okay to stand by while I was raped?" Katrina ground out.

Lorna dropped her hands to reveal tear-stained cheeks. "*Nothing* would have made it okay. Don't think I don't know that!"

Still stunned, Kellie took Lorna's chin in her hand and turned her head so they were eye-to-eye. "What happened? Exactly, Lorna. Tell me *exactly* what happened."

"Does it matter?" Lorna shot back. "I did just what she said, I did. Which was nothing."

"Then there's no harm in telling me more."

Angrily, Lorna wiped at her cheeks with shaking hands. "You need every detail? Fine! I was coming to see Lucille about a big fat dope buy when I was stopped at her cell door by the two enormous assholes she used as bodyguards. They said I'd have to wait to go inside because the boss was uhh . . ." Her gaze flicked sideways and her cheeks flushed. "She was uhhh . . ."

Katrina's eyes shot sparks.

Lorna made a vague gesture with her hands. "She was busy. But I was so impatient that I wouldn't wait. I poked my head between the too-tall guards and saw what was happening." More tears stung her eyes.

"You looked right at me," Katrina said flatly, picking up the ball when Lorna faltered. "I screamed for help and you looked right into my eyes."

"I know." Lorna's voice was a coarse whisper.

"And then you just disappeared."

"I'm sorry."

Katrina went stock-still for a long moment. She was a powder keg ready to blow, but something held her back. A few seconds more and that eerie, familiar mask that she wore like a shield draped over her. She shrugged as though she didn't have a care in the world. "Ehh . . . Don't worry about it, Mally. It's old news."

Her face returned to its normal porcelain shade of white. "It was only a year after that that we became cellmates. Even after our rocky start, we were destined to be a team."

Then Katrina focused on Kellie. "Besides, what goes around comes around." The beginnings of a sly smile peeked through. "Now is my time to be queen."

"Ugh." Kellie's face twisted. "You make me sick."

"What about me?" Lorna asked fearfully. Her voice dropped to a whisper. "How do I make you feel?" Her gaze sharpened and her chest stilled as she held her breath.

Rather than try to process any more of her conflicting feelings before her lover's worried eyes, Kellie dug for more information, trying desperately to find reason where she feared there would be none. "Could you have helped Katrina if you'd wanted to?"

Lorna sniffed a few times. "What?"

"The guards wouldn't have let you in, right? So could you have done anything to help Katrina?"

Lorna looked confused, as though she'd never thought about that before. "I—"

"Who the fuck cares?" Katrina spat. "Her mouth still worked. She could have done or said something . . . anything. She wouldn't lift a goddamn finger!"

Kellie jumped to her feet and grabbed hold of Katrina's T-shirt with both hands. She yanked hard, pulling the larger woman up until she was barely on the bench. "You need to shut your filthy mouth and let Lorna finish," she seethed, eyes smoldering with hatred. "Or, so help me God, I will find a way to kill you myself."

Both Lorna's and Kellie's eyes popped wide open at the surprisingly credible threat. Kellie was livid and past the point of caring what happened to her. They'd seen enough to know that this was the very moment when a woman was at her most dangerous. In disgust, Kellie shoved a shocked Katrina away and stalked back to Lorna. "Well?"

"I thought about helping Katrina. I knew without a shadow of a doubt that it was the right thing to do, but I couldn't make myself do it."

Kellie remembered Lorna's spectacular defense of her during Katrina's attack. What was so different then? "Why?"

"Look what had happened the last time I'd tried to help someone! I ruined my miserable life! It wasn't like I was happy here or anything, but by then at least I had a tiny piece of a life back." Lorna stared across the cell with unseeing eyes. "I was petrified to think of risking that. I thought I'd found a home with the gang and I wanted that more than I wanted to help anyone or anything but myself. So, you see, it wasn't that I couldn't help. I actually forced myself not to."

Lorna continued bleakly, "Instead of yelling or leaving and bringing back the guards, or trying to talk to Lucille, which would have been useless, I just went to the bathroom and threw up. When I came back, I stopped about twenty feet from Lucille's cell. I couldn't hear Katrina screaming anymore, and the stooges were gone. On the floor outside the cell, there was a thin trail of blood that wasn't there before, so I knew Katrina had gone too."

She exhaled heavily. "Then I went in and conducted my business as though nothing had happened."

Kellie sat motionless, staggered and sickened all at once.

Lorna gave her a waxy smile. "Not what you were hoping to hear, huh?"

Kellie didn't answer.

Katrina resentfully rubbed her injured hand. "Aren't you guys going to slap each other and call each other names or something? Fuck!" She made a short, dismissive gesture with her good hand. "At least I can see by the shell-shocked look on Holloway's face that some of that shine you had on you has rubbed off, Mally. Sorry about that."

Katrina glanced at her watch. "Looks like our trip down memory lane is going to be over soon." She giggled demonically. "Time for some fun in the hole!"

"Oh, God," Kellie whispered. She laid a hand on her stomach, sorry she'd eaten dinner that night. "I'd forgotten about that."

Lorna tentatively reached out and patted her knee, obviously expecting to have her hand pushed away. "Just keep talking to me, all right?"

Kellie nodded, her face shadowed.

Lorna took Kellie's hand. "Wherever you are, whichever cell, I'll be nearby . . . thinking about you."

"Awww . . ." Katrina began making obnoxious kissing noises.

It wasn't easy, but Kellie managed to pretend she wasn't there. She knew that she should pity someone who'd gone through what Katrina had. But, Kellie readily admitted, she wasn't that big a person. "I'll do my best to remember that, Lorna."

The lackluster reply caused Lorna's face and spirit to fall even farther. Unexpectedly, she leaned forward and pressed her lips to Kellie's ear, turning them both away from Katrina's prying eyes. "I'm not going to ask you to forgive who I was or what I did. But I care about you, Kellie. And . . ." She paused and Kellie felt tears splash on her shoulder. "I want you to still like me."

There was something oddly childlike about Lorna's statement. Her feelings had never been laid so bare before her, and Kellie found her heart reacting before her head was truly ready. She turned and whispered back, "I'm freaked out by a lot of things right now. But no matter what, I can't help but like you."

She felt Lorna's shaky exhale, and unable to take another emotional scene without falling apart herself, she opted for a change in subjects. "About protective custody . . ."

Lorna leaned back, wiping her eyes again. "Yeah?"

"I'll see you in the yard, right? They have to let us exercise. That's the law."

Lorna closed her burning eyes. "They do. Just not together. You'll be put in a private yard for exercise. And you can do as many sit-ups and push-ups as you want."

"Great," Kellie said dully. They would talk. And somehow she would come to terms with everything, including a stark truth that was impossible to avoid. Deep down inside, Kellie knew that despite everything Lorna had done, and even after all she'd been through, that today, her cellmate was easily a better person than she was. And what that said about the person that Kellie faced in the mirror every morning wasn't exactly easy to swallow.

"You run," Lorna said quietly.

Lorna's words dragged her from her thoughts. "I'm sorry. What?"

"You run."

Kellie blinked slowly, watching to see if she was being tweaked.

"When you're in your exercise yard, run until you get so tired that you go back to your cell and collapse. Sleeping makes the time go by faster."

Kellie grimaced at the thought of sleeping sweaty. A year ago the entire concept would have been patently unacceptable and she would have refused to do it. Now, that was the least of her worries. Still, being dirty always made her feel worse. "What about a shower? Don't tell me they make you wait until morning even after you've been outside in the heat."

Lorna bit her lower lip.

Kellie's eyebrows jumped at the obvious hesitation. "We do get to shower, right?"

"Oh, sure, sure," Lorna said quickly.

"Whew." Kellie wiped some mock sweat from her brow.

"But only once a week and the guards watch you the entire time."

Kellie covered her face with her hands. "I'm going to stop asking questions now."

Suddenly, she heard the cell door open and a horrible odor invaded the room with shocking speed. Kellie's stomach roiled at the putrid smell of feces.

"Oh, fucking Christ!" Katrina snapped. "Not Delia!"

Kellie let her hands fall from her face and took in a sight she never thought she'd see. A small woman with snow-white, close-cropped hair was shoved into the cell by a pissed off looking guard. The inmate was barefooted, and dressed in nothing but a T-shirt and ratty-looking panties. While that in and of itself was odd, it wasn't nearly as strange as the fact that nearly every inch of the woman's uncovered skin was smeared with shit. "Jesus H. Christ!"

"Bad guess," Lorna mumbled.

"Don't think you're going to sit by me, you crazy stinking bitch," Katrina barked. Scrunching up her face, she waved her hands in front of her nose scooting all the way to the end of the bench. "Go sit by the lovebirds over there. They're so full of shit they won't notice you."

The woman waved at Lorna. "Hey," she greeted cordially, seeming not to notice that she had dung dripping from her short hair. "Lorna Malachi, it's been a while. You look all grown up."

"Hey, Delia," Lorna answered, trying to talk without breathing in too deeply. "Long time no see."

Delia gave her a friendly smile. "Staying mostly out of trouble nowadays?"

"Tryin'."

"That's nice," she answered in a robotic voice.

"How long was this stretch in the hole, Delia?" Lorna wondered out loud. "If you don't mind me saying so, you don't look so good."

The woman thought for a minute, a serious expression overtaking her face. "I'm not sure." She tapped her chin. "I think . . ." Then her eyes sparked as she seemed to light on the answer. "Forever, I think."

Lorna winced. "That's rough."

Kellie's gaze flicked back and forth between Lorna and Delia, who were carrying on what could only be described as a normal, calm conversation. Just then a small clump of poop dropped onto the floor. Kellie covered her mouth. Had the entire world gone insane?

"Go sit by Katrina, okay?" Lorna coaxed, shooing her in that direction with a flick of fingers. "I know she misses you. We don't see nearly so many interesting people now that we're in medium security." She turned. "No offense, Kel."

Kellie smiled wanly. "None taken."

"Okay, Mally. I'll sit by Katrina," Delia said dutifully, another drying piece of crap falling from her ear onto her shoulder. But before she had the chance to move, two guards, wearing gloves and protective suits unlocked then threw open the cell door. They grabbed Delia by the biceps and lifted her off the ground as they yanked her back through the door, muttering something about a hose.

"See ya," Delia called out as she disappeared from view. The cell door clanked loudly as it closed automatically behind her.

"Bye," Lorna yelled back, not daring to look at Kellie.

"Thank fuck," Katrina sighed, still waving away the stink that followed Delia out of the cell.

Kellie started to say something a couple of times. Finally, she got out, "Lorna?"

"Yeah?" Lorna was already bracing herself.

Kellie shook her head, visions from the film *The Snake Pit* dancing behind her eyes. "By any chance, are mental patients kept in the hole too?"

"You have to fucking ask after seeing that?" Katrina inserted tartly. "How many normal people do you know that rub their own shit all over themselves?"

"Well?" Kellie prodded Lorna with a nudge of her shoulder.

Lorna's forehead creased. "They aren't exactly mental patients, though some of them clearly should be. Some get drugs. Some get the wrong drugs. Some get nothing. Unfortunately, more than a few inmates in maximum security are criminals and crazy at the same time and they somehow end up here and not in an institution. They're incapable of following a lot of the rules and so spend most of their time in the hole." She grimaced. "I'm talking years and years. That alone would make the sanest person nuts. Some of these women never get out."

Kellie shivered. "That's horrible."

"Tell me about it."

Heavy footsteps drew their attention to the cell door again, where Elaine began unlocking the door. "Holloway, you first. Time to go."

"Hey," Katrina protested indignantly, "why are you taking her over instead of one of the hole *goons*?" She stared at her raw, handcuffed wrists. "And where are her bracelets, or Mally's for that matter? You have to use cuffs. It's policy!"

Elaine lifted her lip in a snarl as she stepped inside, choking a little at the lingering smell. "That's none of your business. But don't worry, one of the goons will be back to get you in just a few minutes to take you to your cavity search." She smiled insincerely. "If Lorna hasn't killed you by the time he gets here, that is."

Katrina's eyes narrowed.

Lorna mouthed 'thank you' to Elaine, who nodded, then motioned for Kellie.

Lorna pulled her lover into a quick hug and spoke in a voice so soft that Kellie barely heard her. "It will be all right." She kissed Kellie's cheek, her lips lingering against the soft skin. "Be good and don't be afraid."

She felt a little like she was going off to war. "I'll t-try."

"And," Lorna's voice grew huskier, "don't forget that I love you."

Eyes wide, Kellie pulled away a little to look into Lorna's eyes. Slowly, she raised her hands to frame her partner's face, watching as Lorna's eyes fluttered closed at her touch. When she smiled in wonder, she got a slightly sheepish look in return. *Forget?*

But as usual there was no time to talk.

"Holloway," Elaine repeated a tiny bit impatiently. "We really have to go. You girls already had time to say good-bye."

"Go on, Kel," Lorna urged quietly. "Elaine did me a solid by coming to escort you. It would be a bad idea to make her wait now." She smiled lovingly at her friend, her eyes conveying a level of strength and raw affection that made Kellie's knees weak. "See you in a month or so."

Kellie stood, throat tight with emotion, her head spinning. *She loves me?* Over the years others had said it, but they'd never made her believe it with a bone deep certainty that Lorna had with just a few simple words. In a reeking cell. In front of the bane of her existence. *Amazing.*

Kellie had so much she wanted to say but no time to say it in. *How long does it really take to say three little words? Dammit! Dammit! Dammit!* "I—" Fear gripped her. "I'll be thinking of you too, okay?"

She caught a flash of white teeth as Lorna offered a small smile that held a ghost of disappointment. Then Kellie faced the empty hallway before her. The passage was long and dark and in the distance the mottled sounds of yelling, crying and moaning welcomed her to her worst nightmare.

For the first time since she met Lorna, she was truly alone.

Chapter 11
Three and a half weeks later . . .

Panting, Kellie looked up at the blue sky from her private exercise yard and wiped the sweat from her brow with the back of her hand. Her hair was braided down the center of her back, accenting high cheekbones that had become far more prominent over the past few weeks, even though she'd disconnected her mind from her belly and eaten everything on her plate.

Some things, she'd discovered, were exactly as Lorna had described them, and she was grateful for what little mental preparation her cellmate had provided. Other things, like where she was now, were nothing like what she'd imagined.

The 'yard' had no grass at all, and was actually a twelve-by-thirty foot concrete slab with fifteen-foot cement walls on all sides and a roof made of chain link mesh that still let in the light. It reminded her more of a dog-run, or something you'd see at the zoo to house the dangerous cats, than a place for human beings. Still, it was sunny and she was thankful to be outside her cell, if only for a while.

"Four days and four hours. Four days and four hours," she chanted just to hear her own voice. "I can make it. I can make it." Her feet slowed, and her run became a quick walk. In that startling second, Kellie understood that all her hopes were pinned on leaving the hole on time. She was slowly unraveling around the edges. And she held on by focusing on the minute when she would leave the hole and never come back, the moment she would see Lorna again, and not the moments between now and then.

She'd been the model prisoner, following every rule to the letter, knowing that if her time here were somehow extended for even another day she might truly go insane.

She could tell by her labored breathing and the sweat that trickled down her back and neck that it was almost time to go back to her cell. The thought of being locked inside was enough to make her scream. There was nothing to do in that cell but sit and think. Stew. And then think some more. She was a doer, not a thinker. But finally she'd been there long enough so that she'd had no other choice but to examine the critical mistakes in her life, lingering over the especially gory ones in vivid detail.

Physically and emotionally drained, she leaned against the concrete wall, pressing her shoulders against the cool surface and scratching her back against the wall.

A bang sounded and then the door to the yard opened. A fresh-faced, young guard whose voice was unfamiliar to Kellie rang out, "Time's up, Holloway." The man stepped out of the shadows and into the bright sunshine, shielding his eyes with one hand. "C'mon, let's go."

Kellie froze. *Impossible!* He looked exactly like the officer she'd shot on that horrible night so many months ago. But how could it be him? A wave of grief engulfed her and she desperately scrubbed her eyes with the back of her hands. But afterward, the picture before her was still the same.

Gaping, she pointed at the guard with a shaking hand. "You . . . you can't be him!"

"No talking, okay?" he reminded kindly. "When I came on shift they told me your time in protective custody is almost up. So you don't want to get in trouble now, right?" He let loose with an engaging smile that somehow managed to make him look even more like a high school football player borrowing his daddy's uniform. "And it's my first week on the job and I don't want to mess with doing the paperwork it would take to keep you here."

Kellie stepped forward slowly as though approaching a ghost, staring at this man's right leg the entire time. "Wait." She stopped and bent at the waist, closing her eyes as she put her head between her knees, afraid she would pass out. Stars paraded across her vision.

The guard stepped a little closer. "Hey, are you okay? What's wrong?"

Forgetting that she wasn't supposed to be talking, she muttered, "Nothing. I—I—I'm just tired." It took several deep breaths before she could stand upright and she raised a hand to forestall him as he began to move forward. *You can't be him. I'm cracking up!*

As loud and clear as a bell, Lorna's words rang out in her head. *We always have choices.*

Bullshit. I didn't choose to shoot him! It was an accident! "Gimme a min-minute . . . another minute," she panted, her chest heaving as she lifted an arm to brace herself against the wall. *Except for the part where I chose to drink myself into a stupor. That was no accident.*

Oh, God. Oh, God. She didn't want it to be true, but it was, and she couldn't escape owning it for another second. It was like being hit between the eyes with a brick. *She* was the reason she was here. Not bad luck. Not a treacherous ex-girlfriend. Not some cosmic accident. Her own bad decisions and even worse actions had landed her at Blue Ridge and worse than that, she'd ruined someone else's life in the process. *My fault,* she thought miserably. *All of it.*

In a far-off way it registered that this was a monumental epiphany. It also registered that epiphanies suck. "I'm so sorry!" Her face crumpled like a sandcastle in the tide. "I can't tell you how sorry I am. I would give anything to take it back. I'm so, so sorry," she whispered in agony.

With a worried expression, the guard cocked his head. "Are you sick or something?"

That's not his voice. Kellie slammed her eyes closed and grabbed hold of herself, holding on for dear life, terrified that she was about to shatter into a million jagged shards.

She drifted aimlessly in her own mind for a handful of heartbeats, too overwhelmed to do more than hang on. But after a few deep breaths, and with as much attention to detail as she could muster, she began sorting through her raging thoughts. Gradually, a sense of real time and context drifted to the forefront, giving her hope. And finally, though it wasn't easy, she began the one-by-one process of discarding the images that didn't make sense and clinging to the ones that did.

It took a long, scary moment for sanity to reassert itself, but Kellie finally understood that her mind was playing tricks on her. This couldn't be the police officer she'd shot.

Reluctantly, she allowed her eyes to open, and nearly collapsed in relief when caught sight of the man's two healthy legs. Her vision blurred for a second until she could blink away the tears. Then hair several shades too dark and a nose far straighter than the one living in her memory came into crystalline focus.

The sound that erupted from Kellie's chest was something between a desperate laugh and a sob. Self-consciously, she mopped the sweat from her forehead and did her best not to look as crazy as Delia.

"Wow, you look wiped out!" Oblivious to her mental struggle, the guard glanced at his watch, his eyebrows hiking up his forehead. "Have you been running the entire time?"

Kellie's throat tightened to a painful degree. "That's it exactly." She sniffed.

"Are you okay now?"

She nodded, but she really didn't think so.

Chapter 12
Four days later . . .

It was after lights out when Elaine escorted Kellie to Ramona's cell for what was Kellie's first night back from solitary confinement, and her first night back on the cellblock with her new roommate. Desperate to catch even a glimpse of Lorna, she looked longingly into her cell as they moved past it, but all she saw was two bodies huddled in bed, sleeping soundly.

Elaine caught Kellie's wistful look. "Lorna made it back just fine a few hours ago. She was in processing before that suicide today slowed everything down."

"Is that what all the yelling was about?"

"Oh, yeah. Jelisa slit her wrists after getting her plastic dinner utensils." Elaine began unlocking Ramona's cell door.

Kellie's brow knit. "She used one of those flimsy sporks?"

"Mmmhmm." Elaine made a tsking sound and pulled open the door. "It wasn't pretty."

Kellie did her best not to gag.

Elaine lowered her voice in deference to the sleeping woman inside. "Welcome to your new home."

"Thanks," Kellie said lifelessly.

"Cheer up, Holloway. You'll see Lorna tomorrow. The second she got back she was peppering me with questions about you."

Kellie laid a hand on Elaine's doughy forearm. "Thanks for telling me that."

Elaine squared her shoulders, clearly pleased with herself. "Go on." She gestured with her chin. "Tonight won't be so bad. I promise. Don't forget this." Elaine handed over her toothbrush. "You really don't want to have to go the dentist."

Kellie eagerly took back her toothbrush. She'd heard the stories about the dentist who came to the prison every other Monday. He had been convicted of vehicular homicide after running down a woman while high on drugs he'd pilfered from his own dental clinic. Instead of serving real time, however, his slick lawyer had worked out a plea where he came to the prison and offered free dental services. The dentist's preferred course of treatment was tooth extraction, no matter what the ailment. In fact, the procedure was so common and he plowed through so many patients in one day, that the entire prison was served soft food for dinner on the days he worked. Kellie smiled and gave her white teeth a healthy chop. "Exactly. Thanks again."

She stepped into Ramona's cell, cringing a little at the loud snoring coming from the top bunk. That was going to take some getting used to.

The cell looked very different from the one she had shared with Lorna. Photographs of Ramona's kids were plastered everywhere. And Dusty, Ramona's previous roommate, it seemed, was an enthusiastic dog lover. Pictures of puppies and dogs of all shapes and sizes were mixed in among Ramona's family photos. A large stuffed dog sat on the metal desk.

Kellie was so bone-tired that she felt a little sick to her stomach. She sat on the lower bunk, elbows on her knees, and closed her eyes, savoring the darkness. It was cloudy and even the small window at the top corner of the cell let in only the barest amount of light.

In solitary confinement, the lights were left on twenty-four hours a day, and prisoners weren't, under any circumstances, allowed to cover their faces, which had to be viewable by passing guards at all times. The result was learning to sleep with the light shining in your face, which was something Kellie had had trouble with from the very start.

Suddenly, the bunk above her creaked and the snoring stopped.

Kellie sighed and said, "Sorry about that. I didn't mean to wake you."

"Not a problem, Princess."

Kellie's eyes popped open wide with recognition.

"I was waiting for you."

Kellie flew off the bed and tore the covers off the woman in the top bunk, smiling wildly. "Lorna!"

"Shh!" Lorna laughed softly and gave her friend a slightly sheepish look. "I couldn't wait to see you."

In the blink of an eye, Kellie went from dead on her feet to so excited she could barely contain herself. "Mind? Are you crazy? Of course I don't mind!" She did a little happy dance in place, and then started to climb the ladder to the bunk.

"Hang on, hang on," Lorna chuckled. "You're gonna fall on your butt if you climb up doing that stupid dance. I'll come down."

"Don't laugh at me!" Kellie said sternly, smiling all the while. "I'm happy to see you!"

Lorna stopped midway down the ladder. "Even after everything I told you right before we got carted off to solitary?" she asked doubtfully.

"Even then," Kellie assured her seriously. "We need to talk about it . . ."

"But not right this second?" Lorna asked with a slight grin.

"Hell, no! I want a kiss!"

A dazzling smile bloomed on Lorna's face. "Thank Christ!"

Kellie suddenly remembered that they weren't supposed to be here together. "Isn't this going to get you into trouble? What if Elaine—"

"She's in on it. For a fee, of course. This is a one-time-only. Roscoe's on vacation or she wouldn't have risked it. You can't say a word—"

"I won't. I won't." The thought of not sharing a cell with Lorna after tonight couldn't bring down Kellie's mood. Over her months at Blue Ridge she'd become quite adept at living in the moment. And this moment was awesome.

"Where's Ramona?" Kellie asked.

Lorna jumped down the last step. "She's next door with her old roomie. They're probably still yakking away in there. The reunion actually made me a little teary-eyed."

Lorna opened her arms wide. "C'mere."

Their embrace was all encompassing and Kellie squeezed Lorna for all she was worth, her heart pounding with joy. "What you said to me, as I was leaving for the hole . . . I should have—"

"No, you shouldn't have," Lorna told her seriously. "Not until you're ready, Kellie. There's no rush. It's not like I'm going anywhere."

Kellie's legs went weak with relief. Her heartbeat sped up just thinking of her new lover. She knew that she was tumbling headlong into love with Lorna. But she was also still reeling from what she'd learned before they went into solitary and what she'd learned about herself while she was there. She wasn't steady enough on her own two feet to be making declarations about her feelings. But she was getting there.

"So how was it in solitary?" Lorna placed a tiny kiss on Kellie's ear. "Are you really okay?" They were cheek to cheek and Lorna closed her eyes at the simple but intimate sensation of warm skin touching hers. She sucked in the closeness as though it were oxygen.

"It was . . ." Kellie found it impossible to put the profound effect of isolation into words.

"You don't have to explain. If anyone gets it, it would be me. I just need to know that you're okay." Lorna pushed her away gently to peer through the darkness to find those slate gray eyes. Craving the physical contact, she left her hands on Kellie's arms.

"I think I went a little nuts there for a few minutes."

Lorna smiled sadly. "I would be more worried about you if you didn't."

"It's been a *very* long month." She lifted her eyebrows. "Bed?"

Lorna nodded and brought Kellie's hands to her mouth and gently kissed each finger, the scent of shampoo from her recent shower still lingering sweetly to her skin. She pressed Kellie's warm palm to her cheek and sighed.

In the lower bunk, mesmerized by the face so close to hers, Lorna traced Kellie's dark eyebrows one at a time with the tips of her fingers, then her cheeks. Her expression darkened. "You've lost weight. Goddammit, Kel! You were supposed to eat that nasty shit!" She half-smiled and added, "Who says I like skinny chicks?"

Kellie reached out and pinched the taut skin on Lorna's belly. She wasn't the only one who'd lost weight.

Lorna leaned forward and gently kissed Kellie on the mouth, allowing her lips to linger, and swallowing her lover's soft sigh. Tentatively, she swiped her tongue across Kellie's lower lip and the sigh turned into something deeper.

When Lorna began kissing her neck a low moan wrenched itself free of her chest. She feasted on Kellie's throat as though the tender flesh were all the nourishment she would ever need. "Nice."

Kellie narrowed her eyes and tried to draw in a calming breath. Her skin was wildly sensitive and a heavy sensation had already settled between her legs. She was starting throb.

Lorna glanced up in question. "Can I—" Her fingertips were poised at the edge of Kellie's bra.

Kellie's nostrils flared. "God, yes."

Reaching around her, Lorna undid the clasp and slipped the bra off, tossing it over her shoulder. She was left with a large expanse of very warm, very soft skin and drew her fingertip down the line between Kellie's breasts. It was dark, but not so dark that she couldn't see what lay before her. "You're really beautiful." She glanced up. "But I bet you've heard that a million times."

"None of them made me feel like you do."

"Good." Lorna leaned forward and kissed the edge of Kellie's breast, moaning into its smoothness. Then she dragged her tongue over Kellie's nipple, her lover's sensual groan thrilling her to the core and causing lust to rise up in her like a tidal wave. Her sex clenched and her entire body shuddered.

This wasn't like the last time. They weren't in a fevered rush. Now Lorna could savor every sight, sound and taste, give and take everything she'd wanted for so long. Somehow it made her even hotter. She was making Kellie writhe under her. *She* was what caused the constant stream of sexy sounds to spill from the gorgeous mouth below her. A heady sense of power filled her.

And suddenly, Lorna stopped moving, panic creeping into every corner of her body.

Kellie's hands were everywhere, exploring the muscles and curves pressed so intimately against her own. She felt excitement thrumming through Lorna as well as her lover's hesitation. Lorna wanted to take control but was fighting it. *C'mon, baby*, Kellie urged silently. *Let go.* "What is it, Lorna?" she whispered.

Face still flushed with excitement, Lorna glanced away, her lower lip between her teeth. "Nothing."

Kellie tamped down on the urge to push Lorna past her reluctance. To simply take what she wanted.

"Oh, Mal-ly!" Roscoe's voice boomed from down the hall and the weak beam of his flashlight filtered through the window on the cell door. "I hear you're back with us tonight. I missed you," he warbled.

"Shit!" Lorna scrambled off Kellie and hastily began rooting around the floor for her T-shirt. "Shit! Shit! Shit!"

Kellie jumped up and began looking for the shirt. "Get back in the top bunk!" She nudged Lorna with one hand. "Go!"

The sound of Roscoe's boots grew louder and louder, the light from his flashlight bobbing up and down and he walked.

"I can't find it." Kellie bounced around on her hands and knees, looking very much like a demented windup toy, the floor cold and hard against her hot flesh. "Just get under the blankets!"

Roscoe stopped outside the cell and trained his light on Kellie's bed, which was empty. He was just reaching for his keys when Kellie cleared her throat and looked up from her position on the floor.

Topless.

"Can I help you?" she asked sweetly.

Roscoe smiled, his hand moving from his belt and dropping loosely to his side. "You already have." Reluctantly, he moved his light from Kellie's breasts to the top bunk. Apparently satisfied that the lump under the covers wasn't up to anything fishy, he refocused on Kellie. "What are you doing on the floor?"

Kellie pressed Lorna's T-shirt against her bare chest. "Nothing. I got hot and tossed off my shirt." She shrugged mildly and did her best to smile. "Then I got cold and wanted it back again."

He grunted, clearly unhappy that his view had been spoiled. "How was solitary?"

The smile melted from Kellie's face. "It sucked."

"Back when you first got here, I warned you that hooking up with Mally would be nothing but trouble. You should have listened."

She didn't want to say it, but she had little choice. Being caught in a sexual situation with another prisoner earned you an automatic thirty days in the hole. Then there was the whole matter of being in the wrong cell after lights out. Punishment would be stacked on top of punishment. They'd be lucky to see each other again for months. "You're right. I should have."

Roscoe nodded smugly and moved on to the next cell.

Each woman held her breath as they waited for the worst.

"Mally," he called out in a taunting voice. "Welcome home."

"She's asleep," Ramona answered sleepily, rolling over and causing the springs on her bunk to whine. "Torment her in the morning."

Kellie's heart was beating so fast she couldn't distinguish between the individual beats.

"C'mon, Mally," Roscoe urged, giving the cell door a rap with his baton. "Wake up and blow us a kiss." He made a few obnoxious kissing noises.

"I'll give you a kiss, asshole," Lorna muttered darkly, her ear cocked toward the cell next door. "Right after I stick that baton up your . . ." The rest of her words disappeared into her pillow.

Roscoe laughed. "Get out from under those blankets so I can see your face." A pause. "Hey! I'm going to break that middle finger tomorrow!" he bellowed, before stomping his way back down the hall. But not before he banged on the door of every cell on his way, waking up the entire block.

Kellie padded the two steps to the wall and gave a gentle knock of thanks, receiving one in return. "Christ." She ran her shaking fingers through her hair as she moved back to the bunks. "I age ten years with every one of these close calls." She was shaking.

Alone on her bed, Lorna allowed frustrated tears to come. "How do people do it? How do they go from being so turned on they might die, to scared shitless, to furious all in the space of a few minutes and not go bonkers?"

Kellie was about to say that most people don't encounter ridiculous circumstances like they just did, but she figured the question was rhetorical. "Come back to bed with me."

Lorna wiped her cheeks and deftly made her way down the ladder, her mind awhirl. Roscoe was the most unpredictable of the guards and loved surprise searches, but he was also lazy and so it was unlikely that he'd traipse back down the hall anytime soon. Still, she needed to be more careful than she'd planned.

Lorna slid under the covers and Kellie gasped when they were together, chest-to-chest. She was now wearing Lorna's T-shirt, but Lorna was still topless. A sigh trickled out at the sensation of warmth. "Are you okay?"

"I don't want him to take this night from us," Kellie whispered fervently.

Lorna kissed her hard. "Then we won't let him," she vowed, her lips still touching Kellie's.

They made love quickly, as though it would be their last chance. Kellie had tears in eyes by the time they were finished.

Sated and exhausted, Kellie forced her mind to forward to keep from falling apart. "I did a lot of thinking while I was in solitary."

"Kel, I know what I told you about my time in maximum security, and about my history with Katrina shook you up," Lorna whispered. "It was lousy to tell you that right before we were going to be separated. I thought about that a lot when I was alone. That was cruel, and I'm sorry."

"It did shake me up," Kellie admitted, feeling her way very carefully. "It still does."

Sighing bleakly, Lorna covered her face with one hand. "I don't know how to change that."

"From what you said, your time with Lucille's gang was working. Why give all that up? What changed?"

Kellie expected a thoughtful pause. But Lorna's answer came easily. "If you're looking for a dramatic event where I suddenly realized that I needed to turn my life around, you're going to be disappointed. There was nothing like that." Lorna lifted one hand and left it fall. "Over time, I started to grow up and think about other people and not just myself."

Kellie kissed her chin again, silently urging her to continue.

"The women I truly respected weren't like me. And they sure as hell weren't like Lucille. They hadn't let Blue Ridge snuff out whatever spark of goodness was still inside them. They were strong in a way that I wasn't and I hated that truth almost as much as I *hated* myself."

Kellie looked at her doubtfully. "So you stopped doing bad things out of the blue?"

"What I stopped ignoring was how doing the bad things made me feel. After that, what was the point in continuing to do them? I just wanted to be able to look in the mirror and not flinch."

Kellie yawned. "Ramona once told me I'd made the second big difference in your life. Was this the first? You wanting to change?"

Lorna thought about that. "Maybe. Was she high on coke at the time? She's been known to indulge every once in a while."

A dark eyebrow lifted. She'd learned long ago not to be deterred by one of Lorna's diversionary tactics. "Can you just leave a gang? Just walk away?"

Lorna propped her head up on her hand, then reached out and fingered a strand of Kellie's dark hair. It was so soft she was hard-pressed not to swoon. "If you go feet first."

"Not funny."

With a soft sigh she let go of Kellie's hair. "I had a little help on my way out. Lucille died and that gave me the opportunity to bolt.

When she croaked there was a lot of infighting and vying for control. The women who wanted Lucille's reins were thrilled that I was blowing them off. They thought I was crazy to walk away, but they let me do it once they saw I wasn't trying to take anyone with me."

"You said she died . . . do you mean she was murdered?" The level of violence here never stopped appalling Kellie.

"Someone fed her rat poison until it killed her. On my way to lunch, I heard a rousing chorus of *Ding Dong The Witch is Dead* coming from Lucille's cell the day she died. I didn't know until later that she was actually in there twitching and dying at the time." Lorna shuddered. "Apparently, Lucille died the way she lived. Screaming and clawing like the filthy monster she was."

Kellie let out a low whistle. Apparently, Lorna didn't have a problem with speaking ill of the dead. "Do you think you know who did it?"

Lorna hesitated before quietly saying, "Katrina's favorite movie is *The Wizard of Oz*. Besides, I'd recognize her wretched singing voice anywhere."

Kellie's eyes widened. "You're certain she did it?"

Lorna nodded slowly. "The state never had a clue, and the other cons only suspected. But I knew. She kept the rat poison in this little Tupperware thing hidden in our cell until I found it and flushed it down the toilet. Guess she got some more."

"You knew and you didn't turn her in?" Kellie exclaimed. "What the hell is wrong with you?"

A storm swept across Lorna's face and her body stiffened. "You didn't see Lucille going at Katrina with that baton! Lucille was a twisted, violent bitch who got off on making other little twisted violent bitches in her image! Whatever Lucille got in the end . . . well, that was between her and Katrina. And whatever I owed Katrina for not helping her when I could have, I paid back with my silence. As far as I'm concerned, all the scales are even!"

Kellie winced at the anger in Lorna's voice. "I'm sorry," she pushed out. "I'm trying not to do that anymore."

"No?" Lorna said warily, hurt sparking in her eyes.

"I didn't understand the journey you took to get to where you are now. And I still don't understand completely, but I feel closer to you because I know you better." Kellie's gaze softened. "I hurt for what those bad years did to you. Good people sometimes do bad things. They make mistakes. Big ones. But that doesn't have to change who they are. And no matter what you did then, you're a good person now. You're someone I want to be like and someone I want to continue to care about."

The air escaped Lorna's lungs in one long rush.

Kellie leaned forward and put her face a hairsbreadth from Lorna's. "I want you to know that even though I'm still a little freaked out, I'm not afraid of you. I'm glad I don't know the person you were then, but I'm lucky and happy to be with you now."

Lorna swallowed a few times. "Me too, Princess."

"You feel so good," Kellie said dreamily, her voice barely audible as she snuggled close.

Lorna settled in for a long night of holding the person she loved most, and watching the door. "Sleep now," Lorna soothed again.

And that was all it took. Like a helium balloon tethered to the earth by a sturdy string, Kellie felt herself begin to float away while being grounded at the same time. She drifted in space for several minutes, wanting to hold on to the safe, freeing sensation as long as possible. But Lorna's soft breath against her neck, and the solid feeling of the body pressed to hers, lulled her closer and closer to a deep slumber. The kind she hadn't had in ages.

The kind filled with peace.

Chapter 13
Four months later . . .

The sound of two sets of sneakers rapidly hitting the track disappeared into the bracing afternoon wind. "Walk?" Lorna asked as she ran, her words sending a cloud of fog into the late afternoon sky.

Kellie slowed to a jog, then a walk. "Good idea." She put her hands on her hips and concentrated on slowing down her breathing.

Fluffy clouds dotted an otherwise sunny sky, and a blindingly white new layer of snow covered the exercise yard. At the completion of the twentieth lap, half of which they walked, Lorna bent to recover the too-small coat she'd left on the ground when she began working up a light sweat. For once, she was eager to get back inside.

"So, today's the big day. Or is it tomorrow?" Kellie teased, lifting her knees high to stretch her tired legs.

Lorna took Kellie's hand as they began strolling back toward the door. "You know it's today. If I put another coat of lacquer on the thing, I'm afraid the shine will blind me." There was a noticeable spring in her step that made Kellie smile.

Kellie grinned, charmed by Lorna's evident excitement. "I can't believe you wouldn't let me see it for all this time. Even Jennings was impressed. You should have heard her yesterday. She said it was the most amazing work she's ever seen. She's pissed that you won't sell it to her."

"She'll live." A beguiling smile creased Lorna's cheeks. "But just barely. It is gorgeous."

"Hey," a guard called out from the perimeter, pointing an angry hand at Lorna and Kellie. "No touching!"

With a low growl, Lorna let go of Kellie's hand and raised both of her own to show her compliance. It was Sunday afternoon, and the only time they could spend more than a few stolen minutes talking. There was no talking during meal times and under no circumstances were they ever permitted to enter another inmate's cell. Over the past few months, she missed her old cellmate, missed even the things that used to annoy her about living with Kellie.

"Why do they bother? It's not like we're hurting anyone," Kellie said.

"They bother because they can." Lorna sneered in the guard's direction. "Peckerwood."

The women crossed in front of the basketball court just as the doors to the inside swung open. Chul stepped outside and gave a shrill blow on a whistle.

"Hey," Kellie bumped hips with Lorna, "don't let him bring down your mood. Today's the big day, remember?" She was nearly as excited to see the piece of furniture as Lorna was to show it. "I can't wait to see your creation!"

Jennings, who was thrilled with her new computer skills, had given Lorna some space in a seldom-used storage room that was located just off the main shop. Other inmates had, of course, stolen glances at the work-in-progress during the months it had taken to complete. But Kellie had promised that she wouldn't look until it was finished. It had nearly killed her, but she'd kept her promise.

"You're right." Lorna wrestled a smile into place. "Let me show you what I made for you."

Kellie stopped dead in her tracks. "For me?"

Lorna's grin grew. "For you." Her gaze strayed to the women filing inside. It was cold, so the line was moving fast. "We'd better get inside." She began walking again.

"I can't take your desk. I can't. It's for when you make parole and get a place of your own on the outside. That's less than ten months."

Lorna stuffed her rapidly chilling fingers into her pockets and rocked back onto her heels. "But there's only four months until your hearing."

Dead silence.

Lorna mentally kicked herself. That had come out far more melancholy than she'd intended, especially on what was supposed to be a happy day. She was thrilled for Kellie's upcoming release, even though she dreaded it.

Kellie looked confused. "I can . . . Did you want me to keep the desk for you until you can take it? I still have the few things that weren't sold off or repossessed in my parents' garage. I'm sure there's room for—"

Lorna sighed. "I don't want you to store it for me." She reached out to take one of Kellie's hands, but pulled back as she remembered the guard that was undoubtedly still watching them. "It's a gift."

The snow began again and Lorna brushed an errant flake from the tip of Kellie's nose before quickly stuffing her hand back in her jacket pocket. "Using the desk will give you an excuse to think of me when you're far away." A tiny crease formed between Kellie's eyes and she nearly had to stand on her hands to keep herself from rubbing it away.

"I won't need an excuse to think of you." Feeling awkward and helpless, Lorna looked away. She didn't want to discuss Kellie's future on the outside. A future that, she suspected, would have little place for her. But soon they wouldn't have a choice. "I'm bad at this." She gestured between her and Kellie. "At us, sometimes."

"Lorna, that's not true."

Lorna gave her a look that made it painfully clear she disagreed.

The line of women ended.

"Hey, Chul," Lorna greeted. "I know it's Sunday, but Ms. Jennings said that I can bring Kellie by the shop to—"

The Asian man held up a hand. "Yeah, yeah, I know. Jennings already told me. Not that she needed to, mind you. The whole cell-block is buzzing." He smiled, his eyes dancing with the good humor of a man about to go off shift. He leaned a little closer to Lorna as he lowered his voice. "Is it true the top has an intricate mahogany inlay?"

Kellie took her place alongside Lorna, who put a finger to her lips. "Shh . . ." she said as they moved inside.

"Oh," Chul laughed as he looked to Kellie. "It's a surprise. Gotcha." His gaze traveled out to the guard tower and he received a hand signal that was the "all clear" sign that he could shut and lock the door to the yard.

The rest of the inmates headed down one of several hallways. One led to the TV lounge and cells, another to the showers and cafeteria, and the third to the woodshop, loading dock and other offices.

Blue Ridge existed on a shoestring budget and the already-gloomy hallway lights were dimmed in the areas of the prison that saw less traffic on the weekends. Alone, Kellie and Lorna proceeded down the third hallway.

At the woodshop, Lorna knocked loudly on the outer door until Patrice Jennings, whom they could see working on her computer motioned them in. The shop door was unlocked.

"Nice job on the desk." Jennings picked up a pencil and began to twirl it with long fingers. "I wish we got enough custom orders to let you do work like that all the time. You have real talent."

Lorna squared her shoulders at the unexpected praise, a smile creeping across her face. "Thank you."

Jennings gave her a knowing look. "Don't worry about her liking it."

Lorna's eyebrows jumped. Was there anyone who didn't know her private business? "No?"

"No." Jennings shrugged lightly. "Any woman would." And with that, she turned, and refocused on the screen as though Lorna wasn't even there.

"Well?" Kellie whispered loudly. "Are you done making nice yet?" Baking now that she was inside, she shed her coat, and thin sweat-shirt, leaving her in her ever-present white T-shirt. She extended a hand.

Lorna passed over her jacket and sweatshirt, watching fondly as Kellie piled them on a nearby table. She was so happy she was about ready to bust a gut. "Now you're the one who's impatient?"

Lorna held her hand in front of Kellie's eyes as she pushed open the storeroom door and flicked on the light. "Here it—" Her words were cut off by an explosive moan that sounded as though it came from a wounded animal.

Kellie grabbed Lorna's hand and pulled it away from her eyes. "Oh, God." Before her was a jagged looking pile with a sheet draped over it.

Lorna's face began to darken with a fiery rage. She marched for-ward and snatched the sheet off what once was the desk she'd labored on. In its place was nothing more than mangled shards of wood that still smelled like lacquer.

Kellie waited to hear a roar of anger. But Lorna just stood there, seemingly paralyzed, her body vibrating with fury, the silence scaring Kellie far worse than the outburst she expected. "Oh, my God." She felt her own eyes well up.

Lorna swallowed audibly and crouched down to run trembling hands over what might have been the top of the desk. She picked up a jagged piece of wood, gripping it so tightly her knuckles turned white.

Kellie's heart felt like it was being torn in two. "How could this happen!"

Lorna stood and Kellie caught a flash of pure violence in her eyes. "Katrina is how." Her voice was so low and even that it sent a chill down Kellie's spine.

Dread began to swirl in Kellie's belly. "We don't know that. It could have been—"

"It could have been what?" Lorna demanded acidly, her face turning from a vivid shade of red to purple. "Look at this." She held the piece of wood that was no larger than a ruler before Kellie's face. "*What* could have done this?"

Kellie looked at the scrap Lorna was shaking in front of her face, and then back at the tangled mountain of rubble, seeing past the wood to little bits of her heart and soul that Lorna had invested in her work. The same pieces that she'd given so freely to Kellie. Her friend had been cut to the quick and beyond, and she felt like she was bleeding.

"We don't know it was Katrina," Kellie whispered in anguish, not believing a word of what she was saying.

Lorna launched the scrap of wood across the room. It banged loudly against the far wall, knocking several small cans of stain to the floor. "I know!"

Kellie's mind scrambled to make sense of what had happened. Jennings was only fifty feet away in another room. Surely someone couldn't have done this while she was at her computer. And yet, she hadn't come to investigate the racket Lorna had just made.

Lorna angrily wiped her eyes with the heels of her hands. "Stay right here, okay?"

Kellie's eyes widened. "No. Not okay! Where—?"

"Please," was all Lorna muttered before taking off like a shot, and slamming the door behind her.

Kellie stood for a split second, stunned. "Oh, shit. Shit!" *She's really going to kill her!* She flung the door open and surged forward, only to collide with Jennings, knocking her to the floor.

"Hey!" the older woman complained, wincing as she rubbed her hip. "What the hell is going on here?"

"Sorry." Kellie tried to move past her to catch up to Lorna, who had already disappeared out of the shop, but was brought up short by a firm hand wrapped around her wrist.

"I said, what's going on?" Jennings boomed, using Kellie's arm to pull herself up, and purposefully not letting go until she got some answers.

"We have to stop her!" Truth was, Kellie wasn't sure she could keep from killing Katrina herself, much less stop Lorna.

"Why?" Then Jennings caught sight of the desk and the breath left her lungs in a single rush. Her face fell. "Oh, no." Jennings jumped out of the way. "Go! Hurry! Bring her back here and I'll call the guards," Jennings yelled after her. "We'll find out who did this."

Kellie raced down the hall, her feet slamming hard against the floor. She spotted Laverne up ahead, her head bobbing in time with the music being pumped into her ears from an old Walkman. She skidded to a stop in front of her. "Where's Katrina?" Kellie demanded.

Laverne smirked as she pulled off her headphones, leaving them to dangle around her neck. "Why should I tell you anything?"

Breathing hard, Kellie grabbed her by the biceps and shook her with all her might. "Goddammit! I'm not screwing around! If you care about what happens to Katrina you'll tell me!"

Laverne jerked away, nearly knocking herself to the floor in the process. Her Walkman crashed to the floor. "What the hell is wrong with you?" She rubbed her arms and bent to pick up the small machine. "You crazy bitch!"

"Have you seen Lorna?" Lorna was less than a minute ahead of her, but that was all it took for her to be uncertain of which way her lover turned when she hit the end of the hall. "Talk!" she roared wildly.

Slack-jawed, Laverne stuttered, "No—no. Not since the yard."

"Where is Katrina?" When the answer didn't come fast enough, Kellie began to advance on Laverne, who threw her hands up in surrender.

"Wait!" Flinching, Laverne shrank back. "Laundry room, I think."

Kellie's gaze darted down the quiet hallway. Most women, she knew, would be in the TV lounge at this time of day. The laundry room was in the opposite direction. Her eyes snapped with anger and fear and her palms grew moist as she fought against indecision. Every second counted. "Are you sure, Laverne?"

Laverne looked at Kellie as though she'd grown a horn in the middle of her forehead. "Yeah, I'm sure."

After a second of indecision, Kellie gritted her teeth and took off toward the prison laundry, not hearing Laverne's muffled snicker as she ran.

"Lorna!" she called as she sped down the hall toward the laundry room, not caring who heard her. She turned the corner and nearly collided with Roscoe.

"Whoa!" he ordered. "Where are you going in such a rush, Holloway?"

"Nowhere," she panted. Bringing Roscoe into this would only bring more trouble. "I mean, I'm late to see my favorite show so I'm hurrying to get there." She smiled engagingly. "You know how it is."

Roscoe appraised her coolly, his Fu Manchu mustache moving with every smack of his wad of chewing tobacco. He jerked his head to the side. "TV lounge is the other way."

Shit. "Umm . . . I left some socks in the dryer in the laundry room. I gotta get those first, before someone steals them."

He nodded doubtfully. "Okay, but why are you calling for Mally? I thought you two were joined at the hip. Now that you turned her into a dyke and all."

His gaze bored into hers and the passing seconds felt like days. "She owes me money for the laundry."

The big man let his hand drop to his baton. "Up against the wall."

"Shit!"

"Do it!"

Kellie faced the wall, spreading her legs and placed her arms above her head, her palms flat against the cool concrete. "Just hurry, okay?"

Roscoe glanced around, smiling to find that they were completely alone.

She grimaced when he slowly ran his hands over her breasts. He crushed his fat belly against her back and squeezed his fingers closed. "What's this? A little contraband maybe?"

It was hard to breathe, but Kellie still managed to whimper in pain. "My nipples aren't contraband," she ground out, unconsciously leaning forward as much as she could in a vain attempt to escape his touch.

Roscoe chuckled, his breath hot on the back of her neck as his meaty hands trailed down her sides. They he strayed beneath the waistband of her sweatpants and cupped her bottom. His hands felt rough and cool against her heated flesh. They also made her skin crawl.

"You're such a bastard, Roscoe." Kellie closed her eyes, the urge to scream growing stronger with every labored breath.

"Don't I know it."

Finally, after a ridiculously drawn out groping, Roscoe straightened and backed away a step. "All clean." He made a show of dusting off his hands. "You can go get those socks now."

Kellie pushed off the wall with a murderous glint in her eyes. She'd been searched dozens of times since she came to Blue Ridge, and she never stopped feeling utterly violated.

"Don't give me that look." He laughed. "It wasn't as bad as all that." Then he winked. "Say hi to Mally for me."

Kellie didn't answer, instead she silently turned, and strode down the hall, breaking into a run once he'd lumbered well away from her. The farther she went, the stronger the smell of industrial bleach and the heavier the air. She burst through the laundry room door. "Lorna? Katrina?" Desperately, she looked around, only to find the room empty.

In frustration, she punched a dryer, denting the metal. For a second she felt nothing. Then a bolt of pain nearly melted her knees. It began to throb with every beat of her heart. Clasping it to her chest, she began running back to the cellblock, her body damp with nervous sweat.

The cell doors were all in the open position until lights out. Katrina's cell was one of the first she passed and she poked her head in, expecting it to be empty because it was so quiet. She almost missed the figure crouching near the foot of the bunk beds.

"Ramona?" Kellie slowly entered the cell, catching a whiff of the metallic scent of blood. Her stomach began to churn.

Ramona turned and Kellie saw Katrina sprawled out on the floor, covered in blood. Clothes were strewn on the floor as well as a newspaper and the lower mattress was slightly askew.

"Shhh, come here . . . quickly," Ramona ordered. "Thank Christ it's you."

Her heart in her throat, Kellie knelt next to the Mexican woman, who had nearly as much blood on her as Katrina. Ramona was pressing Katrina's tattered T-shirt against a nasty-looking gash that bisected Katrina's chest.

Kellie tried to talk but it took a few seconds for the words to make it from her stunned mind to her mouth. "Is," she had to swallow a few times, "Is she—?"

"She's alive," Ramona announced, not sounding especially thrilled by that fact. "Here." She replaced her hands with Kellie's so she could grab a pillow from the bed and yank off the dingy pillowcase. She wadded it up and pressed the cotton against the wound, instantly turning the case a shocking shade of crimson. "I saw her on the floor as I passed by and came to help. Everyone else is watching that stupid television at the other end of the cellblock."

No. No. No. "Oh, Lorna," Kellie muttered, feeling lightheaded from the furious pounding of her pulse. "What have you done?" Bile rose in her throat. *I'm too late.*

Ramona gave Kellie a woeful look. "I saw Lorna running from here toward the showers."

God. Oh, God. To wash off the blood. Kellie grimaced at the damage Lorna had inflicted. Every inch of Katrina's face had been pummeled. One eye was already swollen shut. Her nose was obviously broken. *Just like she did to me.* And several bloody teeth were scattered on the floor next to Katrina's limp body. Then there was the jagged cut that was bleeding more than enough to scare Kellie shitless.

"I called to Lorna," Ramona continued, "but she didn't answer. Katrina, the stupid woman, must have finally pushed her too far. When she wakes up she'll tell the guards who did this." Ramona began to lift her hands from Katrina's chest. "Maybe we should let her . . ."

"No!" Letting the source of so much misery simply bleed to death had a certain, if ghoulish, appeal. But she began pressing the pillowcase over the wound herself, ignoring the throbbing pain it caused her hand. "We can't let her die or Lorna will spend the rest of her life in this hellhole."

"Even if she doesn't die, Lorna will never make parole now. And then they'll add more years for this charge. She's going to be here a very long time."

Kellie couldn't shove down her panic. "Don't say that!" She pressed harder against the wound. "Don't!"

Ramona spoke to Kellie as she would to a small child. "This wasn't just a fight, chica. Lorna came here to kill her." She lifted up her T-shirt and pointed to a bloodstained shank that was half-sticking out of her jeans "This was on the floor next to Katrina, but I'm going to get rid of it. Lorna's my friend too, yes?"

Kellie blinked and pointed. *Lorna doesn't own a shank!* "That's not—"

Ramona exploded, "It doesn't matter if she used this bitch's shank or her own! What matters is that she cut her with it." Frustrated, she got up and cautiously made her way to the doorway, slowly peering outside.

The only activity was far down the hallway. She quickly moved back to Kellie. "Roscoe will take this chance to make sure Lorna never gets free."

The color drained from Kellie's face.

"Unless . . ."

Kellie held her breath, but grew impatient quickly and muttered an encouraging, "Unless?"

"Unless she says it was self-defense, yes?" Ramona latched on to the idea with gusto. "I could be her witness and say that it was Katrina that attacked her."

Kellie shook her head desperately. "No. Lorna had good reason to do this. Nobody will believe it was self-defense. She came looking for Katrina."

"*Dios mio.*" Disgusted, Ramona threw her hands in the air. "She's screwed."

The pressure against Katrina's chest was working and the bleeding slowed from a steady stream to a sluggish pulsing. Kellie let out a shaky breath, glad she was already on her knees. "Lorna won't survive if she's stuck here rotting year after year, Ramona. She's already done that. We've got to do something to help her."

Ramona frowned. "Lorna will be fine. She's strong. I'll hide the shank and be her witness and that will probably keep the charge down to assault. That's a nickel at most."

A five-year sentence. The ache that had settled in Kellie's chest was more than she could bear. "I know how Lorna feels about owning up to her own actions, but Katrina intentionally drove her to this! It's not fair. She shouldn't have to lose another five years." She looked down at the woman whose life literally rested in her hands and felt little more than hatred. "Not for the likes of her."

Ramona chewed her bottom lip. "Maybe there is another way." She sighed and looked down at her hands.

"What? Tell me."

Reluctantly, she glanced up, pinning Kellie with her dark gaze. "You'd do anything to help her?"

Kellie had only had a few moments of absolute clarity in her life. The sort of beautiful, horrible moments that were like scars in the way they marked you, changed you forever. That most of them had occurred while she was in prison was, she was certain, some sort of cosmic joke. This was one of those moments.

"Anything," Kellie breathed, feeling the power behind the words. "I would do *anything* for her."

Ramona paused for a few seconds, as if judging the other woman's sincerity. Finally, apparently satisfied with whatever she was looking for she said, "If you mean that, then you can keep her from taking the fall." She stopped speaking to let Kellie put the rest of the pieces together herself.

Kellie's forehead wrinkled. "I can? But how?" And then, like an arrow in the heart, it struck her and she understood with devastating lucidity exactly what she had to do. "I can say that I did this. I can take the blame." The strangled words barely registered as her own. "Katrina is my enemy too. It was my desk she ruined." Even her swollen hand fit the scene perfectly. "It makes sense."

Ramona mumbled something under her breath and Kellie thought she heard herself called "crazy" for the second time in one day.

Katrina groaned softly and Ramona bared her teeth. "Shut up, *puta*! Or I'll finish what Lorna started by letting your sorry ass die."

Kellie squeezed her eyes shut. A confession would surely mean facing more prison time. The thought of being caged like the most pitiful of dogs made her want to rail against the world and claw her way to freedom.

Anxiety welled within her and she waited for that little voice in her head to agree with Laverne and Ramona and proclaim her unhinged. She expected it to laugh cruelly and say she was too selfish to put someone else's needs above her own, too self-absorbed to lay her future on the line for anyone but herself. Hadn't her actions proven that time and time again?

But there was no voice, the landscape of her mind was as open and clear as a windswept plain. And to her everlasting surprise, it was her heart's reverent whisper that she heard instead. A whisper she was powerless to ignore: *Anything for her.*

Kellie opened her eyes as an odd sense of calm and determination settled over her like a comfortable blanket. This was the rightest wrong thing she'd ever done.

She began to run through a series of scenarios in her head. "What happens when Katrina comes to and says it wasn't me who beat the ever-livin' shit out of her? She hates me, but she's got this sick love/hate going with Lorna."

"Always has," Ramona agreed.

"Then she'll want Lorna to be the one to get in trouble."

"If the evidence shows it was you, what she says won't matter. Katrina is a liar. Everyone knows that." Ramona paused. "Are you sure about this? Once you start, there's no turning back."

There was really only one answer to that question. "I'm sure." Now that her die had been cast, Kellie didn't have time to be startled at the length she was willing to go to spare her lover the pain of more incarceration. "Lift up your shirt again."

Ramona obeyed, her face showing her puzzlement. "What are you—?"

Carefully, Kellie removed the shank from Ramona's pants, making sure to wrap her hand tightly around the hilt. She openly shivered, her face scrunched up in repulsion as she tossed it aside.

Ramona nodded approvingly. "Fingerprints. Good."

Kellie's lips thinned as she thought, *What else can I do?* She glanced down. Blood had stained her fingers through the pillowcase, though she'd managed to keep the rest of herself totally clean. "I need your T-shirt."

Ramona nodded and shot to her feet, removing the shirt in one swift motion. It was bloody from the chest down. "It will be too small," she warned, obviously relieved to be out of the soaked garment.

"No one will notice," Kellie said confidently. "They'll be too busy paying attention to the blood."

Ramona took over the pressure on Katrina's chest as Kellie awkwardly stripped out of her shirt using one hand. Then they traded T-shirts.

Ramona ran a hand through her hair then carelessly tucked the T-shirt into her jeans. When she was finished, she let out a shaky breath. "What next?"

Kellie swallowed hard and steeled her nerves. Ramona's shirt was warm and wet and it clung dreadfully to her skin. She was hard-pressed not to vomit. "Get a guard."

"Elaine's in the TV room. I'll go—"

"Get Roscoe instead. He's heading this way from the laundry room and I want that prick to find me here with Katrina. He's the dumbest of the bunch, but he's still the head guard and what he thinks will carry the most weight. He'll believe an argument got out of hand and I'm helping Katrina now because I don't want to face a more serious charge."

Kellie's face hardened. "When he starts to take me in, I'm gonna take this opportunity to kick him in the balls so hard his ancestors will feel it."

Ramona hummed a little under her breath. "Badass Kellie? Who knew? When Lorna gets out, and you're still stuck here, you won't miss her protection." She beamed. "You won't need it. No one will touch you!"

Including Lorna. Kellie supposed that Ramona was paying her a compliment and smiled grimly in return. "Thanks."

Katrina moaned again as she fought toward consciousness.

Kellie looked up at Ramona, every bit as resolute as she was afraid. "Run."

"You have the right to remain silent."

The metallic scent of blood and the musk of sweat filled the air and Kellie cringed as Roscoe dug his baton into her lower back. "I waive my right and confess to stabbing Katrina. Just like I did thirty seconds ago."

"Yeah, but I have to say this shit anyway." He reached for his cuffs. "Anything you say, can and will be used against you in a court of law."

Kellie watched Chul feverishly administering basic first aid to Katrina, who was still unconscious. She said a little prayer that she would stay that way for just a little longer. She wanted more time to think about her story and make it so believable that it wouldn't matter what Katrina said. And then there was Lorna. If she showed up, all hell was likely to break loose.

A group of women and Ramona, who had bitten her nails down to the quick in the last few minutes, crowded together outside Katrina's cell, watching the unfolding events as though it were their own private soap opera. *And maybe it is,* Kellie allowed privately.

Roscoe had already called for crime scene tape to be laid.

"You have the right to an attorney."

Kellie's second wrist was cuffed and she was yanked away from the wall where she'd been spread-eagled.

"If you can't afford an attorney," Roscoe continued determinedly, "one will be appointed for you. Do you understand these rights?"

Kellie swallowed hard and did her best not to tremble under the weight of what she was doing. "I've become depressingly familiar with the legal system over the past couple of years. So the answer is yes."

The fat man moved close so that she could feel his breath on the back on her neck, the smell of stale cigarettes overtaking her. "I'm going to make sure you get charged with assaulting an officer."

His voice was still a tad higher than normal and a tiny smile cracked Kellie's otherwise serious face.

He shook his head. "If you were missing life in solitary, all you had to do was say something. You're going to rot in there until this is all sorted out."

Katrina's entire body jerked and Chul, in a low calming voice, reassured her that a nurse would be there soon. "I'm ready to go now. How long is this going to take?" Kellie asked nervously. "I . . . um . . . I want to call my lawyer as soon as possible."

A deep frown split Roscoe's face as he glanced around. "What aren't you telling me?"

Kellie froze.

Sensing blood, Roscoe moved in for the kill. "I asked you this earlier," he gave Kellie a violent shake. "And now I want the truth! Where's Mally? I haven't seen her since lunch. I can just as easily throw the cellblock into lockdown and find her in a few minutes, so you might as well tell me now."

"I don't know," Kellie said truthfully, doing her best to edge toward the cell door. "How many places she can be? Besides, she doesn't have anything to do with this."

Roscoe clucked his tongue. "I think she has something to do with just about *everything* you do, Holloway."

Kellie's voice dropped to its lowest register. "Not this."

Roscoe was silent for a long time before saying, "We'll see." With a rough push, they left the cell and entered the hallway.

Several paramedics, an EMT from the prison infirmary, and two guards, one of whom was Elaine, joined the scene.

"Back to your cells," Elaine called out brusquely, pushing gawkers out of her way as she moved. "Go on. There's no show here." But not a single prisoner moved. "Nobody got killed." She turned to the paramedics. "Right?"

One of the paramedics nodded. "Right. Looks like a concussion and a non-fatal stab wound."

Kellie exhaled shakily. *Thank God.*

"Okay, you're getting your wish. Time to go."

"What the hell is going on?"

Oh, fuck. Kellie's stomach dropped.

Lorna, towel in hand, hair still wet, and face still flushed pink from the recent shower she'd taken to cool her temper, neatly sidestepped Elaine and marched up to Roscoe and Kellie, her gaze flicking to the men who were obscuring someone on the floor, before settling back on her partner. She stared at Kellie with wide eyes. There was blood everywhere. "Kel?"

"The blood's not mine," Kellie assured her softly, emotion welling within her.

Lorna let out a shaky, relieved breath. "Why are you in cuffs?"

"Stop right there, Mally." He grabbed a wad of Lorna's T-shirt, holding her in place. "Chul?"

"On my way to secure the shower room."

Elaine pried Roscoe's hand from Lorna's shirt. He left a wrinkled ball of material in his wake. "I've got her." She took out her cuffs, but didn't use them. Instead, she stuck a finger through one of Lorna's belt loops and gave it a discreet tug. It was a friendly reminder to stay put that would be backed up with force, if necessary.

"About the shower room." All eyes turned to Kellie, "I forgot to say before, but I uh, I tried to wash some of the blood off in there before I sent Ramona to get Roscoe. If you check the drain you'll probably find some."

"Katrina's blood?" Bewildered, but not surprised, Lorna was losing patience fast. No one would tell her what was happening. "Tell me what's going on and how you're involved!"

"Shower or sink drain?" Elaine asked Kellie skeptically, her eyes narrowed just a bit.

Sweat beaded on Kellie's upper lip. She glanced over to Lorna hoping for some clue. One never came. "Umm . . ."

"Well?" Elaine prodded, her back going ramrod straight. "Which is it?"

"Both," Kellie blurted. She let out a heavy breath. "Both."

Tension poured off Lorna in crashing waves. "If someone doesn't tell me what's going on, I'm going to—"

"For fuck's sake, Mally," Roscoe boomed, "put two and two together." He scrunched up his face at the gory picture Kellie presented. "Your girlfriend, Lizzy Borden, sliced up that bitch, Katrina." He snorted softly. "And here I thought she had the most influence on you with her dykey ways and had turned you gay-for-the-stay. But it turns out she picked up your fondness for stabbing people."

The color fled from Lorna's cheeks as if she were slowly being submerged in white paint. For a second her belief wavered. "Bullshit!" she finally blurted. "For once, don't be stupid, Roscoe. Kellie wouldn't hurt anyone."

Kellie's gaze drilled into hers. "That's not true, Lorna." The determined voice sounded as foreign to Kellie as the love spell Lorna had cast over her. "I did what I had to do, so there's nothing else for us to talk about." Her eyes begged Lorna to just stay out of things.

Lorna's face went deadly serious and her eyebrows rose to their zenith. "You're saying you stabbed her? *You* did that?" She tried to move closer to Kellie but was brought up short by Elaine's firm grip. "You're—you're actually agreeing with Roscoe?"

Kellie nodded slowly. Heartsick, and her stomach twisting, she muttered, "I had to do it. I told him everything. After the desk, I was just so angry. Then, somehow, she had a shank, and things got out of hand." She sniffed. "Please understand, Lorna. Please."

Lorna squeezed the sides of her own head as though it might explode at any second. It was like standing under an avalanche with her life being smashed to bits. "You *confessed?*"

"Yes."

Defiance flashed in Lorna's blue eyes. "No way." She pointed a furious finger at Kellie. "No way!" Then she whirled around. "C'mon," she begged Elaine. "You're not buying this, are you?" She threw her hands in the air before spinning back to face her partner. "Why are you doing this?" she demanded. Her heart slammed against her ribs with such force that her body shook. "Why?"

"Time to go." Roscoe's said. "Say good-bye, ladies. 'Cause you won't be seeing each other again."

Lorna's head spun. "What?" she screeched desperately, causing Elaine to tighten her grip again. "This is my fault, not Kellie's. The desk—" But everyone but Kellie had stopped listening.

They all had to step aside as Katrina, her upper body, throat and hair drenched with sticky blood, was wheeled out of her cell on a gurney by two harried paramedics. The EMT ran alongside carrying an IV bag that was hooked to Katrina.

Lorna barely gave her a second look.

Chul shivered at the gruesome sight and came to stand next to Elaine. He bounced lightly on the balls of his feet, ready to spring into action if need be.

Kellie was honestly surprised, and the tiniest bit hurt, that Lorna hadn't confessed to the crime to save *her* from more time in prison. After all, Lorna was the one who was actually guilty. *Stop being a baby. She knows it's too late now and what's done is done. It's what you wanted, so be glad it's working.* "I—" Her throat closed when she tried to say something that could convey everything she felt. Everything Lorna meant to her and how much she'd changed her life.

I do love you was poised on the tip of Kellie's tongue. But she wouldn't say it. Not for the first time . . . like this. Not when hearing it under these circumstances would probably only make Lorna feel worse.

Their eyes met again and time came to a crashing halt.

Kellie realized that it didn't matter whether she said it. Lorna already knew.

"Oh, Princess," Lorna whispered, in a stunned, heartrending voice. "What have you done?" Glistening, unshed tears made everything go blurry.

Kellie closed her eyes to block out the vision of hurt before her. She knew it would be hard. But not like this. There was still no soundtrack. Only a sickening silence.

Kellie had the overwhelming urge to crawl into a bottle and never come out.

"Time's up." Roscoe began marching Kellie down the hall. "That wasn't as touching as I'd hoped."

Several inmates sneered in his direction, hatred in their expressions.

"Stay strong, chica," Ramona said proudly as Kellie was escorted past her and through a sea of resentful, but mostly respectful, inmates.

Kellie held her chin high and did her best not to crumble. That, she knew, would happen later.

"Kellie!" Lorna roared from behind her. Elaine and Chul together could barely restrain her. "Take back the confession, goddammit! Take back what you said!"

Lorna's voice was broken by a sob and the sound nearly sent Kellie to her knees. Hot tears streamed down her cheeks. But that didn't matter now. Nothing did.

She finally loved someone more than herself. And that meant she wouldn't take it back.

Not ever.

Chapter 14
Three months later . . .

Lorna sat alone at a corner table in the cafeteria. She stared dully at her tray of food, jaded eyes unseeing. She hadn't heard a single thing from or about Kellie since she was unceremoniously escorted out of the cellblock.

And out of her life, it seemed.

Lorna had scraped and begged the guards for information only to hit a brick wall again and again. Somehow, in a place where secrets were near to impossible to keep, Kellie had simply vanished without a trace. Lorna tried her best to remain strong in the face of losing what she loved most, but the Herculean effort was wearing her painfully thin. What had happened on that terrible day ran in an endless loop in her brain.

Kellie had confessed. *Confessed.* Lorna seethed. Boiled. Twisted. But mostly she cried. She was amazed the human body could produce so many tears.

Confessed? How could someone so smart have done something so stupid? In Lorna's mind's eye, a large crimson pool came sharply into focus, its sickening scent making her wince. First, she would see her father lying in it, his mocking eyes glassy and dead. Then his body would morph into Katrina's. Silent at last. Finally, Katrina's angular face would melt into Kellie's.

It was a waking nightmare with Blood starring in the macabre show.

Was Kellie even capable of that level of violence? *Absolutely.* Lorna knew better than anyone that pushing the right buttons could turn even a gentle woman into a raging volcano. Unstoppable and deadly.

Even so, Lorna was convinced that too much about this entire mess didn't make sense for a reasonable person to believe that Kellie was a would-be murderess. When they had left the woodshop that day, Kellie wouldn't have come looking for Katrina, not even after what happened to the desk. No, even the most casual observer would wager she would have come looking for Lorna first. And even if she had gone looking for Katrina, what could have happened to cause Katrina to pull a shank?

Hatred flowed between the women like water. But loathing alone wasn't a likely motive for what happened. Katrina wanted to toy with Kellie and continually bait Lorna. Killing Kellie would have put a permanent end to her favorite sport. And even in the midst of a full-blown rage, something Lorna had seen Katrina struggle with many a time, Katrina never acted against her own self-interest. Never.

So why had Kellie confessed?

Then, as it had for weeks and weeks, the shocking answer reared up on its hind legs and slapped Lorna in the face. *She came looking for me. She confessed for me. She threw away years of her life for me.* Guilt washed over her all over again. But there was anger too. Anger that Kellie hadn't even considered that she wasn't a cold-blooded killer.

Fractured and lost, she was drowning.

Lorna wasn't completely alone. But despite Ramona's repeated attempts to pull her friend from the dark place she was in, it felt like it.

Most of the room had cleared out as the inmates headed back to the cellblock for the evening. It was time for reading or writing letters, stolen moments of socializing, or even a little bit of television if someone's bad behavior hadn't cancelled that privilege for the group. But Lorna wasn't going to do any of those things. None of them made her even want to get up from the dinner table.

Several inmates still roamed the large room, running mops over the floors and dingy damp rags over the gray picnic-style tables that were connected together like long chains. The scent of grease mixed with industrial bleach made Lorna's empty stomach lurch.

A slender dark-skinned girl in her late teens stopped in front of Lorna's table, rag in hand. She bit her lower lip and rocked back on her heels, waiting for Lorna to lift her tray so she could continue her cleaning. Lorna didn't even know she was there.

Another inmate beckoned the girl over with a frantic wave of the hand and explained that it was much safer to simply leave the con at that table alone. It was as though she wore a flashing "Do Not Disturb" sign. Katrina's cronies, and even the guards, begrudgingly respected it.

From the corner of the room, Katrina, scarred but very much alive, watched Lorna pick at her food. Always watching.

As it turned out, her concussion had been worse than the stab wound, but it was the nasty staph infection she'd picked up in the prison's medical ward that was even worse than the head injury. She'd spent weeks flat on her back, her fever raging and ebbing like a thunderstorm as she was pumped full of antibiotics.

Then there were the half dozen tortuous dental visits it took to replace the teeth she'd lost in her attack. The good news was that her new teeth almost matched the rest of her chilling smile. To say she was bitter didn't put a dent in the truth. But her health had slowly returned, and along with it, interest in her favorite obsession.

"Hello, Mally." Katrina dropped down onto the bench across from Lorna. She rested her elbows on the table. "You look like shit."

The black anger that was roiling just below the surface made a muscle in Lorna's face twitch, but she didn't answer. Instead, she stared at Katrina, who was oddly silent after her opening parry, and wondered what she had been thinking all those years ago when she'd actually spent time with this creature. "I heard you can't remember what happened the day you were attacked," she finally muttered.

"I heard your girlfriend's gone missing in action. Guess she got tired of you."

Lorna pushed her tray away and began to walk back to her cell.

"Wait!" Katrina scurried behind her, moping, disappointed that Lorna didn't want to play. "Wait up. It's Holloway's loss, right?" From the corner of her eyes she could see lines marking Lorna's face that weren't there just a few months ago. Apparently, love wasn't all it was cracked up to be. Luckily, Katrina had never bothered with it to begin with. "We need to talk."

The sarcasm was gone from her voice and Lorna was struck by how alien it made her former cellmate sound. "Katrina?"

The blond woman moved alongside Lorna, huffing a little to keep up. The fast walk made the site of her scar and chest ache. "Yeah?"

"I want you to understand something," Lorna said mildly.

"Okay."

"I have nothing left to lose."

Abruptly, Lorna stopped and focused every ounce of her attention on Katrina. "I'm having trouble actually believing that I shouldn't do the world a favor and kill you." The look in Lorna's eyes was enough for Katrina to gasp out loud.

Katrina glanced around. A few women were milling around a cell about forty feet away. But she knew they wouldn't come to her aid if she needed them. "What about your parole hearing? What is it? Six, seven months away?" She went for bravado. "You'd jeopardize that just to do something for the world? I don't think so."

Lorna cocked her head, a little dismayed that her parole date appeared to be common knowledge. "What part of 'I don't have anything to lose' wasn't clear to you, Katrina? Now go away. I'm tired and you're the last thing I want on my mind before I go to sleep." She began walking again.

"But I need your help."

"Learn to live with disappointment."

"But I'm offering something you want in return."

"You're going to slit your own throat?"

"Okay, I can offer you something else you want."

Lorna disappeared inside her cell. Her cellmate wasn't there yet, and she was glad for the moment of privacy. All except for . . .

Cast in dark shadows, Katrina stood waiting in the doorway. *Just like a vampire,* Lorna thought, *waiting for permission to enter your house so she can suck you dry.*

"Don't you want to know what I can give you?" Katrina tempted, her voice infused with honey.

Lorna stretched out on her lumpy bunk and closed her eyes. "Remember that I warned you. Remember that I gave you a chance to save yourself," she said softly.

But Lorna wasn't the only one with nothing to lose. Boldly, Katrina waltzed into her cell. In this case, however, bold didn't equal suicidal, and she made sure to stay well out of Lorna's immediate reach. "Just listen. I can make us both happy."

The only person here who made me happy is out of my reach. She would never give up on Kellic. But in her heart she was a realist, and her own experience with Meg had taught her that when someone she loved left her life, whether or not they wanted to go, they were gone for good.

"I need money."

"Wow! You were right. I'm thrilled!"

"I know you have a stash someplace. You spent too many years in the black market to be broke now. Then there's your little beauty supply business, which keeps the sows here smelling so lovely."

"My business isn't any business of yours."

"That doesn't matter. What matters is that you have money and I need it."

You've really gone around the bend for good. Lorna considered getting out of bed and strangling her. But Katrina would likely mess her cell and she wasn't up for the stink. Tomorrow in the yard. Yes, that would be better. Cleaner. That is, if her patience didn't run out before then.

"Why do you need money from me?" Lorna asked, not really

caring. "What I'm doing makes me peanuts. You're selling so many drugs in this place that you have to be raking in the dough hand over fist."

"They're sending me back to maximum security."

That got Lorna's attention, and for the first time in weeks, she smiled a real smile, even if it was an ice-cold one. "It couldn't happen to a more deserving person. On second thought, I don't think I will kill you. I like the idea of you rotting your life away in that hellhole instead." She flicked her wrist as though she was flicking a piece of lint from a sleeve. "Good riddance, bitch."

Katrina ignored Lorna's rancor. "It seems my last brush with violence has convinced the warden that I'm . . ." She sneered and her index fingers shaped quote marks. "Not suitable for the medium security environment."

"Well, no shit."

"And that's why I need your money. I need to pay a bribe. A big one." She dug into her pocket and tossed a tattered piece of paper on the desk. It contained the account information Lorna would need for a bank deposit.

The warden wasn't for sale. That much Lorna knew. He was an honest if sometimes brutal man. "You're lying."

"Most of the time," Katrina admitted easily. "Just not now. The bribe isn't for the warden, but it will get the job done all the same."

"Okay, Katrina. If it will get you out of here without my having to get up off this bed, I'll bite. Why do you think I would ever give you a red cent? You have to know that I'd rather set fire to every dollar I have and then stuff the flaming pieces of paper up my own ass before I'd help you."

"Do you whisper sweet nothings like that to your girlfriend?"

"You'll never know."

Katrina couldn't help it; she smiled like the Cheshire cat. She had Lorna exactly where she wanted her, only Lorna didn't know it yet. It was better than foreplay and she was disappointed that she needed to rush through this part and onward to the main event. But she hadn't survived this many years at Blue Ridge by accident. Lorna was a time bomb. One wrong push and Katrina's existence would explode into a world of hurt.

Losing Kellie had clearly broken something deep inside of Lorna. *Tick tock.* But that was okay. Katrina could replace that something with a feeling even better than dominating someone during sex. Together, they would rule the entire prison and everyone in it. "You're not only going to help me, you're going to be glad to do it. In fact . . ." She let out a delighted chuckle. "We're going to be partners again, you and me."

"You have three seconds to get out of my cell or only one of us will walk out of here later."

"What makes you think you can take me?" Katrina snapped.

Lorna held up her index finger. "One."

"Fine!" Katrina barked resentfully. "In return for twenty thousand dollars, and us working together . . ." Her voice shifted into a purr. "I can offer you sweet, sweet revenge."

"No deal." A second finger. "Two."

"And your snotty girlfriend's freedom. At least from the latest charge," she amended.

Lorna was off the bed so quickly that Katrina couldn't even suck in a full breath before strong hands wrapped themselves around her throat and began crushing her windpipe. She was slammed on the floor with brutal force, her legs flopping down a split second after the rest of her body. Lorna followed her down, landing on top of Katrina with her knees pinning her chest to the floor like a rug.

Katrina tried to wheeze, but she couldn't move at all, couldn't suck in even the tiniest breath. Pain exploded in more places that could register at once and the room began to swim.

"Tell me!" Lorna said from behind her teeth. "Now, you shithead!" She squeezed so hard her hands shook. "How can you free Kellie?"

Katrina's face was beet red and when she opened her mouth, not a single sound emerged. Her eyes bulged until they looked like they'd pop out.

Lorna suddenly realized that she wouldn't get answers in her current position and she pried her cramping fingers from Katrina's throat and slid her knees off her chest.

Lurid finger marks stood out against Katrina's pale throat. She choked out a weak, "Damn. Mal—"

With wicked speed, Lorna backhanded Katrina across the face, her knuckles splitting Katrina's snarling upper and lower lips, and spraying a fine mist of blood against the wall.

Addled, Katrina gasped and wheezed a few more times. She brought a quaking hand to her mouth and succeeded more in smearing the blood than wiping it away. "I was—" She wiped her mouth again, and glared hatefully at Lorna. "I was al-already telling you. You—you didn't need to do that."

"I know." Hard as diamonds, Lorna's eyes drilled holes into Katrina. "I *wanted* to do that. *How* can you give Kellie her freedom?" She paused, breathing heavily. "I wouldn't make me wait another second if I were you."

"I—I can tell the pigs who really stabbed me."

Lorna's eyes saucered. She stood, pushed Katrina away and began pacing like a caged animal, stepping over Katrina as she went. "You remember what happened? Since when?"

"This isn't *Days of our Fucking Lives*, Mally. Did you really think a crack on the head made me lose my memory? Knowledge is power. You taught me that." She rubbed her aching neck, hissing a little as her hands touched raw skin. "And what I know is worth something."

Lorna didn't deny it.

Smugly, Katrina sat part of the way up. "I was just waiting until the right time to use the information." She leaned forward a little, wary of moving too abruptly and setting Lorna off again. "And now seems like the right time."

"Bitch."

"Can I get up now?"

"No. Tell me why I shouldn't just beat the information out of you."

"Because if you do, you can't guarantee that I'll testify to whatever it is that you manage to beat out of me." She let loose with a grin that managed to be girlish and ghoulish at the same time. "I can't be trusted, you know."

Oh, she knew. Lorna squatted down over Katrina. "Who did it?"

"Nuh uh." Katrina shook her head, cringing at the pain that caused. Her ears were still ringing. "My money, and you and me back in business, first. Then you'll get your name and you can take whatever revenge you want." Her nostrils flared. "In fact, I'm counting on it."

Lorna stood and put her hands on her hips, and turned to walk out of the cell. But at the last second she changed her mind, stalked back to Katrina, and slammed a wicked kick into Katrina's ribs.

The howling woman rolled to her side, her face contorted. Tears instantly ran down her cheeks and splashed onto the concrete floor.

Lorna yanked the pillow from her bunk and held it over Katrina's face until she stopped screaming. "That's for Kellie! Now shut up!"

It took a few seconds, but Katrina began to control herself.

Slowly Lorna lifted the pillow, not allowing Katrina's bloody, panic-stricken expression to sink in deep enough for her to feel anything other than anger. Neither pity nor kindness could help Kellie now. She needed to be brutal. Cold. "Pray nothing's happened to Kellie while you were keeping this information to yourself. Remember what I said about having nothing to lose?"

Katrina nodded frantically. "I 'member."

"Good." Lorna grabbed Katrina by the collar and began dragging her across the cell. When she reached the door, she used all her waning strength to simply toss her out into the hallway. "You'll have your money." She paused, a low sigh trickling out. "And me, by tomorrow night."

Chapter 15
The next day . . .

Lorna bounced the basketball a few times before taking an unen-thusiastic shot. A thunderstorm had meant that her time in the yard was cancelled, but she was free to use the gymnasium. She retrieved the ball, breathing heavily after only a few minutes of shooting.

It was hard to care, but she knew she needed to start taking better care of herself. As she'd wrestled with all-out depression, she'd let herself go and knew she should be embarrassed by that fact. She vowed to eat dinner even though the food tasted like sawdust with a hefty dose of salt on top.

She tried a layup and missed. *You and me*, Katrina had said. God, just the thought made her sick. In her pocket was a deposit slip showing the transfer of funds from her account into Katrina's. Elaine had easily complied with the request that had wiped out Lorna's savings. Only a hundred dollars and some change remained.

Curious, Lorna thought, that the balance of her account was

almost the exact amount that Katrina had demanded.

Then again, what did she need with the money? Once Katrina got her hooks in her, there was no way she would let go. Lorna was certain that somehow the guards would find contraband in her cell, or that she'd magically be involved in a fight that would guarantee the denial of her parole. The years at Blue Ridge stretched out before her in a hopeless, never ending line.

She gritted her teeth and picked up the ball, making a long jump shot.

"Nice shot."

Lorna closed her eyes briefly, and steeled herself before turning to see Katrina.

The woman's mouth was swollen and a single stitch marred her thin upper lip. "Is it done?"

Lorna glanced around self-consciously before discreetly handing Katrina the deposit slip. She retrieved the worn basketball and set it in a rack along the wall.

Katrina eyed the paper carefully, wary of any tricks as she followed Lorna. "Good job. I wasn't sure you'd think Holloway was worth it."

Lorna's jaw clenched. "She's worth it. How's your memory, Katrina? Getting better, I hope."

"It's suddenly gotten twenty thousand percent better. Thank you for asking."

Lorna sat down on a bench, scooting over a little when Katrina joined her. "So, who attacked you?" She leaned forward a little in anticipation.

"Why did your girlfriend do it?" Katrina was genuinely curious. "Why take the fall for someone else?"

"The name."

"No way. We do a few drug deals together just so I make sure that you're really back into the fold and *then* you get the name."

Lorna looked straight ahead as she spoke. Several women gaped at the sight of them sitting together and having a civil conversation. *Let them look.* "I didn't suddenly get stupid. It's like you said, you can't be trusted. Give me the name and then we'll do business. I already coughed up my money, now it's your turn."

Katrina narrowed her eyes. She recognized the inflexible tone of Lorna's voice. Cement. "Okay," she allowed cautiously. "I'll tell you. And then I assume that you'll be letting this person know how unhappy you are about what they did to me?"

Lorna cast her a doubtful expression.

Katrina rolled her eyes. "Okay, let them know how unhappy you are about them letting your girlfriend take the fall for something she didn't do?" Katrina watched a myriad of emotions crawl across Lorna's face, each one more dangerous than the last. She salivated over the destruction Lorna would inflict. There was something terrifically satisfying about having someone else do your dirty work.

"Oh, you don't have to worry about that." She turned to face Katrina. "You have proof of your claim, other than your no-good word?"

Katrina had been expecting that. "I have enough tidbits to lead the state to the right conclusion without me going down the drain in the process."

Lorna nodded.

"But a confession would really help."

Lorna let go of a chilling grin. "That won't be a problem."

Katrina laughed and gave Lorna a friendly slap on the back. "I can see that, Mally. I'm nearly peeing myself and I'm not the one who'll be confessing."

"A name, Katrina. I want a name."

Katrina wiped her lips with the back of her hand, then leaned over and whispered into her new partner's ear.

Lorna's mouth dropped open. Jesus. "You'd better have proof."

"I do."

Chapter 16
The next morning . . .

Lorna stood in the laundry room folding her clothes. Katrina walked in and ordered the room's occupants to get out. "You can stay," she crisply informed Lorna.

"No? Really?" But she watched in shock when the other women obeyed without question. How had she missed this? Katrina had been growing more powerful while she'd been busy . . . falling in love.

Suddenly, it was very hard to breathe.

"I've got something you've been waiting for, Mally. Wait here."

"Where else do I have to go?" Lorna muttered to herself.

Katrina left the room and for a few minutes Lorna was alone with only the sound of the dryer to break the silence. Shaking her head, she put her container of soap in the bottom of her laundry bag, and then added a pair of well-worn jeans and a sweatshirt. She wanted to help Kellie now. Not later. Not tomorrow. *Now.* Waiting was never her strong suit.

Next Laverne walked in. And she wasn't alone.

Lorna released a shuddering breath when she saw Laverne's companion. *Thank Christ.* This was the beginning of the end of this entire mess.

"Signed sealed and delivered," Laverne muttered, having memorized the words just as she'd been instructed. She glanced around nervously. "I'll just leave you two alone."

The room's third occupant looked surprised when Laverne nearly tripped over herself in her haste to get to the door. "What the hell is going on?"

Lorna set her laundry to one side and lifted her gaze.

Unbidden, the rage inside her began to build. Fiery and destructive. "Did you think you'd get away with letting Kellie take the fall for your crime?" Lorna took a menacing step forward, her chest rising and falling fast. "You're going to make everything all right now." *Or we'll both die trying.*

Chapter 17
Two weeks later . . .

Kellie sat hugging her knees to her chest on her bunk in the protective custody unit of Sugar Land, a women's prison that was located more than a hundred miles from Blue Ridge. This was her new home and she'd yet to see anything other than the processing room, conference room, and the solitary confinement unit. She would be here for God only knew how long.

The guard who'd driven her to her new home, a talkative woman with a thick southern accent, had commented idly that she'd be getting new clothes. *Who the hell cares?* Kellie had thought glumly, having far more on her mind than clothes. But her indifference over shedding her ever-present jeans and T-shirt had quickly been replaced by disbelief the moment she first saw her new garb. She now wore a two-piece white outfit complete with black prison stripes, a la the 1930s.

The facility itself was a little newer, but otherwise identical to the one she'd recently left. She wondered idly if the boring, drab layouts and buildings were part of some master plan. Bore prisoners to death. Make them so depressed they'll kill themselves and save the state some money. Then again, the only difference between Sugar Land and Blue Ridge that really mattered was that Lorna wasn't here.

Kellie sighed and tried to focus on the good times they'd shared. The times that made life in a cage bearable and allowed her to feel human instead of like a nameless con. The laughing and friendship. The kissing. The sex. *God, the sex.* A tremor ran through her.

Kellie knew those memories should make her feel good. A bigger person would be happy to have finally and completely loved someone, even if she lost her in the end. She wasn't, Kellie discovered about herself, a very big person at all. This sucked. All of it. Thinking about what they had and the spectacular life they could have built together did nothing but make her miserable.

Whoever said it was better to have loved and lost than never to have loved at all . . . hadn't been in love with Lorna. No matter how Kellie searched her heart, she couldn't find a way to get over her. Even though her circumstance left precious few other options lest she truly lose her mind.

Her attorney had made it clear that her self-defense claim in Katrina's attack was a loser argument. She simply had no evidence to back her up claim. Considering that the entire story was a complete lie, Kellie wasn't exactly surprised. So now, with her chances at being paroled a thing of the past, she'd serve her entire original sentence, and then the years she'd receive for the Attempted Murder charge she was fighting. All in all she was looking at a minimum of ten more years in prison, but fifteen was more likely.

If Lorna made parole, and if there was a God, she would, she'd be released later in the year. The younger woman had already lost so much of her life, how could Kellie expect that she'd wait for her? She rolled her eyes. She wouldn't expect that of anyone. But what would she do if the situations were reversed? Would she wait? Did she have a choice given how she felt?

She had, she realized, far more questions than answers. A desperate, lonely feeling swept over her.

She stood and began doing jumping jacks in place just to have something to do. "I will not go crazy. I will not!" she chanted, swinging her arms wildly to get the blood pumping. "Think of something else. Anything else before you go mad." She couldn't tell how much of her melancholy was a side effect of her isolation and how much was due to the fact that her life was completely and utterly hosed.

She'd known that going through with her plan to protect Lorna wouldn't be easy. But she'd never imagined that it would mean moving prisons. Apparently—and her lawyer had explained this as though he were talking to a slow child—when one inmate attacks another, and serious injury results, it's common for the women not only to be physically separated, but for any ability to communicate with each other, prison gangs or mutual associates to be severed pending a full investigation by the state. That meant a transfer.

Common sense, she supposed. But it still wasn't something she'd been mentally prepared for. *I didn't really get to say good-bye. Not like I wanted to. Not like she deserved.* One minute she'd been looking into Lorna's ravaged eyes, then, before she knew it, she sat shackled in the back of a prison van, speeding to Sugar Land. *God.*

A shadow darkened her doorway and she stopped her exercise, praying that someone was there to stop and talk to her.

A short, stout guard with a shaved head and heavy, black plastic glasses began unlocking her cell door. "C'mon, Holloway. DA wants a word with you."

Kellie blinked at him. "I'm not supposed to meet with him until the end of next week. My lawyer—"

The guard adjusted his keys on his belt. "Your mouthpiece is already in the conference room waiting for you."

Anxiety began to brew in the pit of her stomach. Absently, she put her wrists together and stuck them out in front of her so she could be cuffed. She was used to this routine. "What's going on?"

"I dunno. But it's big." He fastened the cuffs and they began walking together. "Boss told me to gather your things."

"What?" she screeched. "I'm being moved again? But just to the main cellblock, right?"

The guard shrugged. "Don't know. Was just told to gather them up and bring them back to the processing office."

"Man, oh, man," Kellie whispered to herself. What if Ramona had spilled the beans? Or what if the state had somehow found proof against Lorna that made the confession irrelevant? Or what if Katrina had convinced someone important that Kellie wasn't her attacker. Or what if—

"Lift 'em." At the door of the conference room, Kellie lifted her hands and her handcuffs were removed.

Kellie opened the door to see her lawyer and the DA chatting like they were old friends. Her eyes narrowed. She wanted them to be enemies like she now was with her own government.

"Well, Ms. Holloway, I've got some wonderful news!" Her young state-appointed defense attorney, with his earnest face and cheap suit, beamed.

I'll bet this is his first real case. I'm going to end up in the electric chair.

"Hello, Doogie."

His cheeks turned pink and Kellie rolled her eyes.

"Umm . . . my name, in case you forgot again, is umm . . . Alan Corbin, Ms. Holloway."

Alan pulled out Kellie's chair while still managing to stand as far away from her as possible. His hands shook a little when he pushed the chair in.

She quirked a smile in thanks as she sat and tried to look dignified while wearing an outfit better suited for Al Capone. It was still a mystery to her that anyone would be afraid of her. The kid was a chickenshit and his career was going to eat him for lunch, but at least he had manners. Unlike . . .

"But there are conditions."

Kellie gave Assistant District Attorney Max Greenberg a sour look. Though any reprieve from her cell was a good one, this man was almost enough to make her reconsider her opinion. He reminded her of a more refined, slightly older Roscoe. Same enormous asshole, only with a better shoes, and hair that was graying at the temples.

"Aren't there always?"

He inclined his head, acknowledging the truth in her statement.

"Let's cut to the chase, shall we? I've got a very long drive back home."

Greenberg looked terribly annoyed by that fact, which pleased Kellie. It was immature, she knew, but . . .

With a loud thump, the DA set Kellie's case file on the table in front of him. Then he steepled his fingers and looked right through Kellie. "I know you didn't attack Katrina Nowak."

Kellie's stomach dropped, but she forced a smirk in place. "You do, huh?"

"Someone else has confessed, but this time there is physical evidence to back it up." He gave her a challenging look.

Kellie gripped the arms of her chair so tight she heard the plastic groan. *Lorna confessed? No!*

"And I intend to prosecute the *true* perpetrator of this crime to the fullest extent of the law for this. That means you will recant your false confession immediately."

Kellie raised an eyebrow. "No," she said simply.

Greenberg slapped his open hand down on the table. "What do you mean, no? What is wrong with you? Do you want to stay in prison until you're old enough to be a grandmother?"

Kellie could practically see the wheels in his head turning.

"Is someone forcing you to do this?" Greenberg asked aggressively.

Kellie glared right back. "*I'm* forcing myself to do this." And that was a truer statement than she realized. It wasn't easy going against your own nature, and Kellie had no delusions about her mile wide self-preservation streak. Precious few things trumped it. But it just so happened that how she felt about Lorna was one of those things.

"Ms. Holloway," her defense attorney began in a calming voice, "you don't understand. I would advise—"

Kellie crossed her arms over her chest and kept her focus on the DA. "It doesn't matter what you advise, Junior. My answer is still N-O. My confession stands."

The older man leaned back in his chair and let out an explosive breath. He appeared to be sizing her up.

Greenberg unconsciously fingered with his cuff links. When he spoke, his voice was laced with resentment. "I've already laid out a very agreeable deal with your attorney, Ms. Holloway. You can be a free woman by the end of the day." He spread his arms wide. "What more do you want?"

Years of experience in negotiating her own contracts barely kept her from passing out of the spot. *Free?* Could they want Lorna that badly? "Ex—" she cleared her throat to keep her next words from sounding unnaturally high. She had to have heard him wrong. Yes, that was it. She'd misunderstood. Free didn't really mean free, as in going home. And she'd learned that there were levels of freedom within the prison walls. "Excuse me?"

"I said," Greenberg bit out crisply, "what do you want? Two confessions to the same crime could lead to reasonable doubt, and I won't have you messing up my case. This is going to lead me to a big fish, Ms. Holloway, not a pissant guppy like you. I'm putting you in the catch and release pile . . ." He tucked his pen behind his ear. "For now."

Kellie squared her shoulders and lied through her teeth, putting even the hint of true freedom out of her mind. She'd made her decision. "Lorna Malachi had nothing to do with Katrina's attack. I know that for a fact and I'll testify to that. I won't help you put her away for a crime she didn't commit."

The men looked at each other in confusion. Greenberg's bushy eyebrows contracted. "And who is Lorna Malachi again?" He began thumbing through a thick file in front of him.

Kellie's forehead wrinkled. She was so deeply adrift that she didn't know what to say or when to lie anymore. "I—I." She clamped her mouth shut, deciding silence was the smartest route at the moment.

"There seems to be some confusion here." The DA spoke without looking up from his papers. "I'm not about to divulge information concerning our current suspect, but I can assure you that it's not Ms. Malachi. She's not being charged at all in this case."

Kellie's mouth dropped open. She couldn't stop herself from blurting, "What?"

Greenberg blinked a few times. "I think you heard me."

"She's not being charged?" *What the fuck!* "She's not even a suspect?"

The DA's eyes slitted and he slid the case file aside so he could lean forward, hungry to hear more. "Should she be?"

"I—I . . ." Kellie shot to her feet. "No! Of course not!"

"Ms. Holloway, please." Her attorney glanced worriedly at the top half of the door, which held a large window. An antsy-looking guard stood just outside. "Prisoners must remain seated at all times. Otherwise, they'll shackle you to the table."

Kellie hastily sat back down. Okay, so maybe this was his second case. "Let me get this straight." Her distressed voice rose with every word. "Someone else, as in not Lorna and not me, is being charged with the crime that I confessed to?"

"Yes," the men both said in unison. Their twin sighs made it clear they were relieved to finally be on the same sheet of music.

Kellie couldn't believe what she was hearing. "How do I know this isn't a trick?"

"Why would I do that?" Greenberg spluttered. "I already have your confession!"

"Prove you're not going after Lorna," Kellie insisted stubbornly. "Prove it or I won't take back my confession."

Greenberg's beady eyes caught fire. "I will not jeopardize my case by—"

"Let me see the charging documents," Alan said, holding out his hand. "I can verify you're telling the truth easily enough."

Greenberg ground his teeth. "I haven't even filed them yet. They're only preliminary and—"

"But there's a name on them, right? For Christ's sake, Max, you're going to file them tomorrow anyway." Alan held out his hand again.

Grumbling all the while, Greenberg passed over the papers for Alan to review, then, after a few seconds, he yanked them back and frowned unbecomingly as though his opponent had just peeked at his cards during a game of poker.

Alan confirmed, "Lorna Malachi's name is not there, Ms. Holloway."

Kellie still wasn't sure she could trust him. She wanted to, but her judgment was clearly crap. And hadn't he just called the DA by his first name? They were probably golfing buddies or something equally nauseating and had cooked up this little trick somewhere around the ninth hole. Then she took a good look at them, sitting on opposite sides of the table.

Alan had an open, honest face. He'd probably gone to law school to save the world and crusade for justice. He would be making thirty grand a year for the rest of his rewarding, but disrespected, days. Life was not fair.

Greenberg, however, was pure shark. Public office was no doubt in his future. No, he wasn't spending his time in the minor leagues concocting lies with a state-appointed defense attorney.

Sometimes, she decided, you just have to close your eyes and jump. "Okay, I believe you."

"So long as it's not you being charged, does it really matter who is?" Greenberg asked, clearly astounded. This case didn't appear to have gang implications. Those were the few times where inmates seemed to spare a thought for anyone but themselves. And even those misguided, but genuine, displays of loyalty were rare. Whatever hold this Lorna woman had on Kellie Holloway, it was strong as steel and went right to the bone.

"It matters," Kellie confirmed quietly, still too stunned to think of anything else to say. *Oh, my God. She didn't do it? I . . . She . . . I never even considered that! I just assumed. That's why she looked so confused. Oh, Christ, I'm an idiot! I did this for nothing and if she ever figures out why she's going to hate me.*

Kellie's heart seized in her chest. Lorna had worked so hard to outrun her past and become a better person. And the one person who should have believed in her no matter what assumed the very worst without a second's hesitation. Shame burned inside her.

A visible vein in Greenberg's forehead began to throb in time with his pulse. "I don't know what your game is, Holloway. But you've wasted a lot of people's time with your lies! Normally . . ." His lips tightened as he struggled to control himself. "I'd do my best to make sure that you paid for that."

Kellie's attorney broke into the conversation, which seemed to be quickly devolving into a shouting match. "But in this instance he needs your cooperation and so he's willing to be gracious and make some allowances, right?" Alan waved off the guard, who was now peering worriedly into the window.

Kellie saw a tiny opening, and though she was almost certain it wouldn't work, she jumped on it. "What about a deal for Lorna? If you want my cooperation, you can make allowances for her too."

"Who is this person?" Greenberg asked angrily. "And why isn't she in my file?"

She's everything. "A . . . friend."

His eyebrows crawled to the very top of his forehead. "A friend with direct knowledge of this case that helps the state?"

Kellie hesitated.

"I can see your answer is no." The skin around Greenberg's eyes tensed. "That's not how this system works. Ever. Don't think that I won't proceed with my case without your cooperation, if you insist on something that is *impossible.*"

Kellie could see by his demeanor that this was a deal breaker. She suspected it would be, and wasn't even sure that it would be legal in the first place, but she had to try. She believed Greenberg's threat, but still had to literally bite her tongue to keep from pressing the issue.

Alan gently redirected the conversation. "You were discussing cooperation and allowances for Ms. Holloway . . ."

Greenberg scowled and took a calming breath. "Your confession, Ms. Holloway, complicates my case. I want you to recant. And I want it to happen today."

"And in exchange? Go, on. Tell her," the other man urged.

Greenberg sighed out loud as though this pained him greatly. "In exchange, we drop all charges in this case and accelerate the time frame for your eligibility for parole."

Kellie's jaw sagged and when she tried to speak, her voice was nothing but a croak. She'd expected them to say they were freeing her from solitary confinement so that she could join the rest of the prison population. "Accelerate?"

Greenberg nodded seriously. "There are papers for you to sign, of course. And I'll need a full and *accurate* accounting of what actually happened between you and Ms. Nowak on the date in question."

Alan opened his briefcase and pushed a pile of crumpled but offi-
cial-looking documents in front of Kellie for her review. "I took the
liberty of filling out the paperwork necessary for your parole hearing
on your behalf. It was submitted several days ago in absentia as part
of this special arrangement with the prosecutor's office."

"Can you do that? Have the hearing without me?" Kellie gaped.
"I didn't even get to testify on my own behalf!"

"I can do a lot more than that," Greenberg muttered smugly.

Alan ignored him and spoke in his best lawyer voice. "I've
reviewed the pertinent documents and everything is in order. Upon
compliance with the DA's requests for information, and agreement
to the terms of your parole, which are standard, your request for
parole has been granted, the four-month investigative period waived,
and the length of your reporting period reduced to six months. You'll
be free to go, Ms. Holloway. I've even arranged for a ride into town
once you leave Sugar Land."

The young man grinned toothily. It was obvious that his side
didn't come out on top very often. "Oh, and your first appointment
with your parole officer is Monday morning at seven thirty. I have
that information and his card for you here someplace." He began
rooting through his messy briefcase once again. "Let me see . . ."

Kellie felt lightheaded. *Free.* She sprang to her feet and wrapped
her arms around a startled Alan, knocking the papers in his hand to
the table as she hugged the man with all her might.

Greenberg was too shocked to speak, much less call for a guard.
All he could do was stare with a slightly resentful look on his face.

"You're the best lawyer ever, Alan Corbin," she whispered hoarsely
into his ear. "You saved my life."

He returned her embrace with a hug of his own, albeit a brief
one.

She was shaking as she sat back down and began scanning the
mountain of papers, her heart in her throat. She glanced up nervously. "Tell me where to start."

Greenberg pulled his pen from behind his ear and tossed it, along
with a notepad, at Kellie. "Was Ms. Nowak already injured when

you entered her cell?"

Kellie picked up the pen and positioned the pad in front of her. She gave her lawyer a questioning look.

He nodded confidently. It was time for Kellie to spill her guts. "Yes."

"Then start there." Greenberg kicked his legs out to the side and crossed them at the ankle. They were going to be here awhile. "For now, that will be our beginning."

Kellie almost burst into happy tears. This was someone else's beginning. For her, a living nightmare was about to end.

"What do you mean I can't have any contact with inmates?" Kellie roared as she paced the conference room, gesturing wildly. Her face was brick red and she knew her blood pressure had to be through the roof.

Alan, who was now alone with Kellie, and reviewing the terms of her parole, looked like he wanted to slink under the table. "Ms. Holloway, there are conditions to being released on parole. And that one is standard." His gaze strayed to the door for the twentieth time that day. "Now please sit down. I hate talking to clients when they're chained to the table."

"You don't understand."

He held up a hand to stop what was likely to be an impassioned argument that would be totally wasted on him. "I can't change these conditions. They're set by the parole board and non-negotiable." He stopped and scratched his jaw. "Well, I take that back. You could decide not to accept them and serve out the entire remainder of your sentence instead."

Kellie stopped dead in her tracks.

"Exactly. Besides, what good could come from allowing contact between parolees and inmates still serving time? You're supposed to be transitioning into your new life on the outside, not looking backward by associating with criminals."

Kellie's hackles rose and it must have showed on her face because Alan murmured a quick, "No offense."

Kellie rubbed her temples. She'd been in this room for seven straight hours. "It would do me a lot of good."

He blinked. "How?"

It would let me explain myself to Lorna, you twit! She rolled her eyes at herself admitting that wasn't an exactly compelling argument. Frustrated, she plopped down in her chair. "You don't understand," she said quietly. "I really need to get word to someone on the inside. It's important that she know . . ." *That she's not alone.* "It's just important."

"Let me guess." He offered a sympathetic smile. "Lorna Malachi?"

Bleakly, Kellie nodded, forcing back the tears that had wanted to come all afternoon. They were ridiculous, she knew. She should be turning cartwheels right now. But the stress and fear of a new prison and plain missing her lover were taking its toll. She promised that she'd sleep for twenty-four hours straight upon her release. But because she had exactly eleven dollars to her name and didn't know a soul closer than two hundred miles away—not that any of her former friends or family would give her the time of day now anyway—she'd be sleeping on the street tonight.

That was something she wouldn't have considered in her wildest dreams only two years ago. Under the circumstances, however, it sounded surprisingly doable. Maybe she could find a nice park bench with a drinking fountain nearby.

Alan's voice took on a surprisingly fierce edge. "Don't even think about violating parole. I mean it. Any violation, even one that seems small to you, could be catastrophic. You planted Ms. Malachi's name in Max Greenberg's head. Don't think he won't be following up on your friend." He gave her a meaningful look. "If he ever found out . . ."

Her eyes blazed. "One personal visit? What could that hurt? I don't have state secrets to pass. I can say I'm her sister."

He lifted a doubtful eyebrow to let her know what he thought of that plan. "Then there is your parole officer. These guys are a cross between a foaming-at-the-mouth bulldog and Sherlock Homes. If you mess up, they *will* be all over you. They live to put violators back behind bars."

"A phone call?"

"That's still contact. The conditions of your parole are clear."

"How about a letter?"

Alan loosened his necktie. "Am I still speaking English? You know incoming mail is read. And you'd still be violating your parole. It's only six months." He could see the stubborn set of Kellie's jaw and tried another route. "Your friend wouldn't want you to risk your freedom, would she?"

Kellie nibbled her bottom lip, then dropped her forehead to the table, banging it on the cool wood a few times for good measure. "Crap, Alan," she groaned.

He rubbed the back of his neck for an awkward moment before dropping his hand to gently pat her back. He sighed. "Do you feel better?"

"No."

"Good. Shall we discuss the last condition of your parole? This is the one that makes grown men cry."

"Go on."

He hesitated as if warding off an expected blow. "No alcohol."

She lifted her head and leveled a penetrating gaze at him. "Thank God."

Chapter 18
Two hours later . . .

Kellie stepped out into the fresh air wearing the same clothes she'd had when she entered county jail. They were baggy, but still felt incredibly soft and downright decadent. She sucked in a lungful of air feeling thrilled, uneasy and alone, all at once.

Alan Corbin stood next to her at the curb. "Good luck, Ms. Holloway. Your ride should be here soon. I said six o'clock." He glanced down at this watch. "It's already ten minutes after."

A ride. She'd forgotten. "Is it a taxi or shuttle service?" It was a long ride into town and she hoped somehow he'd be reimbursed for the expense. She certainly couldn't cover it.

"Your parents."

Her eyes popped wide open. "You called my *parents*?" The last time her parents had been called to come get her had been in the fifth grade when she'd thrown up on her teacher in homeroom. And even then her father had sent his secretary because the school couldn't locate her mother and he was busy showing a house. "So they're coming to get me?"

Alan had the good graces to look a little embarrassed. "Their number was in the file, but, umm . . ."

"They had a prior engagement?" Kellie didn't sound surprised.

He looked relieved that she hadn't fallen apart at the news "Yes. But they said they would arrange for someone to come and get you."

Kellie nodded. It would be a cab driver's lucky day then, which was fine by her. That way she could avoid the inevitable, uncomfortable conversation with her mother.

No, the taxi would fine, thank you very much. Not that she'd made up her mind on where to direct it. Alan had given her a list of local shelters and other public or religious facilities for women in her situation, and though they sounded about as appealing as Blue Ridge or Sugar Land, they were probably better than risking a loitering charge. Normally, she wouldn't be released without showing that she had a place to stay. But Alan had personally vouched for her with the parole board. And apparently that was good enough.

The young defense attorney looked genuinely torn about leaving Kellie in the parking lot. "You'll be all right?"

Kellie smiled warmly. He really was cute in a crumpled, bookwormy sort of way. "I'll be fine." She hugged him again and whispered a question into his ear.

He pulled away, considering her words. "That, I can do. You have my card?"

She patted the pocket of her slacks and stepped aside.

With a wave, he began to walk toward the parking lot.

"Mr. Corbin?"

Surprised by the formality, Alan stopped and turned, lifting his brows in question.

"You really are the best lawyer."

A smile as wide as the Mississippi stretched his cheeks. "Stay out of trouble," he reminded her.

"I will." And she meant it.

She took a seat on the curb, setting a bag with her few possessions down next to her, and watched idly as Alan disappeared into the parking lot, not surprised when he drove away in an electric car. "Figures," she chuckled softly.

Kellie stretched out and let the sun warm her face. The weather was balmy and a light breeze danced across her skin, creating a riot of sensations. She soaked in the magic of the moment and fought the urge to worry about what she couldn't control as she waited.

Even when she first left home she'd had a detailed plan. Which college, which major, even which dormitory she would stay in. She'd never truly been at loose ends the way she was now. But for all her planning—Lorna had hit the nail on the head—she wasn't happy.

For now, she decided, she would take things one day at a time.

She could hear a car approaching from around the blind side of the building and she stood and brushed off her pants, hoping it was her taxi. It would be nice to settle in someplace before dark. Tomorrow she would use her money to start making phone calls and rebuilding her life.

A gleaming Cadillac pulled up. The driver rolled down his window. "Ms. Holloway?"

Kellie nodded and silently slid into the backseat, the leather feeling luxurious against her skin.

"I have a note for you, ma'am." He passed back a folded slip of paper.

Kellie fingered the paper as the car pulled away. "Well, what do you know," she said softly, shaking her head in amazement.

The driver peered into his rearview mirror. "Ma'am? Did you say something?"

Kellie sighed. "Hell is freezing over." She crumpled up the note. "The black sheep of the family is being welcomed back into the fold."

Chapter 19

Three weeks later . . .

A Newjack led Lorna to one of Blue Ridge's prisoner visitation rooms, making her all the more uneasy. The new guard had plucked her from the woodshop where she was sanding down a tall curio cabinet. No one ever came to visit her. Everyone knew that. So either this guy was as dumb as he looked, or something was up. She stepped into the room, leaving the guard outside, not knowing what to expect.

"Please sit down."

Lorna narrowed her eyes at the suit that was already reclining in the uncomfortable molded plastic chairs. She jerked a thumb at her own chest. "You're here to talk to me?"

"Are you Lorna Malachi?"

She kept her voice neutral, and except for an almost imperceptible narrowing of her eyes, managed to do the same with her expression. "Who wants to know?"

The man chuckled. With Lorna had come the faint earthy scent of freshly cut wood. And he instantly decided it was much better than the stale cigarette odor he usually had to endure. "I do." He gestured to the empty chair across from him. "Please have a seat, Ms. Malachi."

Dread swam in her belly as she eased into the chair, not bothering to lean back. She wouldn't be here long enough to try to get comfortable.

"My name is Assistant District Attorney Greenberg." He pursed his lips and tapped his chin with his index finger as he muttered, "You really don't look anything like I thought you would."

After his intriguing meeting with Kellie Holloway, he'd researched the mysterious woman who had very nearly cost him his deal. What had the guards he'd spoken to been thinking? Lorna was younger and more . . . wholesome looking than he'd imagined.

She had an impressive reputation to be sure, especially in the maximum security wing, but now as he looked at the face of everyone's All-American kid sister, he scoffed, wondering how well-deserved the reputation could really be.

Lorna sprang up from her seat, her eyes suddenly hard. "I don't talk to *you people*." She straightened, visibly restraining her sudden temper. "So I'll be heading back to work." She turned and headed for the door, then bit back a virulent curse when she found it locked.

Interesting. "I'm afraid my invitation isn't voluntary."

Lorna spun on her heel and marched back to his chair, creating a surprisingly menacing presence as she loomed over him, though he wasn't sure whether it was intentional. "Go to hell, shyster pig." She crisply enunciated every word, and then shocked him by smiling so sweetly it was downright disconcerting.

He grinned wanly, trying not to feel the prickle of worry that made him uneasy. "Guess that answers that question."

Chapter 20
Three months later . . .

The mournful wail of a saxophone filled the candlelit room as men and women dressed in all black and white swayed on the dance floor. Drink in hand, Kellie sat alone at the bar, her silver-colored sequined dress glimmering regally as she stared at the bubbles in the amber liquid in morbid fascination.

No one from Blue Ridge would recognize me. Weeks of jogging in the fresh morning air, along with a healthy diet and a reasonable amount of sleep had transformed her thin body into something fit and healthy. The dark circles that had become a permanent fixture on her face were gone, and her skin had a rosy glow.

The lines that had started to form at the corners of her eyes while in Blue Ridge were still there though, and nothing short of plastic surgery or Botox, something her mother wholeheartedly advocated, would change that. But Kellie had graciously declined her mother's offer to pay to have them removed. She'd earned them the hard way and had no urge to start that particular losing battle.

The first chance she'd had, she'd shorn her long hair, wearing it stylish and short, not wanting to see the lost woman who desperately missed her lover looking back at her when she gazed in the mirror.

It hadn't worked.

She stared at the glass again, knowing its call to be stronger than any siren's. Suddenly, it was hard to remember why she should bother to resist at all. Martini lunches. Client receptions. After-dinner nego-tiations. It was *everywhere* in this stilted world where Lorna wouldn't fit in for even a second.

Lorna was too good for this crowd.

"So . . ." Her father stiffly sidled up to her and gazed out at his guests in satisfaction. He was a short man with a barrel chest, perfectly trimmed silver hair, and a perpetually sugary smile that reminded Kellie of an eager used-car salesman. They didn't look alike at all, except for their stone-gray eyes that would darken when provoked to anger.

Kellie had to acknowledge that he'd made incredible strides with his business in the last couple of years and he was currently at the top of his game, so much so that he could afford to offer a very slender, shaky olive branch to his only child upon her release from prison. He was finally at a place in his career where he could, just barely, afford to risk the raised eyebrows of his peers.

Kellie had reluctantly accepted the branch, still not sure whether it was genuine or whether that even mattered. It was a chance to get on her feet when she desperately needed one and she'd paid her parents back by working hard not to disappoint them.

Mr. Holloway leaned his elbows back on the mahogany bar. "Are you enjoying the party?"

"I'm still surprised you invited me," she said honestly, swirling her drink, and continuing to stare at those tiny bubbles, eyes fixed.

"Nonsense, Kellie!" Covertly, he glanced around the room to see whether anyone had heard her unexpected and rather unflattering comment. "Your hard work is part of the reason we're here."

It was her parents' fortieth wedding anniversary, but what they were really celebrating was the recent sale of a forty-story office building, a deal that, at her father's insistence, they'd worked together, with the senior Holloway taking the lead. Her father's commission would be staggering.

She'd burned the midnight oil for weeks on end, focusing on this project alone while only sparing an hour or so a day to help regain her physical health and nothing else. But like slipping into a well-worn pair of shoes it was frighteningly easy to fall back into most of her old ways. Add a scheming girlfriend and a fully stocked bar at her beck and call and it would be as though the last few years had never happened.

She was good at what she did and now even her parents were forced to acknowledge that fact. Their approval was something that had eluded her for so long she'd stopped trying to attain it and she wasn't sure what to do with her conflicting emotions now that she had it.

"More champagne?" her father asked. "You've been staring at that full glass all night." He made a face. "It must be warm by now."

"It's fine," Kellie assured him absently, waving off the bartender who had scurried over at Mr. Holloway's reproving look.

It was barely nine o'clock but she wanted to go home—which, for now, was a lovely condo her parents sometimes used when they didn't want to fight the traffic on their long drive back to their lake home. They'd offered it to her for as long as she needed it . . . so long as she worked for them. They hadn't come out and said it, but it was clear they wanted to keep an eye on her to minimize the likelihood of any further family embarrassment. Free use of the condo had been another surprise and one with more strings than a spider's web.

Freedom, she decided, was a very relative concept. She smiled inwardly at the pun.

Kellie's gaze flickered around the room. "Where's Mother?"

Mr. Holloway gestured with his chin to a table of women near the dance floor. "She's with Cindy." He took a big gulp of champagne, then set his glass down next to him, eyes still riveted on the younger woman talking to his wife. "Too bad you let that one get away, Kellie." The corner of his mouth quirked upward. "She's a looker."

The muscles in Kellie's jaw bunched and she gripped her glass so tightly she thought it might shatter. Cindy was much more than that. But what made Kellie most ashamed was the knowledge that even after understanding a good portion of what Cindy was, at one time she'd been more than willing to overlook it all on her persistent march to the top.

A seductive cocktail of beauty and raw need, Cindy was truly ugly on the inside, and by the time anyone realized it, her fangs were embedded far too deeply in their guts to be removed without tearing away flesh. The traitor who had very nearly ruined her life had somehow, at the last moment, escaped prosecution and had convinced Kellie's own parents that any wrongs she'd *allegedly* committed were nothing more than fairy tales made up by an overzealous prosecutor or things he'd tricked her into saying. There was no doubt in Kellie's mind that the woman had more lives than an alley cat and claws that were twice as sharp.

In an interesting twist of fate, the wily blonde was currently working with a prominent acquaintance of her parents, a powerful broker whom her parents wanted to keep nice and close. For reasons unknown to Kellie, the broker felt the same way about her parents.

How very convenient for them all.

Cindy openly exploited her sex appeal, though Kellie knew she despised men in general. And the broker was old enough to be her father. She was most certainly doing her best to suck him dry financially, and any other way he required, but Kellie's parents would hear nothing against the woman.

The line between business and family, love and hate, and right and wrong had been permanently blurred. Worst of all, her ex and her mother were actually friends now. *Friends.* They spoke on the phone and "did" lunch. The mutual friendship was now prudent in a way it had never been when Cindy was merely living and sleeping with their daughter. It was like a bad episode of *Ricki Lake*.

Kellie brought the glass to her mouth and let the bubbles tickle her lips. The heady scent overwhelmed her senses and promised sweet oblivion. She closed her eyes, opened her mouth, and tipped her glass, anticipating a flood of profound relief when her mother's voice at a microphone brought her up short.

"Kellie, would you please join me?"

Kellie blinked and lowered her glass so swiftly she spilled half its contents on the bar.

Her father gave her a hearty slap on the back. "C'mon." He slipped his arm around hers and led her to the microphone on the dais alongside the band.

Her mother reluctantly stepped to the side to give Mr. Holloway and their daughter center stage.

"Friends," his voice boomed; he really didn't need the microphone. "Tonight, I'm the luckiest man alive. Not only did I have the good sense to marry the young woman who sat behind me in economics class forty years ago . . ."

Resplendent in Vera Wang, her mother, who could ruthlessly emasculate a four-star general with a few well-placed words, batted her eyes and played coy when Mr. Holloway grinned in her direction. She had nerve. Kellie had to give her that.

"But I now have the very good fortune of celebrating something that Holloway Realty has been looking forward to for several long years. At last, we're celebrating the sale of the Ford Building." Applause rang out. "It was the deal of a lifetime, and I'm especially proud that our daughter was a part of it."

Kellie couldn't believe her ears and she hoped the shock she felt all the way to the tips of her toes wasn't written all over her face.

"She's had a difficult couple of years . . ."

Murmurs of agreement from the crowd at the base of the dais caused Kellie's cheeks to heat and she had the sudden urge to hiss back at them. *Difficult?* They had no idea.

"But she's worked her way through it." Her father turned to her and gave her a look that could only be described as . . . affectionate. "And we're so proud, in fact, that her mother and I have decided to bring her on board as a partner of Holloway Realty." The applause was more subdued and polite this time, but Kellie couldn't have heard it even if it had thundered. Her head was spinning. *Partner?*

Mr. Holloway reached into the pocket of his tuxedo and pulled out a blindingly white envelope. Ever the showman, he held it high for all to see. "Your portion of the commission." He presented it with a flourish as he beamed.

Her mother raised her champagne flute. "To the first of many more big deals!"

The crowd echoed the toast and Cindy, that audacious bitch, who was standing in the front row of guests, raised her glass and winked at Kellie, acknowledging this momentous accomplishment.

Kellie glared at her and let every ounce of the hatred she felt drip from her pores like hot wax. Nowadays it took a hell of a lot to surprise her. But she was actually shocked that Cindy had the nerve to show up here tonight.

Still astounded at her father's words, Kellie was pulled back into the moment by a loud crackle of the microphone. She gazed out to the sea of faces, people who had utterly abandoned her when her own business had begun to flounder. Those people were dead to her and she felt nothing but dead inside when she looked at them.

Her father pumped her hand enthusiastically much like her college dean, a total stranger, had at her graduation and she resisted the urge, now as then, to march off stage to make room for someone else.

"Thank you," Kellie murmured, trying not to think about the drink that was still sitting on the bar. She had to remind herself that she had worked hard for this money and there wasn't anything wrong with taking it. Even though *everything* about tonight felt wrong.

The band resumed playing and she turned to speak to her mother, only to find that she was already busily talking to a business associate from a large commercial real estate firm. She laughed at all the right moments and doled out morsels of information as though she were a miser passing out bits of gold to the worthy, unwilling to miss even the smallest opportunity to work the room. Kellie understood all too well. After all, she'd done it more times than she could count. And yet she shivered when she saw an echo of herself in her mother.

These pillars of the community, vultures who were here for the free bar as much as anything else, were her peers again too. Many were alcoholics and most were workaholics. With their big dreams, sadly neglected relationships, and inflated egos, every one of them would sell his or her soul to the devil for the right commission. And she was one of them again.

She didn't want to be. Not anymore.

Clutching the envelope containing her commission check, she exited the swanky hotel and slowly wove her way through the small throng of smokers clustered around the stone ash cans near the front door. They were a club unto themselves, outcasts who banded together in a pack to fight off their extinction . . . and fill their lungs with carbon monoxide.

At the very fringe of the group, two young men stood close to one another, wide smiles wreathing their faces, heads tilted slightly together as they traded their own stories. Their body language told her they were *real* friends and, as she looked closer, perhaps something more.

She felt a familiar twinge of pain at the obvious camaraderie they shared. Something she'd only experienced for what now felt like a fleeting amount of time. For a second, she considered trying to bum a smoke and join the larger group, but she hadn't sucked on a cigarette in more than twenty years. Another bad habit that she'd only have to work to quit later, she decided. Something she could do without.

Her heels clicked loudly on the sidewalk as she briskly walked farther away from the hotel . . . and everyone in it.

The parking lot was blessedly quiet, with only the light hiss of traffic from the road beyond to mar the silence. She tilted her head back and looked up into the clear night sky wondering whether Lorna was seeing those same twinkling stars from the tiny window high in the corner of her cell.

Even if she was able to contact her lover, would Lorna forgive her for what she'd done? Knowing how important trust was to her, she wasn't sure of the answer.

Lorna loved her. Kellie knew that as surely as she knew her own name. Lorna wasn't the sort to give herself lightly. But the hasty belief that she'd savagely attacked Katrina would undoubtedly hurt her deeply. What would it take to undo that sort of hurt even if she could? And did it matter? She smiled a little. Lorna would be lethal in a little black dress, but wouldn't last more than thirty seconds with the pompous stuffed shirts inside the hotel. Kellie doubted that love, even the sort that made her pulse race and heart swell to the point of pain, would be enough to get them beyond those differences.

As she stood among the fancy cars and big city lights, her lover and her time at Blue Ridge seemed worlds away, as though it couldn't have been real at all. She sighed and spoke to the heavens, sending out a silent prayer to Lorna. "I miss you."

Then she turned to go back inside.

Chapter 21
One month later . . .

"What do you mean it's *now*?" Lorna sat up on her bunk and looked at Katrina as though she'd lost her mind. Which, of course, she had a long, long time ago. She hated the fact that the bitch was in her cell at all. One less confrontation in a life that was, once again, full of them.

"I mean . . . the time for the deal has changed. The shipment is coming in this afternoon instead of tonight."

"Shit!" Lorna rubbed the back of her neck. "Are you just trying to get caught? Last-minute changes like this cause mistakes. You know that!"

Katrina chuckled as she sat down on the bed. "That's why I have you, Lorna, to do all my worrying for me. And, boy, am I glad." Her voice suddenly took on a syrupy Southern accent. "Because I can't think about that right now. If I do, I'll go crazy." She fanned herself delicately. "I'll think about that ta-mar-ah."

Lorna's hands ached for wanting to strangle the smartass. "Who changed our plans?" Furious, she sprang off the bed. "Why didn't I know about? I thought we were *partners*." She spat the word as though it were a curse.

Katrina's expression frosted over. "We are. But I'm still the one in charge. You seem to have trouble remembering that."

"Like I could forget!" Lorna snapped, shoving the cell door open wider. She needed air. She was suffocating. "You're reckless and you're stupid. And one day one of your mistakes is going to cost me." She shook her head gravely. "You're going to push me too far."

Katrina absently touched the long scar that ran up to her neck. "You forget that I'm not so easy to get rid of."

Lorna grated, "You forget I'm far more competent than the last idiot who tried." Her back to Katrina, she lowered her voice and closed her eyes. *Why in the hell am I doing this? Oh, yes. A promise. What could my word mean now anyway?* "The guards this afternoon—"

"Won't be a problem," Katrina finished smugly.

"Same terms and merchandise?" This was their biggest shipment of drugs yet. So big, in fact, that Katrina didn't trust any of her stoolies to meet the shipment and make the payment. She didn't even want Lorna going it alone. It had taken their supplier an extra two weeks to come up with the merchandise, and every one of the parasites up the drug food chain was going to cash in with this deal.

"Of course! Everything is the same except for the timing. You think I'd let our supplier screw us over just because Patrice Jennings insisted her stupid lumber truck deliver early?"

Lorna raised an eyebrow. "I don't know what to think. Besides, we have a big order of furniture coming up for an elementary school and we need the wood."

"Like I care."

"You wouldn't be so obsessed with your dope if you had something else to think about." Frowning, Lorna stuck her head out of the cell to confirm that no one was listening.

"For Christ's sake, Mally, why are you so jumpy?"

Lorna shrugged, her arms wrapped around herself as she eased back inside. "I don't want something messing up my parole," she answered honestly. *I'm so close.* An uneasy feeling bubbled up inside her. *Please, just let me get through today without something going wrong.* "And I don't like you making big moves without me."

Katrina moved next to her and rested her hand on Lorna's shoulder. "It's not like I had a choice. You sure that's all that's buggin' you?"

"Isn't that enough? I don't want to screw up. It feels good to be making real money again." She scrubbed her face. "When I get out of this hellhole, I'll have more options than being a whore or a waitress in some cruddy dinner."

"Hell, yes we're making good money! We're doing even better than I thought we would. Even Elaine is getting rich."

Lorna flinched at that. It had been a blow to find out the guard she trusted most was not only a longtime member of Katrina's payroll, but had fed Katrina information about her own bank account. It had been a cruel reminder—one of many—that screamed *Trust no one.*

Lorna's eyes opened wide at the look of pure ecstasy that swept over Katrina's face.

"I never dreamed we'd be supplying maximum and minimum security so soon," Katrina breathed. "And all from here? Jesus, it makes me hot just thinking about it!" She chuckled demonically and sang "We're in the Money." "I knew that working together we could do anything. I swear I'd forgotten how good you are at all this. You're wicked. A goddamned machine, Mally."

Lorna winced. A newbie who'd recently celebrated her eighteenth birthday had overdosed on some of their drugs the month before. Thankfully, she hadn't died. But it was only a matter of time before someone used that poison to kill herself, accidentally or not. Lorna laid a hand on her belly, which was burning a hole in itself from the inside out. *Way too late for regrets now.* "A girl's got to do what a girl's got to do."

Katrina squeezed Lorna's shoulder and Lorna fought with herself to keep from knocking the clammy hand away. Her skin crawled at the touch and she exhaled shakily.

"With all your money you can finally set your fancy girlfriend up in style, huh?"

Lorna could hear the poorly veiled jealousy in Katrina's voice. But she didn't rise to the bait. "She's long gone and you know it," she said dully.

Katrina snorted. "Wouldn't you be?"

"No." Lorna's voice was stark. "I really wouldn't."

With a look of utter absorption, Katrina drew her fingers down Lorna's arm, her touch shifting from a weak attempt at comfort into something more sensual. "You know," she coaxed softly, "you don't have to be alone just 'cause Holloway is gone."

Now Lorna did knock away Katrina's hand. "Let's just get this over with." She snatched her work gloves from the top of her dresser.

Katrina took Lorna's rebuke in stride. Almost. "Your loss, asshole. Let's go make some money."

At the entrance of the loading dock, a guard emerged from the shadows to meet them.

Lorna's gaze locked with Roscoe's and the corners of his lips turned upward in a sinister smile.

"Hiya, Mally." His meaty hands dangled from his belt loops by this thumbs. "Did you think you could run your little game forever without me ever getting involved?"

The air exploded from out of Lorna's lungs as though she'd been shot. *Oh, shit. Oh, shit. Oh, shit.* Her head snapped sideways and she glowered at Katrina. But the other woman just stood there, a mild expression on her face, cool as a cucumber.

Why wasn't Katrina as surprised as she was? And why weren't they both being arrested? "What is *he* doing here and where's Elaine?"

Katrina slipped on a pair of work gloves in case another guard happened to walk by. This part of the building was fairly deserted on the weekends, but just in case, they needed to look legitimate. "Elaine doesn't come on shift until tonight and I couldn't get a hold of her. Relax, Mally. He's with us now."

Lorna's head wanted to detonate. "Since when?"

Katrina stalked over to Lorna and got right into her face. "Since I needed him to be!"

Roscoe clucked his tongue and inserted himself between the women. "Ladies, there's a truck to be unloaded."

Katrina snorted. "Let someone else do that!" She waved dismissively. "I'll send Laverne and Dusty back here as soon as we're finished."

Roscoe glanced at his watch and then around the dock.

Lorna's eyes narrowed. He was uncharacteristically nervous.

"Fuck," Roscoe mumbled, blowing out a big breath.

"What?" Katrina looked around until she spied the driver standing next to his truck, kicking pebbles as he waited.

"I'm supposed to be off shift soon."

Katrina turned and stared. "You're being compensated for your time, fat fuck! Now keep watch. There are too many new guards around this place lately." She shivered. "They give me the creeps."

Lorna continued to eye Roscoe warily. He wasn't supposed to be here, dammit! "Katrina," she warned softly. "I don't like this."

Katrina ignored her and marched out to meet the truck driver, Joey, who also happened to be the warden's dim first cousin. Lorna watched her warily. The lumber truck was always searched on the way out of Blue Ridge in case a prisoner got any bright ideas about trying to escape. But because the driver was trusted, this vehicle wasn't searched as it entered the grounds. With greasy hair and hollow eyes, Joey was a gaunt poster child for "just saying no." His hands trembled a little as he lit his cigarette. Lorna shook her head, noting his forehead was damp with sweat even though it wasn't the least bit hot. She'd watched him wither before her eyes over the past few months. *I'm surprised he has anything left to sell. Stupid.*

"Well," Katrina asked, irritably pointing at the man. "I don't have all day. Where is it?"

He gave her a look. "Where is it always?" His cigarette was plastered to his lower lip as he spoke and he waved over his shoulder for her to follow him. "In the back."

They moved around the back of the truck and walked up the ramp, with Roscoe bringing up the rear. The compartment carried only half a load of planks and tall stacks of particleboard sheets. The driver stepped over the bundles and climbed to the very back, kicking aside a few errant boards to reveal a small cardboard box that was heavily wrapped in packing tape.

Lorna's heart began to pound when she saw the object of their mission. Such a small box that spelled so much trouble.

"Open it," Katrina demanded, staying right where she was so he would have to come back to her. She took off her gloves and shoved them into the waist of her jeans.

Grumbling, Joey pulled a switchblade from his pocket and slit the tape with ease. He selected a bag from the top of the pile and offered it to Katrina to sample.

Lorna hissed involuntarily when she saw the flash of the blade.

Three sets of eyes swung her way.

Lorna drew in a calming breath through her nose. *Easy.* "You don't think we're just going to trust you, Joey? Katrina picks the baggies to test, not you."

The man scowled but nodded and Katrina selected a bag from the bottom and, from her pocket, withdrew a NIK drug kit—the kind the police used and that was available on the Internet—to test the contents. "Whatever."

She dropped a tiny sample of powder into the small bag of clear liquid, broke the ampoules, and waited anxiously for the color to change. It didn't take long for the test to register positive for narcotics. Just to be sure, Katrina rubbed the powder on her gums, humming a little in appreciation when they numbed almost instantly. "Very nice."

She offered the bag to Lorna for a taste.

"Thanks, anyway, but I'd rather not end up looking like Joey someday."

Joey's eyes sparked. "Hey!"

"Suit yourself, prude." Katrina rifled through the box and repeated the process several times with several different bags before nodding, apparently satisfied. Not wanting to carry the entire box back inside the building, she crammed a few bags into the pockets of her jeans, then tossed the box back to Lorna, who silently began stuffing baggies into her own pants pockets. When they were full, she lifted her shirt.

As she padded her bra with Ziplocs containing cocaine, Lorna waited for one of Roscoe's inevitably vulgar comments. But it never came. *Why is this taking so long?*

Katrina smiled at Joey and he grinned back crookedly through his cloud of smoke. Happier than Lorna had ever seen her, she removed a thick roll of bills from her pocket. "Nice doing business with you." Negligently, she tossed the wad of cash at the man's chest and he cursed as he dropped his cigarette while he fumbled for the money.

Then, before Lorna could take another breath, so many things happened at once she could scarcely make sense of it all.

From out of nowhere, a male and a female police officer burst into the back of the truck, wearing bulletproof vests. Their guns were drawn and they were screaming their fool heads off. "Freeze!" Instantly they spotted the glint of Joey's knife and swung their weapons in his direction. "Drop it, motherfucker! Drop it!"

Shots rang out and Joey and Katrina panicked at the exact same time. She dove for cover, but then, like a stack of dominoes, she tripped over some planks and fell into Lorna, who hurled into Joey. All three bodies collided violently as they crashed into the wall and then the floor. Katrina cried out when her elbows smashed into some wood and then the metal bottom of the truck. Lorna's forehead slammed against a plank of solid cedar and her world exploded into a million stars.

"Don't move!" the cops shouted. "Don't move!"

Joey's knife was wrenched out of his hand by someone's knee and he bit into the thing nearest his mouth. Which happened to be a woman's hand. Katrina screamed again. Lorna blinked a few times and tried to rise to her feet, only to be yanked back down by her hair. "Ugh!"

Rising to her knees and wrapping a skinny but strong arm around Lorna's throat, Katrina pressed Joey's blade into the soft skin of Lorna's cheek hard enough to pierce it.

Lorna sucked in a surprised breath when a trail of warm blood dripped down her face and splashed onto the floor. *Christ!* How had Katrina come up with the knife?

"Stay b-back," Katrina stammered to the cops. She was breathing so fast that Lorna worried she'd pass out and slit her throat on the way down. "Or I'll kill her!"

Lorna's gaze flitted around the truck. She could smell gunpowder and consoled herself with the thought that at least no one was dead . . . yet.

Roscoe was only two paces from Katrina, grinning like a moron, his gun pointing right at Katrina's head . . . or maybe it was Lorna's. Without thought, Lorna began to struggle and the knife at her cheek cut deeper. She hissed as the blade went through her cheek and into her mouth, coming to rest painfully at the very edge of her gums.

Katrina jerked the knife back a fraction of an inch and Lorna let out a relieved breath.

Joey was too stunned to move. He stood quaking with his arms in the air, his face as white as snow.

"Outside now!" the female officer ordered him. There wasn't room to secure him where he was. "Go! Move!"

She stepped aside and he crept by her at a snail's pace, every bit of his focus welded to her gun. A second later the male officer grabbed him and dragged him outside by his collar. Joey cried out as he was roughly thrown onto the ramp of the truck, his arms wrenched behind his back.

The female cop never took her eyes off Katrina, remaining in her crouched position with her weapon drawn and poised to fire. "Keep him out there, Frank," she called to the other officer. "I've got this under control."

You do? Lorna thought woozily.

The familiar sound of handcuffs being slapped on hazily registered in Lorna's head. Everything had gone to hell. "Let me go, Katrina. It's over."

"Shut up!"

The knife dug deeper again and Lorna swallowed a cry of pain. She knew if she could see behind her she'd find Katrina's icy eyes were wild with fear. "Katrina?" She considered trying to elbow her, but her head was yanked so far back and the knife was in so deep that she was certain any drastic movement would only make her situation worse.

"I said be quiet!" Katrina boomed. "I'm thinking!"

"A hostage only works . . ." Lorna swallowed hard, her neck muscles straining as she spoke, "It only works if the person pulling the trigger is afraid to shoot because he doesn't want to kill the hostage."

Complete stillness behind her.

"Roscoe," Lorna said in a calm, conversational tone that was truly ridiculous under the circumstances, "How would you feel if you missed Katrina and hit me instead?"

He cocked his gun, the noise unnaturally loud in the small space. "Like it was two-for-one night at my favorite bar."

Katrina dropped her head against Lorna's shoulder and the knife slipped a little in her hand. "Shit! Shit! I don't know what to do."

"Drop the knife!" everyone yelled.

Several charged seconds that felt like years ticked away with no one saying another word. No one even dared breathe.

"Roscoe?" Lorna finally said, closing her eyes tight and bracing herself for whatever came next. "Shoot this bitch already."

Katrina threw the knife to the floor as though it were on fire. She raised her hands in surrender.

Roscoe surged forward and snatched her up by the hair, much the way she'd grabbed Lorna.

Lorna let out a shuddering breath and moved aside, her knees like jelly.

Katrina shrieked in pain.

"Hurts doesn't it?" Lorna mocked. She lifted her hand to her face and it came away sticky and stained crimson.

"Roscoe was in on this," Katrina blurted, futilely trying to pry his hands from her head. Desperate to get him off her, she looked to the police. "Arrest him too!"

"Nobody is arresting me. I'm one of the good guys, dumbshit."

Lorna blinked slowly. *A good guy?* She was in the *Twilight Zone*. She had to be. Her addled mind sluggishly processed the news even as her ears still rang from the hit on her head.

Roscoe spun Katrina around and shoved her hard against the wall of the truck, making the entire compartment vibrate and knocking out her front dentures in the process. Not surprisingly, that quieted her down.

Wearily, Lorna addressed the female cop who was helping Roscoe cuff Katrina and doing her best to keep him from violating every one of her civil rights. "What took you so long?"

The woman blew a braid out of her face as she leaned into Katrina. "We thought this was going down tonight. If we hadn't gotten a call from Roscoe here, we wouldn't have made it at all."

Katrina's head jerked sideways and her eyes bugged. Her incredulous expression left her jaw dangling. Her gaze bored into Lorna with palpable force. "*You're* a rat?"

Lorna stiffened, knowing she'd done what she had to do, but still stung by the undeniably true statement. She looked away, wiping her bloody cheek on her sleeve as a woozy feeling crept over her. "I warned you not to push me too far."

"Mally?" Katrina demanded. "I trusted you!" Her eyes softened for just a second. "Maybe I even loved you."

Defiant, Lorna lifted her gaze to Katrina. "Love? I'm not even sure you know what it is."

"You turncoat bitch! Goddammit!" She thrashed wildly and it took both officers to hold her in place long enough to finish getting both wrists cuffed. "I don't believe this. How much money did it take to turn you into a filthy rat? Huh?"

"Money?" Lorna laughed humorlessly. "I *lost* money doing this. I won't get to keep a dime of what we made and I lost everything I had before that, too. I'm flat-ass broke."

"Frank," the female officer called behind her. "Radio for an ambulance." A worried expression settled on her face and she quickly slipped on a rubber glove and pressed something cool against Lorna's cheek. She winced in sympathy. "Oh, man, the bleeding isn't stopping. It's going to have to be stitched." With a gentle hand, she turned Lorna's face to study it, squinting. "Your eyes don't look right either."

"What the hell kind of deal did you make, Mally?"

Lorna tried to step out of the truck but stumbled back onto a pile of lumber, her bottom hitting the wood with a loud thump. She sat there numb. It was finally over. She could scarcely believe it. Months of working with Katrina had very nearly wrecked her. She wasn't sure whether it was relief, or loss of blood, or the fact that her head was pounding like a snare drum that was making her weak. Maybe it was all three. "The DA made me an offer I couldn't refuse."

"You're getting out in a few months anyway!" Katrina's face contorted with rage. "What could they possibly give you?"

Lorna shook her head. "You should never have hurt her," she mumbled to herself. "Never."

"What are you taking about?" Katrina writhed in Roscoe's grasp and spat. "You gave up all that money for nothing! For that snobby girlfriend who's probably fucking someone else by now? Retard! You won't have a thing when you leave and you'll be back in this place inside six months."

Roscoe began walking Katrina out of the truck. "What could the pigs offer to turn you into one of *them?* when you'll always be one of *us*?"

Lorna's chest seized at Katrina's jab, but she lifted her steely gaze and squarely met Katrina's. "They offered me you, Katrina. Your head on a plate."

Chapter 22
Two and a half months later . . .

Lorna stepped lightly off the bus from Sugar Land prison into town, her feet kicking up a puff of dust as they hit the ground. Just behind her another woman exited. They were both carrying canvas duffle bags made in the prison sewing room that were sold to inmates at cost upon their release. Lorna's was barely half full with everything she owned in the world.

A white sedan pulled into the small parking lot as the bus drove away and three children with neatly combed hair but tattered clothes flew out of the car before it had completely stopped. They were obviously here to pick up their mom.

Lorna couldn't help but smile. "Good luck," she said sincerely, though her chest was filled with a painful ache. No one was here to pick her up. She hadn't heard from Kellie since Katrina's stabbing, and didn't even know if she'd been released from prison, though her first parole eligibility date had come and gone. Even though a tiny bit of her had tenaciously clung to the hope that Kellie would be here when she stepped off the bus, her head had warned her heart that things would be just this way.

The woman smiled distractedly and wished Lorna good luck too, then bolted for her children, scooping them up in her arms as they shouted with undisguised glee, "Mommy's out of jail! Mommy's out of jail!"

The only man Lorna had ever seen who would dwarf Roscoe lumbered out of the car on the heels of the children and anxiously waited his turn for attention. Every last one of them was crying, and when the small group came together, they hugged each other ferociously.

It wasn't exactly a Norman Rockwell print, but it was the closest that Lorna had ever seen.

Sighing, she turned to survey her surroundings. The bus had dropped them off at a diner on the edge of town. The building was painted pink and the shingles and siding were shabby, but the delicious smell of fried chicken that poured from its smokestack made more of an impression than the decor.

Lorna's stomach growled loudly, but she was so enthralled at being outside that even her hunger couldn't force her inside right away.

Tall pine trees towered all around her, their strong scent mingling with the smell of grease. It was heavenly. Her eyes drank in her surroundings. They were in the midst of a late Indian summer and everything looked so colorful! She hadn't watched much television over the years and she suddenly regretted that fact because it made her feel like even more of an alien marooned in a strange new land.

The cars looked different and people's hairstyles and clothes didn't match her memories. One passenger on the bus worked on a laptop computer so skinny it looked like it would snap in half with the least bit of force. She'd seen commercials for iPods and cell phones, but had no idea they were really that *tiny*.

A teenaged couple exited the diner and she watched them curiously as they walked past. Their shoes were unlaced and hanging open. The girl's pants were skintight and everything that could possibly be pierced was. By contrast, the boy's blue jeans were ten sizes too big and the waist sat closer to his knees than his stomach. Lorna grimaced when she caught sight of his underwear hanging out of the top of his pants. "Yuck."

She had less than one hundred dollars and her duffle contained her picture of Megan, a small toiletries kit, and three changes of used clothes she'd purchased on eBay through a guard just prior to her release. *Normal* clothes that she now suspected were at least fifteen or twenty years old. But the other adults, unlike the teenagers on the bus, had been wearing clothes that fit, and that, at least, gave her some hope she'd blend in somewhere.

In her pocket, alongside her parole officer's business card, was a slip of paper containing the name and telephone number of an elderly man who lived in town and rented spare rooms by the week on the cheap to women recently released from Sugar Land. The larger rooms housed three women each and were the most economical. And she found it funny, in an ironic sort of way, that if she let a room there she would actually be in tighter quarters with other cons than she had been in Blue Ridge or Sugar Land.

Something red caught Lorna's eye and she approached the diner window, reading the Help Wanted sign in the window with interest. She needed money, and if she worked there she could probably earn tips right off and not have to wait two weeks for her first paycheck. They might even offer her discounted meals like the burger joint where Lorna had worked as a teen. She thought about the crack she'd made to Katrina about working at a cruddy diner and smiled wryly, knowing she'd be lucky to get a job there.

"Hey." The woman from the bus approached Lorna, frowning.

Lorna jumped a little, having forgotten she was there at all.

The woman picked up the smallest child and rested him on her hip. "Is someone coming for you?"

Lorna felt some color rise in her cheeks. "No."

"Do . . . you . . . um . . . do you need a ride?"

The man, her husband or boyfriend maybe, nodded his approval at the offer. "We're heading into the city. You don't want to hitchhike on this road. It can be dangerous."

Lorna knew that most inmates headed right into the city upon being released. There were a half dozen smaller towns between here and there, but jobs were harder to come by far away from the big factories and shopping malls.

Lorna had grown up in that city full of smokestacks, tiny houses crowded with too many children and hopeless parents, and memories she wished she didn't have. She didn't care if she ever went back. "No, but thanks for asking." She wished she could remember the woman's name. Kindness was all too rare.

The woman shrugged. "Suit yourself." She waved and Lorna waved back, smiling at one of the little girls who reminded her a little of her sister Megan.

She lifted her bag higher on her shoulder and stepped around an older station wagon as she headed toward the diner and some much-wanted dinner. A bell rang as she opened the door and her stomach growled again at the smell of sizzling burgers and smoky bacon. The room was fairly crowded and the sound of silverware hitting plates and coffee cups coming to rest on Formica rang out, creating a sea of white noise that she found comforting and familiar.

She moved to the bar and sat down, trying not to gape at the prices on the board above the grill. The chicken dinner she'd been hankering for since she stepped off the bus was out of her price range completely. But she should be able to afford a ham and cheese, dammit! Six dollars and ninety-nine cents for a sandwich, fries and soda? Were they kidding? A moment of panic seized her and she realized with sickening certainty that her money was going to run out far faster than she'd planned.

Maybe she should have bulked up before leaving?

A harried waitress came out of the kitchen and set a large 'to go' order near the register to wait for its owner.

"Umm. How much for the ham and cheese sandwich alone?" Lorna asked. "I don't need a fries or drink"

"Four bucks."

Lorna nibbled her lip. She would find a grocery store for the rest of her food. But for now she was starving, having missed both breakfast and lunch while she completed her out-processing. "Okay."

"Everything on it?"

"That would be great." Lorna screwed up her courage. "And an application for the job, please?"

The waitress lowered her note pad, her gaze flicking to Lorna's duffle bag. Apparently, she saw a lot of those. "Sugar Land?" she asked needlessly.

"Yes."

"For?"

Lorna swallowed. She didn't think she wanted to know about how she had to be transferred from Blue Ridge once she'd turned rat. She was a little surprised to find herself having to explain her situation so soon. She'd only been free for an hour. She toyed with the idea of lying. But . . . "Murder."

The waitress tried not to show her surprise. "Sorry . . . I um . . . I can give you an application." She lowered her voice and looked truly contrite. "But it won't do any good. The owner isn't interested in violent offenders."

Silently, Lorna sighed. Who was going to be? The thought of lying made her depressed, but she could see she'd have little choice. She did her best to smile. "Never mind then."

"Hey, you . . . uh . . . you want a salad with your sandwich? On the house. I know they don't give you a lot of fresh vegetables on the inside." The waitress gave Lorna a meaningful look that told her she'd once been in Lorna's shoes.

Lorna's smile warmed. "That would be great. Thanks."

When the waitress disappeared, she dropped her head into her hands. *What am I going to do?* And the thought that had plagued her for months came roaring back to the forefront. *How am I going to find her?* Kellie might have given up on her, but that didn't mean that Lorna felt the same way. She was glad she had on comfortable sneakers, because she'd walk halfway across the country to find her if she had to.

"Is this seat taken?" a disembodied voice from behind asked.

"No," Lorna said absently. "Help your—" She turned her head and every bit of the air in her lungs rushed out.

"Hi."

Lorna's throat closed. There stood Kellie, looking more beautiful, and nervous, than she'd ever seen her. She raised a slightly trembling hand in greeting, suddenly feeling as though she had no idea what to say, despite having dreamed of this scene a hundred times.

"Is it still okay if I sit down?"

Kellie was painfully unsure of herself and Lorna felt a pang in her own chest. She cleared her throat so that she could speak. "I," she began, feeling foolish when it came out as nothing more than a croak. "I—I can't believe you're here. I didn't think—"

"I was always coming," Kellie assured her quickly. "Your bus was early. It wasn't supposed to be here for another ten minutes."

"I—I didn't know that." A pause. "I . . . I missed you." *So much that it felt like I was dying.*

Tears leapt into Kellie's eyes despite her visible attempt at keeping them at bay. "I missed you too," she said softly. "More than you probably know."

Not only does she think I'm a savage killer, but she's been free and never tried to contact me. She let me twist in the wind for months! Resentment warred with her profound relief at seeing Kellie and her desire to forgive her anything so long as they'd stay together. Lorna didn't want to feel angry or hurt. She wanted a fresh start. And she wanted it with Kellie by her side. *Why does everything always have to be so complicated?*

An awkward silence fell.

"How about a hug?" Kellie asked, a sad but hopeful lilt to her voice. She swallowed thickly. "I know I could use one."

Lorna couldn't refuse her. On suddenly unsteady feet, she jumped up and wrapped her in a fervent embrace. *Finally,* her mind sighed gratefully.

"I'm not letting you go," Kellie breathed raggedly.

Lorna's knees went weak. "Me neither." So many emotions were racing through her body that she couldn't decide whether she wanted to break down into hysterical tears or laughter. She placed her lips to Kellie's ear, smelling the clean scent of shampoo, and feeling the body so close to hers begin to shake with silent sobs. "I'm glad you didn't make me track you down."

"Would you have?" Kellie whispered and then held her breath. "Even after—"

"No matter how long it took, Kel," Lorna swore fervently. "I've lost too much in my life already. There was no way I was losing you too."

Kellie pulled back to see Lorna's face, leaving her hands on Lorna's arms, unwilling to lose physical contact with her for even a second. "I know we have a lot to talk about." She was as serious as Lorna had ever seen her. "And we will. But I have something I need to say first."

Lorna nodded, a little mesmerized just being in her lover's presence again, and a little anxious about what she'd hear next.

Kellie gave her a helpless, watery smile. "I love you."

A sharp intake of breath.

"I *really* love you. The 'with all my heart' and 'forever and ever' kind," she said in a clear voice, just so there'd be no question. "I know this isn't the most special place to tell you, but I can't risk waiting another second." Kellie lifted a hand and let it drop. "God only knows what's going to happen to one of us next!"

Lorna's heart sang. She wanted to crawl *inside* Kellie and stay. "You know I feel the same, right?"

Kellie smiled through her tears. "You never gave me a reason to doubt you." She swallowed again and studied her shoes, shame heating her face. "I wish that you could say the same for me."

Lorna frowned. "Kellie—"

"Ahem? Excuse me, ladies?" The waitress was back and she handed Lorna a paper sack that held her sandwich and the promised salad. "I thought you might want to take this and take your conversation outside." By way of a none-too-subtle hint, she inclined her head toward the door. "Even though this is way better than *General Hospital,* I'd rather the customers eat, pay and leave, instead of sitting here gaping at you." Her words were stern, but not unkind.

Kellie glanced around. Every eye in the diner was riveted on them. "Not a problem." With one hand she hefted Lorna's duffle bag and with her other she grabbed hold of Lorna and began walking toward the door. "I know someplace we can go to be alone."

Still a little stunned, Lorna snatched the sack from the waitress and managed to toss a five-dollar bill on the counter before nearly being dragged outside.

The outside air was cool and fresh; the diner had been so hot. The contrast left Kellie a little lightheaded. Or maybe it was the relief coursing through her faster than her blood. *Things between us aren't beyond repair. They're not,* she chanted gratefully. *Thank you. Thank you!* She'd been half-expecting Lorna to tell her to go to hell when she asked to sit down at the diner counter.

"Do you have to check in someplace?" Kellie's eyes suddenly turned to slits and she reached up and grazed her fingers over a small scar that wasn't there the last time she'd seen Lorna. Worriedly, she glanced up in question. *Who hurt your beautiful face?* she thought darkly. *'Cause I want her dead.*

Lorna took the fingers from her face and kissed Kellie's palm.

The contact sent a bolt of heat tearing through Kellie and her eyes grew hooded.

"I'll catch you up on that later." They had so much to talk about that she didn't know where to begin. But it sure wasn't going to be at the end. "There's a boarding house in town. I have the phone number."

Reluctantly, Kellie nodded and allowed the matter to drop . . . for now. *You'll stay in that clap trap over my dead body.* "You can call in later tonight though, right? Not right this minute?"

Lorna shrugged. "Sure."

They stopped outside a late model pickup truck. Kellie gave it a pat. "This is mine."

Lorna's eyes widened a trifle at her choice of vehicles. "I guess I shouldn't be surprised you bought something already. You're really smart."

"Thanks for saying that, but smarts had nothing to do with it." Kellie smiled and used the keyless entry to unlock the door.

Lorna's eyes widened even further and a childlike grin overtook her face. "Whoa! That is so cool!"

Charmed, Kellie said, "It is, isn't it? It's easy to forget how neat things like that are."

"Is it a laser? Can I try it later?" A frown. "It's not easy to break, is it? I can't afford to—"

"You can't break it and you can try right this second. No more waiting for what you want when there's no reason." Kellie handed over the keys and fell a little bit more in love with Lorna. *Precious.*

Her former girlfriends hadn't looked half as delighted when presented with jewelry or designer clothes. They were too concerned with appearing sophisticated and bored with everything to be fazed by anything so simple. But Lorna, who could be as jaded as anyone when it came to assessing human nature, was always heartbreakingly earnest in the way she expressed her own feelings.

After a few times locking and unlocking the door and one mishap with the panic alarm, they climbed into the truck.

Not taking her eyes off Kellie, Lorna said, "You seem . . ." She struggled for the right words. So much had changed. It wasn't just the loss of her long hair in favor of, what was to Lorna, an even sexier style that was every bit as lively as Kellie herself, or the weight she'd put on in *all the right places,* but the way she'd taken charge when she'd pulled Lorna from the diner. It was . . . "Different."

Unconsciously, Kellie's brows drew together and she touched the back of her bare neck.

Lorna let her awe show. "And not just your hair. You're friggin' gorgeous."

Relieved, she beamed, and felt relaxed enough to give Lorna a frank, appreciative look of her own. The look she'd been holding inside since she saw her sitting in the diner. "So are you." Her voice dropped to a happy purr. "And I *love* you wearing that color."

Lorna was always attractive, even in her plain white T-shirt. That, and the occasional sweatshirt, was the only thing Kellie had ever seen her in. But today she wore russet brown corduroy pants and a soft cotton blouse that was a bright cornflower blue. It was an alluring shade that, somehow, still couldn't match the depth and soulfulness of Lorna's eyes.

Lorna muttered a slightly embarrassed, "Thanks." She watched the landscape fly by, her bag clutched to her chest as they rode.

Kellie's gaze strayed from the road. Lorna had grown quiet as though a pensive mood had settled over her. "Are you okay?"

"It feels . . ." She chewed on her lower lip for a moment. "I feel weird, I guess." She laid a hand on her stomach to indicate its upset.

"Is it riding in a car after all this time?"

"No. I mean . . . I guess that, too. But it feels strange not to have anyone watching me. You know the sort of worried feeling you got when you ditched school when you were a kid?"

Kellie nodded even though she didn't know.

"It's sort of like that. Like at any minute your folks are going to find out what you did and beat the shit out of you. Like you're on borrowed time."

Kellie reached over and took Lorna's hand. "Nobody is *ever* going to touch you in anger again, Lorna," she said, barely able to keep her own fury in check. "And you're not on borrowed time. This is *your* time. No one is going to take it away from you."

Lorna let out a slow breath, a little overwhelmed. "I guess."

"Why don't you eat your dinner? I know you've been dreaming of food for years."

Still tense about where things sat between them, Lorna shook her head. "I'm not hungry." Her stomach chose that second to growl. Loudly.

Kellie gave her a reassuring smile and read her mind. "Go ahead and eat. I'm not going anywhere."

With that, Lorna's appetite returned with a vengeance and she tucked in, moaning around the sandwich as though she were orgasming with every bite.

She has no idea what she does to me. Kellie squirmed a little in her seat, the low sounds coming from Lorna's chest sending an electric current between her legs.

When she was finished eating she slowly licked her lips and Kellie thought she would die.

"Kel?" Lorna crushed the sack into a ball and stowed it in her duffle, not wanting to mess up Kellie's truck. "You have a strange look on your face."

"I'm fine," Kellie rasped, squirming a little more, her hands gripping the steering wheel with all her might. They'd driven close to thirty miles. "Not too much farther now. Aren't you going to tell me what an idiot I was for confessing to a crime I didn't commit? For nothing?" Kellie sighed. All those months in solitary at Sugar Land had left her feeling like the walking dead. "What a jackass I was."

"But I love you anyway," Lorna deadpanned.

The embers of inquisitiveness that had been sleeping inside Kellie sparked to life. "Speaking of my ill-fated confession . . ."

"You want to know who really stabbed Katrina."

Anticipation brewed in Kellie's belly. "It was Roscoe, right? I ran into him while I was looking for you, but he still could have done it earlier." That deep pool of blood she knelt in was still the stuff of Kellie's nightmares. "Katrina had been on the floor for at least a few minutes by the time I arrived and she needed to do nothing but taunt him."

"It wasn't him, though I'd wondered if he did it myself." Anger made Lorna's body stiffen. "You're not going to like the real answer."

"You're wrong," Kellie told her seriously, patting Lorna's leg to try and remove some of the tension she felt there. "Any answer that's not you or me is a good answer."

"It was Ramona."

Kellie's heart stopped. "What?" she shrieked.

Dejected, Lorna could only add, "I know."

"Ramona?" Kellie blinked stupidly. Her heart sank. "But she was our friend!"

"I think—" Lorna shifted in the seat so she could face Kellie. "I think she really was our friend, at least she thought she was. She just couldn't resist trying to save herself, no matter who else's life she had to ruin in the process."

In her mind's eye, Kellie could clearly see Ramona crouching over Katrina's barely alive body when she entered the cell. Ramona'd been trying to save Katrina, hadn't she? Kellie had to admit that that was only what Ramona had told her. She could have just as easily been trying to finish the job. She was the one who had the shank tucked in her pants. She was the one who'd been covered in blood. It's why Kellie had traded T-shirts in the first place. To look more convincing.

To look exactly the way Ramona had.

Kellie shivered.

"Oh, and she was so slick about it too," Kellie remarked bitterly as the long missing pieces of this mystery slid into place. "She didn't exactly encourage me to confess, but reminded me at every turn what would happen to you if I didn't. She played me for a fool!"

"She played us all. For months after you left, when I felt like I wanted to curl into a ball and not get up, she actually comforted me."

Stunned, Kellie asked, "Why did she do it to begin with?"

Lorna made a face. "Why would she do everything to save her own skin? Why does anyone?"

"No. Why stab Katrina? We all hated her, but Ramona barely spoke to her! What possible reason could she have?"

"The same reasons people have been killing each other forever. Drugs. Money. And love."

Kellie blanched. "Please don't tell me Ramona was sleeping with Katrina."

"I said love, not sex. Dusty is her best friend in the world. When Katrina arranged for you and I to be separated . . ."

Kellie's jaw dropped. "The move separated Ramona and Dusty too! They both complained about it constantly."

"She was devastated by it."

"And the drugs?"

"Ramona had always smoked a little dope. But when Katrina moved from maximum security to medium, the flood of poison really started to flow. It was easier to get and so Ramona used more. She started having trouble paying and went to Katrina for help."

Kellie wrapped her arm around her stomach. "Oh, God."

"I know." Lorna sighed sadly. "It was like asking the devil herself to save your soul. Katrina knew Ramona was struggling and so she fucked with her constantly, making her wait for her dope, stringing her on about bringing her into the fold, and even occasionally making her pay double when she really needed a fix."

"Ramona told you this?"

"Katrina told me this. She wasn't even ashamed. It was all just business to her." Lorna's mouth quirked. "Until she pushed Ramona too far one day and she snapped."

"I still can't believe it. What made Ramona finally confess? The DA told me he had her confession when he cut me the deal."

Lorna went stock-still.

Dread made Kellie's mouth go dry. "Lorna?"

"I helped her along in that department," Lorna admitted. Her eyes flashed. "Don't ask me to be sorry for it, all right? I'd do it again in a heartbeat!"

Kellie stroked Lorna's thigh. "I wasn't going to ask you to do that. But if you beat the crap out of her to get a confession, it'll never stand up in court."

"I didn't lay a finger on her." Lorna shifted uncomfortably.

Kellie braced herself for a serious 'but.'

A storm erupted in Lorna's eyes. "But she knew I was up for parole soon and I threatened the people she loves most."

Holy shit. Her sons. "And that worked?" Kellie scoffed, truly surprised. "Duh. You would never hurt her children."

The storm blew over as quickly as it had come and Lorna dared a tentative smile. She wasn't proud of what she'd done, but desperate times had called for even more desperate measures. "No, I never would. But I can be very convincing when I want to be. And I was very, *very* motivated."

Although Ramona's deceit hurt, it was something that Kellie could file away for later examination.

Kellie turned off the highway and entered a small town, winding through several old residential neighborhoods before she reached the end of a quiet cul-de-sac and started up a long gravel-lined driveway.

Lorna's lips curved at the sight of the modest, brick red Victorian home near the back of the tree-filled lot. The place needed a lot of work, but its wraparound porch, shingled gable, and columns with gingerbread filled it with character. "What's this?"

"This," Kellie smiled proudly, "is home."

"Whose home?"

"My home, of course." Kellie gave her an incredulous look. "Did you think I was taking you to a stranger's house?"

Lorna blinked. Kellie had told her about the ultra modern, luxury lakefront home she'd lost before coming to Blue Ridge. This place seemed worlds away from that. "You bought this house to live in?" *Please let her invite me to stay for just tonight.* It was ridiculous, she knew, but the thought of being alone tonight both terrified and thrilled her in equal measure.

Kellie killed the ignition, frowning as they stepped out of the truck. "I know it doesn't look like much now."

Dismayed, Lorna said, "That's not what I meant."

"It was listed as a 'Charming Victorian with Great Potential for Right Buyer!'" Kellie smiled wryly. "That's real estate speak for a small money pit that needs a Bob Vila living in it."

Despite the less than perfect condition of the house itself, Lorna's face lit up as she spun in a circle as she took in her surroundings. It was truly beautiful here. "Don't say it's a pit. It's not! It could be fantastic." She gave Kellie an apologetic look that still managed to be a little lovesick. "But you're no Bob Vila."

I know, but you are. Kellie held back the wild grin that threatened to overtake her. Lorna loved it as much as she did. She could just tell. And she hadn't even seen the best part. "It was a steal, so it was still a good investment. And it's not really what I sunk my money into." She gestured toward a wooded area behind the house. "C'mon. There's more to see."

"Just let me get my bag."

"Leave it," Kellie laughed, shifting from one foot to the other like a little kid. She was excited to show her the rest. "You can get it later."

Lorna retrieved her duffle anyway, holding it close to her body. "I don't mind carrying it."

"But—"

"Someone might steal it."

Kellie's expression softened. "Oh, honey, your things are safe out here. It's a really quiet neighborhood. Nobody is going to—" She stopped at the anxious look on Lorna's face and changed her course. "You're right. I should be more careful too." She stepped around her. "I'll get the door."

Lorna watched unhappily as Kellie closed, and then locked the doors. "I'm being paranoid, right?"

Kellie shook her head. "Nope. It's your bag, and it makes sense for you to want to keep it safe." She held out her hand and wiggled her fingers invitingly, thrilled when Lorna took her hand without question. "Let's go around back. You haven't seen the best part."

They kept walking up the driveway for another twenty-five yards until a large outbuilding emerged from behind a thick grove of trees. The gray shingles were worn but intact and the same red paint from the house was chipping away in spots, but the windows were so new they still had stickers on them. "Big garage." Lorna murmured. "Nice."

"It is big." Kellie's heart thumped unevenly. She unlocked the metal door. "G'wan, look inside." Even though the early evening sun was pouring through the windows, she reached inside and flicked on the lights.

Lorna gave her a strange look, but complied.

Kellie waited outside with her fingers and toes crossed. "Please like it." She heard a thump when Lorna's duffle bag fell to the floor.

"Holy shit, Kel! It's fantastic!"

Thank you. Relief made Kellie want to sink to the floor and a wide grin stretched her face. Doing a happy dance, she joined Lorna inside.

The space wasn't nearly as large as the woodshop at Blue Ridge, but it held the basic tools and machines necessary for cabinet-making and there was plenty of empty floor space to add more later. The walls were lined with tall pine shelves and sturdy cabinets that held an assortment of stains, brushes, paints and other supplies. There was even a cache of lumber already neatly stacked along one wall.

Kellie nodded in satisfaction. Everything was neat and in its place. She hadn't been in here since the equipment was delivered.

The smell of machine oil and wood reminded her of the prison shop, which was something she could live without. She was worried that Lorna would feel the same way, but her reaction told her she needn't have been concerned.

Lorna ran her fingers carefully over the shiny metal blade of a table saw and she moved from machine to machine, each one set on large rubber mats for the comfort of the workman. "The whole place is amazing," she whispered in awe.

"The salesman at the local Sears thinks I'm a goddess."

"He's not the only one," Lorna whispered under her breath.

Kellie heard the faint words and her heart skipped.

"I guess this means you're back in business." She cast the machinery another appreciative glance. "Your workmen must love this stuff."

"I am back in business, but not like before. I'm not only going to tear things down now, Lorna. I've got a small crew of contract workers in the city and I've been doing some real flipping. It's a ninety-minute commute, but I don't have to do it every day. Me and the guys are really getting the hang of this home repair thing."

Lorna lifted a playful eyebrow. "Are any of these guys cute?"

"Not as cute as you," Kellie shot back. "Why, are you looking?"

"No." Lorna swallowed hard. "I've already found who I'm looking for."

"Me too."

Lorna glanced down at her shoes and grinned. "I'm glad we got that settled. Are you happy doing what you're doing?"

I am now. But she gave Lorna's question its due. "I handle the business part of things and the guys do the real construction and refurbishment. Together we make a good team and it feels . . ." She shook her head, a little surprised at how true this was and how deep a cord it struck within her. "I know it sounds hokey, but it feels good to be making something better instead of just making way for something else."

Lorna's eyes took on an excited gleam. "I know just what you mean. There are some old places, like your house, that are just waiting for someone to love them and bring them back to life. How did you do this? You said you lost almost everything before coming to Blue Ridge."

Kellie watched Lorna carefully as she made her way back to her. There was something about the steady way she moved and curiously examined everything in her path, taking in every detail, that was filled with self-assurance and intelligence. It was an incredible turn-on. The slow burn of arousal that had started the moment she saw her was growing stronger and stronger by the second. He lips parted, and for a second she forgot Lorna's questions.

"Kellie?"

"Oh." She licked her lips. "Sorry."

Lorna's grin held a hint of satisfaction and it was obvious that she recognized Kellie had taken a lustful detour from their conversation. But she didn't seem to mind.

"I'm still not sure why, but my parents really came through for me and let me work with them for a while. Things were good, and business was . . . lucrative. But . . ." She shrugged one shoulder. "I decided to strike out on my own again." She made a sweeping motion with one arm. "I just bought this place last month."

"Big step."

"I want a different life than the one I had before we met. I *need* it to be different."

Kellie wanted to scream from the rafters that she wanted that new life with Lorna, but she could see that Lorna, who was holding her bag again, was feeling a little spooked. And who wouldn't be after spending so many years in prison, only to be dropped off in a diner parking lot one day and expected to just adapt?

"I am so proud of you, Kel. This is awesome. I can't believe you have so much going in such a short amount of time. I think it would have taken me years and years to do this. And you look so—" Her gaze sharpened and she hesitated, the words hanging from the tip of her tongue.

"Yes?"

"You've stayed sober."

Kellie let out a deep breath. "You knew that?"

"I've seen the pull the bottle has on people. And I know it takes more to stay sober than just wanting to. So I wasn't sure how you'd do once you got out," Lorna admitted. "But I had faith in you."

At the word 'faith,' Kellie flinched inwardly. When the chips were down, she hadn't had much in Lorna and she'd all too easily believed the worst. They'd both paid for her poor judgment.

"You're a strong woman. You just thought your only strength was work, and that's never been true." Affection laced her words. "And now you have proof that you can tackle anything."

Stunned at the analysis, Kellie blurted, "That's the nicest thing anyone's ever said to me!"

Lorna couldn't stop herself from throwing her arms around her lover. She pressed her nose into Kellie's soft, dark hair and breathed contentedly. "I knew you could do it, Princess."

Kellie chuckled, besieged with emotion. "I don't think the war is over yet, but I'm finally winning a few battles."

"Speaking of battles, it's going to take one to get me away from you. You know that, right?

Kellie smiled tentatively. "I do now."

"You're gonna be sorry that you showed me where you live," Lorna teased.

"Nuh uh. Not possible."

Lorna sighed and untangled their arms, placing her forehead against the other woman's. "I have a phone call to make."

"I have one more thing to show you. Please don't make your call until you've seen this."

In the back of the shop, a narrow staircase led to a second story room. "This used to be an office," Kellie explained, her fists clenching and opening nervously. "But I made some changes." She turned and looked directly into Lorna's eyes. "For you."

Wondering what else Kellie could have up her sleeve, Lorna opened the door. Her jaw sagged. "This is—"

"A studio apartment. It's not much, but it's a start, right?"

The large room was painted a cheerful yellow, and apple green curtains hung from two large windows that faced the main house and thick, colorful rugs were scattered across the floor. The furnishings were simple but functional. A maple bookcase and dresser were pushed against the wall near the low bed draped with a fluffy quilt. And a desk was strategically placed under one of the windows. There was even a small living area with a coffee table, television and red leather love seat. In the far corner, a small kitchen island, stove and mini-fridge completed the scene.

Kellie chewed on her lip. "The people at IKEA love me too."

"Can you . . . can you afford this?"

Kellie nodded and didn't look the least bit sorry when she said, "I sold the furniture that my folks were storing for me."

Alarmed, Lorna opened her mouth to protest.

Kellie raised a hand to forestall her. "I wanted a new start, remember? That sale more than covered all the renovations in this room here. And even if it hadn't, I earned good seed money while I was working with my folks."

"I think your definition of seed money might not match mine." Lorna's mind reeled at not just the money Kellie had spent, but the loving attention to detail. This room was obviously intended to be as warm and inviting as possible. "You did this all for me?"

"All for you. Though I'm hoping you won't want any of it."

Lorna placed her hands on the side of her head. It was starting to throb. "I think I need to sit down."

"Here," Kellie quickly took her hand and led her to the sofa, stowing the duffle bag near their feet. When they were both seated she said, "Are you freaked out yet?"

"A little."

They exchanged nervous smiles.

"What did you mean when you said you hoped I didn't want this?" *I don't remember her being this crazy.*

Kellie took both of Lorna's hands in hers and closed her eyes for just a second before saying, "I want you to live *with me*. I want you to share what I hope will be *our* scruffy, beautiful house," Kellie pointed out the window, "and sleep in *our* bed, every night."

She cupped Lorna's cheek and as though drawn by a magnet. Lorna leaned into the touch. "But in case that's too much, in case you're not ready for that, I was hoping you'd consider this a first step. It's not exactly living together." She looked at her in question. "Please consider it."

The gears in Lorna's head were spinning a million miles per hour.

Kellie reached up and tangled her fingers in Lorna's auburn hair, reveling in the feel of the wavy, thick strands. She gave her a gentle nudge. "I love you. I haven't said that nearly enough, but I'm going to fix that starting now."

Lorna nearly melted into a puddle. "That's good, because I don't think I'm going to get tired of hearing it. I love you too."

Lorna glanced around again. "It's beautiful, Kel. All of it. But you live out in the middle of nowhere in a tiny town. I don't have a car, and I need to be able to get to work."

Kellie gave her a strange look. "What do you think that wood-shop downstairs is for?"

Lorna returned the look. "For your workers."

"For you."

"I—"

Kellie cut off her words by crushing her mouth against Lorna's.

The kiss caught Lorna off guard, shoving her deeper into the loveseat cushions. Without conscious thought, her body responded with abandon.

After a few steamy moments, Kellie wondered whether Lorna would make a move to slow things down. Instead, she slid her tongue into Kellie's mouth and stroked her to a near frenzy in a matter of seconds.

"Kel—" Lorna moaned quietly against those impossibly soft lips. She threaded her fingers in a handful of dark hair.

"That's it," Kellie mumbled back, encouraging her every move, already eager to shed her clothes and help Lorna do the same.

Control, Kellie had come to understand, was a big issue with Lorna. It had been wrenched from her time and time again in her life and this was one area in particular that Kellie knew she longed for it, but had yet to assert herself. She'd always held a part of herself back.

That was going to change. Right now.

Kellie covered one of Lorna's breasts. Gently squeezing its exquisite fullness, she felt a rush of heat flood her body. Even her toes curled. *Oh, God,* she thought desperately. *How am I not going to tear her pants off right this second?*

Somehow, though, Kellie maintained enough control to keep her caress featherlight. Teasing. Making Lorna want more. But even that resolve came under attack when Lorna tentatively slid her hand under Kellie's blouse and bra.

Kellie returned the favor, groaning freely at the feeling of smooth bare skin and a hard nipple that strained against her palm.

Lorna leaned into Kellie, trying to force more of her breast into Kellie's hand. She half-moaned, biting her lip at the last minute to stifle the sound.

Kellie could see that Lorna was trying to be quiet, to hold in the sound out of force of habit. She'd never hated Blue Ridge as much as she did at this very moment. But even that couldn't stop her from growing painfully aroused under Lorna's touch.

Their tongues dueled for long moments, tasting, plunging, and teasing, leaving their bodies coiled with lust. But Kellie didn't escalate things beyond the intensely erotic kissing. She continued petting Lorna's breast in a fashion that was far gentler than she knew her lover yearned for.

Breathless, Lorna backed away first and gazed at Kellie from behind hooded eyes. She blinked her eyes slowly, looking dazed. "I want you," she growled.

The words were like flint violently striking stone, and a shower of sparks exploded between them. Then Kellie saw it, lurking behind Lorna's barely restrained demeanor. That burst of energy that was just so . . . her. That compelling mix of assertiveness and kindness that was so damn sexy she could barely stand it.

Kellie raised a challenging eyebrow. "So *do* something about it."

Lorna's chest heaved and a light coating of perspiration beaded on her face and between her breasts. Color rose in her cheeks, but she didn't move, unwilling to take too much.

"Are you afraid?"

"I—" An uncertain pause. "No."

Kellie's mind railed at the unfairness. *They've made her afraid to take what she wants even when it's being handed to her! Not tonight!*

Not ever again. They'd both been denied this too long. This closeness. The intimate feeling of another heart beating so close to yours that you can't distinguish the beats. The taste of flesh coated with passion. The searing heat of two naked bodies writhing against each other. Nothing was going to stop either one of them from getting exactly what they wanted. What they *craved.*

"No?" Kellie said mildly. She batted her eyes looking at Lorna through a fan of dark lashes. "I thought you wanted me."

"I do," Lorna bit out in a throaty voice. "So much." She hadn't been shy or even especially tentative during their other sexual encounters. But she'd been . . . careful. Careful not to be a user like Katrina. Careful not to dominate Kellie because she was physically stronger and it felt good to be the one with the reins. She'd gratefully let Kellie take the lead. But now . . . Lorna's hands clenched and unclenched with the strain of going against her own grain while she waited helplessly for Kellie to make a move.

Kellie didn't say a thing. Instead she got up from the sofa and purposely walked across the room. She was closer to the bed, but also the door to the stairs.

Lorna's eyes widened with panic. "Where—" The words died on her lips when she saw Kellie's blazing gaze meet hers and her hands reach for the button on her own slacks.

"I'm glad you want me, love." Kellie had no idea how she kept her voice so steady. "Because I want you."

Lorna leaned forward, face flushing hot when Kellie wiggled the pants over her hips and they dropped silently to the floor. She stepped out of the pool of material and carelessly knocked it away with her foot.

Lorna swallowed convulsively. Kellie's panties were lacey, jet black, and very brief, coming to rest well below her hipbones. Her eyes darkened with unconcealed hunger. "You . . ." A ragged exhale. "You did—didn't have those before."

Kellie smiled wantonly. "You're right," she said simply. "I didn't."

With exaggerated slowness, Kellie began working her blouse buttons. First the cuffs, then, one-by-one, starting at the bottom, her shirt began to part and tantalizing peeks of creamy flesh came into view. She lifted the sides of her shirt and let it drop off her shoulders, revealing the bra that matched the panties and still allowed a generous amount of her breasts to spill over its top. She reached up with both hands and pinched her nipples through her bra, letting out a lusty cry.

Lorna's nostrils flared at the sight and her stomach clenched with need. She was on fire.

Then, unexpectedly, Kellie spun around and faced the wall, reaching high over her head with both arms and moving to her tiptoes. "Have I shown you this clock?" she said softly, her lips curving into a broad grin when she heard Lorna leave the sofa and begin to cross the room. She twitched her ass enticingly, excitement thrumming through her and making her wet. *That's it, baby. Come and get me.* "I put it up high so you—"

Lorna molded herself to Kellie's back, pinning Kellie's wrists high on the wall with one hand. She rubbed her cheek against her lover's; their bodies touching, coming together in an explosion of sensation as slightly rough cloth slid against soft skin, bring every nerve to life.

"You're *such* a tease," Lorna whispered thickly, her nose pressed in Kellie's hair as she drew in a deep breath of the clean scent.

Kellie's eyes closed of their own volition. *Keep going.* "Am—am I?"

Lorna pushed Kellie's hands against the wall. "Stay," she commanded, her voice an octave below normal as she slowly dropped her own hand while Kellie left hers in place. "And you know you are."

Lorna eased back slightly to survey the woman before her. Presented before her. "You are sooo hot." She slid her hand around Kellie's side to cover her belly, then gave her an unexpected jerk.

Kellie gasped as she bent at the waist. The movement sent her bottom higher in the air, her palms still plastered to the wall, albeit much lower than they were before. Her sex ached. *Please. Please.*

"And now you're even hotter." Lorna kissed up and down Kellie's back, then up into her hairline. Her mouth traveled to a pink ear. At the same time, she fondled one of Kellie's breasts beneath her bra with one hand, while she reached around and palmed between her legs with the other. She groaned, unrestrained this time, but not loudly, at the wetness that greeted her. "Jesus, you're driving me *wild*."

Kellie whimpered.

"But you," Lorna's kisses moved to the side of Kellie's throat where she bit down softly, "already knew that." She removed her hand from Kellie's breast and skimmed her fingers lightly down Kellie's stomach. "I adore you," she whispered, the hand between Kellie's legs beginning to slowly stroke the length of her.

Lorna's touch was just enough to drive Kellie insane with lust, but not quite enough to make her come. *Paybacks . . .* she admitted to herself, *were a bitch. What was I thinking?* She widened her stance, silently begging for deeper contact.

Lorna murmured incoherent words of love and devotion against Kellie's skin, kissing and stroking her all the while. *Worshipping* her.

Kellie's mind and body were engaged in a raging war with one another. She'd intentionally, and surprisingly successfully, enticed Lorna into action. But now that she had, it was maddening to be at her mercy. Her lover was relentless and didn't seem to be in any hurry. "Please," she finally cried, when Lorna's fingertips just skimmed the outside of her clit. Her entire body jerked. "Please."

Lorna removed her hand from between Kellie's legs and the dark-haired woman rested her forehead against the cool wall, eyes squeezed shut in frustration.

"Please what?" Lorna said quietly, her tongue darting out to taste Kellie's shoulder. "Don't you trust me, Princess?"

The odd tone of Lorna's question caused Kellie to freeze. There was something behind the words. She tried to turn around but Lorna would have none of it.

"No. Stay just like you are." Her voice was firm but not unkind, and each word was punctuated by another loving kiss.

"Lorna—"

"How can you trust me to do this?" Lorna entered her from behind with one long, smooth stroke.

Kellie threw her head back and cried out.

"And still think I'd do something as crazy as try to kill Katrina," a kiss between Kellie's shoulder blades, "knowing it would separate us . . . maybe forever?" Lorna added a second finger. "When I would never intentionally do anything that would keep us apart. Never."

Kellie's head thrashed from side to side. "You—you want to talk about this right . . . Oh, God . . . *right now?*" Hearing Katrina's name right now was like having a bucket of ice water dumped on her. And yet Lorna was unyielding in her demands on her body and mind.

"Tell me why you did it," Lorna ordered softly, keeping her strokes deep and steady.

"Be—because I lo—love you," Kellie ground out, on the verge of coming, or screaming, or spinning around and pinning Lorna on the floor to take her herself. Maybe she'd do all three.

"And?" She reached up and pinched one of Kellie's nipples through the slightly rough lace of her bra.

Kellie felt it all the way to her toes and she cried out again. "Yes!"

"And?" Lorna stopped her stroking completely.

Frantic, Kellie's eyes popped wide open. "Because I wanted to kill her myself and she deserved it!" The words spilled from her in a desperate stream. "It wasn't that I didn't trust you to do the right thing. It was that, at that moment, killing didn't seem like the wrong thing. I was afraid for you. I trust you with *everything*."

Lorna murmured her agreement at the heartfelt sentiment and molded her body against Kellie's again and curled the fingers that were planted deep inside the other woman, massaging her.

The movement brought a wave of sweet relief and Kellie gasped, feeling the first stirrings of her impending orgasm. She gasped and tried to remember what they'd been talking about. *Oh, yes.* It was a struggle to speak and though she knew they would discuss this again later, she still needed to say something now. Even if the timing was surreal. "I'm sorry."

"Shh . . . s'okay," Lorna soothed, rubbing her cheek against the sweat-slicked skin on Kellie's back and purring like a contented jungle cat at its incredible softness. "I don't blame you, Princess. I just needed to know." She shifted upward and grazed her teeth along the tender column of Kellie's throat as she plunged her fingers inside again and again. "Does this feel good?" she rasped.

The question was genuine though it sounded like seduction. Something that was totally unnecessary at this point. *Good?* "God, yes," Kellie panted, mindless as she thrust back onto Lorna's hand.

"I love you so much. I want you to feel good. Tell me—"

"Faster!"

Lorna obeyed instantly.

Kellie didn't have enough time to suck in another breath before a mind-blowing orgasm was upon her, ravaging her from the inside out. She shuddered violently, safe in Lorna's arms as she came again and again, hearing a far-off cry that only vaguely registered as it was rent from her own throat.

"Easy," Lorna murmured. "I've got you."

One of Kellie's arms slipped from the wall and she nearly toppled over, but Lorna held her tight.

It took a full minute of panting before Kellie came back to her senses enough to mumble, "Jesus Christ." Her legs were wobbly and she groaned as Lorna's fingers slowly reappeared from inside her.

Lorna kissed her tenderly. "You're fantastic."

Kellie smiled weakly. "I think I'm the one who should be saying that."

"Was that . . . was that okay?" Her voice begged for absolution. "I didn't hurt you or—"

Kellie spun in her arms and pinned Lorna with a look that would melt steel. "It wasn't just okay. It was so good I don't think I'm going to be able to walk tomorrow!"

Lorna's eyes widened. "I'm—"

"If you say 'I'm sorry' I'm going to have to hurt you."

Lorna's mouth clicked shut.

Kellie relaxed again. "Thank you."

"I can't believe you let me do that," Lorna persisted, still a little shell-shocked over the way she'd behaved. "I held you in place and then . . ." She paused and lowered her voice as though she was saying something terribly naughty. "From behind."

Kellie knew why Lorna was upset. They'd both seen guards take prisoners that way, not bothering to look the woman in the face

as they fucked her. But this was *nothing* like that. "Let you?" she
snorted. "I was damn near begging for it." She was delighted when
Lorna's chagrin turned wolfish.

"I know. I couldn't wait another second."

Oh, boy. Kellie mused briefly that she'd very likely just unleashed
a lovely, potent monster. *Lucky me.* "I'm not made of glass and I
know what I want. I know it's not easy for you . . . especially after
everything you've seen. But you need to believe that you'll never take
me someplace I don't want to go."

Lorna shook her head in amazement. "You looked . . . you were
just so . . ."

Kellie hoped the word that she was looking for was 'fuckable,'
but she decided to spare Lorna the effort of trying to come up with
it. Softly, she clucked her tongue as she dragged her gaze up and
down Lorna. "If I looked half as edible as you do right this second, I
wouldn't have held out as long as you did."

The front of Lorna's blouse was damp with a mixture of her own
perspiration and Kellie's. It clung sensually to her breasts, raising
the temperature in the room all on its own. Her lips were swollen,
and a deep red. *Temptation personified.* And those eyes that so easily
mesmerized Kellie fairly blazed, her pupils still dilated with arousal.
The auburn hair at Lorna's temples was damp and dark and Kellie
lifted a hand to brush it back.

Lorna's skin was hot enough to make her hiss in reaction.

Lorna leaned forward and brushed their lips together, then deepened a kiss that soon turned blistering.

"You need to be naked," Kellie muttered after several more minutes of kissing. "*Now.*"

Lorna didn't need to be told twice. As though her life depended
on her speed, she tore off her own clothes until she was standing
before Kellie totally naked. There wasn't a trace of modesty and when
Kellie surveyed the proud, beautiful body before her, she could see
why. Lorna was gorgeous.

She ran the back of her hand from Lorna's navel up and over
nipples that stood proudly at attention.

Lorna trembled.

"There's something I want to do, Lorna," Kellie said, continuing to touch her softly.

"Anything," Lorna vowed reverently, "I would do *anything* with you."

Kellie groaned inwardly, her heart thudding so hard it threatened to burst free from her chest. Lorna trusted her in a way no lover ever had. Without reservation.

Grinning, she dashed for the bed, and after a second of surprised hesitation, Lorna ran after her, tackling her onto the soft blankets and laughing. They wrestled and, not unexpectedly, Lorna came out on top. She straddled her lover and leered provocatively. "Well, Princess, is this what you had in mind?"

Kellie teasingly wrinkled her nose, feigning dismay at being captured so easily. "Not quite. Lie next to me instead?"

Lorna scampered off her and settled right next to her. Elbow on the bed, she propped her head up with the palm of her hand.

Kellie mirrored the pose, so close to Lorna they were sharing the same breath.

"So . . ." Lorna began, her eyes growing hooded again, "You've got me here. What are you going to do to me?"

"Everything," Kellie breathed, watching Lorna's throat as she swallowed convulsively. "I'm going to start here," she leaned forward a few inches and kissed the very tip of Lorna's nose, "and then work my way down, kissing *every* inch of you."

A rush of heat at the words made Lorna shiver. Her eyebrows jumped. "Everywhere?" she whispered, in a tone that Kellie couldn't read.

"Uh huh." Their eyes met and held. "Is that okay?" *Please say yes!* Kellie was dying to take Lorna with her mouth. She knew Lorna had never experienced that pleasure and wanted to show her how much she loved her while taking her to new heights through that devastatingly intimate act. Plus, she simply loved doing it.

Every second they were together in Blue Ridge had been an opportunity for the guards to catch them and, at a minimum, toss them in the hole, or worse, separate them for good. There simply hadn't been a good time or the right opportunity to avail themselves of that facet of lovemaking.

But those days were over.

Lorna's heated expression and rough voice set Kellie's blood ablaze when she said, "Anything you want is yours."

Kellie's chest ached with love and her mouth watered. She began her exploration with Lorna's face, kissing eyebrows, chin and cheeks, and tasting her lips for so long that she lost track of the time until Lorna's whimper, and her hands clutching frantically at the sheets, drew her attention farther south.

She lavished Lorna's breasts with attention, gently biting, licking and sucking her nipples until Lorna was out of her head with want and nearly squirming off the bed. The sight was the most erotic Kellie had ever seen and her own sex pulsed in time with her heart.

Dizzy from desire and panting harshly, Lorna urged Kellie's head down with both hands. "Jesus, Kel, don't make . . ." a guttural groan forced her to push out the words, "me wa-wait anymore!"

Kellie had a pang of empathy for Lorna. She, herself, had already come several times. *Hard.* And she was already so turned on again that she could barely think straight. Lorna had to be on the verge of madness, and the fact that she could talk at all was an impressive feat.

Sometime during their lovemaking the sun had set and Kellie realized she could see the wetness between Lorna's thighs glistening in the moonlight. Her own sex clenched painfully at the seductive picture.

On hands and knees, Kellie turned the opposite direction so she was facing Lorna's feet. Then she gently eased apart thighs that were shaking with anticipation and rubbed them soothingly. God, how she'd dreamt of doing this.

Kellie kissed her slick inner thighs, and Lorna thought that alone would be enough to make her die from pleasure. But when Kellie turned her head and laved the length of her in one long, solid stroke, Lorna cried out in rapture, unrestrained.

Kellie encouraged her with a loud, throaty moan that sent a wave of glorious vibration through her entire body.

Lorna's eyes slammed shut and her mouth parted as pleasure sang through her. *Sweet Jesus!* It was, she decided, a very good thing she hadn't known how good this felt. If she had, she would have *never* been able to resist having Kellie this way.

Lorna's orgasm raced closer like a freight train careening out of control. Nothing could stop it now. If Kellie ceased what she was doing, she would die. It was as simple as that. Still, a maddening curiosity overwhelmed her.

Kellie's perfectly shaped bottom was only inches from her face. She gasped when an especially delicious stroke of Kellie's tongue circled her clit and then she gave in to her curiosity. *What if. . . ?* She edged her fingers under Kellie's panties and slid them through the copious wetness she found there.

Kellie shuddered and moaned again.

That was all the permission Lorna needed to shove Kellie's panties aside and grasp that sweet ass to bring Kellie down onto her own mouth, pausing only the second it took for Kellie to move so that she had one leg on each side of Lorna's head. Lorna wasn't sure exactly what to do, so she copied what Kellie had done to her, and what had made her want to explode in a million pieces.

Kellie lifted her head and groaned out a mind-bogglingly sexy, "Hell, yes!"

Then they simply devoured each other.

Unaccountably, Kellie came first, her legs shaking as a ferocious orgasm tore through her.

Lorna *felt* her come, and that, in combination with Kellie's valiant attempts to continue what she'd been doing, despite the fact that her entire body was quaking, sent Lorna over the edge of her own cliff.

She screamed raggedly and her legs closed around Kellie's head, but sure hands kept her from suffocating her lover. For a few seconds she saw stars as she spasmed relentlessly.

Kellie wrung every ounce of pleasure from her until Lorna could take no more and had to gently push her head away.

Still breathing as though she was running full out, Lorna sank bonelessly into the bed, but instead of crashing back to earth, she floated down blissfully, in a place so sweet it didn't seem real.

A few light kisses and the warm weight of Kellie's head resting on her thigh brought her back to reality.

"Hey," Lorna said, hoarsely, taken aback by the flood of sudden emotion that swamped her. She blinked a few times, scattering crystalline tears. At that moment she loved Kellie so much it actually hurt.

"Hey," Kellie answered back, and Lorna could feel the lips against her skin curve into a smile.

"Come up here."

And Kellie did, moaning a little as she stretched out limbs that had begun to cramp. She lay down next to Lorna on the same pillow and tenderly brushed away the tears with a single finger, choosing not to comment on them. Her eyes told Lorna that she understood exactly what she was feeling.

"I . . . um . . ." Lorna cleared her throat after they'd spent a few moments of silence simply reveling in the closeness they shared. "I really like this bed."

Kellie burst out laughing, happiness rushing out of her like a geyser. "You do, huh? Well, so do I," she admitted.

"And I really like you in it."

A wry smile twitched at Kellie's lips and she kissed Lorna's cheek before pulling back just enough to rub noses. "Likewise. Does that mean you're staying?" she asked hopefully. "At least for the night."

If Lorna said yes to one night it was likely to turn into forever, and she knew it. "That means you might need a crowbar to get me out."

Chapter 23
The next morning . . .

Slowly, Lorna began to stir from a deep slumber. She burrowed into her soft pillow feeling puffs of warm air caress the back of her neck with every one of Kellie's breaths. The sensation was delicious and she sighed contentedly and she wondered why she'd been uneasy about sleeping with someone at all.

The guards!

She bolted upright, her eyes wildly darting in all directions, her heart pounding so fiercely that the sound drowned out even her harsh breathing. The head rush left her dizzy.

It was still dark outside and it took a long, terrifying moment for her mind to reconcile exactly where she was. And who was sleeping so peacefully beside her. And that they were safe.

She ran a trembling hand over her face as her heart slowed. Lorna still felt spent, but she was tired in a good way. And, thank God, if she'd dreamt she couldn't remember about what. She and Kellie had worked each other's bodies so hard and for so long that she'd been thoroughly worn out when she finally closed her eyes last night for the final time, she'd slept like the dead.

She glanced at the clock high on the wall and started to feel a stab of guilt over how she'd behaved when Kellie stood under it. But Kellie looked so sweet and contented, her face creased with lines from her pillow, a tiny strand of drool connecting her to the bed, that Lorna paused in her self-recriminations to smile.

Still caught in the throes of slumber, but sensing her lover had moved, Kellie murmured a soft, "S'gonna be okay," and laid her hand on Lorna's thigh. She nuzzled a little closer. "Love you."

Get over yourself and look at her. She's dreaming something happy. We both wanted last night. With every heartfelt sigh, moan and heated whisper, Kellie had conveyed again and again that what they'd done, and how Lorna had behaved wasn't just okay, it was welcomed. And Lorna let that thought serve as a balm on her battered spirit.

Throwing her reservations to the wind, Lorna decided to simply trust that they would develop a give and take that they could both live with. If last night was any indication, it was going to be a hell of journey.

Kellie had, quite literally, rocked her world.

Gently, so as not to wake her, Lorna lifted the slender hand from her leg, and examined it, noting the symmetry through a haze of happy tears. Who knew people could cry from being happy? It was an interesting, but still a little disconcerting, experience.

She refocused on their joined hands. They were a perfect fit. She brought Kellie's hand to her mouth and tenderly brushed her lips against it. "I love you, too," she whispered, her voice catching. Affection swelled within her until she thought she might burst.

She felt *so much* that she had an unstoppable urge to flee. But not far. Just to the fresh air outside where she could gather her scattered wits and feelings into a manageable ball.

A tiny thrill skittered down her spine. She could just walk out there as though it were nothing out of the ordinary. No one would stop her or question her.

Lorna slipped out of bed and tucked the sheet and blanket

around Kellie, kissing away her mewing protests that erupted at once. From the floor, she retrieved the quilt that had been kicked off the bed while they were rolling around like weasels.

Yawning, she wrapped it around her shoulders, shoved her feet into her shoes without bothering to tie them, and padded outside.

It was just before sunrise, and the sky and yard were an ethereal purple color that cast everything in a magnificent, dreamlike hue. "Whoa," she breathed, awed. Eyes wide, she spun in a circle, taking it all in.

The yard was large and very private, with trees and shrubs completely obscuring any houses that might be nearby. For a city girl, this was as foreign as if she'd just been dropped off on the moon. There were no buses whizzing by, no barking dogs or streetlights, no far-off car alarms blaring insistently.

A feeling of peace swelled within her, and like the sun on a foggy morning, she let its intensity burn away many of her fears.

Closer to the main house, she spied a bench and slowly walked to it, determined to watch the sunrise. Only one thing was missing . . .

"Lorna?" Kellie questioned softly, worry marring her face. "Are you okay? I woke up and you were gone."

Lorna glanced up and smiled warmly. Kellie was wrapped in the throw blanket from the sofa and had haphazardly thrown on Lorna's shirt, failing to button it correctly and there was a piece of paper sticking out of her pocket. But blue eyes swept over it quickly, more concerned with the woman than what she was wearing. A serious case of bed head had the shorn hair standing up at odd angles. "You look beautiful," she whispered back, giving her a love-drunk smile.

Kellie's brows spiked. "I'm sure I do," she muttered wryly. *If I'm lucky, this love-is-blind thing goes on forever.* She bumped Lorna's legs with her hip. "Scoot?"

Lorna nodded and did more than that, opening her blanket to let Kellie sit down before she wrapped them tightly together.

Their bodies relaxed when they came into warm contact. "You didn't answer my question," Kellie prodded gently. "Are you all right?"

"Uh huh. I just wanted . . ." Lorna's voice tapered off.

"To escape for a minute?"

"Mmm . . . something like that."

And I came and hunted you down. Ugh. Nothing convinces a woman to stay with you like coming off as hopelessly needy. "I should go."

Lorna shook her head and bussed Kellie's cheek. "You should stay," she corrected, her voice low in deference to the quiet. "I didn't necessarily want to be alone, I just didn't have the heart to wake you so you could sit outside in the cool breeze and the dark with me."

Kellie's eyes narrowed as she tried to gauge the sincerity of Lorna's words. "Okay," she finally allowed. "So what are we doing?"

"We're watching the sunrise. It's got to happen soon." The stars were already beginning to fade and the birds in the trees were beginning to stir. "I love it here," Lorna decided out loud.

Kellie grinned. She could see it as though it were a visible link between them. Their lives were knitting together here just as they had at Blue Ridge.

"But how were you able to do all this so fast?"

And then they talked. Kellie explained the deal she made with the prosecutor and how she'd been paroled early but couldn't contact Lorna until she was free from Blue Ridge.

Lorna let out a shaky breath. "Fuck me. I should have thought of that."

Realization dawned and Kellie looked at Lorna as though she had two heads. "You thought I was just blowing you off?" Half of her was wounded that Lorna would ever believe something so absurd. The other half of her wept for what her friend must have gone through during those long and lonely months, wondering if she was truly alone in the world. "God. If I had an inkling you'd think that, I would have—"

Lorna grabbed her hand. "You did the right thing." Disgusted, she scowled. "I just can't believe that I made myself crazy for nothing."

"Lorna—"

"Shh . . . It's old news. I want to look forward now."

Kellie nodded. "So do I, which is why I'm dealing with my past." She fingered the slip of paper that she'd grabbed, on impulse, from the pocket of her slacks as she headed out to find Lorna. She'd practiced doing this a million times, but now that she was down to the wire, the right words seemed to elude her. "I did something while I was waiting for you to be released."

Lorna frowned, obviously sensing Kellie's unease. "Is it a letter to me or something to the cop you shot?"

"I wrote him last month. His wife wrote me back telling me to go hell and threatening to have my parole revoked if I continued to harass him."

"Ouch."

"S'okay." Kellie lifted her chin. "As much as I was apologizing, I was easing my own conscience. I can't expect his support in that."

"So?" Lorna reached out and touched the paper that was sticking out of Kellie's breast pocket. "Do you want me to keep guessing? You don't have to tell me if you don't want to."

"I found your sister Megan."

So much blood drained from Lorna's face that Kellie thought she was going to pass out.

"Shit! Here," Kellie eased her forward, leaving her hands on Lorna's back and feeling her lover's heart pound wildly. "Put your head between your legs."

Lorna waved her off, but did as Kellie instructed. "You found her?" she asked weakly. Her wide, glassy eyes looked purple in the waning light. "But the guard who did the search for me—"

"Either he just did a bad job or there wasn't as much information on the Web at that time. This was years and years ago, right?"

"Yeah, but . . ." Lorna grabbed onto the seat of the bench with her hands and closed her eyes. "Is she . . . is she dead?"

"No!" Kellie hugged her, feeling horrible for scaring the life out of her. "She's a newspaper reporter and is married with a baby boy. They live in a Chicago suburb."

Lorna opened her eyes and looked at Kellie as though she were speaking a foreign language. "A reporter? That takes college, right?"

Kellie smiled. "If you work for a big paper it does. And she does."

Lorna let go of the bench and covered her mouth with her hand and spoke from behind her fingers. "She got out then." She shook her head in disbelief. "Somehow."

"Her address is on the paper." Kellie lifted her eyebrows in question. "Don't you want it?"

Lorna reached out with a trembling hand then stopped cold. "Will you keep it for me?"

"Of course." Puzzled, Kellie searched Lorna's face. "But I don't—"

"I just need some time, Kel." Lorna looked a little like a soldier that had just returned from battle. Happy to be here, but still traumatized and more than a little dazed.

Frustrated, Kellie cursed herself for not waiting to give Lorna the news. But it was good news, dammit! And she'd been so happy when she found it that she'd cried for half a day herself.

Lorna said, "I'd hoped she was alive for all those years, but I was never sure. And even if she was alive, I figured she'd still be back home, reliving my mom's same horrible life." Her worried gaze pinned Kellie. "How would she feel to have a convict sister waltz back into her life? Maybe her husband doesn't know anything about how we grew up and what I did to Dad and—"

"Whoa. Whoa. It's okay," Kellie reassured her, stroking her hair. "I'll keep it as long as you want, and if . . . when you're ready, we can decide what to do then, all right?"

The tension drained from Lorna's body. "Yes." She released a deep breath. "That would be perfect. I can't say thank you enough for this. I can't." She smiled just a little, the lines around her eyes easing to nothing. "She's really alive?"

"She really is."

Lorna let out a loud whoop, scaring the birds.

Kellie did a dance on the inside. That happy yell was the reward for the hours and hours of work she'd spent researching Megan Malachi. "Hey, look," Kellie turned her head and Lorna mimicked the move. "We're about to miss the show."

The sun peeked over the horizon, splashing the sky with brilliant streaks of pink and purple.

Captivated, Lorna's face was transformed into one of childlike wonder. "Wow."

Comprehension came over the horizon along with the rising sun. Enchanted, Kellie asked, "This is your first sunrise, isn't it?"

Lorna beamed, white teeth flashing in the early morning light. "Looks like you're going to be around for a lot of my firsts." With extreme care, she adjusted the blanket that covered them and released a contented sigh. "So I'm just going to sit back and enjoy."

When she finally tore her gaze away from Lorna's face and looked out into the distance, Kellie didn't see the sun that had blinded her so many times during the years of her painfully early morning commute. Or the sun that had shone through her bedroom window, making her pounding hangovers feel even worse. Or even the sun that she'd cursed for setting when there was still work to be done and she didn't want to have to stop.

It was all brand new.

For both of them.

Spinsters Ink titles

by Blayne Cooper

Unbreakable

and from Other Publishers

The Story of Me—*written under the pen name Advocate*

Castaway—*co-written by Ryan Daly*

Cobb Island

Echoes from the Mist

Madam President—*co-written by T. Novan*

First Lady—*co-written by T. Novan*

The Road to Glory—*co-written by T. Novan*

The Last Train Home

Undercover Tales—*co-written by SX Meagher & KG MacGregor*

Publications from Spinsters Ink

P.O. Box 242
Midway, Florida 32343
Phone: 800-301-6860
www.spinstersink.com

MERMAID by Michelene Esposito. When May unearths a box in her missing sister's closet she is taken on a journey through her mother's past that leads her not only to Kate but to the choices and compromises, emptiness and fullness, the beauty and jagged pain of love that all women must face.   ISBN 978-1-883523-85-5 $14.95

ASSISTED LIVING by Sheila Ortiz-Taylor. Violet March, an eighty-two-year-old resident of Casa de los Sueños, finally has the opportunity to put years of mystery reading to practical use. One by one her comrades, the Bingos, are dying. Is this natural attrition, or is there a sinister plot afoot?   ISBN 978-1-883523-84-2 $14.95

NIGHT DIVING by Michelene Esposito. *Night Diving* is both a young woman's coming-out story and a 30-something coming-of-age journey that proves you can go home again.
                    ISBN 978-1-883523-52-7 $14.95

FURTHEST FROM THE GATE by Ann Roberts. *Furthest from the Gate* is a humorous chronicle of a woman's coming of age, her complicated relationship with her mother and the responsibilities to family that last a lifetime.   ISBN 978-1-883523-81-7 $14.95

EYES OF GRAY by Dani O'Connor. Grayson Thomas was the typical college senior with typical friends, a typical job and typical insecurities about her future. One Sunday morning, Gray's life became a little less typical, she saw a man clad in black, and started doubting her own sanity. ISBN 978-1-883523-82-4 $14.95

ORDINARY FURIES by Linda Morgenstein. Tired of hiding, exhausted by her grief after her husband's death, Alexis Pope plunges into the refreshingly frantic world of restaurant resort cooking and dining in the funky chic town of Guerneville, California. ISBN 978-1-883523-83-1 $14.95

A POEM FOR WHAT'S HER NAME by Dani O'Connor. Professor Dani O'Connor had pretty much resigned herself to the fact that there was no such thing as a complete woman. Then out of nowhere, along comes a woman who blows Dani's theory right out of the water. ISBN 1-883523-78-8 $14.95

WOMEN'S STUDIES by Julia Watts. With humor and heart, *Women's Studies* follows one school year in the lives of three young women and shows that in college, one's extracurricular activities are often much more educational than what goes on in the classroom. ISBN 1-883523-75-3 $14.95

THE SECRET KEEPING by Francine Saint Marie. *The Secret Keeping* is a high-stakes, girl-gets-girl romance, where the moral of the story is that money can buy you love if it's invested wisely. ISBN 1-883523-77-X $14.95

DISORDERLY ATTACHMENTS by Jennifer L. Jordan. The fifth Kristin Ashe Mystery. Kris investigates whether a mansion someone wants to convert into condos is haunted. ISBN 1-883523-74-5 $14.95

VERA'S STILL POINT by Ruth Perkinson. Vera is reminded of exactly what it is that she has been missing in life.

ISBN 1-883523-73-7 $14.95

OUTRAGEOUS by Sheila Ortiz-Taylor. Arden Benbow, a motorcycle riding, lesbian Latina poet from LA is hired to teach poetry in a small liberal arts college in Northwest Florida. ISBN 1-883523-72-9 $14.95

UNBREAKABLE by Blayne Cooper. The bonds of love and friendship can be as strong as steel. But are they unbreakable?
ISBN 1-883523-76-1 $14.95

ALL BETS OFF by Jaime Clevenger. Bette Lawrence is about to find out how hard life can be for someone of low society standing in the 1900s. ISBN 1-883523-71-0 $14.95

UNBEARABLE LOSSES by Jennifer L. Jordan. The fourth Kristin Ashe Mystery. Two elderly sisters have hired Kris to discover who is pilfering from their award-winning holiday display.
ISBN 1-883523-68-0 $14.95

FRENCH POSTCARDS by Jane Merchant. When Elinor moves to France with her husband and two children, she never expects that her life is about to be changed forever. ISBN 1-883523-67-2 $14.95

EXISTING SOLUTIONS by Jennifer L. Jordan. The second Kristin Ashe Mystery. When Kris is hired to find an activist's biological father, things get complicated when she finds herself falling for her client.
ISBN 1-883523-69-9 $14.95

A SAFE PLACE TO SLEEP by Jennifer L. Jordan. The first Kristin Ashe Mystery. Kris is approached by well-known lesbian Destiny Greaves with an unusual request. One that will lead Kris to hunt for her own missing childhood pieces. ISBN 1-883523-70-2 $14.95

Visit

Spinsters Ink

at

SpinstersInk.com

or call our toll-free number

1-800-301-6860